FLAMES OF DECEPTION
COCKED PISTOL

TEAM TEXARKANA

TRAVIS DAVIS

Flames of Deception: Cocked Pistol

Copyright © 2024 Travis Davis

(My Random Thoughts, LLC)

Second Edition: 2025

Printed in the United States

All rights reserved. No part of this publication may be reproduced, distributed, or transmitted in any form or by any means, including photocopying, recording, or other electronic or mechanical methods, without the prior written permission of the publisher, except in the case of brief quotations embodied in the critical reviews and specific noncommercial uses permitted by copyright law.

ISBN – 13: 979-8-9901382-5-4 (Paperback)

ISBN – 13: 979-8-9901382-4-7 (Hardcover)

ISBN – 13: 979-8-9901382-3-0 (ebook)

Published by My Random Thoughts, LLC

Bulk orders of this book may be obtained by contacting My Random Thoughts, LLC at www.randomthoughts.llc

Public Relations Dept. – My Random Thoughts, LLC

972-897-8872

travis@randomthoughts.llc

My Random Thoughts, LLC

972-897-8872

travis@randomthoughts.llc

AUTHOR NOTES

The events and characters in this novel are entirely the product of the author's imagination.

I want to dedicate this book to the men and women who work seven days a week, twenty-four hours a day, supporting the mission of the National Geospatial-Intelligence Agency (NGA) and the greater GEOINT community, both military and civilian. The NGA was established in 1996 as the National Imagery and Mapping Agency. In 2003, it was renamed the National Geospatial-Intelligence Agency and is headquartered in Springfield, Virginia. Thank you for everything you do. Most of us will never fully appreciate your contributions and sacrifices in defending the United States and our allied nations.

I also want to express my gratitude to my wife, Martina, for supporting me wholeheartedly while I wrote Flames of Deception. Additionally, I want to thank a dear friend of mine for over thirty years, my former Scout Platoon Leader, Colonel (Ret) Scott Bertinetti. He was the first person I shared my book idea with, and he responded, "Go for it. It sounds like a good premise," so I took his advice. I truly appreciate your support.

MAIN CHARACTERS

United States

Justin (Tex) Adkins – Assistant Director of the National Geospatial Agency GA

Kim Barnes (aka Natalia Fedorov) National Geospatial Agency Analyst

Tyler Brown – National Geospatial Agency Analyst

Bob Weager – Senior Manager NGA

Sally Castel – Project Manager at the National Reconnaissance Office

Mark Chung – Director of National Intelligence

Jesse Dorn – Secretary of Defense

Marsha Fields – Director of the National Geospatial Agency

Master Sergeant Green – Boom Operator, Unites States Air Force

General Ralph Harris – Joint Chiefs of Staff

Chief Warrant Officer Ryan James (Grumpy) – MH-60 Pilot

Jenny – National Geospatial Agency Manager over Will and Kim

Peter Johnson – Director of the National Security Agency

Jordan Jones – United States President

Sean McGill – Director of the Central Intelligence Agency

Ed Mullings – Secretary of Energy
Captain Richards – Commanding Officer of AM Blueberry Hill
General Kurt Robinson - Major General Army Operations
Dr. John Russel – Chief Scientist for Mission-Related Technology
Mr. Toby Walters – Oil Expert for the Intelligence Community
Captain Lynn Vogel – AH-64 pilot

China

General Chen – Chief of Staff, People's Liberation Army (PLA)
Ai Yin (Fugu / Lucy) Chung - Commander of the Chinese cyber unit 34564
President Yang – President of the People's Republic of China
General Yen – Commander Chinese Cyber Command

Russia

Admiral Balakin – Commander Russian Northern Fleet
General Popov – Commander of Russian Forces
President Stoval – President of the Russian Federation
Minister of Energy – Igor Volkov

India

General Patel – Commanding General Indian Armed Forces
President Kumar – President of India

PROLOGUE

In December 1991, the Soviet Union collapsed after an unsuccessful coup attempt. The economy was in disarray. The only dependable industry was petroleum, which held the country together. It was believed to ensure their cohesion in the future, maintaining their superpower status and securing their place in history—or so they thought. Over the next twenty years, their goal was to rank among the top five energy exporters in the world. Their estimated reserves alone could last for many decades, ushering in affluence and prosperity while forging and sustaining a powerful military influence for their country and its allies for the foreseeable future. With this newfound wealth, they could amass influence and power over their adversaries, politicians (both in office and out), lobbyists, business leaders, and academia, and they certainly did just that.

That is, until 2001. Maxim Andreev, the Minister of Energy for the Russian Federation, sat in his office, gazing out the window on a beautiful spring day. All he could think about was the upcoming long weekend at his dacha south of Moscow. He had been planning this weekend for weeks, anticipating the start of fishing season and spending some much-needed time with his wife. Suddenly, a knock disrupted his thoughts.

"Yes, what is it?"

"Sir, the new report on the West Siberian petroleum basin you requested has just arrived. It's marked urgent, and I haven't reviewed it—it's for your eyes only."

"Okay, give it to me. Don't leave just yet. Sit down. Let me look at this to determine if I need you for anything."

"Yes," replied his assistant.

He opened the manila envelope and read the report from the ministry's chief petroleum engineer. Although he was usually very calm, this report made him uneasy. He unfastened the button on his shirt collar and loosened his tie as he read. He kept reading it over and over, unable to believe what he was seeing.

He leaned forward in his chair and reached for a water decanter with his right hand. As he poured a glass, he began to sweat. He thought, "I need something stronger with a little more punch." He set the glass of water on his desk, opened the top-right drawer, and pulled out a bottle of his finest vodka. He didn't bother with the glass, opting instead for a big gulp.

As Maxim took a swig from his glass of vodka, Ivan watched in amazement. He had never seen him react to a report like this in all the years he had worked for him.

After downing his vodka, he lowered his head and rubbed his temples to relieve stress.

After a minute, he looked up and yelled, "Ivan, get me the chief petroleum engineer on the phone now!"

"Sir, do you mean Petrov?"

"Yes, whatever his name is—*now*, please!"

Ivan, his assistant, got up, picked up the phone on the desk, dialed a number, and waited for an answer.

After two rings, a voice on the other end said, "Hello, this is Petrov."

He handed the minister the phone.

"Minister, Mr. Petrov is on the line."

"Petrov, this is Andreev. I just read your report. I won't go into any details about it. I'll ask you a few questions. Please answer yes or no—no details or lengthy discussion are needed. Do you understand?" The FSB warned him that the Americans, British, and Germans were monitoring his calls along with the other ministers. In his mind, he knew the Russians monitored all his calls.

"Yes, sir."

"Are you one hundred percent sure that everything in the report is correct and accurate?"

"Yes."

"This is extremely important. Has anyone else seen it?"

"No."

"How many copies of this report did you produce? If more than one copy, who has one? Do you have any in your possession?"

Again, he replied, "No copies. You are the only one. It's the original."

"Have you verified everything in the report? Did you explore and examine more than one location in the basin?"

"Yes, and yes."

"Thank you. Don't share or discuss this with anyone," the minister instructed.

"Yes, sir," replied Petrov.

Two U.S. National Security Agency analysts listened to the entire conversation in a building in downtown Moscow. One agent told his partner, "I wonder what that was all about."

"It had something to do with energy since the Minister of Energy called him. Who was that Petrov character?"

"No idea, but he's not much of a talker. He sounded like he had created a report for the minister. I could hear some concern in his voice and in the minister's voice, which is out of character," the agent replied.

"What do you mean? Out of character," he asked.

"I have been listening to his conversations for months, and he never sounds stressed."

"Okay, let's mark this one and save it."

His partner nodded in agreement.

After his one-sided conversation with his engineer, Maxim quickly called his contact at the Federal Security Service. "This is Andreev. Take down this address. Please go there and pick him up. He is not needed anymore." The line went dead.

Typically, he would call the president of the Russian Federation, but he realized he needed to convey this information in person. The information he shared with the president that fateful day triggered a series of events and actions that brought the world to the brink of destruction in just twenty-six years.

DECEMBER 2001 MARKED a pivotal moment for China and the world, as it joined the World Trade Organization with the assistance of a former president. Western companies were eager to introduce their products and services to over one billion consumers using inexpensive labor. To achieve this, they had to relinquish intellectual property and trade secrets, some of which could be. They would be used in military equipment that might one day be employed against the country that had allowed the technology transfer.

In the following years, China emerged as the leading exporter to the United States, dominating the global production and manufacturing of over eighty percent of all components, systems, and software utilized in the Green Revolution sweeping the Western world. They manufacture everything from solar panels to wind turbines, charging stations, car batteries, and the software needed to operate them, distributing these products globally. The U.S. became one of the largest importers of this "Green Technology." One day, China could control the very power on which the U.S. depends to sustain its way of life, and they were aware of this, wanting the U.S. to recognize it as well.

～

In July 2021, President Taylor aimed to reduce the United States' greenhouse gas emissions by 50 to 52 percent. His ambitions for the U.S. to become 90 percent carbon-free, eliminate the import and export of oil, and reduce drilling for it, natural gas, and coal mining by ninety-five percent by 2030 were within reach. By 2024, the U.S. and most of the Western world, along with Japan and South Korea, were on track to cut greenhouse gas emissions by over seventy-five percent due to innovations in solar, wind, and other renewable energy sources. However, this could not be said for Russia, China, India, Central and South America, and Africa. They still rely on fossil fuels and consume all the fossil fuels the U.S. and the Western world would have produced. In 2021, the global oil demand was 96.5 million barrels per day. By 2027, the market was expected to reach 125.5 million barrels daily. Pollution levels were not experiencing dramatic reductions, greenhouse gas emissions were rising, and climate change remained a concern.

In the years after the U.S. announced it would transition away from fossil fuels, wind farms and solar panel arrays appeared from coast to coast. Every new home featured solar panels, and electric cars outnumbered gas-powered vehicles three to one.

Ninety-five percent of all solar panels, components for charging stations, and wind turbines were manufactured in China, utilizing minerals and rare-earth elements like cobalt from the Democratic Republic of the Congo, Russia, and nearby countries. Furthermore, eighty-five percent of all wind turbine components were produced in China.

A joint venture involving Chinese and US technology companies developed software to operate solar panels, charging stations, and wind farms. However, the Chinese government mandated that all development occur in China. The federal government approved the plan because it was a joint venture. The project advanced with support from China-friendly lobbyists, primarily former federal officials, employees, and politicians from both parties.

The United States transitioned from being sixty percent reliant on oil from OPEC, Russia, Venezuela, Iraq, and Iran to being ninety percent dependent on China for green technology.

In 2025, OPEC formally announced its restructuring under a new name. In the future, OPEC will be rebranded as the Organization of Energy Exporting Countries, or the OEEC, and will move its headquarters to Moscow, Russia. In a press release, an OPEC official stated, "We believe that 'energy' includes petroleum and its products, green energy, the manufacturing of solar panels, charging stations, wind turbines, and all the hardware components, including the software to run these solutions. We provide end-to-end solutions to power the world today, tomorrow, and for hundreds of years."

"With this new strategy, we are restructuring OEEC with its founding members and reorganizing what they contribute to the organization.

China – Green technology
India – Green technology
Russia – Petroleum
Iran – Petroleum
Iraq – Petroleum
Saudi Arabia – Petroleum
Venezuela – Petroleum

"The members of the old OPEC can apply for membership. However, no additional countries will be added in the foreseeable future."

ACT ONE

I

PRESENT DAY - WEST SIBERIA BASIN, RUSSIA

As the managing director of the West Siberian Basin, Boris Ivanov, who has over thirty years of experience in the oil business, inspected an oil derrick in one of the basin's oil fields. He couldn't believe what he saw. He had never encountered anything like it in all those years working on a rig or in any of his management roles. At one of the drilling sites, the flare stack was not burning. He looked around at the other wells, which flickered, appearing as though they could be extinguished at any moment. He stood there in amazement for what seemed like hours, though it was only a few minutes. Coming out of his trance, he walked over to the well, checked the pressure, and ensured everything was operational. He glanced down at the pressure gauge—it was nearly at zero. He looked to his left and right, and all the flare stacks were out. Only a few were still lit, but none were burning at full capacity.

Boris knew he needed to check the other wells in the deposit before calling his boss, the minister of energy for the Russian Federation. As he walked towards his truck, he looked back and shook his head. He climbed into his vehicle and drove to another well. It was the same situation: no pressure and the flare stacks were out. He repeated this process over and over with the same results.

After several hours of inspecting more than eighty percent of the wells, he pulled out his phone, took a deep breath, opened his favorites, and tapped the first name on the list.

RUSSIAN FEDERATION MINISTRY OF ENERGY

The Minister of Energy, Igor Volkov, sat at his desk in the Ministry of Energy building at 42 Shchepkina Street in Moscow, Russia, reading a report on the current quarter's energy exports. When his phone rang, it startled him. He picked it up, glanced at the contact name, and held it to his ear.

"Hello, Minister. Many of our wells are shut down or shutting down across the entire basin. I'm not sure what is going on. What would you like me to do?"

He rose from his chair behind his desk and asked, "What do you mean by shut down? I want details. Details, Director!" Minister Volkov ordered, his voice raised.

"First, while inspecting one of the drilling sites, I noticed that no flames were coming from the flare stacks at one well, so I checked the other wells and found no pressure there either. I then turned off the pump jacks to prevent them from seizing up. I sent a couple of teams to investigate the other wells, and they were the same—no pressure, no flame."

"How deep are those wells? Are they all at the same depth?" the minister asked.

"Yes. They are all at the same depth, approximately 2,800 meters deep. We can't go any deeper and haven't yet installed the horizontal drilling capabilities."

The minister understood it wouldn't matter if they had horizontal drilling.

"Okay. You know what to do. I will inform President Stovol."

"Yes, sir. We should be up and operational in a couple of days. I can send a message about why we aren't producing as much product—something regarding mechanical issues."

"No, send all inquiries to me. Your job is to implement the plan. Again, if there are inquiries, please send them to me, not anyone else. I'll take care of it. You must enact the plan, and I will send it to you later today. Do you understand?"

"Yes, sir, I fully understand."

The line went dead.

The energy minister knew what he had to do, but thinking about it made him sick. He had always hoped he would be gone before the time came to do it. He picked up the secure phone and called President Stovol of the Russian Federation.

After his conversation with President Stovol, Igor Volkov walked to his cabinet, entered the combination, opened the secure door, and pulled out a report. He intensely reviewed the alarming information from a group of petroleum engineers and geologists. The report had to be reviewed yearly, but this year was different. He needed to review it now after speaking with Boris. The findings must be verified yearly with new on-site tests, surveys, and rig inspections. It wasn't the first time he had read this report. He couldn't believe it would be the last. It made no sense, yet he discovered the findings were accurate. Everything was true.

After all, this report was over twenty-five years old, and every Minister of Energy knew it. Each of them had to review it, which he had done twice since he became the minister of energy two years ago. However, it wasn't until Boris's call that a Minister of Energy had to confront its contents and implement a plan to address what was happening in the basin. Only a small group of people at the highest levels of the Russian government were aware of or had even seen this document. He shook his head. What are we going to do? What can we do? Unbeknownst to him, a plan was already in place. This was merely the first step in a long march.

Before putting the file back in the cabinet, he pulled out a piece of paper, reviewed it, and placed it on his desk. With the report in hand, he leaned forward, tapped the intercom button on his desk, and said, "Kir, please come in here."

No sooner had he settled back in his chair than a knock sounded at his door. Although he had just instructed Kir to enter his office, the knock caught him off guard. He closed the report and composed himself. After all, he was the Minister of Energy for the Russian Federation. "Yes, please come in."

"Yes, sir, what can I do for you?"

"I need you to review this press release, update it, and return it to me. I need it returned immediately," he replied, tense.

He handed it to Kir, who gazed at it in amazement and asked, "Sir, is this real?"

He pulled out a pack of Apollo-Soyuz, took one out, and examined it. Rubbing his temples, he replied, "Yes, it's real, very real."

"Sir, I thought you quit smoking?"

"I did until just a few minutes ago. Well, I haven't lit one, but I really want to," he replied, bringing it to his lips without lighting it.

Kir looked at him, confused, and said, "I'll get it back to you immediately."

The minister took the unlit cigarette from his lips and put it back in the pack.

Kir updated and verified the information in only ten minutes. Then, he selected the print function in Word, gathered the printed press release, and knocked on the ministers' door. Lost in deep thought, the knock brought him back to the present: "Come in."

"I have the press release ready. Would you like to review it? Sir, do the other countries know about this press release?"

"No, but I need to. This is going to go over like a box of rocks." He recalled an old Russian saying his mom used to tell him: "You can't avoid that which is meant to happen. Yes, they have been pre-warned and approved," Igor said.

Draft Press Release

With the OEEC's approval today, the Russian Ministry of Energy announced that Russia and member countries of the OEEC will reduce oil exports to non-aligned partner nations by seventy-five percent within the next 90 days. The affected countries are in Western Europe, including Germany, Italy, Poland, Finland, Spain, and France. South Korea, Japan, and South American countries are also affected, as is the United States.

OEEC members and North Korea are excluded. Satellite countries like Belarus, Syria, and other selected countries will continue receiving imports.

This course of action is being taken because of the unwarranted sanctions imposed on the Russian Federation during our invasion of Ukraine, which are still being imposed today. We will now only support and provide oil to our friends and allies.

We have also been notified and permitted to include that the OEEC members will reduce oil exports to those countries within the same timeframe.

No further information will be provided.

There were other reasons. The main one was difficult to comprehend fully, and only a few knew it. China was privy to the actual reason. The other members of the OEEC were oblivious, as if too many people knew it would cause a leak, and they weren't ready for that. It wasn't time yet.

Igor continued to review the release. He didn't want to, but he complied with his instructions. That's what you do in Russia. After all, he had only served as the energy minister for four years. Before his appointment, he had been the COO of Gazprom, one of Russia's largest energy companies.

He thought, "What a stupid move—working for the government." But you don't turn down a government position in Russia if you are selected. You can't."

"This looks good. Please send it out."

"Is there a specific time and day you want it released?" the assistant asked.

"Now is as good a time as any. It isn't improving with age."

"I'll schedule it for tomorrow afternoon. It's a Friday, so maybe it won't get as much attention."

"Good thinking. Maybe no one will even read it," Igor mused.

"Minister, if nothing else, I'll schedule this and call it a night. Is there anything you need before I head out?"

"Kir, let's share a drink before you go for the night. We'll need it."

"We'll need it, sir?" he asked.

"Just a figure of speech, Kir."

"Well, thank you, sir. I think I'll join you for one." He sipped his drink, tasting the whiskey's fruitiness, spice, and oak. After savoring the whiskey, he asked, "Mmmm, what kind of whiskey is this, Minister?"

Igor replied, "That, my friend, is Jack Daniel's ten-year-old Tennessee whiskey. It's smooth."

"Sir, it is. Can I have another shot?" Kir asked.

"Yes, of course. If you don't have any plans for the evening, we might as well sit here and drink the rest. We're not getting any more."

Kir wasn't sure what the minister's last comment meant. "Minister, I don't have any plans. That sounds great."

"Drink up. Hell, order us some food. We can't drink on an empty stomach!" said Igor. "Get the chief petroleum engineer on the line, please."

Kir picked up the phone on Igor's desk and made the call.

Once the call connected, Igor began, "Hello, old friend. Please explore the eastern part of the Chayanda field. I reviewed some old data last week and believe it's promising. I need it ASAP."

"I'll do that, Minister. Give me a month or two. I've looked at the same data, and it looks promising. It may be bigger than the Western and Eastern Siberian Basins." The line went dead.

"Where were we?" Igor asked.

The two men sat in Igor's office the entire evening, savoring American whiskey one last time. Before they realized it was gone, they had forgotten why they had started drinking in the first place. They would feel it in the morning.

2

SPRINGFIELD, VIRGINIA

It was a beautiful early summer morning in Northern Virginia. As he drove to work in his new Gun Metal Silver Audi S4, Tyler Brown was blasting "Take It to the Limit" by the Eagles, jamming along with the music without a care. He worked in a Sensitive Compartmented Information Facility at the National Geospatial-Intelligence Agency. He was a member of a Geospatial Intelligence cell responsible for Western Russia east of the Ural Mountains. This cell typically included a GEOINT officer, an imagery collection and production manager, a geospatial collection and production manager, a visualization, systems, and data expert, a GEOINT plans and requirements expert, a National Geospatial-Intelligence Agency support team (NST), and an NST liaison officer.

Tyler drove into the parking lot, parked, and got out. As he walked to the entrance, he glanced back at his car, smiled, and thought, *Man, can I park a car? It's perfectly within the lines.*

He walked into the NGA headquarters, went through security, and headed straight to his cubicle in the SCIF, thinking today would be another relaxing day as an imagery analyst sitting in front of his three twenty-seven-inch Dell monitors. Last year, he was a twenty-eight-year-old Army veteran stationed at Fort Hood, Texas, who had several deployments with the Green Berets and Delta Force under his belt before arriving at Fort Hood, and now he works for the NGA. Glancing at the news on the television monitor on the wall, he thought, *With everything happening in the world, from the Middle East to Ukraine and Southeast Asia, I'm just here looking at pictures from a frozen wasteland. Man, I miss the days when I was working with full-motion video. I need to get back in the game.*

His current mission was to analyze the latest images and video footage from an area in Russia. He was always amazed at how quickly the images and videos could be retrieved from their databases. As he typed in a search, the images appeared on the screen in seconds. Being tech-savvy, he loved this stuff. His area of interest has recently been the petroleum fields in West Siberia, Russia.

He reviewed images from earlier in the day. Something on the screen caught his attention. There weren't as many drilling sites as usual pumping or extracting oil, and the oil derricks' sucker pumps were not moving. Additionally, there was no thermal heat signature from the burn-off gas outlets or flare stacks in over half of the wells across three oil fields. For some reason, these were extinguished, and no activity was present around them. One would think maintenance crews would be on-site to find out the reason for the shutdowns.

Tyler knew very little about the energy industry. He quickly conducted some Internet searches and discovered the four common reasons the flare stack would be extinguished:

1. Wells are not operational.
2. Maintenance of the wells.
3. New well(s) exploration.
4. Capturing of the burn-off gas.

Puzzled, he researched thoroughly and found that Russia hadn't installed the necessary equipment to capture the gas. While he was uncertain about the reason, he could make a reasonable guess—

perhaps it stemmed from a lack of concern for the environment or the reality that the extra costs would cut their profits. After all, they needed the money to fuel their war machine.

He knew they were older wells, so he believed the third reason didn't apply, but he would leave that decision to the higher-ups. It was above his pay grade. He removed his fingers from the keyboard, clasped his hands behind his head, and pondered, "If those wells could produce tens of thousands of barrels of oil daily, why aren't they pumping?"

He reviewed images from the past days and weeks to identify the wells where the flare stacks and pump jacks were operational. According to his assessment, this number of wells had never been offline or extinguished simultaneously. Sometimes, just one or two, but never this many all at once. It felt like someone had blown out all the candles on a birthday cake. That doesn't make sense since they were pumping yesterday and the day before. It seems like they just dried up. Maybe they were under maintenance, but why all at once? It simply didn't add up.

Tyler's job was to analyze the images and intelligence, not to make assumptions. Other cells and teams had that responsibility, but he needed a second set of eyes.

He asked Kim Barnes, another imagery analyst with several more years of experience, to review the images. Most would agree that Kim, also twenty-eight years old, was extremely attractive with her long black hair and green eyes. Standing at five feet eight inches, she stood out. Make no mistake: She could hold her own. She had an eighth-degree black belt in Krav Maga and was tough as nails. Additionally, she spoke fluent Russian and Mandarin, having served as a linguist in the army.

He poked his head out from his cubicle and asked, "Hey, Kim, can you come here, please?" Her head appeared around the cubicle. She replied, "Sure," and got up.

He glanced at her as she walked toward Tyler and thought, *She resembles a young Harris Faulkner from Fox News. Wow, she's stunning.*

She approached and said, "What are you staring at?" He smiled but didn't respond. After a moment, she tapped him on the top of his head. "What can I do for you?"

"Oh, sorry, do you have a minute? I'd like you to look at these images."

Kim leaned over his right shoulder and viewed the images.

"Okay," she said. "What was I looking for?"

"Kim, do you notice anything strange or unusual in those images? Hold on before you answer. First, check out these from last week. They are the same wells."

She leaned over again, examined the images, ran her fingers through her hair—just as she did when lost in thought—and said, "That's strange. Over half the wells have extinguished flare stacks, and many aren't pumping. It seems that a large portion of the oil field is non-operational. Is this the same place?"

"Yes," Tyler answered. "Strange, right? I thought it might be maintenance, but they would cycle through only one or a small group of wells in the past—never this many at once."

"Let's try this. Can you access and display some thermal images of the same area from yesterday and today?" Kim asked. "Let's verify what we're seeing.

"Sure, of course. Here, let me drive," he said as he leaned over Kim. Getting a brief smell of her perfume.

Leaning over her, he said, "You can see the thermal signatures of the flare stacks in yesterday's images but none today. Can you check a few more days back?"

Looking over the images on his screen, she noted, "Interesting... out of five days' worth of imagery, yesterday is the only day with the same anomalies, but they weren't as widespread. Puzzling, to say the least. But today, they are all out."

He replied, "Maybe this is just the first puzzle piece."

Kim glanced at him. "What puzzle?"

He smiled and answered, "The puzzle of this mystery we're trying to assemble."

"Assemble? Couldn't you have just said 'put together'? You don't need to use big words around me, Tyler."

He smiled and began to laugh. After a minute, she nodded and said, "Okay, so let's start putting it together. I think you might be onto something, but to be sure, let's review some images from the Timan-Pechora Basin from today, yesterday, and a week ago."

They walked over to Kim's cubicle. She sat down, typed "Timan-Pechora oil field" on her keyboard, and hit enter.

The database retrieved information about the oil field within seconds. She then selected a group of images.

Kim brought up the images and started the review. After about five minutes, they observed some behavior in those fields. "Interesting. There are a few, but nothing unusual compared to a week ago. However, yesterday, over a quarter of the wells in the oil fields we are monitoring were shut down and remain down today."

Tyler added, "Since they invaded Ukraine, the importation of replacement parts and other infrastructure needed to maintain the fields has greatly decreased. Still, they have been able to get what they need from China, Iran, and other countries, so I don't think acquiring parts is an issue."

"I agree, but this doesn't seem to be maintenance. Let's take it a step further and check for human heat signatures. Let's filter out all the noise. I want a clearer picture. This will show us if they're fully manned and operational or just running a skeleton crew. It's strange. There were no human heat signatures at some of the wells, while when I reviewed those same wells in the previous images at the same time on the same day, there were about the same number of people each day based on the heat signatures."

"I agree. I don't think it's maintenance either, but what on earth could it be?"

"Right. If maintenance were done on and around the wells, you'd think there would be more heat signatures than usual. Yet, there's not a single one at the site, which is unusual." Tyler started biting one of his fingernails.

"Knock it off," Kim scolded.

"A nervous habit, sorry. Maybe they're on strike."

"The oilfield workers? That's hilarious, Tyler. There are no worker strikes in Russia."

"They'd be sent to Siberia if they did, so maybe they are on strike," Tyler laughed.

"Do you always find your jokes funny?"

"Someone has to!"

"Okay, funny man, enough with the jokes. I think we have something," Kim said.

Tyler shook his head. "I think you're right."

"Let's escalate this intelligence. We'll create a package with the images and our analysis, then submit it to Jenny Goodspeed by the end of the day. What do you think?" Kim proposed.

"Definitely! Let's do it!" Tyler replied.

Kim and Tyler worked on the package for about five hours. When they were almost finished, he asked Kim, "Do you want to call Jenny so she can watch for the package?"

Kim replied, "I like your idea, Tyler." She picked up her phone and called their boss. Jenny, I wanted to give you a heads-up. Tyler and I created a detailed intelligence package. Look for it in your inbox today by COB."

Jenny had worked at the NGA for over ten years and was a well-known and respected professional. She rose from an entry-level analyst position to lead analyst and team lead and now serves as the production manager of a cell.

"That sounds good," Jenny replied. "I'll look for your email. Is there anything you need now? You sound a little excited."

Kim's voice trembled slightly. "Once you review it, I think you'll be excited, too. Thanks."

"Hold on, what's it regarding?" Jenny asked.

"The West Siberian petroleum basin."

"All right. Talk to you tomorrow after I review the package."

That was strange, Jenny thought. In all the years she had worked with Kim, Jenny had never called to inform her that she had sent something.

Sure enough, the email arrived in her inbox at 5:30 p.m. Since Kim was intrigued, she decided to jump right on this. Jenny reviewed Tyler's and Kim's analysis along with the accompanying images. The intelligence findings were exciting—potentially disturbing—and warranted further investigation.

She glanced at her watch. Damn, I need to pick up the girls. I'll be late again—the second time this week, and it's only Tuesday.

As Jenny drove to get her daughters, she couldn't understand why so many oil-producing wells would suddenly shut down. We need additional assets, she thought. She began formulating her plan to escalate the intel without sounding panicked or alarmed. I'll clear my calendar for tomorrow morning. I need to conduct a detailed review without interruptions.

3

RUSSIAN MINISTRY OF DEFENSE

Sitting at his desk, General Popov was reviewing reports when his aide de camp knocked on his door, peeked in, and said, "Sir, we just received word from the Ministry of Energy that the press release will be issued tomorrow afternoon."

"Excellent planning. It coincides with our upcoming meeting in the next few days."

There would be no turning back, and he knew the ramifications could catapult the world into a war the likes of which they hadn't seen since the end of World War II in 1945. He was following orders, after all. He was a soldier, and soldiers followed their orders.

General Popov, the unassuming General of the Russian Armed Forces, who worked his way up from Private to General, opened the cabinet door, pulled out a folder marked "Top Secret – Operation Moose," and began his review of every detail of the plan. This mission had been in the planning phase for years, intensive not only in the man-hours spent planning the operation but also in the money spent on preparing equipment for the operation. Now, it was complete and ready to be executed. He was confident that the operation would be successful. However, he had felt the same way as a battalion commander during the invasion of Ukraine. This time, we are better trained. Supplies have been staged, and we know why we are fighting.

Operation Moose's true objectives were revealed only to the Russian and Chinese governments, securing oil exclusively for them, and they were uniquely positioned to achieve this. He had access to the Ministry of Energy's information, which he had known for years. Now, it was time to take action. Some of these governments are so foolish, he thought. He rose from his desk and poked his head outside the door. To his aide, he commanded, "Call Admiral Balakin of the Northern Fleet on the secure phone."

"Yes, sir," replied his aide. After a few minutes, the aide entered his office and said, "Sir, Admiral Balakin is on the secure phone."

He picked up the secure phone and said, "You old son of a bitch." General Popov replied, "Right back at you, old friend. What can I do for you today?"

"First, I have just one question."

"Sure, what is it?"

"How effing cold are you?" General Popov asked.

"It's not too cold. I'm wearing shorts and a T-shirt. It's only minus five degrees Celsius today. But that's not why you called, right?" he replied.

"No, it's not. Let's proceed with our part of Operation Moose."

"General, we've already started preparations. I can provide an update now if you'd like."

"That would be great, Admiral."

Admiral Balakin began his update: "General modifications have been made to several of our submarines. We tested one of them yesterday, and it worked flawlessly. We received confirmation from the tracking stations along the route, and the test lasted over twelve hours. I have some exciting news regarding what we call the mimic.

They are one hundred percent operational and perform better than we anticipated."

"Sorry, Admiral, I wasn't aware of this mimic," General Popov said. "If you have some time, I'd love to learn more. I'm fascinated. Let's wrap this up, and once the operation is complete, we can review it in depth. I'm a technology enthusiast."

Admiral Balakin responded, "Sir, we can do that, but let me give you a quick overview. When one of our submarines leaves its pen, the Americans detect it using sonar, an underwater detection system, or satellites. Most of the time, we can avoid detection by their satellites since we know when they're scheduled to watch us and when their satellites are overhead. We plan around those times. However, evading their sonar and underwater detection systems (SOSUS) is more complicated."

"So, we've modified several drone submarines to emit the same passive signature, propulsion noise, and vibrations as any of our submarines. They can travel at the same speed and depth and have similar maneuverability. We can even add sound if we want them to detect noise or human activity underwater! It's amazing. Any one of the drones can mimic any of our submarines. It's simple: The operator selects the submarine to mimic from the list, and off it goes. We'll use these well into the future as we develop new and more advanced submarines," Admiral Balakin explained.

General Popov spoke excitedly, "So you launch the sub out of its pen without the Americans picking it up because we'll launch a couple of mimics first to lead them on a wild goose chase?"

"Basically, General, we'll pre-program its course as if it's on a routine mission. All the while, Generalissimo Suvorov and Prem will set sail for their battle stations," Admiral Balakin answered proudly.

"Can they detect them when they leave their pens?"

"No, let me explain. We've modified them to mimic a surface ship. It's like modifying a car, or as the Americans say, 'thinking outside the box.' It's all been tested," Admiral Balakin replied confidently.

"Even if they're submerged?"

"Yes. In that case, they'll initially go only to the depth or draft of one of our largest tonnage ships, which we've positioned at the base," Admiral Balakin said. "We've modified their hulls and lowered the height of their conning towers to meet specifications. We'll slip them out when US satellites aren't in use."

"The other modification is to the Ural, one of your newest nuclear icebreakers, which will be completed early next week. She will be ready to take on the complement of marines once they are aboard. She will then set sail. We have provided the maritime agencies with information about her voyage. We will sail her from her home port along the Northern Sea Route. We want it to appear like a regular cruise. From the outside, there is no difference. All the modifications are internal," said Admiral Balakin.

With the phone in hand, General Popov stood up from his chair. "Admiral, this is fantastic. Excellent work! Now, tell me about the airborne units."

"Sir, we have not yet moved them in large numbers to indicate anything unusual, though we have sent a company to the staging areas weekly. I didn't want to execute a massive troop movement while the other ground units were getting positioned in Syria. I thought it best to keep some in their garrisons. We will have three waves, and since there are currently very few United States ground units even close to the vicinity of the objective, we have plenty of time. I estimate it will take the U.S. and Canada almost a day to launch a counterattack with their airborne troops. Most of the 82nd Airborne Division is still deployed in Europe, and the 11th Airborne Division is not fully manned or combat-ready." Which makes no sense, Admiral Balakin thought.

"What about the Canadians? If we attack the U.S., it could provoke NATO's Article Five," General Popov inquired.

"Sir, most of their units are stationed closer to urban areas. Since the trucker convoy, they have grown more concerned about managing their population, which isn't a factor."

"But what about the UK, France, Germany, and the other NATO countries? They could join the conflict."

"General, as you know, there's no way those countries could mobilize a large enough contingent of troops to the U.S. They lack the transport aircraft, and we could secure the sea lanes and the skies. They won't be able to deploy enough NATO troops on the battlefield. All we need to do is reposition some of our forces to their eastern flank. That would halt them in their tracks. You and I both agree that NATO has never planned for a war in North America, only in Europe. Considering the Chinese and their actions in the Pacific, we can't be stopped."

"Yes, yes, that's excellent thinking. Airborne troops on the move usually signal that something is about to happen," General Popov replied.

"Exactly, General."

"How long will it take them to be in a position to jump on the target once you receive the go-ahead?"

"I need four hours for the initial troops to be on the ground. I will start prepositioning additional aircraft to support the drop."

"How many sorties are you planning, Admiral?"

"Sir, we are currently finalizing our number. I have a call with the airborne units and the Air Force commander later this morning."

"Just out of curiosity, how many more soldiers could we deploy if we wanted to increase our forces?" General Popov asked.

"Well, sir, we currently have sixty thousand soldiers in the airborne units. There's no way we could or would deploy them all at once. We're considering half a division for this mission, so around thirteen thousand soldiers will initially be on the ground. We could always send reinforcements if needed.

"We plan to drop them south of the objective to cut off any advancement the Americans attempt. The Marines from the icebreaker will land to the north and secure the area. They will have support from the helicopter units on the ship."

"Concerning the Americans and Canadians, I will let you know if the plans change or if we notice any movement from them. Is there anything else you need from me at the moment, sir?" Admiral Balakin inquired. "I have a lot of planning to do to execute the mission."

"No, Admiral. I'm very impressed. You'll hear from me. Have a nice day, and stay warm."

"Yes, sir, and please say hello to my sister."

"I'm heading home when I'm done, and I definitely will. Bye."

The line went dead.

A couple of hours later, General Popov called for his aide. "My car, please. Have it meet me in five minutes at the back entrance. I'm going home for the evening." He wanted to spend time with his family, understanding that time would be in short supply in the weeks ahead.

"Yes, sir. Have a wonderful evening with your family," his aide said.

"I suggest you do the same. Things are about to get hectic," replied the general.

He rose from his desk and returned Operation Moose to the secure filing cabinet. Afterward, he secured the cabinet and smiled as he walked out of his office and down to his waiting staff car.

4

PYONGYANG, NORTH KOREA

Beak Hyeon, a lead computer programmer and member of Bureau 121 of the Korean People's Army, had been working on the code for weeks with other members of the unit. The bureau's customer wanted the programs by the end of the day. He was slightly behind and understood the consequences of failure. There was immense pressure to finish. His former roommate had faced the repercussions of not completing his program on time. Beak missed him, along with other coworkers and friends.

He believed the code was about ninety-nine percent complete. He just needed to test it with a few more lines before moving into alpha testing.

The program was finished, and only one hour was left until his deadline. Beak sighed, put his hands behind his head, and relaxed. His relaxation was blissful yet short-lived.

He saved the program on the group's shared drive and will begin alpha testing tomorrow. As he started working on this test plan, the group commander and leader suddenly tapped him on the shoulder. He immediately stood at attention, looking straight ahead.

"Sir, I have completed the program. Junior Officer Choi, how may I assist you?" he asked.

"I was notified that your mission was complete when you saved it to the network drive. Our Great Leader thanks you. Please remove all documents, lingering code, notes, and anything related to this project, and format your hard drive. Wipe it clean now. I will monitor this. Start now," Junior Officer Choi commanded.

"Sir, I haven't tested the code yet."

"Soldier, that is not your responsibility. Do what you're ordered to do now!"

"Yes, Sir Sojwa."

Beak had completed many projects like this one before, and nothing seemed unusual except for the frequent updates he had to provide. However, this order was extraordinary. He was instructed to remove every remnant of code and documentation and format the hard drive. Beak had never had to do that before, but he also knew better than to ask questions. You don't ask questions in North Korea.

What Beak Hyeon didn't know, however, was that his program was just one of many small programs finished that day. Developers all over North Korea had received the same orders from their leadership.

It was like they were wiping their hands of anything to do with this project as if it never existed, he thought after complying with his orders. It was as if they didn't want anyone to know they had anything to do with the consequences the code could cause. Why? They usually boast about their accomplishments. Oh well, it was time to move down to the buses. He got up, turned off the lights, and went downstairs.

All the commanders of Bureau 121, who had their teams working on the project, reported to the chain of command that the mission had been completed.

Pacing in his office, Sojan Hu, the commanding general of Bureau

121, awaited confirmation that all the programs had been completed. As he paced, there was a knock at his office door. He stopped pacing, saying, "Come in."

His aide opened the door and reported, "Sir, all the programs are complete and on the main server."

"Thank you. Now get out!" He sat at his desk, entered a command on his keyboard, and accessed the central server. He opened a secure website and transferred all the programs to another server—not a North Korean server, but the customers' server. Once all the programs were on the server, he picked up his phone and made a secure call to his contact. He spoke just one sentence: "The fields are ready to grow crops. You can plant your seeds." The line went dead.

He leaned back in his chair, clasped his hands behind his head, and muttered, "Damn, I'm glad this project is done. It's been a real big pain in the ass." Rising from his desk, he looked outside and wondered what their client would do with the programs. He had no idea what the finished product was or what it did, and he liked it that way. As he watched his programmers being led to the waiting buses for their journey back to the barracks, he thought, "I'll authorize additional rations for them. They did an outstanding job."

BEIJING, CHINA

Twenty miles outside Beijing, Ai Yin Chang, the commander of PLA Unit 34564 of the People's Liberation Army, was sitting at her computer in a typical office tower. She studied one of her four twenty-seven-inch monitors, reviewing the code she had received the night before. She quickly ensured that she had all the code and that her team of programmers would be ready to start. Only a few people knew the purpose of these applications, and she was one of them.

Commander Chang was recognized as an exceptional programmer and an even more impressive project manager and leader. She had quickly risen ahead of her peers through the ranks in the PLA. She was on track for higher leadership roles, leading her to the top of the PLA Cyber Command. Her unit was tasked with consolidating all the various programs into one. This would require significant time and effort, but she lacked time. She raised her arms and stretched, enjoying a moment of relaxation. She had twenty days to complete her mission—there was no time like the present to begin. Without delay, she called a team meeting with her developers and program managers.

Once the team had gathered around her, she said, "Today, we embark on a glorious mission to defend the People's Republic of China. Never before has such an ambitious goal been set, and we are at the tip of the spear in achieving it. I can't share the specific details of the mission. Still, I can outline our objective: review all the code and consolidate the individual programs into one application within twenty days. Before you know it, those twenty days will be gone, so I'm canceling all passes. You are restricted to this area. Are there any questions?"

She waited a moment. "Since no one has a question, return to work. Program managers, I expect daily updates in my inbox by 6:00 p.m. Please use the templates provided. Dismissed!"

As she returned to her office, portraits of China's most significant leaders lined the walls: Mao Zedong, Li Xiannian, Jiang Zemin, Hu Jintao, and the current leader, Xi Jinping. Her team's work was poised to change the course of human events and elevate China to the position of the most powerful country in the world. She stopped at President Xi's portrait and smiled. All she wanted was to make her uncle proud of her.

After sitting at her desk for two hours, she stood up, looked out her window, and gazed at the citizens going about their daily lives. They had no idea what was about to be unleashed, but it was all for their benefit and that of their children.

She had her orders, and she would follow through on them. She had never failed before, and she would not fail now. There were four hundred eighty hours left, and time was ticking away.

She took a burner phone from her top desk drawer and texted via Telegram.

> A Finished product in 20 days.

Once she had sent the text, she deleted the app and destroyed the phone to ensure no one could trace it back to her or her contacts. Meanwhile, another burner phone buzzed with a new text message. Its owner read the text, deleted it, removed and ruined the SIM card, stepped on the phone, and tossed it in the trash bin outside his office. He thought it was time for a drink, but he still had work to do.

5

NGA HEADQUARTERS – SPRINGFIELD, VIRGINIA

The day after Kim and Tyler sent Jenny the intelligence package, Jenny called them into her office. "I had the chance to review your intelligence package last night and today. To say the least, it's fascinating. I have something for you two to do."

"Sure, what is it?" Tyler asked.

"I want in-depth reconnaissance and analysis of this area over the next few weeks. I want concise daily updates. They shouldn't take up much of your time—just a quick overview of new intelligence and planned activities. If you're knee-deep in work, email me the update. I don't want to cut your time on target or interfere with your mission. This is your priority until I tell you otherwise. Once we complete our mission, I'll decide whether to take it to Tex. In the meantime, I'm going to request another asset to be placed so we can obtain some 3D images of the target," Jenny explained.

"Sounds good. When do we start?" Kim asked.

"Now," replied Jenny.

"Another asset with 3D imaging capabilities, Tyler. That sounds really cool."

"Have you ever worked with those images before?" he asked.

"No. How about you?"

"I did a few months ago, but I heard they launched another asset with enhanced imagery. I hope that's the one we'll work with. That would be awesome."

"I remember seeing something about that in the paper a few weeks ago," Kim added.

"Okay, you have your instructions," Jenny interrupted. "Now, get back to work."

Once they left her office, Jenny called an old friend at the National Reconnaissance Office (NRO). "Sally, how are you?" Jenny asked.

"I'm good."

"Can we go secure?"

Sally replied, "Sure, give me a second... going secure." A double beep on the line indicated that the call was secure. "Jenny, what can I do for you?"

"I need a favor. I can't provide many details because I don't have them. I'm hoping you'll be able to help fill them in."

"Ask away, and I'll let you know if I can help."

"I have a team monitoring a target in the West Siberia Basin—the oil fields, to be specific. Would it be possible for you to deploy an asset with 3D capabilities in the target area for a few days, maybe a week or two?"

"Don't you guys have your eyes on it now?" Sally asked.

"Yes, but I believe the 3D would provide us with better information for analysis. I can't tell you much more than that right now."

"Have you discussed this with Tex and gotten his approval?"

"Sometimes it's easier to ask for forgiveness than to seek permission," Jenny replied.

"I can't tell you how often I've used that strategy," Sally laughed.

"So no, not yet. I want to keep an eye on the target for a couple of weeks before I approach him to ensure that what we've observed is long-term, not just a fluke."

"Okay, but this is outside the standard asset request. I'm sure you know about our new 3D capabilities. Somehow, it made it into the newspapers. We need to clamp down on leaks and hold those responsible accountable! Ah, sorry, I digress."

Sally continued, "What the press failed to mention is that it's not 3D—it's 4D. We've utilized the same technology in ultrasounds to provide the most remarkable imagery in real-time or still images. It no longer matters: day, night, fog, clear skies, overcast clouds, or completely obscured. We're experiencing a few glitches and want new features, so your request is perfectly timed. We need field assistance to work out the bugs and add those features. How does that sound? Are you in?"

"Are you kidding?" Jenny asked. "We'd love to help you and your team! After all, it's for the greater good. The images have to be amazing."

"They are," Sally said. She continued, "I would send you one, but I first need to request access for you and your team. Please send me all their information, and I'll start the paperwork. For justification, I'll state that your team will help conduct system-wide tactical expertise testing, identify known and unknown bugs, and evaluate new capabilities. Once approved, I'll position the asset for thirty days."

"That would be fantastic," Jenny gushed. "I can't thank you enough!"

After their conversation, Sally got to work. She wanted to explain to Jenny that the new capability included the force of movement, determining how much something weighs based on its force on the ground and the vibration a mechanical device produces, using Newton's third law concerning ground reaction force. Their new technology could also identify the types of liquids flowing through a pipeline by sensing the vibrations caused by the friction against the pipe's walls. The analyst could determine the speed and density of the liquid moving through the pipe or in a storage tank when combined with the new thermal capabilities regarding liquid movement.

The satellite's sensors can detect movement, which generates force and heat, and vibrations, which create shock or sound waves. Then, using their software, they calculate the weight of any object and the speed at which a liquid moves, even if it is contained within something. Embedded Palantir Analysts can then identify the substance using its artificial intelligence (AI) since different materials produce varying temperatures when traveling at specific speeds.

Intelligence analysts can retrieve all this information about a target with just a right-click on the object.

Truly remarkable, she thought, and this is only the tip of the iceberg.

After the conversation, Jenny leaned back in her chair and gazed into space. What have I gotten my team into?

THREE DAYS HAD PASSED since her talk with Sally, and the team was busy reviewing images. So far, nothing had changed, which felt odd. That day, Sally called Jenny.

"Jenny, go secure."

"Will do—going secure."

Sally said, "I have great news! You and your team have been granted special access to the asset, which will be positioned tomorrow for thirty days. One of our IT team members will arrive at your office no later than noon today. Please ensure your team members are at their workstations. He will install the necessary software, which should only take a few minutes. Additionally, I have scheduled training for tomorrow at our location, starting at nine and ending around four or five. They should meet at the guard office at the main entrance, and they will be on the day's visitor list."

"Sally, I can't thank you enough," Jenny said.

"No need for thanks. You're doing me a huge favor! Until tomorrow," Sally replied.

Jenny jumped up, throwing her arms in the air as if she had just won the 100-meter dash at the Olympics. She leaned out her door and shouted, "Kim and Tyler, come into my office!"

They peeked around their cubicle wall at each other. Both said in unison, "Something's going on."

Walking to Jenny's office, they asked, "What do you think it is?"

Tyler wondered, "Is the mission canceled?"

They entered Jenny's office with trepidation.

"Hey! I need you guys at your workstations all morning," Jenny stated. "An IT technician from NRO will install the software on them. Please clear your schedules for tomorrow. We're returning to school. I'll send the calendar invite with the instructions and logistics shortly."

"Do you all want to carpool or just meet at the NRO?" Tyler asked.

Jenny replied, "I'm just going to drive myself. I have some errands to run in the morning. I'm fine. I will meet you there."

"Tyler, could you pick me up since I'm on your way? If you don't mind," Kim smiled.

"I'll pick you up around eight," Tyler said. "Traffic going into Chantilly is terrible at that time of day. Honestly, it usually sucks most of the time!"

They left Jenny's office with a little extra pep in their step. They were heading back to school—and for new exclusive technology, no less!

Jenny's secure phone rang almost immediately after they left. She glanced at the number warily. "Hello, Tex," she said.

Tex said, "I just received an email stating that your team has been granted access to an NRO asset. Your team has access to a highly classified intel asset, and somehow, I now have access, too. Can you explain why you, your team, and I need this access?"

"I might have added you to my request, just in case," she replied.

"Why the request, Jenny? And why didn't I get a heads-up or warning about it?"

"Tex, one of my imagery analysts, Tyler Brown, noticed some unusual activity in the oil fields of Western Siberia. He brought in another analyst, Kim Barnes, to verify his observations. She confirmed it, and they provided me with the intel. I reviewed it and felt it warranted additional time and resources to gather the best intelligence. So, I called an old friend at the NRO, Sally."

"I know, Sally. Please continue," Tex said.

"I shared as much information as possible regarding the unusual request with Sally. She informed me they have a new asset, but it's facing a couple of minor issues, and they also want to add some functionality. She believes our team would excel at identifying all the bugs, giving feedback on the functionality, and providing input on the new features. I assured her we would be happy to assist. That's about it. You're up to speed."

"Now I'm intrigued about what you all are watching. When can you give me a briefing?"

"A week or two?" replied Jenny.

"Of course. If you need more time, reach out. By the way, thank you for including me in your request."

"I'm looking forward to reviewing your intelligence. Keep me updated," he replied with a smile.

"Tex, I almost forgot—we will be in training all day tomorrow at the NRO. If you need to reach one of us, please call Sally. I'm sure she'd love to say hi."

"Sounds good. Have fun, and take the team to lunch tomorrow. I'll cover the bill."

"Thanks, Tex. Do you want to join us?"

"Can't. Bob and I have a meeting at the Pentagon tomorrow."

"Before we hang up, did you catch the recent press release from the Russian Ministry of Energy?"

"Yep, that's why we're meeting at the Pentagon. Have fun at school tomorrow."

"Catch you later, Tex," Jenny said.

At 11:00 a.m., the IT guy arrived to install the new software on each workstation. However, he informed them that they wouldn't be able to access it until after they completed their training, during which they would receive their login information.

The team returned to work and reviewed new images of the target area. Before they knew it, it was time to head home for the night. They couldn't wait to look at the photos from the asset.

6

NATIONAL RECONNAISSANCE OFFICE – CHANTILLY, VIRGINIA

Being prompt, at precisely 8 a.m., Tyler pulled up in front of Kim's apartment in Manassas Park, VA, to take her to Chantilly. He stopped and waited for her. Only three minutes later, Kim walked out and got into his car.

"Are you ready for school?" Tyler asked with a laugh.

"Yep," replied Kim.

The drive to Chantilly took forty minutes, leaving plenty of time to park and find the classroom.

As they approached the main entrance, Tyler marveled, "Wow, this building is stunning with its modern architecture. It's huge! I'm glad I have the room number, or we'd wander around all day."

"No, you would wander all day. I would stop and ask for directions or help. You men!" Kim joked.

They entered through the main entrance and approached the guards sitting in front of the security turnstiles.

"We're looking for room 2-275. It's a secure classroom," Tyler said.

One of the guards asked, "May I please have your badges? I need to scan them."

"Of course, here you go. This is mine," Kim said as she handed the guard her ID.

The guard scanned the badges—green lights for everyone.

"Let me make a quick call. You both require an escort. . . . Hi, Ms. Castel. Your guests are at the main entrance."

"Excellent. I'll be right down. Thank you!" she replied.

"Before Ms. Castel arrives, please hand over all your electronic devices, including phones, USB drives, and smartwatches. You can pick them up here when you leave. Thank you."

Shortly after, Sally walked up to the welcome desk.

"Ms. Castel, these are your guests."

"Thanks, Marvin," she replied to the guard. "You must be Tyler and Kim. I'm Sally. Are you ready for today?"

"Yep, I think we are. This is a beautiful building, Ms. Castel," Tyler said.

"Please, call me Sally." As they started walking, Sally shared some history with Kim and Tyler. She enjoyed discussing the NRO. "It was built in 1994 and is larger than it appears. It consists of four buildings and sits on 68 acres of land. The campus features beautiful green spaces, not just concrete and blocks. The architects did a fantastic job. We're in the main building on the second floor. I've been at this facility for about nine years and love it."

They ascended the stairs to the classroom, where the instructor had not yet arrived. The classroom was in a SCIF converted into a learning space. Instead of cubicles, it had desks equipped with a keyboard, mouse, and two 27-inch monitors capable of 4K resolution. The classroom remained secure, with no connections to the outside world, so there was no Internet surfing on those computers.

"Well, here we are," Sally said. "Please take a seat. June, the instructor, will be here in a minute or two. If you'd like something to drink, it's down the hall to the left in the break room, and the restrooms are to the right. I kindly ask that you only go to those two locations. Please let your instructor know if you need to go somewhere else. She will escort you. There's a phone in the break room if you need to use one. If you need to make a secure call, inform the instructor, and she will take you to a secure phone in one of the SCIFs."

Sally's cell phone rang. "Ms. Castel, your other guest has arrived," a voice said.

"Thank you. I'll be right down." She hung up and said, "Jenny is here! I'll be back in a moment."

At the main entrance, Marvin greeted her, saying, "Hi again, Ms. Castel. Two visits in one day? I'm a lucky man!"

"Thanks, Marvin, you're so kind. Have a great day." She smiled and continued, "Good morning, Jenny. You look amazing!"

"I was about to say the same thing, Sally, and thanks again," Jenny replied. Sally escorted Jenny to the classroom, where the instructor was ready to begin the training as soon as they arrived.

Once everyone was seated, Sally exited the classroom. Before she left, she said, "I want to express my gratitude for your assistance, and we welcome your feedback. June is a fantastic instructor, and you'll learn a lot today. Jenny, feel free to call me later if you need anything."

"Hi, everyone. As Sally mentioned, I'm June, and I'm excited to be your instructor for today's training. We'll explore the most advanced and latest intelligence-gathering satellite technology globally, but there might be bugs or issues. If you encounter any, please note them so we can add them to our list of issues to address. It's always beneficial to get fresh perspectives on a new product. Please introduce yourselves and share your knowledge of imagery and expectations for this training."

Jenny herself and her team. "Hi, June. I'm Jenny, the cell lead.

Tyler and Kim are experienced imagery analysts who have held their positions for several years and come from military backgrounds. A couple of weeks ago, Tyler noticed some unusual activities in the Western Siberian Basin, and since then, we've utilized all our available resources. A few days ago, I reached out to Sally to see if the NRO could provide any new or additional resources. She agreed to arrange this training for us but didn't specify the capabilities of the new assets since I didn't have the necessary clearances at that time. Now that we have the clearances and the assets in place, we're excited about what we can collect moving forward. We're all yours today. Abraham Lincoln once said, 'The best way to predict your future is to create it.' Let's get started."

After the introductions, June said, "Well, let's dive right in. You guys have some great experience, so I'll go fast and furious. Feel free to stop me anytime. We only have nine hours."

They all exclaimed, "Nine hours?"

"We'll take a few breaks, and I'll have lunch from our on-site cafeteria. A menu is on your desk. Please mark what you would like and hand it back to me."

"Let's start by looking at an image from the asset. Please focus your attention on the flat screen. I will give you an overview of the images, and once I'm finished, we will work on the images on your monitors so you can start having fun. Although the image on the screen is still excellent, the images will be more detailed and precise on your computer monitor." June began to discuss every aspect of the image.

"Ladies and gentlemen, this is 'Thoth.'"

She then proceeded to demonstrate Thoth. "As you can see, the image can fill the entire real estate on your screen, but there are two flyouts: one on the left and the other on the right. The left flyout gives the analyst the exact location, relative direction, time, date, and weather conditions. By clicking on it, the flyout will disappear, giving you more real estate on your monitor. Click here, and it will reappear. Click on the small tab on the right, and the right flyout provides any previous analysis and notes, if available, and this is where you can add your notes or comments."

June paused and said, "Any questions?"

Tyler raised his hand, then lowered it.

"Tyler, do you have a question?" June asked.

"I have one, but I'll wait. You might tell us later," he replied.

June nodded and continued, "Under each entry, you'll find the initials of the analyst who provided any intelligence or information. Some notes have checkmarks next to them to indicate that another analyst has verified them. Only some entries will be checked. If you are reviewing the images, you can mark them as verified by right-clicking on the entry."

"Now, I'm not assigned to your mission, nor do I have any details. But I will cover all of the features of the new technology. When I start to cover a feature you believe will directly impact your mission, I can park on it and provide more details. However, you can try them all out when you receive images from your target area. The best way to put it is that you will have access to 100% of the technology.

One feature is the ability to right-click on an object and view the heat it radiates, its height from the base, its weight, and any vibrations it produces. Remember, these are still images, but the asset can provide live feeds or saved footage. Now it's time to view some images and video streams on your computer monitors. Launch the Thoth application and open the Test Images folder.

"June, why is the application called Thoth?" Kim asked.

"Hey, that was my question, too," Tyler said, laughing.

Kim extended her right arm, tapped him on the shoulder, and said, "That's why we make a great team."

The smile on his face was contagious.

"Thoth is the Egyptian god of knowledge," June replied.

"That makes perfect sense," Jenny said as Tyler and Kim nodded.

"Hold on, everyone," Tyler said.

He continued, "Did you know he was also associated with fertility?"

Kim turned to him and said, "What? How do you know that? I've never heard of Thoth until today."

Tyler replied, "That's why we make a great team." The entire classroom erupted in laughter.

Kim kept looking at him, smiling.

"Okay, everyone, let's get back to work. Did everyone open the folder? Now click on the first image."

"You were right, June," Kim remarked. "The image on the monitor didn't do it justice."

June continued to guide them through the app for nine hours, taking a couple of breaks to explain how Thoth worked and to share valuable tips and tricks. When it was over, Jenny, Tyler, and Kim were exhausted but utterly amazed. They couldn't wait to review Thoth's images from their area of interest the next day.

"Before you all go, I want to give you your login credentials," said June. She approached each person and handed them their credentials. June walked the team out of the building, and they thanked her.

"You did a great job, June!" Jenny exclaimed. "Let's grab a drink."

"What about your kids?" Kim asked.

"My husband can pick them up today."

Kim and Tyler exchanged glances, and Tyler said, "Is Jenny married?"

TYLER AND KIM arrived at the office earlier than usual, eager to see the new imagery. Around 9:00 a.m., they discovered that the asset was positioned and ready for them to view its imagery. The first images and intelligence appeared on their monitors in just a few minutes.

Tyler and Jenny sat in awe at the images and information from Thoth.

"Hey, Kim, can you believe how clear these are? They're incredible! Just like June showed us—not only the images but also the information embedded in each one," Tyler said.

"I can see everything, and the ability to switch to thermal on the fly is amazing! Wow, click on that oil pump right there. Yes, that one," Kim replied.

"Wow, look at all this information! It's unbelievable! It would almost be overwhelming if they didn't build in some great AI technology. Check this out: It indicates that the pump operates at nine hundred revolutions per minute and that the temperature is within normal limits."

"Jenny is going to freak out when she sees these images. Okay, let's tone down our excitement. After all, we are professionals," Kim said. They both started laughing and fist-bumping.

"Yes, you're right, but this is really cool."

Throughout the week, the team kept providing and building their intelligence package, and every day, they discovered new ways to work with Thoth.

They provided their updates and attended their daily sync-up meeting with Jenny. At each meeting, it was evident that she was becoming increasingly excited and curious. The questions flowed to them like water from a fire hydrant.

After a few days, she asked her team to compile the images and film footage into a single product for analysis. She wanted it by the next day.

Tyler and Kim stayed up late that night to assemble everything into one product. When they finally finished, it was almost 11:00 p.m. Thankfully, they enjoyed spending time together.

"Kim, send it to Jenny. I think it's time for us to head out. It's been a long day," Tyler said.

"Sending it now, and yes, it certainly has been, Tyler," Kim replied.

As they walked to her car, he was about to leave when Kim said, "Hey, no hug?" Tyler turned around, and Kim hugged and kissed him on the cheek. "Thanks for walking me to my car. I'll see you bright and early tomorrow."

Tyler turned back and walked to his car, unsure whether his feet were touching the ground.

7

NGA HEADQUARTERS, SPRINGFIELD, VA

The intelligence product that Tyler and Kim assembled included thousands of images, hundreds of feet of film footage, a detailed analysis of each image, and a synopsis for every foot of film. They also added background information about the area, its history, and statistics on output, revenue generation, and oil production trends over the last five years. It was the most comprehensive product Jenny had ever seen. She believed this was what every product should include.

After reviewing it, she took it straight to Tex, a choice outside protocol and standard operating procedures (SOP). SOP requires monitoring the target area throughout the entire specified period. Once another team had gathered, reviewed, and analyzed all the intelligence, it would be sent to the next link in the chain of authority.

Jenny was known for being a stickler for policies and procedures. However, she had a gut feeling—something wasn't right. What the hell? If I'm going to step outside of protocol, this is the perfect time.

She printed the intelligence package and placed it in a folder marked 'Top Secret.' Jenny then took the folder and walked briskly down to Tex's office

Tex, whose real name was Justin Adkins, was a senior GEOINT officer and the assistant director at the NGA, responsible for Western Russia and the Black Sea regions. Standing at just five feet eight, his demeanor gave the impression that he was much taller. You could tell he took pride in his appearance and cared for himself, displaying that confidence daily. His closely cropped, graying hair and piercing blue eyes exuded friendliness. He never met a stranger, perhaps because he grew up in an Air Force family and moved every three years until he turned twelve.

Tex's door was slightly ajar, so Jenny peeked in. "Tex, do you have a minute?"

"Sure, Jenny. What's on your mind?"

"Wow, Tex, you look great! Is that a new suit, or do you have an interview?"

"Hilarious, Jenny," he sighed, smiling.

It was common knowledge that Tex wore the same suit daily, meaning he owned at least five identical suits. When asked about it once, he replied that mixing and matching would take too long.

"I don't have the time or the energy for that, so I just buy the same suit, shirt, tie, socks, and shoes. I can't even imagine how much time I've saved over the years. Plus, the blue shirts make my eyes pop," he would say with a laugh. "I suppose it also comes from my twenty years in the army. Back then, I always knew what I would wear."

Tex retired from the army as a first sergeant. He enjoyed being called "Top" around fellow veterans. At work, he was Tex.

"So, Jenny, what's on your mind? Please have a seat."

She handed him the 'Top Secret' folder and said, "Remember the oil fields in the West Siberian Basin that my team has been monitoring?"

He placed it on his desk and answered, "Yes, I sure do."

"They uncovered some fascinating and unusual occurrences in the oil fields."

"Jenny, what do you mean by 'unusual'? Can you be more specific?"

As Jenny spoke, he opened the folder and looked through its contents. Under his breath, Jenny heard him murmur, "Fascinating." He closed the folder and focused completely on Jenny.

Jenny continued, "Of course. Let me explain: a functional and operational oil well typically includes the oil rig, the pumping station, several tanks, and a flare stack. The flare stack burns off excess gas and releases pressure from the oil well. Tyler, one of my team members, discovered that multiple flare stacks from a significant number of oil well sites in various fields were not emitting heat or showing a flame."

"Maybe they're doing rig maintenance?" Tex asked, though he knew better. He was fishing for information.

"This is where it gets interesting. Many older wells aren't pumping. The derricks aren't operational; from what we've observed, they've stopped producing oil using our new asset. There's no liquid in the pipelines."

"Stopped pumping?" asked Tex with a puzzled look. "I've worked in the oil fields of West Texas and have seen many of those derricks not pumping. This can happen for various reasons. A typical oil derrick's lifespan is between twenty and thirty years. Some of those oil wells and sites in West Texas are much older than that, so maintenance might need to be performed on them. It could cost more to bring the oil to the surface, or the oil deposit could have dried up, which is known as a dry hole. I would love to know the reason."

"Dried up, dry hole?"

"Yep. The well might not have had as much oil as they thought. It happens all the time."

"Tex, if I'm not mistaken, the Russians have repeatedly stated that the oil field has fifty to sixty years of oil left. Knowing this, do you think we should move on? I want to make sure we're not wasting our time, money, or resources," Jenny said.

"No, I don't believe you are wasting your time with so many wells out of service. There's no way they all ran dry at the same time. The question is, have any of them been replaced with new equipment among the non-operational ones?"

She replied, "No, not that we've seen."

"Okay, let's move on."

"The oil wells and fields in Russia are newer than that, and with their technology, those derricks should last at least forty to fifty years with proper maintenance," Jenny continued. "Oil is currently $190 per barrel so that those wells could generate a significant amount of money. Why would they shut them off and decide to do maintenance on such a large number all at once for weeks?"

"Great points. This is becoming interesting." Tex stood up from his desk, looked out the window, and then back at Jenny. "How long has your team been observing this area? When was the first time it was identified?"

She replied, "They identified it about a week and a half ago, and we've been actively monitoring it since then."

"Has your team reviewed other regional drilling sites to see if this is specific to these fields or more widespread?"

"In Timan-Pechora, Russia, we observe the same pattern, though not to the same extent."

"Jenny, you've given me a lot to digest. What do you need from me now?" Tex asked.

"I'd like to continue observing this area for thirty days. That would give us enough time to identify if we see an anomaly, a pattern, or more."

"Let me review what you sent, and I'll get back to you tomorrow," Tex said. "Is that okay? Once I review the intelligence package,

I'll reach out to Sally at NRO about extending the time the asset can be on the station since it was originally scheduled for only thirty days. That shouldn't be an issue. They appreciate your team's feedback and recommendations. Jenny, great job—both you and your team!"

"Thank you. I also sent a link to the online package."

As she left his office, Tex called out, "By the way, I don't think we'll need the full thirty days."

A strange sensation stirred in her gut again. Did he believe it wouldn't take the entire thirty days? Does he know something?

Tex sat at his desk and opened an online version of Jenny's package. He reviewed the images, removed his hands from the keyboard, leaned back, and took a deep breath. After a moment, he leaned forward again, resumed examining the material, and continued for the next hour.

During his review, he thought, "Wow, these images and the analysis are excellent. I've never seen anything like this. Jenny was right. These are disturbing. We need more intelligence." Before leaving, he emailed Sally, asking her to keep the asset in place for another two weeks, possibly more. He then closed the files and turned off his computer for the night.

Driving home, he couldn't shake the thoughts of what he had read and seen. It makes no sense at all.

Once home, he started calculating the Russians' revenue losses. An average oil well can produce 21.9 barrels daily, and at the current price of $190 per barrel, that amounts to about $4,200 per well daily. Nine hundred wells are currently not operational, leading to a loss of around $3,800,000 daily, translating to a potential monthly loss of $114 million.

"What the hell!"

THE NEXT DAY, Tex called Jenny. "After reviewing the intelligence material, I agree with you. Continue to monitor the target area closely for the next thirty days. I want to be briefed every few days and notified immediately if things change or there is any more unusual activity."

8

RUSSIAN MINISTRY OF DEFENSE – MOSCOW, RUSSIA

General Chen, Chief of Staff of the Chinese People's Liberation Army, and General Patel, the commanding general of India's Armed Forces, sat with their staff in a conference room at the General Staff building in Moscow, near Arbat Street and Arbatskaya Square.

"Welcome, everyone, to Mother Russia," General Popov began. "We're glad you could make it on such short notice, but we believe it's essential for this meeting to be held on-site and in person. We have much to review before we launch Operation Moose—the beginning of the end of the United States' dominance. We are poised to put them in their place. For too long, they've bullied all of us, but no more, my friends, no more!"

Everyone stood up, stomping their feet and applauding. The sound was deafening, and the enthusiasm was euphoric. The applause lasted for five minutes. All in attendance raised their glasses in unison, shouting, "Victory, victory, victory!"

Once they had calmed down, they sat back down and reviewed their operational plans.

"Comrades, please turn your attention to the flat-screen monitor. It shows each of our theaters of operation. Your theater will be updated based on your words as you provide your update. It is voice-activated."

The other generals had never seen anything like this and wanted one.

"To begin, I would like you to provide a status update on your forces. Let's start with General Chen."

General Chen stood up and walked around the table as he gave his update: "Thank you, General Popov. We have moved the bulk of our four army maneuver divisions into position along our border with Laos and coordinated their movement across the border. Our 150,000 soldiers are currently prepared and conducting training and equipment maintenance along our border with Laos."

Pausing briefly, he continued, "China's People's Liberation Army is ready to mobilize when ordered. The commanding general of one of our four army maneuver divisions, along with his brigade commander for the leading infantry unit, has already coordinated with the commander of the border checkpoint north of Ban Souan-teng, Laos. This coordination will facilitate movement into Laos. We are also wrapping up a naval training exercise along the Taiwan Banks, and four of the participating ships are heading to Vietnam before proceeding to Singapore. Once this operation is complete, we will take steps to establish control over Taiwan. We have already initiated internal espionage efforts. Hong Kong has proven to be an excellent location for redefining our internal leadership structure and personnel management. Taiwan will allow us to dominate the semiconductor industry, aligning perfectly with the green initiatives pursued by the West. China will expand its economy and vision of dominance in Asia and beyond. However, you, my friends, need not worry. Do you have any questions for me?"

"No, General. Excellent! General Patel, you're next."

"Thank you, General," General Chen replied with a smile as he sat down.

Leaning over the table, General Patel began his update on the Indian forces involved in Operation Moose: "General, the upgrades on the INS Vikramaditya are complete and ready to set sail with her task force upon command. They are on a twelve-hour alert to depart. We have added four additional vessels and a complement of marines to the task force. We don't anticipate any issues with moving into position. We have announced a planned naval exercise in the South Indian Ocean, so nothing will seem unusual when she sets sail. Additionally, we have stationed more forces along the border with Bangladesh. We are closer to our naval bases if we need to assist in pushing down the Malaysian peninsula."

General Popov commented, "General Patel, those four vessels or the soldiers were never part of the original plan, but thank you for adding them."

"Gentlemen, that is all I have. Are there any questions?"

"How many helicopters will support the operation?" General Popov asked.

"As of now, we have nine. We can deploy fixed-wing aircraft in the region once some airfields are secured. We are ready to commit five squadrons—eighty aircraft."

Standing up, General Popov walked toward the monitor on the wall, faced it, smiled, turned around, and said, "Very nice, General. I guess it's my turn to address the heightened tensions in the Middle East since the overthrow of Bashar al-Assad. With much persuading, promises, and money, the new interim government has permitted us to move our ground forces into the country's interior. Now that the Americans have abandoned their fire bases in Syria and moved them to Jordan, our freedom of movement allows us to deploy our forces quickly. The Russian army has positioned four armored and three infantry divisions along Jordan's border with Syria for our push to the Red Sea. Our aircraft are in position and have been conducting reconnaissance missions for the last three weeks. We have noticed that Jordan is mobilizing its forces, but they will not match us."

"General, what about the American forces in Jordan? How do you plan to bypass them? We don't want the Americans to react too soon," asked General Patel.

"General, we have mapped out all their positions. Our routes of advancement steer us clear of them. As long as Jordan doesn't request American intervention, we won't face any issues. Before we advance into Jordan, the Russian government will notify them. We are not at war with them. We are merely passing through," he replied with a smirk.

"Passing through?" General Chen responded.

"Gentlemen, I will leave it to the diplomats to choose their words. I'm a soldier. I wage war."

Everyone at the table thought that was what had happened in Ukraine, but they would never express their opinion. They could only hope Russia had learned its lesson.

"Now, let's continue our operations in the Greenland Sea towards the Labrador Sea. We are positioning a surveillance ship halfway between the Greenland and Labrador Seas. The mission of the Ivan Khurs is to monitor the situation and observe the construction of a new small U.S. naval base at Taslilaq. However, we all recognize how crucial this piece of land will be in the near future."

"We have not identified any increased activity from the United States or its allies," Popov continued. "Do you have any questions for me, my friends?"

Everyone fell silent. The giant screen went blank.

He didn't even mention Admiral Balakin's mission as part of Operation Moose. Only Russia and China were aware—well, China believed they were aware. There was no mention of naval activities or cyberattacks against the U.S. Only Russia and China knew about them. India was merely a pawn in this chess match.

"Comrades, it's time for dinner and tonight's activities. I have cars ready to take you back to your hotel so you can attend to any personal matters, change, and prepare for dinner. I will meet you in the lobby at 8:00 p.m." With that, General Popov returned to his office. He still had a substantial amount of work to complete before dinner.

9

NGA HEADQUARTERS, SPRINGFIELD, VA

Over the past couple of weeks, Jenny has provided Tex with regular updates from her team. After just fifteen days, he decided it was time to call Jenny about his decision to move forward with the mission. Despite years of experience in the military and intelligence community, he was unaware of what was happening in the Russian oil fields. It was time to advance to the next level, so he picked up his desk phone and called Jenny.

She was arriving at her office early to review Tyler and Kim's latest analysis when, suddenly, her phone rang. She glanced at her watch and wasn't expecting a call at this hour. When she checked the number, it was Tex's.

She answered her phone, but before she could say hello, Tex asked, "Hi, Jenny. How are you this beautiful morning?"

"Yes, it is beautiful, Tex, but why are you calling so early?"

"The early bird gets the worm. I should ask why you are at work so early. I was going to leave a voicemail, but since I have you on the phone, I'll tell you now."

Leaning back in her chair, she replied, "I just wanted to get a jump on the new intel from Tyler and Kim."

"Well, that's why I'm calling. Good news! Although it's only been fifteen days, what's happening in the oil fields requires a larger team and additional skill sets. I wanted to inform you that we are moving forward and creating a new cell."

She thought, "Wow, this is moving fast."

"I want to let you know what I've decided. I want Bob Weager to lead the larger team, but I must clarify one thing. This is not a demotion. You will report to Bob only for the duration of the mission. Under your leadership, your team is doing great work. I want you to continue focusing on the intelligence and analysis your team is gathering. Bob will handle the administrative and political challenges I'm sure will arise."

"That's no problem," Jenny said.

Jenny shifted in her chair and continued, "I've been playing this game for a long time. Something's happening in Russia, and I want to be part of it. So whatever you need me to do, I'm in."

Tex smiled. "I couldn't agree more."

They knew something was amiss in Russia. It didn't make sense.

"So, inform your team about the new larger group being formed, and we have our first meeting tomorrow at 8:00 a.m. I'll see you and your team at the SCIF next to my office."

Tex hung up, put his feet on his desk, leaned back, and closed his eyes. I wonder what Marsha is up to. I'll have to let her know, but not now. He put his feet down and called Bob.

Jenny left her desk and walked out of her office toward Kim and Tyler's cubicles. She wanted to tell them in person and see their reactions.

"How are you two doing?" she asked casually.

"Good," they both replied.

Kim added, "I'm just busy and tired, but the images are fantastic."

"Aren't we all? It's been hectic for the last few weeks, but nothing compared to the last few days. The girls are already in bed by the time I get home. They aren't even awake when I leave in the morning." She glanced at her wristwatch. "Oh no, I'm going to be late again! I'm taking them to school. Let me text them. But before I go, I want to thank both of you for putting in the extra effort to get the package done so we could send it to Tex. He praised your work! You all have just set a standard for the other teams. Can you come into my office for a quick huddle?"

"Sure, we're right behind you," Tyler said.

"Hmm, our next sync-up is next week," Kim said softly. "Why do we have one today? We just met yesterday."

"I have no idea. I hope we can leave here on time today. I have a date tonight," Tyler replied.

"A date? I didn't even know you had a girlfriend."

"This is our first date." Tyler smiled. "It won't go over well if I'm late or have to cancel."

"If we leave here late, you can take me to dinner—means you're paying."

They both laughed.

Tyler grinned. "Sounds good. I'm not sure she and I would have much to discuss anyway. She isn't read in on the mission." They cracked up, staring at one another for a moment.

In her office, Jenny informed them about the larger team being formed to support their mission and the meeting scheduled for tomorrow morning. She advised them to go home after lunch, get some rest, eat something, and relax. She knew they were about to get even busier and that their stress levels might rise.

"I guess my date is on," Tyler said. "Hell, yes!" Kim felt disappointed as she walked out of Jenny's office. *I guess I'll be eating alone again tonight. What is it going to take for him to ask me out? Honestly, I might as well ask him.*

During those fifteen days, Jenny knew Kim and Tyler had reviewed every image they had in the area and knew it like the back of their hands. They even tracked when shift changes occurred for each rig. The amount of data they gathered was astounding, and their analysis was precise.

They were ready for the meeting, and she was confident. The team was prepared to take it to the next level.

As she was about to turn off her computer to leave, she heard Bing—a new email had just arrived. Knowing it was regarding tomorrow's meeting, she turned off her computer and said, "It's time to pick up the girls and take them to school." She would have the rest of the day to address whatever came up. But right now, her sole focus is on the Russian oil fields.

10

NGA HEADQUARTERS, SPRINGFIELD, VA

Kim and Tyler met on their way to Tex's conference room. Kim asked him, "How was your date?"

"We sat there for about an hour. She asked about my job and what I was working on—a casual conversation to get to know each other. She said, 'Wow, you don't say much, do you?' I replied, 'Nope, not too much.'"

"What? You talk all the time! Is a second date on the horizon?"

Looking down, Tyler responded, "Nope, I don't think so. She called an Uber to take her home."

"Well, maybe next time you can take me out?"

"I like your idea. At least we can have a conversation."

They laughed and met Jenny while heading to Tex's conference room.

Kim saw Jenny sitting at the conference table and had to do a double take. Before she could say, "It's summer. Why are you wearing a sweater, Jenny?"

Jenny burst into laughter. "I'll answer your question briefly, but I need to know how Tyler's date went."

Jenny continued, "Tyler, how was your date?"

"He told me it sucked. She took an Uber home," Kim replied with a smile. "So, why the sweater?"

"Now, getting back to your question, Kim, I've been in too many meetings with Tex," she said with a mischievous smile.

Tex walked in and sat at the head of the oval conference table. His assistant, Bob Weager, was to his right, while Jenny was to his left. Kim sat next to Jenny, and Tyler sat beside her. Two Cisco secure IP phones with speakers were placed on the desk. Everyone had a water bottle. The only items missing were notepads and pens. The room had no windows, and the temperature was uncomfortably cold.

Kim wished she had brought a sweater as well. She tapped Jenny on the arm.

Jenny glanced over and, smiling, said, "Brrrr."

At one end of the conference room, a whiteboard stood. At the opposite end, an 85-inch flat screen displayed original images alongside Thoth's newer ones. Tyler thought it was an amazing monitor. *I need one of those for gaming.*

Tex stood up and began, "I want to say, great job pulling together the images and completing your analysis. Jenny sent the package to me the other day for my review and that of my staff. I received an email from Ms. Castel, and she wants to express her gratitude to you and your team for the feedback you provided them. Based on your recommendations and findings, they believe that Thoth will be fully operational in fifteen days. She also mentioned they would keep the asset where it is so you can continue using it until it's no longer needed and asked for further feedback. Forgive me, have you met Bob?"

Tyler replied, "No, sir, we haven't met him before."

"Bob, please introduce yourself."

"Going forward, I'll be collaborating with both of you, along with Jenny and a few other analysts we're currently identifying," he said. "You both have done fantastic work, so we've decided to create a cell based on your expertise. Our mission has been given the code name Flames of Deception. You'll continue to report to Jenny. She will be my right hand. I'm excited to be working with her, finally. I've known her for years but have never been on the same team or cell. She's well-respected throughout the agency as a reliable and fair manager, leader, and intel analyst. We synced up last night and are eager to get this mission underway!"

"I know she's a poker player. I believe she's taken at least a buck or two from me. I enjoy playing poker. It's relaxing. You can learn a lot about people when they play the cards dealt to them, and we will engage in interesting conversations. Do either of you play?"

"No, sir, but I'm eager to learn," Kim replied.

Bob smiled. "What about you, Tyler?"

"Yes, sir, my dad taught me when I was ten. When I turned twenty-one, he took me to Las Vegas, and since then, I've been a couple more times."

"Outstanding! Let's all get together this weekend if you're free. I know Jenny is all in. The rest of the team will join us this weekend. We can all get to know each other better since we'll be spending a lot of time together. This could be a learning session for you, Kim. There's no money involved. We'll play for fun."

Tyler and Kim exchanged glances, and they agreed. "We're in. Sounds good."

"Excellent. I'll have my assistant send you the details. Please don't mention it to anyone or where you're going. Let's keep this between us for now. Tex, you're welcome to join us, but don't bring it up yet."

"Thanks, Bob, but I'll let you and the team start bonding," he replied. "Kim and Tyler, the information and intelligence you provided are excellent. We ran your analysis through a couple more teams, and they couldn't find any faults or errors. I want to ask both of you some questions. Have you ever seen a large cluster of wells where the burn-off fires or the wells are not operational?"

"No, sir," Tyler answered. "I've seen maybe one to three at once, but never all in the same area. They've always been at least 2 miles or 3.2 kilometers apart but never clustered like we see now."

"Kim, what about you?"

"No, sir, I've only noticed the same things Tyler identified. We're in sync on this."

"How long have you both been working on this mission?" Tex asked.

Tyler replied, "After nine months on the mission, I noticed the strange activity a few weeks ago. Once I saw that the burn-off fires weren't lit, I researched as far back as five years. I didn't find any mention of whether this type of activity had been reported in Russia."

"I have some contacts who monitor Saudi Arabia, and I asked if they could go back and search for anything resembling what I saw. One mentioned that something similar had occurred about six months ago in the Khurais oil field. But now they are all operational again. They didn't find anything beyond that, so it seems contained to Russia. Of course, that's my assumption."

Tex looked at Kim. "What about you?"

"I was working on another mission before this, so I've only been on this one for a few weeks. Tyler asked me to analyze the images and share my thoughts, which is how I got involved."

"It would be interesting to gather information about how much oil Russia exports from its ports on the Black Sea and the Sea of Azov. I need an average for the last three years, if possible," Tex said.

Bob replied, "It might take some time, but I'll see what I can find."

"I'm interested in the pipeline that runs from the oil fields in West Siberia to Novorossiysk on the Heracles Peninsula," Tex continued.

Jenny chimed in, "Tex, we have some information on that pipeline. It's over 2,466 miles long, and we're unsure of its exact capacity since it just came online a few months ago. Tyler or Kim, do you have any additional information you can share?"

Tyler replied, "Of course. Here's what I know: the pipe's diameter is forty-seven inches, which is considered large for a pipeline moving a substantial amount of oil. Based on that, we estimate it can transport approximately 250,000 barrels per day. However, we used Thoth's technology to measure vibrations, velocity, complex measurements, still images, and full motion video, and we obtained an exact flow volume through the pipeline."

He continued, "I researched because certain things weren't adding up. A few months ago, the Russian Ministry of Oil announced their plan to move 240,000 barrels daily through the pipeline. However, as mentioned earlier, Thoth can detect vibrations and friction, generating heat. Even though the pipelines are insulated against heat and cold, they still produce a tiny amount of thermal energy."

"So, what are you telling us, Tyler?" Bob asked.

"The amount they claim to be transporting through the pipeline differs significantly from what's actually being moved. It's almost half—around 120,000 barrels."

Everyone looked up.

"You're saying they're exaggerating the quantity of oil they're transporting," Tex said.

"Yes, I believe they are."

Bob asked, "Tyler, did you do all this with Thoth?"

"Yes, sir, all with Thoth," Tyler replied like a proud father.

"If your estimate's correct, that's a lot of lost revenue each day," Bob said.

Tex stood up. "Team, how are we going to verify this? This is good, but it's not enough to take it to the higher-ups. I have an idea, though. We know where this oil is headed—I want some eyes on the southern Black Sea at Novorossiysk and Rostov-on-Don along the coast of the Sea of Azov. Let's monitor the oil tankers leaving the ports. I'll see if we can get an asset at each port."

"What are you looking for, Tex?" Tyler chimed in.

Tex replied with a mischievous grin, "Great question. Based on the amount of oil they loaded, I want to determine if the tankers are sitting at the correct depth. If it's too high, it's lighter than it should be, or they didn't load as much oil as stated on the manifest. If it's too low, it might not even be oil. Remember, liquids don't all weigh the same. They have different densities."

Kim added, "We can also monitor the Murmansk and Druzhba oil pipelines. I believe we'll find that the number of barrels flowing through the Murmansk pipeline is lower than what they claim is being sent to Novorossiysk. The Druzhba oil pipeline is a different situation. It should align with their statements."

"Why is that?" Bob asked.

Kim responded, "That's the only one being monitored outside the Russian Ministry of Energy. The EU oversees it. Unless the regulators are compromised, it should reliably match what they report is moving through it."

Bob said, "I'll reach out to some Navy personnel to see if they can help. Accessing the Black Sea is tough, but they can gauge how much fuel they've consumed by traveling from one of the ports to the Bosporus Strait's exit on their way to the Sea of Marmara. Sir, what do you want the Navy to observe?"

"Yes. I want visuals of those ships," Tex replied. "I want to know if the oil tankers leaving those ports are riding higher or lower in the water than they should be according to the oil volume they say is in their storage tanks. We can compare their observations and calculations with what we capture from our satellites."

Everyone looked at Tex.

"Now that's thinking outside the box!" Jenny said.

Bob replied, "I'm on it after this meeting."

Jenny continued, "Tex, what's happening? Do you have a hunch, or are you keeping something from us?"

"Nope, you guys know as much as I do, but I have a hunch. The information Thoth provides turns my hunch into more of a possibility."

Tyler couldn't resist. "Thoth is badass! Excuse me, sir—I meant incredible."

"No, Tyler, it is badass!" Tex replied.

"Sorry to throw the conversation off track—where were we?" Tyler grinned.

Just as Tex was about to continue, there was a knock on the door: Larry, Tex's administrative assistant, peeked in. He was the only one who would think of interrupting one of Tex's meetings.

"Excuse me, Tex. You asked me to let you know when Mr. Walters arrived."

"Thanks, Larry. Please come in, Mr. Walters," Tex said.

"Please call me Toby," said the man who entered. He found an empty seat and sat down.

"Team, I want to introduce you to Mr. Walters—I mean Toby," Tex began with a grin. "Toby is an industry expert and the go-to person for oil and gas matters. Most of the other agencies also reach out to him. He holds the highest clearance and access controls and has reviewed your intelligence. I invited him here to provide details, insights, and recommendations for further exploration or any additional activities we should undertake."

With his right arm pointing to the east, Toby said, "Thank you, Tex. I apologize for being late. The traffic on D.C.'s George Mason Memorial Bridge is terrible." He lowered his arm and surveyed the room.

He continued, "Thank you for that excellent introduction. I must say, the intelligence I reviewed is the best analysis I have ever come across. Who are Tyler and Kim?"

Tyler and Kim raised their hands.

Toby continued, "Tyler and Kim, I understand you initially uncovered this intelligence. Great job! Let's review some fundamental concepts of oil drilling and provide some background on the West Siberian petroleum basin."

Toby paused briefly and stood up, walking toward the monitor on the wall. He took a laser pointer from his front pocket and aimed it at the screen, circling an area on it. "I am going to concentrate my briefing on the oil aspect of the basin, not the natural gas, which, by the way, is enormous. Now, back to oil. It's the largest hydrocarbon basin in the world, covering roughly 2.2 million square kilometers, and it's also the largest oil and gas-producing region in Russia. Six hundred oil fields hold reserves of over 146 billion barrels. It comprises 107 giant fields, one mega-giant, and ten super-giant fields. Since 2019, nine new giants have been discovered. It accounts for over 70 percent of Russia's oil and gas production. Any questions before I proceed?" He put the laser pointer back in his pocket and walked toward his chair.

"When did the Russians discover oil in that area?" Tyler asked.

Stopping short of his chair, he placed his left hand on his chin and replied, "Mmm, good question. The first hydrocarbon was discovered in 1953 when a gas well was tested in the Berezov field on the western margin of the basin. Most of the giant oil and gas fields that contain the bulk of the basin's reserves were discovered during the 1960s and 1970s. Large-scale production began in the early 1970s, and currently, the basin produces over three-quarters of the oil and gas in Russia. Despite extensive drilling and seismic surveys, the basin remains only moderately explored, particularly in its northern regions. Only three wells have been drilled offshore in the Kara Sea, and they discovered two potentially giant gas fields."

Tex stood up and asked, "Toby, how many barrels does it produce daily?"

He replied, "Well, they report 6.2 million barrels daily."

"Thank you, Toby," Tex said.

Tex continued to stand and pace in the back of the room. Everyone could tell he was deep in thought.

Sitting down, Toby continued, "Given your keen observations

and the intelligence I've read, let's discuss the basic steps to extracting oil from the ground. This may be the most important step. There are six fundamental steps to extracting oil from the ground in Russia and virtually anywhere else in the world."

"The tasks are: 1. preparing the site; 2. drilling; 3. cementing and testing; 4. well completion; 5. production; and 6. well abandonment and land restoration."

"Identifying so many flame stacks not ignited simultaneously is fascinating and disturbing, as we have been told these wells are still producing and will continue to do so for the foreseeable future."

Toby glanced around to check for any questions before continuing. "The vertical drilling depths in this basin range from five thousand to twenty thousand feet. When moving into horizontal drilling, the lengths can reach up to forty thousand feet."

"Is Russia beginning to engage in more horizontal drilling?" Jenny asked. "If so, would that require the well to be shut down for a long time?"

Clapping his hands, Toby responded, "Another excellent question. Tex, you have an impressive team. They are transitioning to fracking. However, it wouldn't require an extended shutdown, so no."

Toby continued, "Let's discuss flare stacks, but we don't need to delve too deeply into the details. Understanding what you've identified is crucial to extracting oil and is quite interesting. Let me illustrate it on the whiteboard."

He got up, shoved his hands into his pants pocket, and pulled out a black marker. Before writing on the whiteboard, he checked to see if it was a permanent marker. Smiling, he glanced at Tex and said, "This one is erasable. Remember last time?"

Tex nodded and replied, "Sure do. It took me half an hour to erase your last drawing."

"Okay, here goes. There are four major components. I'll start from the well to the flare stack. The first is the liquid knockout drum, which separates oil or water from the relieved gas. Second, the flashback seal drum prevents any flashback from the flare stack. Third, you can think of the spark-igniter device like the pilot light on your water heater. It's on all the time to ignite the gas."

Toby took a breath and surveyed the room. Everyone was absorbed in his briefing.

He continued, "And fourth, the flare stack is where the flame exits and features a flashback prevention system. The typical height of the stack or flare boom is based on the thermal radiation that is acceptable for equipment and personnel. The minimum diameter is six feet, and the height is at least forty feet. They are also designed to minimize noise and obscure the flame. Any questions?" asked Toby.

Kim inquired, "Why are there flare stacks at drilling sites?"

Toby replied, "I should have started with that. There are three reasons: first, to test and stabilize the pressure and flow. Second, to burn off the gas that can't be captured or processed, and third, to release pressure in emergencies—a major safety precaution."

Tyler raised his hand.

"Yes, Tyler?"

"What can cause the flare stack to go out?"

"Typically, if the well is not producing, during maintenance, or if they have just begun drilling more for exploring new deposits."

Kim asked, "Toby, does the height of the flame mean anything?"

"There are many factors. Pressure from the well and the wind can affect it."

Toby paused. "Hey, Tex, I need to head to another meeting, and he outranks all of you. If you have any additional questions, please consolidate them and send them to me."

"Thanks, Toby. You'll hear from us soon. Have a great day," Tex said.

Once Toby left the room, Tex sat down and said, "I think it's time I gave Director Fields a heads-up. I was going to wait, but I believe we have everything we need to bring it to her attention. I want her input in case we discover any more abnormal activities so we can move faster to inform other agencies and find out what's happening in the West Siberia oil fields."

"I think you're absolutely correct," Bob agreed.

"I can handle this. Your team needs to get to work. Bob and I might catch up with you all this weekend for poker and beer," Tex added. "You did say there would be some beer, right?"

"Yep, I sure did." Bob shrugged, glancing at Jenny.

Jenny smiled and remarked, "I heard Tex enjoys his beer."

Bob grinned and looked down at his phone. He noticed a new email. He opened it, read it, and said, "Tex, before we head out, I have the answer to your question about oil shipments from the Black Sea ports. According to information released by the Russian Ministry of Energy and Commerce, it's approximately four hundred million metric tons annually."

"Wow, thanks, Bob. We have a lot to do, so let's get to it."

After the meeting, Tex returned to his office and logged into his computer. He fired up the DuckDuckGo search bar and entered "Ministry of Energy, Oil Press Releases Export." The results appeared on his monitor, and he clicked the first one.

With the OEEC's approval today, the Russian Ministry of Energy announced that Russia and member countries of the OEEC will reduce oil exportation to nonaligned/partner nations by 75 percent within the next 90 days. The affected countries are in Western Europe, including Germany, Italy, Poland, Finland, Spain, and France. South Korea, Japan, and South American countries are also affected, as is the United States.

The excluded countries are OEEC members and North Korea. Satellite countries like Belarus, Syria, and other selected countries will continue receiving imports.

This course of action is being taken because of the unwarranted sanctions imposed on the Russian Federation during our invasion of Ukraine, which are still being imposed today. We will now only support and provide oil to our friends and allies.

We have also been notified and permitted to include that the OEEC members will reduce oil exports to those countries within the same timeframe.

No further information will be provided.

After reading this, he knew it was time to discuss it with Director Marsha Fields. He considered calling her but opted to drop by instead. He needed to tell her in person and wanted to see her. It couldn't wait any longer. He required additional resources from other agencies.

11

BEIJING, CHINA

Commander Ai Yin Chang's team finished assembling the individual programs into one application two weeks ahead of schedule. Then, it was time to perform internal testing in a simulated environment before handing the application to the manufacturers.

"Let's review the testing plan," she told her team.

They intended to test the app's performance in a simulated environment using solutions that U.S. power companies employ to identify incidents of compromise or IOCs. Infosec professionals utilize IOCs to detect intrusion attempts and malicious activities. The application was also evaluated against various security tools, including antivirus software and malware.

Thanks to her team's exceptional proficiency, the testing took only a few hours. Once she was informed that it was complete, she approached her lead developer and asked, "Did we uncover any issues during our tests, or are there any reasons we shouldn't proceed to the next phase of the project?"

"No, we knew it was running and couldn't detect anything. No issues at all. I believe we can proceed, Commander," he responded.

"You have done an outstanding job. The People's Republic of China thanks you. You are the warriors of the twenty-first century."

She returned to her office and decided her team deserved a celebratory speech. However, her team was already ahead of her. When she stepped out of her office, all the developers had gathered in the open area on their floor, clasping their hands and bowing to her. She waved at them and exclaimed, "You are the best developers in China—not just in China, but the entire world! My cyber warriors! We still have work to do, but we will move on to the next phase tomorrow. What you have accomplished quickly is incredible and will set the standard for other projects. However, this is not the time to let up or allow anything to slip through the cracks. The People's Republic of China needs you at the top of your game."

One of the developers shouted, "Commander!"

"Yes?"

"We should name the application."

"That's a great idea. What should we call it?" Commander Ai Yin asked. "Does anyone have a suggestion?"

Everyone replied, "Qi."

"Wow, that was quick—and very fitting. So, Qi it is."

The room erupted in cheers as they shouted, "Qi, qi, qi!" She left the room, her team still chanting. She headed into the office of her lead developer and waited for him to return from the celebration.

The lead developer copied the application to a folder on a secure file server. Once the file copy was completed, the manufacturer installed the firmware update on just over five thousand devices in the United States in about an hour. These will be the alpha test devices.

The manufacturer would notify her once the deployment was complete.

In under two hours, she received confirmation that the application had been successfully installed and no issues had been detected.

It even passed the United States' verification process, which checked for malicious code or malware, as it aimed to ensure the security of its power grid.

Once she received the information, the software was installed. It was time to notify her chain of command. They would approve the next phase of the project, which would include the same five thousand devices located in Northern Virginia.

She picked up her desk phone and called General Yen, the commander of the Chinese cyber units.

"Sir, the initial testing was completed, and no threats were detected. I need your approval to move forward," said Commander Chang.

"Excellent, Commander. Please proceed," he replied before hanging up the phone.

After receiving approval, she got up from her desk, went to the secure file cabinet, entered the combination, and retrieved the file labeled "Lights Out." She grabbed a pen, struck through "Lights Out," and wrote "Qi" in its place. The file contained the locations, dates, times, and durations of the "blackouts." The first item on the list was for the upcoming alpha testing. She reviewed the information, returned the folder to the drawer, and closed it, ensuring it was locked and secure.

She picked up a burner phone from her desk, tapped the Telegram icon, and typed a message containing the beta test details, including the location, time, and duration.

> Done early - 38.8048° N, 77.0469° W - 0900 Zulu, two tests lasting a minute.

Once finished, she confirmed that it had been sent before removing the SIM and destroying the phone.

WASHINGTON, D.C.

Commander Chang's contact was pacing in front of a government building when his burner phone started vibrating. He took it from his pocket, unlocked it, and read the message. After reading it, he removed the SIM card and destroyed the phone. He then walked back into the five-story government building, took the elevator to the fourth floor, entered his office, and called the CIA Director, Sean McGill.

"Sean, could you please contact DHS? They need to inform the local government about a test on its critical infrastructure. Please prepare for a simulated power outage in the Alexandria area within the next twenty-four hours. Also, ensure that the Security Operations Center monitors the situation and that their security measures and endpoints are updated."

"Thank you. I don't need any further information." The line went dead.

BEIJING, CHINA

Commander Chang arrived at her office early to ensure all the testing equipment was configured correctly and ready for alpha testing. She walked down the hall toward the developers, spotted the lead developer, sat beside him, and instructed him to start the beta test. He launched the application, entered a few commands, and pressed Enter on his keyboard. She was always amazed at how casual and distant it felt to execute a cyberattack. She never felt any guilt about it. After all, most of the previous attacks had targeted banks, tech companies, and social media firms—which she believed were the demise of Western civilization—so they didn't hurt anyone. This attack was different. Many people could die. She had to make sure it performed better than expected.

The command entered by the lead developer into the application instructed the code on the location of the attack. It also deciphered which power companies and grid locations would be impacted and the duration of the surgical strike. That was the beauty of the code—it was undetectable and hidden in the devices' firmware. The North Koreans did an excellent job. It wasn't their first time assisting the Chinese or executing their cyber warfare attacks.

Commander Chang had to wait for the results, which could take about an hour. She decided to get something to eat before the test results came in and thought, *How can I be hungry and so relaxed about what I just unleashed? It was only a test to start, and they won't even realize it's a cyber attack.*

She left her office and walked down to the chow hall. It was empty. All her soldiers were still at their desks, monitoring the cyber-attack. She approached the food line, selected some soup, noodles, and fried pork, looked around, found an empty table, and sat down. While she ate, she glanced at her watch, realizing that she had been sitting there for over thirty minutes. Looking down at her plate, she noticed she had hardly eaten anything. Her mind was elsewhere. She got up and walked back to her office.

Upon returning to her office, she received an email from the lead developer with the alpha test results. It had gone even better than she expected. Although the power companies used the most sophisticated software, tools, and protocols on the market, the latest and best security software failed to detect the code executed on the devices. Not a single security engineer was alerted in their operations center.

Commander Chang was confident. As the test became more complicated, they still wouldn't detect anything. Security engineers in the Security Operations Center at Potomac Electric Power might suspect something abnormal, but they could never pinpoint or stop it. China controlled everything. The beauty of the program lies in its design. The best part was that it didn't require anyone to click on a link or download an attachment. All it needed was an internet connection to download the software update. In the event that the device loses its internet connection after the update, the code will still complete the last command it received. However, the devices had multiple network cards to ensure a connection, allowing the power companies to control them. Commander Ai Yin thought, "*Thank you, 5G.*" It's embedded in the firmware and automatically updated by the manufacturer. She laughed, "*We are the manufacturer.*"

Commander Chang took out a burner phone and sent a short text.

> The alpha phase was successful. The next phase will be at the exact same location: one minute at @9:00 EST.

After confirming the text was sent, she removed the SIM card and destroyed it with the phone. She always had more burner phones.

12

NGA HEADQUARTERS – SPRINGFIELD, VIRGINIA

Tex took the elevator to the third floor and headed to Marsha's office. Her administrative assistant greeted him.

Tex asked, "Betty, can I see Marsha? I only need a couple of minutes."

She replied, "Tex, you don't have an appointment, but she's on a call right now."

"I just need a few minutes of her time," he said.

"You know as well as I do that she'll stop a meeting to talk to you. Go ahead. I won't even let her know," she said with a big smile.

Tex smiled and replied, "It'll be a surprise."

Tex knocked on the door and walked in.

Sure enough, Marsha was sitting at her desk on a conference call. She heard the door open and looked up. She said, "Hey, all, I need to go. You know what to do."

She got up from her desk, and they hugged each other. "It's great to see you, Tex. How can I help you on this beautiful day?" she asked, a twinkle in her eye. "Please, have a seat."

They sat down on her couch.

"Marsha, I'll get straight to the point. I know you're busy. My team has uncovered some fascinating and unusual behavior in Russia's largest oil fields in the West Siberian Basin. Something seems off. I don't want to say more than that right now. We need to gather some information, and I plan to do just that with your approval."

"I'm intrigued, Tex, to say the least. Can you send me an intelligence package to review? Your team can continue working on its mission. I agree in principle, but I'll give my final approval after reviewing all the intelligence."

"Marsha, that's all I can ask for. I sent it earlier. Please check your email."

As their eyes met, Marsha looked away and stood up from the couch. She returned to her desk and said, without looking at Tex, "I need to get back to work. Let me review this package first, and I'll notify you in a day or two."

"Sounds good, Marsha," he said amicably as he walked out of her office. She didn't look back until her door closed.

Her administrative assistant asked, "Is she okay?"

"All good," Tex replied.

She thought she had seen an email from Tex earlier today. Marsha sat down at her desk, moved her mouse, and entered her password on the keyboard. She opened her email and found the message from Tex. Right-clicking on the file, she saved it in a private folder. Then, she double-clicked a different folder and searched for the Word document she had received from the CIA yesterday. After reading the document, she opened the folder where she had saved Tex's team intelligence package and began reviewing it.

As she reviewed the images Thoth provided and Tex's team's analysis, Marsha was reminded of her youth as an imagery analyst. While attending Virginia Tech, Marsha interned at the NGA. After graduating with a degree in Geographic Information Systems, she took a GS-11 level position and, over the years, moved into leadership positions. While on TDY to Fort Stewart, she met a young soldier, Tex, a Scout Section Sergeant assigned to the 3rd Infantry Division. It may not have been love at first sight, but their affection grew daily. Her three-month TDY was ending. Tex proposed to her, and they married shortly after. Within two years, they had a beautiful girl, Janis.

Coming out of her daydream, she thought, *What the hell is going on? Could this be connected to the other?* She closed the files, stood up, looked outside, and muttered, *Wow, that traffic is crazy. I'll wait to go home.*

She didn't notice the power outage until she returned to her desk and her computer rebooted.

Damn Windows. She didn't think it would be Windows 11 that caused the power to go out, but she couldn't think of anything else to blame it on.

By the time she finished reading and processing the intelligence, it was almost nine o'clock. She was exhausted but needed to clear her mind, so she picked up her phone and called Tex's cell. "Marsha, how are you? Is everything okay? It's been a while since you called me this late."

"Very funny, Tex. Can you meet me at Yard House in Springfield Mall in twenty minutes?"

He smiled. "Of course. Wow, that was quick—does this have to do with the package I sent you?"

"I'm sorry. I can't answer that on the phone. See you in twenty."

Tex replied, "Of course. See you there."

YARD HOUSE, SPRINGFIELD MALL – SPRINGFIELD, VIRGINIA

Marsha walked in and saw Tex already sitting at the bar. He watched her as she approached him with a big smile.

"Hey, sailor. Mind if I sit down?"

"No," he said, laughing. "And it's 'soldier.' Of course, you can sit."

They both laughed.

"Tex, you've always made me laugh."

"Well, Marsha, you look beautiful. It was great to see you today."

"Thank you, Tex. You're looking mighty handsome these days. I might need to keep my distance from you," she teased, sounding somewhat seductive with a smile.

"Are you flirting with me?"

"Yes, I am."

"Please don't stop. It's been a while since I've seen you laugh. How long has it been since we had a drink together?"

Looking into Tex's eyes, she said, "It's been way too long. I miss this."

Tex reached out, took her hand, squeezed it gently, and said, "So, Marsha, what's on your mind that's so important we had to meet at this hour?" She shifted her feet on the floor and, grinning, replied, "What's on my mind, or what do I want to talk to you about? How about a drink first?"

"Bartender, one Russell's Reserve Single Barrel Bourbon on the rocks and one Corona Light," Tex ordered.

"Corona Light?" Marsha asked.

"Yes, it's almost swimsuit season." They both laughed.

"Let's get a booth," said Marsha.

They got up from the bar and walked to a booth in the back of the restaurant. Sitting next to each other, Marsha turned to Tex and said, "What I'm about to tell you is just between us for now, okay?"

"Of course. We have plenty of secrets between us."

She smiled. "After you left, I opened the link you sent and reviewed the intelligence and a document from the CIA. Your team is onto something. We believe there's a conspiracy involving Russia, China, India, and potentially the entire OEEC. We're not certain, but it seems related to oil production, specifically refining around known strategic oil reserves in Russia. I want the NGA to play a pivotal role in determining what is happening. Man, what I wouldn't give to be an analyst now. I truly miss the hands-on work."

"Hold on, Marsha, oil reserves... are you referring to what's underground?" He leaned closer to Marsha. He could smell her perfume—Chanel, Coco Mademoiselle. Memories began flooding back. "Does this relate to the Russian press release the other day regarding oil exports?"

She moved closer to him and smiled. "That's your job, and that's all I can tell you today. Because we really don't know, there are some unusual troop movements that we are monitoring. But I want you to concentrate on the oil fields. With that, I've decided to create a working group to figure out what's going on. I'm going to include other agencies and departments. One more thing, your intelligence will be in the President's Daily Brief tomorrow." She gave him a quick kiss on the cheek.

Suddenly, the power went out in the restaurant.

"What the heck? The power went out in my office earlier, too," Marsha said.

"No clue. It's been happening more frequently," Tex replied. "I agree about involving the other agencies. Just let me know what you need me to do."

Marsha responded, "First, please compile a list of people, agencies, and departments you think will provide the most value and help solve this puzzle. I need the list by tomorrow before noon."

They could hear the jukebox when the power returned after a minute.

Marsha leaned over to him and said, "Tex, they're playing our song!" They could hear "I Want to Know What Love Is" playing on the jukebox. "Let's dance!" she urged.

Tex looked confused. "You want to dance?"

"Yes. No one will see us here."

"Are you sure?"

"No." They started laughing. Marsha commanded, "Get your ass up!"

"Okay, here goes. It's been a long time since I danced. The last time was with you, and we both know how that turned out," Tex said softly.

"Yes, I do." She rested her head on his shoulder and closed her eyes, feeling secure in his arms—a sensation she had missed. The feelings had never vanished. She had merely suppressed them.

After the song, they finished their drinks, paid, and stepped outside.

Tex opened Marsha's car door. "Bye, Marsha. See you tomorrow."

Marsha asked in a sultry tone, "Tex, aren't you getting in?"

"I guess I can pick my car up tomorrow. No one will steal that piece of crap anyway," he chuckled.

"Tex, get your ass in the car, please, before I change my mind."

He climbed into her car, and they drove off. "Is this electric?" he asked jokingly.

"No way! I love the roar of the engine in my 1969 Chevy Camaro SS. It's like music to my ears."

"Well, let's hear it," he said, and they sped off.

13

BEIJING, CHINA

Commander Chang called her commander. "Sir, the second test was more successful than we anticipated. It was conducted at two different times and locations for a predetermined duration without any flaws. We did not find any evidence that it was intercepted, nor did we see any investigations. We will monitor the Security Operations Center to determine if any investigations have been initiated since the attack."

"Thank you for the update. Please refrain from additional testing until you receive a message from me. The next operation will not be a test but fully operational. The time for testing has ended. Great job. Your team deserves extra food rations for the coming week. Continue to isolate them until I notify you."

"Yes, sir." She jumped up and down, yelling, "It worked! We're good."

She took out another burner phone. Every text she sent went to a different number. This one read

> Testing complete. No need for further testing. The program is operational.

She tapped the Send button, took out the SIM card, and destroyed it with the phone. She only had two phones left, but that was all she needed.

14

NGA HEADQUARTERS – SPRINGFIELD, VIRGINIA

After meeting with Marsha the previous night, Tex received official written approval via email to form the interagency team and proceed with the mission.

When Tex returned to his office, he formulated his communication plan for the broader team and evaluated which departments and agencies needed to be included. He aimed to ensure no one was left out while keeping the communication as succinct as possible to avoid mired discussions on unnecessary political issues. The only Cabinet secretaries involved would be from the CIA, NSA, and Defense.

Tex decided to reach out to his counterparts at the Central Intelligence Agency, the National Security Agency, and the Department of Defense to review the intelligence he had received. Each secretary or director could contribute their expertise in the oil industry and Russia. However, participation would be limited to two representatives from each agency. He believed that this issue warranted inviting only the heads of these agencies. Tex asked his executive assistant, Larry, to send out the meeting invites for next week's kick-off meeting. He thought *I have a lot of work to do and prepare for before the meeting. Where should I start? I suppose I need a list.* He worked on the logistics for the inter-agency meeting, and by the time he finished, it was nearly 8:00 p.m. He turned off his computer, switched off the lights, and headed to his car. He needed to stop by the store before it closed. He hadn't eaten all day. He had to maintain his strength to combat the government bureaucracy he sensed was approaching.

Representatives from each department or agency gathered around an oval table in a large Sensitive Compartmented Information Facility (SCIF) at the NGA. The participants included Sean McGill, Director of the CIA; Peter Johnson, Director of the NSA; Jesse Dorn, Secretary of Defense; and Marsha Fields, Director of the NGA, each accompanied by their experts. General Ralph Harris from the Joint Chiefs of Staff was also present, along with Jenny, Tyler, Kim, Bob, and Tex.

This was the first time Jenny, Tyler, and Kim had met with a secretary or director from any agency or department, and they felt a bit nervous.

Kim leaned over to Tyler. "Why are you sweating?" She laughed out loud.

Marsha asked Kim, "Okay, what is so funny, Kim?"

"It's just Tyler, Ms. Fields. I apologize," Kim replied.

"Let's get down to business. Tex, please provide the latest intelligence," Marsha said.

Tex looked at Tyler and Kim and asked, "So, how much money did you lose in the poker game last weekend?"

Kim replied, "I must have had beginner's luck. Check out my new shoes!"

Tyler glanced down and initially said nothing but smiled and remarked, "Look at my old shoes."

CIA Director Sean McGill interjected, "Hold on, Tex. Before we start, can you explain why everyone calls you Tex? Were you born there, for those who don't know?"

Tex started laughing. "I wasn't born in Texas. When I was younger, I worked a lot in the oil business before joining the Army in West Texas— that sweet crude. One day, my boss said, 'Hey, Tex.'" No one turned around, so he repeated it. I looked at him and said, "Are you talking to me?" "Yep," he replied. "My name isn't Tex. It's Justin." "Not anymore. At work, you're Tex." And ever since that day, everyone has called me Tex. I was born in Bald Knob, Arkansas, and I'm a proud Razorback." Tex laughed and pointed his middle finger at Sean.

Tex stood up and began to explain the purpose of the meeting: "About a month ago, in June, Tyler Brown—please rise, Tyler—Tyler here observed some unusual activity in the West Siberia petroleum basin."

"He asked Kim Barnes—Kim, please stand—to share her thoughts on what he was observing. The thorough intelligence from Tyler and Kim has sparked a chain of events, which is why we're all here today. I'll let Tyler and Kim take it from here."

Tyler took the lead. "Yes, thank you, Tex. During some routine analysis, I observed that many flare stacks used to burn off gas were extinguished at the wells, and several drilling sites weren't pumping. Please direct your attention to the display. Image one clearly shows the drilling site from a week before I noticed the anomalies last month, providing a frame of reference."

"As you can see, all the flare stacks were lit and burning."

Tyler clicked the remote and displayed the second image, taken just last week. The two images appear side by side to highlight the dramatic differences between the two timeframes.

Director McGill inquired, "Excuse me, Tyler, but are these images of the same location?"

"Yes, sir," Tyler replied.

Tyler continued, "As you can see, no flames are coming from

many flare stacks. They have been extinguished. With Kim's help, I reviewed some images from previous days and weeks, which you can see on the monitor."

Kim stood and said, "One significant piece of new intelligence is that most flare stacks are now lit. This happened within the last few days and seemed to rotate among the wells like a timer for our lamps. They appear to be on a schedule as if trying to trick us. They know we're watching these fields as closely as they do ours."

The Director of the NSA, Johnson, stood and said, "Those images are incredible. I haven't seen this level of quality or detail before. What asset are you using?"

"Jenny, could you brief us on Thoth?" Tex asked.

"Thoth?" Director Johnson said. "This should be interesting."

Jenny took a few minutes to explain Thoth's capabilities.

"I thought we had some impressive technology, but this is really cool," Director Johnson commented.

Tyler snorted and said under his breath, slapped his hands on the desk, and exclaimed, "Hell yes, it is!"

Not realizing he said it loud enough for everyone to hear, Everyone turned to Tyler and laughed. He and Kim continued to present all the intelligence they had gathered over the past few weeks. Their presentation lasted just over sixty minutes, and everyone remained silent the entire time, a rare occurrence for government bureaucrats. In closing the presentation, they asked if there were any questions.

Director McGill of the CIA then spoke up. "I want to ask the team —Jenny, Kim, Tyler, and Bob—based on your intelligence, what does this all mean? What's your gut feeling? Let's not forget that they seem to be on a timer now. As you know, the Russians are skilled at deception."

Bob looked at Tyler, who replied, "I can take that one, sir. Does anyone from the team want to chime in?"

After a few seconds, Tyler continued, "I have narrowed my conclusions about why a flare stack would not burn. First, it could be routine maintenance. The average duration for a well in the fields we monitor is two weeks, so we have ruled out maintenance. Second, there are new wells that are still under exploration. All the wells we observe are already established. Another team oversees new wells, and there are no new wells or exploration in the field. Third, they don't capture the gas, similar to how we operate in our oil fields. Alaska is at the forefront of technology. However, to the best of our knowledge, Russia does not use this technology. The CIA may have more information." Sean shook his head.

"Lastly, a large number of oil wells have been shut down and are no longer operational. There have not been any drilling crews at the site, which is odd. They want us to believe that everything is normal in the basin. However, the team suspects they may be shutting down the basin. Why that is, we do not know. But we need to find out—and quickly."

"You still believe this even after the flare stacks are operational at the previously inactive wells?" Secretary Dorn asked.

Kim replied, "Yes, sir, we do."

"Why is that? Can you explain?"

"Using Thoth, we monitored the temperature of flare stacks in the Timan-Pechora oil fields and then in the West Siberian basin. We observed a significant reduction in heat and radiation from the flare stack in West Siberia," Tyler stated.

"What does that mean? Maybe the oil is a little different, but I'm no expert in oil, that's for sure," Director McGill said.

"We believe the flare stacks are not burning off the gas from an oil well," Kim responded.

"Do you think this is just a ruse?" Director McGill asked.

"Sir, it's not my responsibility to determine that. I only provide the intelligence," Tyler replied.

"I understand," Sean said, "But again, what is your gut telling you?"

"Sir, I believe this is a ruse. What they're saying and doing are two different things."

"Great," Director McGill said. "What do you mean by two different things?"

"Tyler, do you mind if I take this one?" Kim asked.

Kim continued, not waiting for a reply, "Based on our intelligence, we believe the Russians are producing only half of what they claim, considering the flow-through of their pipelines and the number of oil wells we've observed that are not operational."

"So, they want us to believe they're at 100 percent production, correct?" Secretary Dorn asked.

"Yes," Tex replied.

"Does this account for their recent press release about reduced oil exports to nonaligned countries?" Director McGill asked.

"Yes, sir, we believe this has been happening for at least a year, possibly longer," Jenny replied.

Secretary Dorn asked, "Wait, what did you say?"

General Harris, the joint chief of staff, inquired, "Are you suggesting they are intentionally deceiving us and the rest of the world? Why would they do that?"

Jenny stood. "Yes, General, only two things the Russians have that keep them relevant: nuclear weapons and oil exports."

"Don't forget about their vodka. I mean, their vodka is excellent." General Harris smiled.

Jenny continued, "If they can't sell oil, they can't support their economy. The latest information indicates that oil exports comprise 40 percent of their federal budget revenue and over 50 percent of total exports. Their economy would collapse without oil, and they couldn't sustain their nuclear arsenal or military capabilities. It nearly happened with the fall of the Soviet Union in December 1991."

"Damn, we can't allow the Russian government to become unstable. Who knows what will happen to their nuclear weapons?" Marsha said.

"You're absolutely right, Marsha," Director McGill replied.

Tex stood up. "Last week, through Peter, I asked a friend at the NSA to do some research for me. I requested that they use the

Wayback Machine to look for any communication or metadata with specific keywords and phrases. Surprisingly, they only found one message. Please direct your attention to the monitor."

Message Body
Start
Date: 10 June 2001
To: President of the Russian Federation
From: Russian Ministry of Energy
Sir, following my visit, our assumption was correct. I have reviewed and verified the data again. As we discussed, I have siloed all the information. There is no single data source but rather a group of investigations. I didn't want anyone to have all the information except for me and the future Ministry of Energy. We have shared the information with three individuals.
The President of the Russian Federation
The Minister of Energy
The Commanding General in the Ministry of Defense
I will keep you informed if there are any changes or updates.
End

"As you can see, this isn't alarming by itself. It seems like everyday communication could mean anything. Another notable aspect of this communication is that no replies acknowledged it. That's strange, but nothing in it would immediately raise any alarms. Since Russia was still shipping oil to the world, we didn't conduct any further investigations, and no follow-ups were necessary," said Tex.

Peter stood. "Tex, what do you want us to do?"

"Peter, can you dig up any information, call logs, or recordings from around that time frame from the Ministry of Energy to the president of the Federation?"

"Sure, Tex. We'll get right on it, but it will take some time."

Tex continued, "We need to monitor using all our assets. Secretary Fields, can you request that Thoth stay on target for an unlimited time?"

"I don't think that will be a problem. I'll reach out to Sally. Another initiative launching next week is focused on southern China to monitor troop movements along the border with Laos. So, consider it done. For the next few weeks, I need your agencies to monitor intelligence regarding any abnormal, unusual, or unknown patterns related to oil drilling, new drilling sites, new pipelines, the movement of drilling structures, and the shipment and processing of oil in Russia, China, and India," Marsha said.

"I have a question, Sean."

"Go ahead, Tex."

"Do we keep track of their strategic oil reserves? Everyone knows how much we have and where it's located."

"Yes, we monitor them and have been doing so for a long time," Sean replied. The difference now is that they don't specify how much they have or where it's located, but we have a general idea based on the size of the storage tanks and some human intelligence we have in those countries."

"Marsha, can we assemble a team and allocate an asset to gather intelligence on them? It could be useful. I'm looking to obtain additional intelligence. We need to monitor the strategic oil reserves in Russia, China, and India. Are they increasing their reserves?" Tex asked.

"Of course," Marsha answered, appearing in great spirits.

Tex continued, "You all have different methods, sources, and techniques for gathering intelligence. I only ask one thing: Please don't share any information outside your agencies. In the event you have to share it with me. I will disseminate it to the other team members. Keep it compartmentalized as much as possible. There will be no communication between the agencies. This needs to be siloed until we meet again. You'll see why in our next meeting when we'll piece everything together. I'm just curious about what the final puzzle will look like."

"Tex, what could this activity tell us?" Peter asked.

"My guess is—and please take this with a grain of salt—they are worried about a long, sustained disruption of oil to their countries. I mean China and India. I think Russia has a supply issue. Perhaps some wells are running dry and need time to locate new drilling sites."

"Tex, may I interject something?"

"Of course, Sean. What is it?"

"Regarding your earlier comment about increasing strategic oil reserves, I didn't think it was a big deal. However, our intelligence indicates that the Chinese have constructed two substantial storage tanks, each capable of holding 600,000 barrels of oil, at their tank farm in Datong. They are also building a couple more tanks. As of last week, the tanks have not been filled, nor is there any process underway to fill them. We believe they currently lack the pipeline capacity to do so. However, we have been closely monitoring the extensive construction of pipelines from Eastern Siberia to Datong. The official statement is part of their Belt and Road Initiative."

"Thanks, Sean," Tex said. "Team, it's imperative that we surface this type of information. We need to put all the pieces together, so please get in touch with your teams when you return to your offices. Does anyone have anything else? If so, please speak up."

"Hey, Tex."

"Yes, Peter."

"Last month, we intercepted a message from Gazprom headquarters to their field office managing the Druzhba oil pipeline. They were instructed to test reverse flow from the storage tanks in Germany and extract ten thousand gallons from it, which would take seconds."

"Why reverse the flow?" Tex asked.

"We're unsure, so we've forwarded this information to the Department of Energy. They think it was just testing some pressure in the system."

"Do you, or anyone else, still believe that based on what we know?" Sean asked.

Everyone, in unison, shouted, "Hell no!"

"Can we get Toby on a secure line?" Tex inquired.

"Yes," Marsha responded.

Toby picked up his phone immediately.

"This is Marsha. Can you go secure? I'm going to put you on speaker."

"Sure, I'm going secure. What's the occasion for this call?"

"Toby. I have Tex, Sean, Peter, Jesse, Tyler, Kim, Jenny, and Bob in the room. I think you know everyone."

"Sorry, Marsha forgot I was on speaker. Yes, I know them all. How can I assist you?"

Marsha asked, "Why would someone reverse the flow in a pipeline for a short period—only to reverse it and remove oil from a storage tank? And the test lasts just a few minutes?"

"That's intriguing," Toby responded. "Are you referring to removing oil from a storage tank?"

Marsha answered, "Yes."

"Hmm, they might be testing some emergency protocols. If the tank becomes unstable or a leak is detected, it could also involve checking the pressure in the line or possibly an error," Toby noted.

Toby continued, "What's interesting is extracting oil from the storage tank. They could empty it in short order. I hope the operators will notice the reduction in oil levels in the tank and implement emergency procedures to stop it or transfer the oil to another tank. All the pipeline operators have controls—most, if not all- countermeasures are automatic and set up for this scenario. If you ever see tanks at half to three-quarters of their storage capacity, it's not because they can't fill them. It's because they don't want to. I'm not a conspiracy theorist, but consider this: What if the company that owned and controlled the pipeline also supplied the software and applications to monitor the flow and storage facility? The operators might be unaware of what is happening. When you take a little from here and a little from there, it all adds up to a lot of oil. You could be talking about tens of thousands of gallons. Did you notice any unusual activity at the storage facility when you monitored this activity?"

"No, we didn't," replied Tyler and Kim.

"Toby, thanks for the information and insights. You've given us a lot to think about," Marsha said.

"One last thing," Toby asked.

"What is it?" Marsha replied.

"Have you noticed any activity or construction of additional oil storage capacity?" Marsha responded, "Yes, it seems there is some construction in China. However, there is not a lot of intel on it yet. I will let you know if we come up with anything. Why, do you ask?"

He replied, "Just wondering. I heard some rumors they are building a new pipeline."

"Great, Toby. Please let us know if you hear anything else. Again, thank you, and we will be in touch." The line went dead.

Marsha leaned back in her chair, placed her hands on the table, and asked. "What the hell is going on? This is strange."

"Tex, based on your team's intelligence, what do you think is happening?" Peter asked.

Tex replied, "I'm not sure, but whatever it is—the troop movements, communications, alliances, construction, and the ruse in Russia—it's all connected. We need to figure it out pretty damn fast. Does anyone have anything else to add before we go? There's a lot to do."

"One second, Tex, I have one more thing," Marsha said. "I want Tex to lead this mission. He's the right choice. You are in a unique position, having served in the military and worked at the CIA, plus you have the right contacts at the NSA. Not to mention, you also worked in the oil business. Does everyone understand or object?"

"Thank you, Marsha," Tex smirked.

Before leaving, Sean said, "I want to let you know the president is aware of the intelligence the team has gathered. It has been included in his PDB for the last few days."

"Alright, everyone, we know what we need to do. Let's get to it," Marsha stated. "If you need anything to complete the mission, contact Tex. We don't know where this is headed, but one thing is clear. Something is happening, and we need to figure it out. Now, let's get to work, and please send weekly progress reports—not the intelligence—to Tex and Tex alone. We can review the intelligence as a group."

"Hey, Tex, before we leave, when is our next meeting?" Sean asked.

He replied, "I'll send out a meeting invite for early next week."

Marsha said. "If there are no more questions, let's get back to work."

15

TEX'S OFFICE, NGA HEADQUARTERS – SPRINGFIELD, VIRGINIA

Over the past few weeks, Tex realized they needed operatives in Russia to validate what they observed in the imagery. Tapping his pen on his desk, he summoned the team into his office.

Everyone gathered in Tex's office and sat on the six-foot leather couch while Tex settled into the leather chair opposite them. He began, "Thanks for coming on such short notice. We have some incredible imagery, and what we have started to uncover is, to say the least, disturbing and troubling. Something is happening, and we need some 'boots on the ground.' With that said, I recommend we deploy a team to Russia.

Jenny asked, "A team?

He answered, "Yes, a team. It would help validate what we are seeing, and I think the team should include me, Kim, and Tyler."

Everyone exchanged looks of surprise, remaining silent.

"Bob and Jenny, I need you and the rest of the team to stay and support us while we continue gathering intelligence.

"Okay, Tex. Why us? The CIA already has assets in the country, and they're trained. We're not field operatives," Kim said.

"Great question, Kim. Let me explain my reasoning. I chose you because of your language skills, hand-to-hand combat abilities, and field experience. So don't sell yourself short. Tyler, you'll be joining us for some fun—just kidding! Your extensive background in special operations and Army training will be valuable. So, who's in? This is completely voluntary," Tex stated.

Kim was the first to speak up. "I'm in! Sign me up."

Next was Tyler. "If Kim's going, I guess I can go to protect her."

Bob and Jenny agreed with Tex, emphasizing that they needed to stay back to keep the team's focus, gather more intelligence, and support them while on the ground.

Tex shifted in his chair and replied, "Don't mention anything outside this room. Got it?" Everyone nodded.

"So, when do we start?" Tyler asked.

"I haven't discussed this with Ms. Fields, so once again, no one should say anything to anyone. Don't even mention it in the office. I'm figuring out the best time, but we'll start within the next week at the latest."

Tex thanked everyone, and they left his office. He then called Sean to update him on his plan and get feedback.

LATER IN THE WEEK, at their weekly meeting, once everyone was seated, Marsha began the meeting. "Has everyone had the chance to review the intelligence for the week?" she asked. Everyone nodded in agreement.

After a minute or two, General Harris opened a binder on the table. Inside was the latest intelligence on Russian troop movements in Syria.

He cleared his throat and said, "The Russians are deploying additional ground troops into Syria at the request of the Syrian government. These troops include armored units and mechanized infantry. They have also increased their fixed-wing aircraft, including the SU-25, and raised the number of MI-24Ds to twenty-five. We have decided to keep our troops in the country and have not observed any provocation toward them."

"That's interesting, Ralph. Our HUMINT sources have confirmed your statement about keeping our troops at a distance."

"Why would they put so many troops, aircraft, and helicopters in Syria? Is it just a staging point for operations against Israel or Jordan?" Tex asked.

"Good question, Tex. That's what we're trying to figure out. The positive aspect is that we haven't observed any unusual activity from their naval forces, not even in the Gulf, to support their ground troops," Secretary Dorn replied.

"Thanks, Jesse," Tex said.

"What about the Chinese, General?" Marsha asked.

"They continue to engage in training exercises with the Laotians. Their air and naval forces regularly harass Taiwan. But nothing out of the ordinary," he said.

"Well, does anyone have anything else?" Marsha asked.

As the meeting ended, Sean asked, "When is our next meeting?"

"You'll have a meeting next week," Tex replied. "I'll be in Russia—or, should I say, we will be in Russia."

"What the hell? Russia?" Marsha asked, looking stern. She continued, "Everyone is dismissed. Now, get to work! Tex, I'll see you in my office in thirty minutes." Storming out of the meeting, she thought, *You're going to Russia over my dead body!*

Everyone looked at Tex, shaking their heads as they left the conference room.

Sean said, "Wow, Tex, that didn't go over well."

MARSHA'S OFFICE - NGA HEADQUARTERS – SPRINGFIELD, VIRGINIA

Marsha's assistant greeted Tex. She looked at him, shook her head, and said, "She's waiting for you. Tread lightly, Tex."

Tex knocked on Marsha's door.

She called out, "Get the hell in here and sit down! You know what? Don't sit down. This won't take long. You somehow decided to spring your mission into Russia on me in a meeting? With no advanced notice."

Tex had not seen her this mad in years. He stood there without saying a word.

Marsha continued, "You are not going to Russia. You, Mr. Adkins, are no longer a field asset. Those days are over, do you hear me? Your job here is to lead this operation from here! Why didn't you come to me before bringing it up in the meeting?"

"Marsha, I'm really sorry about that. I wanted to discuss it with you first, but Sean asked about the next meeting, and well, it just came out. I wanted you to please believe me. Can I explain my decision?" he pleaded.

Marsha responded, "What the hell, Tex. Your decision? It's not your decision to make—it's mine!"

"Can I at least explain why I'm the right person for this mission?" He could see that she was fuming, and she had to be careful about what might come out of his mouth. She pointed to a chair in her office and said, "Go ahead and sit down."

"We need to get some eyes on the ground to ensure that what we see from above is accurate. I have complete trust in our assets. However, something of this magnitude requires someone to touch them and verify our intelligence. Frankly, I'm that person, along with my team."

"So, let me humor you. Who's on your team?"

"Tyler, Kim, and I," Tex replied.

"Why aren't they working on the imagery? They aren't field assets either."

"Marsha, you're right, but they have been training some new team members to work with Jenny and Bob," Tex explained. "The team won't skip a beat. We'll only be gone for a few days to a week or two."

"And why did you choose Tyler and Kim?"

"Kim is fluent in Russian and Chinese and can hold her own. Did you know she's an eighth-degree black belt in Krav Maga? She gained field experience while working at the CIA. Tyler also has field experience and knows how to handle weapons and communication equipment. The best part is that no one knows the oil basin better than he does."

"Where did he learn all this?" Marsha asked. "I know he was in the Army, but I thought he was only doing FMV missions."

"There's a lot you don't know about Tyler. I had a chance to review his military 201 file, and it's heavily redacted. He completed multiple field operational missions with Special Forces in various countries. I even reached out to some SF guys he worked with, and they couldn't say enough good things about him, like how cool and collected he is under pressure."

"Impressive. Okay, I see those two, but I can have the CIA connect them with one or two of their field operatives in country. Why you?"

"I'm the only one with real-world experience in oil fields, CIA field operations, and the military. This mission needs a leader who already knows the team and has worked with them," Tex continued. "We don't have time to waste with the Russians; Chinese and Indians are on the move. You and I both know that. We'd better figure out what's happening quickly and determine if everything is connected."

"All right, all right. Damn it, Tex," she muttered as she stood up from the desk, walked to the window, and stared outside while tapping her right foot. "Have you discussed this with Bob, Jenny, Tyler, and Kim?"

"I wouldn't have brought it to you unless we were all on board."

Marsha turned around and said, "I'm done. You can leave now, and Kim and Tyler will meet us in SCIF #2 in ten minutes."

Tex exited Marsha's office, pulled out his cell phone, called Tyler, and told him to get Kim and meet them in SCIF #2 as soon as possible.

For the first time, he couldn't tell if Marsha was a yes or a no. He'd thought he knew her pretty well.

As he passed by her assistant, she shook her head again and said, "I haven't seen her this mad in... well, I don't remember."

"She was a bit mad, to say the least. I didn't even get a hug."

"You're lucky her foot isn't lodged in your butt," she said with a laugh.

After Tex left, Marsha called an old friend and colleague. "I know you just returned to your office, but can you meet me in SCIF #2?"

"Hell, you're in luck. I haven't left yet. I'm still in the building. I'll be there in ten minutes. Is this about what Tex mentioned?" he replied.

"Yes, and thank you."

SCIF #2 - NGA – SPRINGFIELD, VIRGINIA

It took everyone about ten minutes to reach SCIF #2. Ms. Fields was at the head of the table, with Tex on her right. Kim sat to his left, and Tyler was next to Kim.

"Please call me Marsha."

"Yes, Ms. Fields—I mean Marsha," Tyler replied.

"Do you know why you're here?" she asked.

Kim answered, "We think we have an idea, but we're unsure since there's so much happening."

"That is an understatement," said Marsha. "Tex is trying to

convince me and get my approval for his field mission, which I understand you know about. As of now, I have not approved it. Tex, please give us a high-level overview of your proposed mission. After that, I want to hear everyone's thoughts, opinions, and the chances of its success."

Everyone in the room acknowledged Marsha's request.

"Tex, please provide everyone here with the details you have right now, and let me know who will support you and your team," Marsha said. "Share everything from how you plan to get there to how you will return, including all the details in between. Don't forget the proposed timeline."

A knock resonated at the door, and Sean peeked his head in.

"Sean, please take a seat," Marsha said.

He sat beside Tex, punched his arm playfully, and remarked, "Have you lost weight? It seems like some of your ass is missing."

"I think I left it in Marsha's office."

"Alright, children, let's stay focused," she admonished. "Sean, I've asked Tex to outline the mission. I need your input because I believe your team will work with this one."

"Roger that, Marsha. Sounds good. I'll chime in as needed."

"Tyler, Kim, and I will fly from Dulles to Kennedy and then to Moscow with Russian passports."

"Hold on, Tex. Russian passports? You don't speak Russian," Marsha said.

"Excuse me, Marsha. They don't need to, though Kim is fluent," Sean interjected.

Looking puzzled, Marsha nodded and replied, "Fine, go ahead, Tex."

Tex continued, "We'll meet one of Sean's teams at a safe house in Moscow to review the plan and make any adjustments based on their experiences or concerns. Sean's team will provide us with a vehicle to reach our destinations. They will also supply the equipment we need for the mission. I don't want to take it on the plane. It will be sent via State Department courier to our embassy, where

Sean's team will pick it up and transport it to the safe house. Any questions so far?"

Since there were no questions, Tex continued. However, Marsha's expression showed she was unconvinced about the idea. "Please hold your questions until I have completed the mission briefing. The mission will be divided into three phases. The first phase is from Moscow to the Western Siberian oil fields. Sean's team will provide us with a car painted in the Gazprom color scheme and markings. This is where we will confirm what our imagery shows us."

Marsha was about to say something but stopped short, mumbling, *"How far is that drive?"*

"Marsha, do you have a question or comment?" asked Tex.

"No, please continue," she said, opening her leather binder and jotting down her notes and questions.

"From Perm, we'll take a short flight to Rostov-on-Don. We'll pick up another car painted in Lukoil's color scheme and markings. Once we have the car, we'll drive to the oil refinery and pipeline pumping station in Rostov-on-Don. At this location, we'll confirm the amount of crude being processed and moved through the pipelines that the facility supports."

"Everyone good so far?" Tex asked.

The entire group nodded.

In the third phase, from Rostov-on-Don, we'll drive to the Sea of Azov and the Black Sea, conduct our intelligence activities, and travel to Novorossiysk. Afterward, we'll head to a safe house in Sochi, leave our equipment, catch a regional flight to Istanbul, and take a flight to Dulles using our US passports. We'll be back here before you know it. This will give us a complete picture of the Russian oil industry from extraction to movement, processing, and shipment of the finished product." He paused. "There you go. Any questions?"

"Tex, that's a lot of driving. Are you guys up for it?" Marsha asked.

"We'll drive according to a schedule where at least one person sleeps. We will also stay in several hotels to rest, review the next day's activities, and receive any updates from the team here."

"That was a ten-thousand-foot view of your mission, which is what I asked for," Marsha said. "Sean, can your team support this?"

"Yes, Tex contacted me yesterday to check if it could be done," Sean replied. "I have already sent instructions to my team in country. We will move it into position once we get their equipment list."

Marsha asked, "Tex, when could you have the list ready?"

"I'll have it to Sean by COB today."

"Sean, how long will it take them to be 100% operational once they have all the logistics and equipment set up?" Marsha asked.

"One week at most," he replied. "That gives us enough time to create their identities and obtain their passports, other identification, and paperwork. We're even preparing badges for the locations they may visit in case the authorities in Russia request them. I've asked the team in Russia to review the plan and suggest changes or modifications based on their understanding of real-time events."

Marsha turned to Kim and Tyler. "What about you two? You are under no pressure to participate in this mission, and there will be no consequences for your current roles or any future assignments."

"Marsha, can I say something real quick?" Sean interjected. "Before you speak, everyone must understand that the U.S. government will not acknowledge or accept any responsibility if you get caught. You'll likely be treated as spies, meaning you might not be coming home soon or possibly not at all. Russia doesn't treat spies very well. This isn't a game. It's about to get serious. I need everyone to give me a verbal response."

Tex said, "Yes."

Kim replied, "Yes."

Tyler chimed in, "Yes."

"Thank you. Marsha, I'm finished. I appreciate your time, but we must tackle this immediately."

"Marsha, we're all in and ready to go," Tex stated.

"I have a question. How will the team communicate with us when they're on the ground?" Marsha inquired.

"They won't," Sean replied. "Not in the usual way. They'll have cell phones loaded with contacts for Gazprom and Lukoil and other regular contacts, with no links to us or any locations in the country. I'll have Dr. Russel explain this to the team tomorrow. It's really impressive, and if intercepted, they wouldn't know what to look for, like searching for a needle in a haystack. Any other questions?"

Everyone stayed silent for a moment.

Marsha said, "Tex, please get me the equipment list before you send it to Sean."

Sean interrupted, "One more thing—sorry. This mission is classified as a 'Black Operation.' The president will not be informed about it. The funding will be sourced from an NGO funded by USAID. I guess we can move forward if Marsha gives her approval. Before you all head out, I'll send Tex an address. I want everyone there tomorrow and the day after to plan. Along with the address, I'll provide other important information. Attire is casual, and no electronics, including USB drives, will be permitted. Don't leave your home with them or in your car. Oh, and no smartwatches. Don't bring anything that connects to the Internet or has Bluetooth. If we discover any, I'll call off this mission before it starts. Sorry, these are just standard protocols. We're a bit paranoid. No badges. Just bring your driver's license. Everyone has one, right?"

"Yes, Sean, we all have one," Tex replied.

Tyler added, "I've driven with Kim, and I'm unsure if she has one." He smiled at her.

"Hilarious. I do have one," Kim said with a shrug.

"Do you want to carpool, Kim? I can pick you up," Tyler said.

"I guess so since I can't drive," Kim replied, though she felt pleased to spend time with Tyler.

"I'll pick you up at... well, I'm not sure since I don't know where we're going. Let's wait until we get the address. I'll message you later."

"Transfer control of the team to Bob until you get back," Marsha added. "He's leading the team for now. The mission is a go."

"Roger that. Will do, Marsha," Tex said. "I'll touch base with him once I return to my office. He's expecting it."

"One more thing—I'll devise a reason why you all aren't in the office simultaneously, maybe a TDY assignment. Let me figure it out. Sean, can you stay for a minute?" Marsha asked.

"Of course."

After everyone had left, she asked him, "What are the odds of success?"

"I give them a 50 percent chance. This operation has many moving parts, so there are several points of failure. However, I know Tex, so I'll give them even odds. Historically, we've had only a 70 percent success rate, if that's worth anything. The risk must be taken."

With that, they both got up and walked out of the SCIF.

"I agree," Marsha said as they left, thinking, *What am I approving Tex to get into?* Today, of all days, I'm putting him in danger. I need to go home and relax, but not right now. There's work to do. Where can I send all of them on TDY? Then it hit her—NRO was a perfect cover story. I'll work with Sally on this.

Sean looked at Marsha. "Are you alright? You seemed a little distracted just now. I know it's a tough day for you and Tex."

"Thanks, Sean. I want progress reports while they're in the field. I think I'll call it a day. We have a lot to do, so let's get to it."

Later that day, in his office, Tex looked at his watch. There was nothing more he could do—he had already sent the equipment list to Sean—and it was getting late. Tex decided it was time to go home, relax, and watch something on TV. He didn't care what it was—just anything to keep him from thinking about work for a few minutes.

He got in his car, started it up—no electric car for him—and pulled out of the parking lot, making his way home. On the way, he decided to call Marsha to see if she wanted to hang out. He missed her. He had been feeling a little down all day but never showed it.

"What are you up to tonight?" he asked when she picked up.

"Nothing, just opened a bottle of Stag's Leap. Do you care to come over? Hate to drink alone," she replied.

"I'd love to. Friends don't let friends drink alone. Give me twenty. See you soon. Do I need to bring anything?"

"I don't think so. We can order Chinese for delivery," she said.

"Sounds good." He loved spending time with her. It had been so long.

"You still have a key, right?"

"I sure do."

"Just let yourself in. I'll be in the tub," Marsha said.

"Make it fifteen minutes or less," he replied, smiling.

MARSHA'S HOUSE

He arrived in less than fifteen minutes. After exiting his car, he walked up to the front door, pulled out his keys, and unlocked it. Stepping into Marsha's house, he locked the door behind him. He ran up the stairs and knocked on the bathroom door. "Is anyone in there?" He asked.

"Yes," she replied.

"Are you decent?"

Laughing, Marsha answered, "No. Now get your ass in here."

Tex entered and said, "Hey, I know you."

She looked at him intensely and said, "Get in the water. It feels amazing."

"Okay, but close your eyes first. I'm bashful."

"My eyes are closed. Go ahead." She peeked briefly and said, "Hey, I remember you."

He stepped into the water, which was pleasantly warm. "This water's great," he sighed before briefly submerging his head. He resurfaced, looked at her, and asked, "What are we doing?"

"I don't know," she admitted. "The other night brought up some emotions, and today was tough for both of us. I don't want to talk about work tonight, okay?"

"Yeah, it was. No work talk tonight, I promise," Tex replied, meeting Marsha's gaze. A tear slid down her cheek.

She looked at Tex. "Why did we get divorced?"

"You know, losing Janis took a heavy toll on us, and we blamed each other. I blamed myself. I was always deployed. I wasn't there to look out for her."

"I wasn't there all the time either. We did the best we could. She was a good girl. It was an accidental overdose of fentanyl, Tex."

"Yeah, I know. She was a good girl.

They raised their glasses and said, "Happy twenty-fifth birthday, Janis. We love you."

They both lay in the tub, eyes closed, arms extended along the sides. Tex lightly touched her arms, gently squeezing them. She opened her eyes, said, "Thank you," and then closed them again. After a few more minutes, they got out of the tub and headed to her bedroom, where they lay down. She rested her head on his shoulder and soon fell fast asleep. She hoped everything would be okay. She hated putting him in danger, but she had a job to do, and he knew that. In the end, she still loved him.

16

CIA LOCATION, NORTHERN VIRGINIA – DAY 1

Everyone arrived the next day at a beautiful home in an established community in Northern Virginia. Tex was beaming when he got there, with a bit of extra pep in his step. The homes in the neighborhood were at least 3,500 square feet or larger. The house was a two-story Victorian with a three-car garage. The yard was immaculate, resembling a putting green, with everything in its proper place. However, it was definitely lived in.

They approached the front door and knocked as instructed. An elderly gentleman opened the door and said warmly, "Please come in and sit in the living room." They entered the living room in silence and sat down.

No more than two minutes had passed when Sean came in and remarked, "Nice place, right?"

They all smiled and replied, "Very nice." Tyler asked if it was an Airbnb.

"Ha, ha, no, but that's a good idea. Please follow me. Thanks for being on time. We have a full day ahead of us."

Sean led them to the basement, where they were introduced to Dr. Russel, a man who looked like a mad scientist. He wore a white coat, had long gray hair all over the place, and had half-glasses resting on his nose. He walked with his hands stuffed in his coat pockets.

"Tex, Tyler, and Kim, this is Dr. Russel. He oversees our equipment team."

"The equipment team?" Kim asked.

"You can think of them as gadgets," replied Sean.

Dr. Russel, his face turning red, looked everyone in the eye. "These are not gadgets! They are devices used to execute your duties and keep you alive. Sean, do I have to repeat this every time?"

Sean started laughing. They had worked together for so long that he knew all the right buttons to push.

"Please follow me," he huffed, exasperated.

"Excuse me, Dr. Russel, do you have a first name?" Tyler asked.

"Yes, and you have been using it. Doctor!"

Tyler glanced at Kim and shrugged. Nobody said anything more until they arrived at the workbench.

Tyler started to pick up one of the items on the table. Dr. Russel shouted, "Don't touch anything until I give the order. The first piece of equipment is the cell phone. You will each receive one. The phones come preloaded with contacts for Gazprom and Lukoil—the standard contacts for anyone in the oil fields—and, yes, the numbers are functional. If you were wondering, the contact number will connect you to a linguist at your mission operation center. Each linguist speaks perfect Russian, with a specific dialect available if needed. A female linguist will answer the call if the contact is a woman. You don't have to worry about anything during a call."

"Cool," Tyler said.

"Cool? Damn, youngster, what is the world coming to?" he sighed. "You can access it with facial recognition. Let's set it up on each of your phones."

They set up facial recognition on their phones and tested them twice each.

"It looks like everyone is ready. Please leave them here. You can pick them up tomorrow. By the way, if anyone in Russia wants to check, the cell phones were bought in three different places in Russia. Each phone comes with micro earbuds. When they're in your ears—which, by the way, can't be seen—and the phone detects a language other than English, it automatically translates and plays through the earbuds. They'll provide you with a response in Russian or whatever language you hear. Any questions?"

"Dr. Russel?"

"Yes, Tyler?"

"Everything on the phone will be in English, right? The apps, names, etc."

"Tyler, my boy, that's a great question. Press the bottom-left button for three seconds. Everyone give it a try."

Tyler exclaimed, "It's all in Russian now. That is so effing cool! How did you do that?"

"That's a secret," Dr. Russel responded, beginning to laugh, and soon everyone joined in.

Sean realized it was the first time he had ever heard him tell a joke or even laugh. *What is this world coming to?*

"Okay, let's get serious," Dr. Russel said. "The next piece of equipment is this microchip, which allows us to track you. They won't be inserted until you arrive at Moscow's initial safe house. This is just an example. We don't want to risk having you identified as you go through security."

"Where will they inject them?"

"Good question, Tyler. Please come here, drop your pants, and bend over."

Tyler replied, "Tex, I hereby resign from the team. Here is a little secret, guys. I don't like the sight of my blood. Others, no sweat. One more thing, I tend to pass out, and I hate needles."

Everyone laughed. "I'm just messing with you, son. In your right forearm," Dr. Russel chuckled.

Tyler said, "Okay. I'm in."

Damn, that's two. Sean couldn't believe it.

"Since we understand your mission plans and the locations you'll visit with the implants, we can determine if the mission goes off track. Sean will assess the locations of the emergency extraction sites in relation to where you are during your mission. There's no need to worry about communications. In an emergency, call us and use the contact named Travel Agent. If you become separated, please head to the nearest extraction point, which will be texted to you. Go there, and we will retrieve you. Again, we are here to assist. We will get you out.

Dr. Russel continued, "Our team will pre-pack your vehicle with toolboxes when you arrive at the safe house. These will contain the typical tools an oil field worker would use in the field, as well as work and casual clothes since you can't wear work clothes twenty-four-seven. A handheld thermal scanner will display temperature and friction to gauge the velocity of the oil or substance flowing through the pipeline. This information can be relayed back via satellite in real time. No data is stored on the device itself. All of it is saved on a secure cloud and viewed and analyzed at the command center. The communication link to the satellite can be detected, but it's merely a burst of information, and we change the transmission signature, so it's impossible to pinpoint. If any of you own a smartwatch, you must leave it here. We don't want anything on you that could be tracked."

"When do we get our watches?" Tyler asked.

Dr. Russel replied, "Follow me."

They made their way down the workbench until Dr. Russel stopped.

"In front of each of you is your watch and a pair of ballistic sunglasses. The watches are old Russian analog watches."

"What does it do?" Tyler asked. "Can it be a locator or something cool like that?"

Dr. Russel smiled and looked at Tyler. "It tells time. Do you think you are 007?"

Three in one day! I need a drink, Sean thought. I think he likes this kid.

"Lately, we don't allow any CIA assets to conduct missions without eye protection. These Wiley XP-17s provide the best safety. I recommend wearing them during reconnaissance at the designated locations. They also look cool. I have a pair myself and love them. That's it. Any questions? If not, team, that concludes my part in your training. If you need anything, reach out to Sean. Good luck."

Everyone thanked Dr. Russel. As the group left, he tapped Tyler on the shoulder and said, "Kid, take care of yourself."

"I will," Tyler replied.

Dr. Russel whispered, "It's John."

"What's John?"

"My first name."

"I will, John."

Sean didn't hear the whisper. If he had, he would have passed out, and they would have had to pick him up off the floor. Dr. Russel never shared his first name, and Sean even had to look it up in HR records.

"Next on the agenda is how we'll communicate while you're in country, and we're even going to try it today," Sean said.

The team was led into a room with three gaming computers, each featuring a thirty-six-inch monitor. Tyler was salivating. On each monitor was the most popular multiplayer game in the world: Minecraft.

Anderson Perkins stood at the front of the room. Anyone who knew anything about Minecraft recognized him from his YouTube channel, "I'm Just a Builder!"

Tyler was the only one familiar with him. Does he work for the CIA? Wow, that's so cool—a nerd and a spy.

"I can't wait for this," Tex said.

"Hi, everyone. Please call me Andy. I will give you a crash course on how to play the game and how you will communicate with us at the Mission Operations Center. Has anyone played before?"

Tyler volunteered, "Yes, I've played a few times and love your videos!"

"Thanks, Tyler. Anyone else?"

No one else responded.

"Okay, everyone. Please pick a gaming station and take a seat. Your name, login ID, and password will be on the whiteboard. Please memorize these details. This is how we will communicate during your mission. Other team members and I will be monitoring the game. When you log in with your user ID, we'll be alerted. Is everyone good?"

"I'm going to leave you with Andy," Sean said. "He'll be escorting you for the rest of the day. Tomorrow, we have a surprise. Andy, they're all yours! Tex, please have your team here again tomorrow at the same time. We still have a lot to prepare for your mission, which starts three days from today."

"Thanks, Sean, we'll be here," Tex replied.

Andy began, "I want to familiarize you with the interface and commands for communication. You'll be able to hear me, but you won't be able to communicate via voice, only through the chat function, which I will demonstrate later. We want to make sure no one can overhear you. Here's how you can provide updates, and this is how we'll inform you of any changes to the mission or other important information. This system will help us track our progress as you log in from one site to another. Naturally, we can also monitor your progress through the microchip implanted in your arm. You can use the game's chat function to send any information besides your updates. Let's practice that function. Is everyone following along so far?"

Everyone nodded.

"When you arrive at the safe house, you will be provided with a laptop," Andy continued. "You can log into the laptop using your user ID, which is the same one you use for the game. The laptop has a persistent internet connection via Starlink, allowing you to send and receive updates while on the move. All information sent back and forth is encrypted if intercepted."

"Andy?"

"Yes, Tyler?"

"What about being able to locate us using the IP address when we are online?"

"Good question, Tyler. Your IP address changes randomly every few minutes. It will change even when you send data, but you won't lose the connection."

"How can you do that?" Kim asked.

"Russia currently has four Internet providers, each offering a variety of IP addresses to their customers. When a computer starts up, it receives one of these addresses. This enables users to access the Internet, just like you do here. There's no difference. We know the locations and ranges of those IP addresses. We have preloaded this information onto the laptop's network card."

"When you log in to the laptop, you'll receive an address for that region. After you get it from the provider, a program we installed on the network adapter will piggyback a random IP address from the list of current IP addresses, even if it's already used by someone else in the region. There are no IP collisions, so we've handled that. It would be best to consult the developers for more detailed information, but it's quite effective. We use it regularly in other countries. It's so fast and random that when someone traces you, it shows you at a different location."

Tex looked up and said, "Andy, I lost you at 'IP address.'"

"Good thing it's all automatic, Tex, so there's nothing you need to do!"

"Thank God. Why are we using a multiplayer game for communication instead of normal options like our cell phones or drop sites?"

"Good question," Andy replied. "Let me explain how it works. This game is hosted on multiple servers in the cloud—hundreds, if not thousands. Players can log in from anywhere in the world where the game is available, and Russia is one of those places. A player can log in and enjoy the game without worrying about a single server login. There's no need to know the IP address you're logging in from or the server's name. Just double-click the game launcher icon and log in as you would at home. This all takes place in the cloud's backend."

"Since many users play from different locations worldwide at any time, monitoring every conversation—even searching for keywords or sifting through metadata—is challenging. You could be out of the country if and when anything is uncovered, despite the fact that we've been tracking player information with Log4j for years."

"Log4j?" Kim asked.

"If you want to learn more, we can talk offline. Just give me your number," Andy replied.

"I know about this vulnerability," Tyler chimed in. "I can explain it on the drive home if you'd like."

Kim thought, *Is Tyler getting jealous?* She liked that idea. "Okay, Tyler, it's a deal. We can move on now, Andy."

"Let's get started if there are no further questions. Your character has been active for a long time rather than being a new user. This adds to your credibility as a longtime player since new user accounts can be easily monitored, as every account requires a credit card for a monthly fee. Please log in to access the game and turn on your headphones to connect to the communication link. Can everyone hear me?"

Everyone gave a thumbs-up.

"Great—let's get to it."

The team spent most of the day learning to navigate and communicate using the game. Andy covered every detail of the game, and each member practiced sending and receiving messages using the messaging features. They could hear Andy giving them instructions through the headphones, and everyone listened carefully to the precise directions in unison.

Andy's last message to them was, "We are done for the day. It's time to go home."

They removed their headphones and confirmed they had signed out of the game. If someone forgot to sign out, the game would automatically log them out after ninety seconds of inactivity, or Andy could sign them out remotely.

"Let me take you to the garage," Andy said.

Tyler thought to himself, "The garage? What kind of car are we getting?" Looking at Kim, he said quietly, "I knew there was more."

"What did you say?"

"We're getting a car! I bet it has some crazy technology and weapons."

"You should get out more," Kim said. They both laughed.

Tyler asked, "Andy, are you going to the garage to get our secret agent's car?"

"What secret agent car?"

"You know! Like how all spies get badass cars."

"This is the way out," Andy answered. "We moved your cars to the back."

"How did you move our cars? I still have my keys in my pocket."

"Hey, we are the CIA!" The group laughed together.

"Damn, I really do need to get out more," Tyler leaned over to Kim and whispered, "Hey, Kim, what are you doing tonight?"

She turned to him and replied, in a soft voice that he could only hear, "I'm going out with you. Please pick me up at 7:00 p.m. Also, remember to tell me about Log4j. That sounds so romantic," she replied with a smile.

"See you all here tomorrow at 9:00 a.m. By the way, how was today's training?" Andy asked.

"It was fantastic!" Kim replied. "I can't wait for tomorrow."

Tyler and Tex echoed her excitement.

"Okay," Tex said, "I'll see you guys tomorrow. Don't stay out too late." He got into his Chevy Blazer and drove off.

Kim hopped into Tyler's Audi S4, and they drove away. "Okay, Kim, so Log4j is—"

"You can stop right there. I don't care, silly. It's almost seven. Do you want to go to dinner now?"

"I would love to."

"What are you in the mood for?"

"I love Greek food. I know a fantastic place on Centerville Road—Katerina's Greek Cuisine."

"Let's go. I'm starving."

17

CIA LOCATION, NORTHERN VIRGINIA – DAY 2

Tyler arrived at Kim's at 8:15 a.m. for the trip to the CIA location. Tex met them at the front door, and, like yesterday, they knocked and were let in. Sean and Toby were in the living room.

"Toby, I didn't expect to see you here today," Tex said.

"Who else will ensure your mission is successful? Come with me. Let's get started."

They walked into the conference room, which had a large whiteboard on one side and an 85-inch flat screen on the other.

"I'm not getting into the logistics. I'm just prepping you with the information you need for the three sites you'll visit. Let's start with your first location, Perm. Please turn your attention to the flat screen." Toby provided detailed information about the oil drilling sites in western Russia. "Each drilling location will have a pump jack powered by steam, an internal combustion engine, and electricity or natural gas. A flare stack will be on site, and near the pump jack will be some holding tanks, ranging from two to five."

"There will also be a building housing unit to power the pump-jacks and other electrical necessities, such as lights. A sign will provide information about the site, including its location, the latest maintenance done, the well's owner, and other important details, such as the oil's viscosity from the well. Please direct your attention to the monitor. Here's a picture of one of the wells in West Siberia, and as you can see, roads connect to every well. Any questions?" he asked.

"No, Toby, thank you," Tex replied. "We're good. We have more images of this place than we know what to do with."

Everyone laughed.

Toby continued to brief the team. "Now, let's focus on Rostov-on-Don. This is not a drilling site but a refinery and oil shipping terminal for the Sea of Azov. The third location is the port at Novorossiysk, which facilitates Russian oil exports into the Black Sea shipping channels."

He examined all the information about those locations, supplying sufficient intel for the team to adjust their plan. They would collect additional details and the most recent information concerning their mission objectives in Moscow.

After Toby finished the briefing, there were no questions. The team was ready to go, and the mission was set to start the next day.

The team expressed their gratitude to everyone at the training facility before heading back to their cars.

"Come on, Tyler. I'm taking you to dinner," Kim said.

"It might be a while before we enjoy a great Mexican meal," Tyler replied. Hey, Tex, would you like to join us?"

"Thanks for the invitation, but I have plans. We'll see you at the airport. Please try to arrive two hours early. Have a wonderful evening, and see you tomorrow."

"Tex, where are you headed?" Kim asked.

"That's a secret," he laughed, getting into his car.

ACT TWO

18

EN ROUTE TO MOSCOW

After their flight from Dulles to JFK, they boarded Aeroflot SU123, a Boeing 777. The flight took off from JFK right on time, bound for Moscow, and was scheduled to arrive at 5:20 PM. After clearing security without any issues, everyone settled in for the long journey. The team chose to sit in different parts of the aircraft, preferring not to appear as a group or draw attention to themselves.

During the flight, they tried to sleep as much as possible. It would be a couple of long weeks. When they weren't sleeping, they reviewed their individual responsibilities along with the overall mission. So much relied on this mission, yet they had no idea just how much.

MISSION OPERATIONS CENTER

Everyone took their positions in the Mission Operations Center, ensured everything was operational, and waited for flight SU123 to land in Moscow. Then, they notified the Russian operators that the operation was underway: "We are live. I repeat, we are live."

"Okay, everyone, let's stay on our toes. We're facing a few long days ahead, so ensure all our systems are operational. We can't pick them up or track them until they get their implant," Andy said. "I just confirmed that their flight has landed in Moscow. We'll wait until they arrive at the safe house. The team there will keep us informed."

SVO – MOSCOW INTERNATIONAL AIRPORT

Aeroflot's Triple 7 landed twenty minutes late. Strong headwinds caused a slight delay, but the flight was smooth overall. Tex, Kim, and Tyler retrieved their luggage from the overhead bin. After all, they hadn't checked any bags since they were coming home from a short vacation in New York City. They thanked the crew and exited the aircraft.

At the terminal, they made their way to the "Green Line." They took about twenty minutes to clear customs with nothing to declare and carrying less than the Russian equivalent of $3,000. They approached the border control agents and showed their passports. The agents reviewed the documents and said, "Dobro pozhalovat' domoy"—Welcome home. Briefed on the potential questions or comments from the agents, each replied, "Thank you. It's great to be home," in flawless Russian. Their papers were stamped, and they went to get a cab.

Outside the terminal, they looked at each other. Kim said, "Well, so far, so good. I hope it doesn't take too long to get a cab."

"I'm starving," Tyler said.

"You're always hungry."

"Hey, I'm a growing boy!"

They didn't want to use Yandex, as it would have required them to use their phones and an app that tracked where and when they were picked up. They had to stay off the grid for as long as possible.

Everything was monitored in Russia, which had reverted to its communist ways.

After five minutes, a cab drove up. They all got in, Kim gave the driver the address, and off they went.

In Russian, Kim gave the driver the address of the Lesnoy Country House, located on Ulitsa Shkolnaya, directly across the street from the safe house. This was all part of the plan.

"How long will it take to get there?" Kim asked.

The driver replied, "This is rush hour, and traffic is terrible. Maybe in about forty-five minutes."

LESNOY COUNTRY HOUSE, MOSCOW, RUSSIA

The ride to the hotel took exactly forty-six minutes, and the cab driver was great. Tex thanked him and gave him the fare and a generous cash tip. Everyone exited the cab with their bags and entered the hotel.

Kim approached the desk clerk to begin checking in for their rooms. Tex knew Kim could speak Russian and had heard her before, but this was the first time he had heard her in a real conversation, off the cuff. It was Tyler's first time. They exchanged impressed glances before turning around when they heard the hotel doors open. Two men in dark suits walked in, approached the front desk, and stood behind Kim. After lingering for a moment, they headed to the elevator without looking back at the group.

Once the conversation and check-in were completed, Kim returned to where Tex and Tyler stood.

"Sorry, everyone. We only have two rooms available. Tex, here's your key. You and Tyler will be sharing one room."

Tyler's jaw dropped. He looked at Tex and said, "You don't snore, do ya?"

Laughing, Tex replied, "I guess you're about to find out."

By this time, Kim had a big smile, started laughing, and said, "Tyler, here is your key. We are just messing with you."

"Funny. Who is hungry? He replied as he took the key.

Good idea, but let's get cleaned up first," Tex said.

Kim grabbed Tyler by his arm and said, "It's this way. Tyler, follow us."

They all stepped into the elevator. Kim pressed the button for the second floor.

Once inside, Tex asked, "Kim, did you notice the two guys standing behind you?"

"I didn't see them, but I heard their conversation. They were discussing their last sales meeting. It was pretty generic," she replied.

The elevator reached the second floor. The doors opened, and they stepped out, standing outside the elevator. They agreed to meet in the lobby in forty-five minutes. Once they got to their rooms, they showered, changed, and got ready for dinner.

Tex and Kim were the first to arrive in the lobby. Now, they just had to wait for Tyler. A few minutes later, he walked down the hall like a new man. "Aren't those awesome showers, man? I need to get one of those showerheads."

"Come on, let's go," Tex said.

They crossed the street to Yakitoriya, a Japanese restaurant, to meet their contacts. The safe house was located just behind it. Kim entered first, followed by Tyler and Tex. The hostess greeted them and led them to their table.

The waitress took their drink orders, and as she left, a tall man with a dark beard walked into the restaurant. The hostess said, "Hi, Alex." He returned the greeting and approached their table.

Tex stood, hugged him, and greeted him in Russian, "My old friend! It's so good to see you again. Please, have a seat."

Alex took a seat. "It's been way too long. How was your vacation?"

Anyone watching would think they had known each other since childhood. Tex introduced him to the others.

"Have you all ordered yet?" Alex asked.

"Just our drinks," Kim replied.

"What are you drinking?"

"Beers," the group responded.

"Guys, you have to try their bento box," Alex insisted. "They're fantastic—the best I've ever had, and I've been to Japan! Just tell them what meat you want—chicken, beef, pork, or fish. I usually go with the fish."

They ordered dinner, and each person received a bento box. Tyler got chicken, Tex got beef, and Alex and Kim chose fish. Once dinner arrived, they chatted and got to know each other.

"Wow, that was an amazing dinner!" Tyler exclaimed.

Alex suggested, "You all should come get a drink."

"Before we go, what's for dessert?" Tyler inquired.

"Ice cream at my place. Let's go."

"Absolutely!" replied Tyler. "We'd love to come over! Lead the way."

As they walked the three minutes to Alex's house, they became increasingly aware of their surroundings to ensure they weren't being watched or followed.

So far, so good.

19

CIA SAFE HOUSE – MOSCOW

They arrived at the safe house and walked in.

"Lovely place you have here," Tex said.

"Thank you. I want you to meet my wife," Alex replied. "Sonja, we missed you at dinner."

"Maybe next time. I have a lot to do before your adventure starts bright and early tomorrow," Sonja replied. "We don't have much time. The hotel door locks at 11:00 p.m. After that, you'll need to ring the bell to get back in, which we want to avoid. It's best not to raise any suspicion. We have about four hours. Let's head to the living room. Please, have a seat."

Tex, Tyler, and Kim settled on the couch while Alex and Sonja occupied the loveseat. "Let's start with your laptop," Sonja continued. "It's preloaded with Minecraft and all the applications you'll need, but first, I want to ensure each of you can log in. Can you all please try logging in to the computer, not Minecraft?"

All three of them were successful.

"Great," Alex said. "Tyler, please put the laptop back in its backpack."

"Sure."

Alex continued, "Here are your wallets. Inside each one are your badges and driver's licenses. You'll need them to enter all the facilities. We matched them with your other documentation. Here's the equivalent of ten thousand dollars in rubles, which should last you without any problems. I recommend splitting the money up, just in case. There's a bank card in each wallet. The PIN is the last four digits of your cell phone number back home. We also included Gazprom and Lukoil gas cards—only use them after you apply the decals and only at Gazprom or Lukoil stations. Is everyone following me so far?"

Tex replied, "Have you done this before?" as they all smiled.

Sonja took over. "Here are the keys to your new BMW X5 SUV. It's painted white, as Alex thought you would stand out in a vehicle with the Gazprom color scheme while in Moscow. It's parked in the hotel parking lot. You shouldn't miss it. It's the only one there. Inside, you'll find your toolboxes, some work uniforms, casual clothes, and other items we've typically seen in Gazprom workers' vehicles. The insurance and registration are in the glove box. Having a BMW X5 indicates that you are either a manager or director in the company and should allow you access to some areas without being challenged. It's filled up and ready to go. Next, let's go over the route in detail."

Alex spread out a map on the table.

"It's about seven hours to Kasten. From there, it's another eight or so to Perm. You're looking at roughly fifteen hours of driving if all goes well. I recommend driving straight through and booking a hotel in Perm. We suggest the Hotel Eva. We can handle the reservations for two nights if you'd like. We can make the reservation appear as if it came from the Gazprom travel section. It's in the city center, near some perfect places to eat.

"When you leave here, you'll take the M7. It will take you to Perm, passing through Kasten, Vladimir, and Nizhny Novgorod, which is a little over halfway to Perm. There, you will stop to apply the Gazprom decals. Here's a picture showing where to place them. The decals are located under the front right seat. After applying the stickers, you must change the license plate, as the white BMW is registered to a private citizen in Kazan. Just pull off the old plate. There is another one registered to Gazprom behind it. Are we still good?" Sonja asked.

"Please make the reservations," Tex replied.

"Will do. Are you all up for the first part? The drive from here to Perm?" Alex asked.

"I think we'll take turns driving and turn up the music," Tex said. "It shouldn't be a problem."

"Is everyone all right, or do we need to take a break? We can take a break." Alex inquired. "It's been a long day, and you have an early start."

"Let's take a quick break," Sonja suggested.

"Do you have a beer?" Tex asked.

"Hell, yes. It's a Russian beer called Baltika No. 3. Ever tried it?"

"As a matter of fact, I have, a few years ago."

Alex looked at Tex, confused.

"It's a long story, Alex."

"If you're hungry, some snacks are in the fridge," Alex said.

Tyler and Kim walked over to the fridge.

Tyler glanced at Kim as they walked to the fridge and said, "We have a lot of driving ahead in the next few days, but it's in a BMW. You can sit beside me."

Kim smiled at Tyler.

He hadn't expected that, but he liked it.

Tyler opened the freezer and pulled out some ice cream. "Kim, do you want some?"

"Of course, I want some. Are you crazy?"

"You know what? I'm sitting in a CIA safe house in Russia, and I'm thinking, yep, I might be crazy. Here, let me help with that," he said as he tried to wipe some ice cream from her lips.

She slapped his hand away.

"Ouch! You're lightning fast." He looked down at his hand.

After their break, they returned to the living room, and Alex continued the briefing.

"Now, we're proposing a change to the second phase of your mission. Instead of driving to Rostov-on-Don, you will fly out of the regional airport in Perm. The flight should only take a little over two hours."

Tex got up. "Why the change in plans?"

"After Sonja and I reviewed the initial plan, we realized it would have required you to drive almost two days straight, exposing you to a greater risk of danger and potential interactions with authorities. There's been increased military movement and activity in the last few days, along with more checkpoints. We informed everyone back home and received their approval. Tex, it's your and your team's decision whether to proceed with the initial plan or this revised one."

Tex looked at Kim and Tyler. "What do you guys think?"

"I'm in favor of the revised plan. Those two days of driving can really take a toll," Tyler replied. "There are always potential mechanical issues with a vehicle, checkpoints, and, well, the uncertainty."

"Those are valid concerns," Kim said. "I agree with Tyler. This can save us two days in country. Let's be honest. The sooner we're done, the faster we can get home. Sonja and Alex, no offense."

"None taken, Kim," Alex and Sonja replied.

"To be honest, I'm not interested in meeting any of the notorious FSB agents," Kim said.

"All right, it's settled then. We were hoping you would agree with the change. Let's review phase two," Alex continued. "Your flight is set for the day after you finish reconnaissance of the oil fields and departs at 10:35 a.m. Here's the flight information and tickets. Keep using the same passport, ID, and documents. Park the BMW X5 in long-term parking, remove the Gazprom sticker, and toss it in the trash."

"What do we do with our equipment?" Kim asked.

"You can leave everything except the heat sensor," Sonja answered. "We recommend you destroy it. Your new vehicle will have everything you need: uniforms, clothes, a gas credit card, a toolbox, and a sensor. To destroy the unit, type the command 'good night' and press enter. This will initiate a chain reaction that wipes out all the drives, destroys the memory chips, and fries the wiring. It will turn into a metal box of nothing."

"Wow, that's really cool!" Kim replied.

"You guys are impressive," Tyler remarked.

Sonja continued, "Once you arrive at Rostov-on-Don in Parking Area One, there will be a white Mercedes with the Lukoil logo." The keys will be located in the right rear wheel well. The license plate number is Y495YA 761. It's fully fueled with all the equipment you'll need."

Sonja paused and glanced at everyone. After a few seconds, she continued. "You should have plenty of time to complete your mission in Rostov-on-Don. When you arrive at the main gate, ask for Chief Engineer Antonov, our contact. He'll help you access the facility where you can review information about the oil processing and production at the refinery. He can also take you into the refinery pipelines that supply and distribute the final products."

"You need to be there at 1:30 p.m. The main gate is marked with the number one."

Alex got up, walked over to a desk, opened the top drawer, and took out two USB sticks. When he returned to the group, he held out his hand and said, "Also, please give him this USB stick and request that he upload its contents to his work computer. He will need to install it as if it were a new version or an update of the maintenance manual. No code is running on it, so it will pass all their malware and antivirus checks. Once he uploads the file, ask him to go to the restroom and flush it down the toilet.

"Won't it clog the plumbing?" Kim asked.

"No, it will dissolve in water. Here, let me show you." Alex took the other USB stick and said, "Follow me."

They watched him drop it into the toilet. By the time he flushed, it had dissolved.

"Amazing," Tex said.

As they returned to the living room, Tyler remarked, "Now that was cool." While Kim combed her hair with her fingers, Tyler thought she must be lost in thought.

"When you're done in Rostov-on-Don, make your way to Krasnodar," Sonja said. "It should only take about four hours. We've booked you three rooms at the Mozart Hotel. It's east of the M4, so you'll need to get off the highway. It should take you around fifteen minutes once you do, and it's easy to locate. It also has a business center if needed."

"You'll leave early the next day for the drive to Novorossiysk. It's just a three-hour drive. We didn't book you a hotel there. After you finish your work, drive to Sochi, approximately seven hours away. It would be best to arrive around dusk or sunset, so keep that in mind."

"Stay the night at our safe house in Sochi, send your updates, and catch your flight to Istanbul the next day, then to Dulles. You'll receive tickets and flight information in Sochi. I think that covers everything." Sonja paused. "Hold on, just one more small procedure before you go—and you thought I would forget. Please roll up your left sleeve. Who's first? Once I insert the chip in your arm, it will automatically transmit your location to the Mission Operations Center."

Tyler, Kim, and Tex exchanged glances and groaned.

"I was hoping they would forget." Kim sat up, rolled up her right sleeve, and extended her arm.

Alex took her arm. "This might hurt a little."

"Go ahead. Let's finish this up."

Alex put the injector on her forearm, pulled the trigger, and said, "There you go, all done. Next!"

Kim remained silent. She turned away and rolled down her

sleeve. Next was Tyler. He rolled up his left sleeve and asked, "Kim, how did it feel?" By the time he finished the last syllable, Alex had pulled the trigger and injected the microchip. "Ouch! Damn, that hurt."

Kim looked at Tyler and said, "Come on, Nancy, man up." He just glanced at her and sat sulkily on the couch.

Tex stepped forward, his sleeve rolled up. "Let's do this."

Alex put the injector against his forearm and pulled the trigger.

"Ouch." Tex pulled his arm back, shaking it. He looked at Kim and warned, "Don't even say it."

Kim looked disappointed.

"Okay, go ahead."

"Come on, Nancy, man up!"

Everyone just started laughing. They needed something to lighten the mood.

"Alex and Sonja, we want to thank you so much," Tex said. "You guys have been great. When you're back in the States, please look me up. Dinner's on me."

Everyone hugged each other goodbye.

MISSION OPERATIONS CENTER

"Folks, it looks like we're going live. We can start tracking their movements. I have three—count them, three hot ones. They're still at the safe house," Marsha announced.

"They're returning to the hotel," Sean added.

Marsha said, "It will take them a couple of minutes."

CIA SAFE HOUSE

The group left the safe house and walked back to the hotel.

"My arm still hurts," Tyler said.

Under her breath, Kim murmured, "Nancy."

"You still love me, right, Kim?"

"Oh, yes, Tyler, I still love you." She smiled. It was hard for her to control her feelings for him, but they had a mission to complete, and she hoped there would be plenty of time afterward.

Tex looked at Tyler and said, "Nancy."

The three laughed. Their intelligence, strength, and toughness made them a great team—and they had Tyler for laughs.

They spotted their ride at the hotel, just where Alex and Sonja had said it would be. They entered the hotel with minutes to spare, and everyone said good night and went to their rooms. They knew it would be a long few days, and tonight might be the best sleep they'd get for a while—jet lag was kicking their butts. They were out like lights when they settled into their rooms.

20

LESNOY COUNTRY HOUSE - MOSCOW, RUSSIA

The team gathered in the breakfast dining area at 6:00 a.m. the next day to enjoy a hearty breakfast before starting their long journey. Each had two pieces of toast, two hard-boiled eggs, and coffee. Before leaving, they filled their coffee cups.

"My head hit the pillow, and I was out," Tyler said. "How about you guys?"

"Me too," Kim replied. "The bed was so comfortable that I didn't want to get up. And you?"

"Like a baby!" Tex chimed in.

"Let's sort out the driving rotation," Kim suggested.

"I'll take the first five-hour shift," Tex offered. "Then Tyler can take over, followed by you, Kim. How does that sound?"

Kim and Tyler both said, "Sounds good."

Before they left, they checked all the gear and equipment to ensure they had everything they needed. Once everything was accounted for, Tyler got in the front seat with Tex, and Kim sat in the back so she could rest.

Their SUV pulled out of the hotel parking lot and took the M7 to begin their long, and they hoped uneventful, drive.

Before Kim went to sleep, Tex said, "Let's go over what we'll do if we encounter any checkpoints. Make sure to put in your earbuds so you can understand what the police or soldiers are saying or asking. Second, Kim, you will be the main communicator between them and us. Since your badge says 'Director,' you'll take the lead, and everyone else will act normally."

"Maybe not you, Tyler," Kim replied.

"Tex, do you mind if I turn on the radio?" Tyler asked.

"Go ahead."

"Where can I find satellite radio?"

"They don't have satellite radio in Russia. Let me find a station," Tex said, scanning the channels when suddenly "Take It to the Limit" by the Eagles came on.

Hearing the song, Tex said, "I love this song! One of my favorite bands. I saw them in Dallas at the American Airlines Center back in the day. I think it was around 2009. It was awesome."

Tex and Tyler talked about the music they liked for several hours. They discovered they both enjoyed the same bands and genres, and a bond was formed.

After a brief gas stop and seven hours on the road, they reached their first milestone, Kasten. They decided to grab a bite to eat and stretch their legs. There were another eight or more hours of driving to Perm—the goal was to get there before ten that night, which should get them there by sunset. They were all feeling jet-lagged.

The team returned to the SUV and found a secluded area to apply the decals. It took five minutes to do so. Tex backed away from the SUV and said, "Just like out of the factory."

It was time for Tyler to take over driving. Tex got into the back seat for a much-needed rest while Kim jumped into the front passenger seat.

"Okay, Tyler, let's go," Kim said.

He eased back onto the road, accelerated, and matched the speed of the surrounding traffic. He didn't want to give any reason for being pulled over. Kim turned to Tyler and said, "We've been working closely together for a couple of months now, and I still don't know much about you."

"What do you want to know?"

"Tell me everything. You can start with where you were born."

"I was born in Plano, Texas, and raised in Allen, Texas. I lived in the same house until I joined the army. Hell, my parents still live in that same house."

"Your parents still live in the same house? That's so cool."

"Yep. A year or so after high school, I joined the army, and here I am."

"So, that was your whole life? You guys are all the same. I guess you haven't traveled much since you've lived in the same town your entire life?"

"Let's see . . . I've been to Hawaii a couple of times, Aruba, the Cayman Islands, Italy three times, and Germany at least fifteen times."

"Wait, you've been to all those places?"

"Yep, and a few more. Once, we stayed overnight in Liechtenstein, the sixth-smallest country in the world. Can you believe we paid twenty euros for a schnitzel?"

"Is that a lot? I've never had one."

Raising his eyebrows, he said, "You've never had one? I'll tell you this: next time my parents are in town, you're coming for an authentic German meal."

"Authentic! Really? Is your mom German? So, do you speak German?"

"Ja, ich spreche etwas Deutsch."

"I'm guessing you said, 'Yes, I speak German,' or something like that?"

"Very good," he replied. "She is. That's why I've been to Germany so many times."

"That makes sense. How did your dad marry a girl from Germany?"

"He retired from the army a few years ago, and besides being stationed at posts in the U.S., he was stationed in Germany three times. One of those times, his unit—Third Squadron, Seventh US Cavalry—was tasked with patrolling the 'Iron Curtain,' the border between East and West Germany, before the Berlin Wall came down. My mom's from a small town called Coburg, where the units patrolling the border had their barracks. It was called Camp Harris. Now, I believe they demolished it and built a new regional hospital. My mom always says my dad had to choose between bringing back a beer stein or a German girl. He chose a German girl."

"That's so cool. Please tell me more." Kim looked at him with a twinkle in her eye. She was beginning to like him. There was something about him, though she couldn't quite put her finger on it yet.

"My oma still lives there, along with two uncles and cousins," Tyler continued. "When I take you there—if you ever want to visit—there's a beautiful, massive fortress on a hill called the Veste Coburg that you can see for miles. My mom and dad got married there. Here's an interesting fact about Coburg: Queen Victoria of England's husband, Prince Consort Albert, was from Coburg."

"Now that is interesting. I remember seeing pictures of her. She always wore black."

"Yep, after his death, she never remarried. One more thing about Coburg—they have the best bratwurst in the world!"

"In the world?"

"Yes, in the world! Once you try one, you'll agree."

"So, I can try one when you take me to Coburg?" Kim asked.

"Sure! You'd love it there," Tyler said. "I can be your guide. I love riding the city buses."

"Is there anything else I should know about you?"

"I have two sisters and a lot of nieces and nephews. They live in Arkansas. My oldest sister works in the medical billing industry, and my other sister owns a flower craft store in Beebe, Arkansas."

"What's her store called?"

"Blooming Bee," Tyler replied. "But enough about me. It's your turn."

"I was born in Northern Virginia. We moved around a lot. My dad works for the government and is often away. He's been stationed all over the world but is home now and has been for a few years. It's great to have him so close. We hang out all the time. You can join us for dinner when we get back. I think he would like you."

"So, where did your dad meet your mom?" Tyler asked.

Kim was about to answer when, suddenly, Tyler interrupted, "Hold on, Kim. Crap looks like a checkpoint ahead. Tex, time to get up."

Tex rose from the backseat. "What's going on? I was just at a beach in Hawaii."

"It looks like we have a checkpoint ahead. Everyone, put in your earbuds." The X5 drove up to the police officer standing nearby. Tyler rolled down the driver's window.

In Russian, Kim leaned toward Tyler and said, "Good morning, officer. How can I help you?"

"Passports, driver's licenses, and identification cards, please," the officer requested. Everyone provided their documents. The policeman examined them and inquired, "Where did your travels begin? What is your destination?"

"We started in Moscow and are headed to Perm," Kim replied. The guard raised his eyebrows. "You're driving from Moscow to Perm? That's quite a long trip. Why didn't you fly?"

"I don't like to fly, and I'm in charge," Kim answered. "Plus, this part of the country is so beautiful this time of year. I decided we would drive."

The policeman glanced around to ensure no one was listening, then said smilingly, "I hate flying, too. I've only flown a few times, and the flights were so bumpy that I got sick, so I understand why you prefer to drive. And you're right. It's beautiful out here. What brings you to Perm?"

"We work in the oil fields. We're petroleum engineers."

Tyler and Tex listened to Kim's conversation with the policeman through their earbuds.

In Russian, the guard asked Tyler, "How long have you been driving today?"

Without skipping a beat, he replied in Russian, "About a couple of hours."

The policeman stepped back and walked around the X5, stopping at Kim's side. He started to return the papers but shifted his attention to Tex in the back seat and asked, "What university did you attend?"

"Gubkin in Moscow."

The officer handed them their papers. He touched Tex on the shoulder and said, "Could you please exit the car?" Just as Tex was about to open the door, an urgent call for assistance came over the officer's radio. The officer placed his hand on the door and said, "It's your lucky day." He smiled and added, "Have a nice day, and drive safely."

Kim yelled to the officer, "Thank you and wished him a nice day. They drove away, and after about a mile, they began to breathe easily again.

"Holy cow, these earbuds are kick-ass!" Tyler said.

"Kim, great job," Tex said. "You were so calm. I think he liked you. Beer's on me tonight!"

Tyler turned up the radio.

Tex added, "I love this song. It's 'Here Comes My Girl' by Tom Petty." They all joined in singing:

> "But when she puts her arms around me
> I can somehow rise above it.
> Yeah, man, when I got that little girl standing right by my side..."

Kim remarked, "Well, at least they have good taste in music," then continued singing.

Ten miles from the checkpoint, Tyler glanced in the rearview mirror. To his surprise, two police cars with their emergency lights were in the distance. They were speeding and would reach them in minutes. "We might have some company."

Tex and Kim turned around. "Man, they're moving fast," Kim said.

"Crap, they're gaining on us. Tyler, slow down a bit, okay?" said Tex.

"Will do, Tex."

The police cars were still gaining on them. Tyler's heart raced, and he was sweating. Crap, they're right behind us. "I'm going to pull over. Did we leave something at the checkpoint?"

"Be ready to take off when they get out of their car. Give them a few seconds to figure this out. I'm checking the map for the nearest extraction point," Tex said.

Tyler pulled over, and the police zoomed past them.

"Crap, this is getting real," Tyler said.

"Yes, it is," Kim and Tex replied in unison, then burst into laughter.

"What the hell is so funny?" Tyler asked, out of breath.

"Look in the mirror," Kim replied. "You're sweating like a pig. Here's a towel."

"I always sweat when I think of you." The next thing he felt was her hand on the back of his head. "Ouch! Or when I get pulled over by Russian police, in Russia, in a car bought by the CIA, on a secret mission to figure out why Russia has been lying about their oil reserves—I mean, production output."

Nobody noticed the "oil reserves" at first.

"Come on, enough of this playing around. Let's go," Tex said.

Tyler shifted the X5 into drive and got back on the road. After a couple of hours, Kim took over the driving duties. They pulled into the Hotel Eva in Perm a little after sunset, having made good progress.

HOTEL EVA - PERM, RUSSIA

They met in the hotel lobby and asked the receptionist if an outdoor dining area was nearby. The receptionist told them about the Boston Café across the street.

"They have some outdoor seating. It was such a beautiful evening. I wish I could join you," she said, winking at Tex.

Tex started to walk away, then looked back, and she winked again. He turned around, smiled, and said, "I still got it."

"What did you say?" Kim asked.

"Nothing," Tex replied and kept walking.

"Tyler, did you hear Tex say anything?"

"Nope, I didn't hear a thing."

"You need to get your hearing checked."

"What did you say?"

Kim slugged Tyler in the arm and said, "Smart-ass."

"The beers are on me!" Tex called out.

They went to the café, sat outside, and ordered beers. When they arrived, Tex told Kim, "It's time for you to get a raise. Cheers."

"Hear, hear!" Tyler said as they clinked their glasses together.

When the waiter returned, they ordered dinner and more beer. Before they knew it, they had been sitting at the café for two hours, drinking, eating, and having a great time.

"Tyler, after Kim slapped the crap out of you, you said something that has stuck with me," Tex said.

"What's that? I might have had a slight concussion."

"Nancy," Kim replied.

Tex looked around, realizing they were alone. He leaned in and said, "You mentioned something about Russia lying about its known oil reserves, then shifted to oil production. Why did you refer to known oil reserves?"

"As for why they might say one thing and do another, maybe they overestimated their known oil reserves. Perhaps their production numbers are inaccurate, and the wells are shut down. Are the wells dry, with no oil left in the deposit?"

"I suppose that's a possibility. Very interesting," Tex said.

"Aren't the known oil reserves validated by external agencies to prevent this kind of situation?" Kim asked.

"I have no idea, but it would be helpful to know," Tex replied. "In our next update, could you ask ops to check with Toby if outside agencies monitor or verify in-ground oil reserves? Let's go."

They got up, paid, and walked back to the hotel. Tex greeted the receptionist and winked.

"You know she's a little older than you, my friend," Kim said.

"I know, but I've still got it."

"I heard you say that when we were at the café!"

Tex just smiled and walked away.

Kim focused her gaze on Tyler. "Did you hear it this time?" she asked.

"Hear what?" replied Tyler.

"Never mind. It's time for bed."

They met in the lobby at 7:00 a.m. for breakfast. After breakfast, they headed to the X5. Tex asked, "How did everyone sleep?"

"Like a baby, but the lady in the next room was snoring," Tyler replied.

"I was in the room next to yours! I'll kick your butt when we get back," Kim said. "Was I snoring?"

He just looked at her and smiled.

Tex said, "Boy, it looks like you're in for an ass-whipping when we get home."

Tex drove with Kim in the passenger seat and Tyler in the back. He thought it would be best to keep them separated for a while.

21

GAZPROM OIL FIELDS – WEST SIBERIA, RUSSIA

As they drove into the oil field, some workers waved and smiled at them as they passed. Tyler said, "What's that smell?"

"The smell of money! I remember my first time in Midland, Texas. We were on a family trip to California and stopped for the night. I got out of the car and said the same thing you just did. My dad replied, 'Son, that's the smell of money.' Okay, Tyler, which way?"

Tyler used reference points for the area that featured specific flare stacks and drilling sites they had seen in the Thoth images. "Over there, the second one on the left."

Kim asked, "How do you remember which ones they are?"

"It's easy. I've been looking at the images for so long that I've noticed the unique features of each one. Honestly, I think I could even find one in my sleep. The first one has five holding tanks and a generator on the left side of the pumpjack. It's the only one with this configuration on the right side of the road that goes through the field."

Incredible, Kim thought. *He can't hear worth a damn but has the eyes of a hawk and a memory like a pachyderm. Go figure.*

"To the right," Tyler instructed.

Tex pulled ahead a bit, drove forward, and stopped.

Once the vehicle halted, everyone got out and grabbed their toolboxes. They wanted to blend in with the regular maintenance crew. They noticed a few people in the fields and minimal activity at the other well sites.

Tex glanced down at his watch. "It's ten after the hour. Let's meet back here at, say, thirty. Is that enough time?"

"That should be plenty," Tyler replied.

"Let's split up. Kim, you and Tyler head over to the storage tanks and shed. I'll go to the pump jack and then to the flare stack. Keep an eye out if one of the oil field crews shows up. Tyler, can you hand me the scanner?"

Kim and Tyler approached the five storage tanks about ten feet apart. A windsock perched atop the second tank, and a walkway ran between each tank, allowing maintenance workers to move from one to another. Ladders on the first and last tanks provided access to the tops.

"Hey, I'm going to climb up," Tyler said. "You can check out the base of the tanks. If you need me, shout."

Kim nodded.

Tyler climbed the ladder and reached the top of the first tank. He wanted to check the lines between the tanks to see if they were being maintained, which would clearly indicate the well's productivity.

While walking between the second and third tanks, he noticed one of the connections had never been properly attached, but it was not leaking fluid. He tapped the tank with his hammer—it sounded hollow—and took a picture of the connection.

"Can you tap this tank I'm on right now?" he yelled to Kim. "What does it sound like?"

She tapped the tank with her hammer. Thanks! "It sounds empty."

"That's what I thought. Let's move to the next tank."

As Tyler and Kim were at the storage tanks, Tex made his way to the jack pump. As he neared it, the machinery hummed, bringing back many memories. He hadn't been in an oil field since he decided to join the army. He smiled, but then he noticed something strange. The sucker was only going into the well a couple of feet, and when it made its way up, there was a gap. The sucker was only ten feet—it wasn't even pulling any oil out of the ground. It was fake.

He noticed a truck approaching the drilling site. "Kim, come over here," he shouted. "We need your language skills."

By the time Kim reached Tex, a Gazprom SUV had pulled up, and two individuals dressed in the same uniform were getting out and walking toward Kim.

Kim walked up to them and greeted them.

Before she could get another word out, the taller individual said, "What are you doing here? We weren't aware of anyone scheduled to be here today."

"Excuse me," Kim replied. "Who the hell are you? I don't need to ask you or anyone when and where I can inspect."

"I'm Petrov, and this is Smirnoff. I'm the manager of this field section. So, are you here for an inspection? I was never informed."

Kim thought *I could use some Smirnoff right now*.

"There must have been a mix-up in communications. We arrived from Moscow last night, and we're here to check a couple of the sites—this one and the one over your left shoulder."

"I need to verify and clear this," Petrov said. "By the way, who are you?"

"I'm Chief Engineer Fedorov, and these are my team members," she said, pointing to Tex and Tyler. "Keep working! We're on a schedule. I'll tell you what, let me call my boss, and you can talk to him to sort this out. We all have a lot to do, and there's a lot of pressure on us. How does that sound? His name is—"

"I know who your boss is," Petrov replied.

Kim took out her phone, opened her contact list, and found the contact. She tapped on the number and handed the phone to Petrov.

As Kim held up her phone, it captured Petrov's face. Using the most advanced facial recognition software, the servers in Northern Virginia pulled up details about Petrov—how long he had been with Gazprom, where he lived, how many kids he had, and where he went to school. Everything known about him was displayed on the monitor in front of one of the agents working the mission.

At the other end of the conversation, the agent in the Mission Operations Center said, "Hello, Natalia. What can I do for you?"

"Sir, this is Petrov from the Perm oil field."

"Petrov, what are you doing on Natalia's phone? Is she okay?" the agent asked.

"Yes, sir. I wasn't informed that there would be a visit from the corporate office today. I'm just calling to confirm," he replied.

"Thank you for being so diligent, Petrov. How long have you been working for Gazprom? Almost ten years, right?"

"Yes, sir."

"Have you ever had an unannounced inspection during those ten years?"

"Yes, sir."

"Then why are you calling me about this one? Listen carefully, Petrov. Let my team finish their work. They are checking two random drilling sites and sending me the information directly. Then, I'll forward it to the Minister of Energy. I can either speak highly of you or not. It's up to you to decide."

"Yes, sir. Here's Chief Engineer Fedorov," Petrov said.

He returned the phone to Kim, thanked her, and asked if they could do anything to assist her and her team. She politely declined.

"I'm sorry to have bothered you, Chief Engineer," Petrov said, "but I'm just doing my job. There's been a lot of activity lately."

"No problem," she replied. "What kind of activity? We haven't encountered any in the other locations we've inspected."

"They're installing equipment like this in some of the no longer operational wells. We're just replacing the equipment to make it look new and updated. I don't know why— I do what I'm told."

"Please stay right here," Kim said. "I need to speak with one of my team members."

She walked over to Tyler and Tex, who were far enough away that their conversation wouldn't be overheard.

"He admitted the well isn't operational."

"Absolutely," Tex and Tyler replied.

"Go along with him and see if you can gather some more information," Tex suggested.

She raised her voice so the other crew could hear, "That's enough. Get back to work, both of you! We need to finish." Tex and Tyler returned to their positions and continued inspecting the site.

She walked back to Petrov. "That's what we're inspecting. Once we wrap up here, we'll move to that one. Is there any information on that well or others in the field? I don't want to waste my time since we randomly select wells."

"The one over there"—he pointed to the next one they were heading to—"is still pumping oil, but I don't know how long that will last. The same is true for most of the wells on this side of the road. We've been told they're relocating production and have found a larger deposit, but they won't disclose where. They're taking a lot of the equipment out of here and prepping it for somewhere else, almost like they're winterizing it. We need to move, Chief Engineer. I apologize for any inconvenience I may have caused."

"Petrov, you've been wonderful, and I'll inform my boss. Look for something extra in your next paycheck."

Petrov smiled at Kim as he and his coworker headed back to their truck.

Kim approached Tex and relayed everything Petrov had said. "Amazing," Tex said.

MISSION OPERATIONS CENTER

Marsha and Sean listened intently to the entire conversation, gazing at each other in amazement. The agent's technology was flawless. During the call, it assessed the caller's stress level, anxiety, and distrust, enabling the agent to fine-tune the dialogue. When he noted his awareness of how long Petrov had been with Gazprom, he could sense that Petrov's voice was anxious. After the call, Marsha and Sean expressed their gratitude to the agent and continued to monitor the mission.

Sean reached out to determine the equipment's destination, where it was being staged, and whether another large deposit had been discovered.

He mused, "They haven't found another site. If they had, they would have announced it. After all, they control the price of oil."

GAZPROM OIL FIELDS

Kim returned to the storage tanks with Tyler, while Tex returned to the pumpjack.

Kim and Tyler finished their inspections quickly. She rejoined Tyler, saying, "That phone worked like a charm, but I don't think we should linger here. Let's head over to Tex and discuss all our findings, then move on to the next drilling site."

"What did he say to you?" Tyler asked.

"Let's wait until we get in the truck if you don't mind."

"Sounds good."

"You look a little puzzled," Kim noted as they approached Tex.

"Just look at that flare stack and tell me what you see."

Tyler and Kim gazed up and then exchanged glances for a moment. "What the hell?" they exclaimed.

"My thoughts exactly. It looks like a flame, but it's not. It's some silicon with heat coming out of the stack, but it doesn't burn off. It's a different fuel source altogether. Have you ever seen those air dancers in front of a tire store? It looks like one of those, but whatever they use is silicon that can withstand extremely high temperatures without radiating heat off—it can store it".

"This drilling site is like those used in World War II to mislead the Germans when the Allies prepared for their invasion of Europe. The Allies deployed dummy tanks to convince the Germans they had more tanks than they actually did. They even moved these tanks around the countryside to create confusion."

"Think about it. The Russians want us to believe they have more operational oil wells than they do, so no one has noticed their production decline. These are the twenty-first-century dummy tanks," he said. "Did the data upload successfully?"

"Yes, it certainly did," Tyler replied.

"Great. Let's move to the next one and get out of here. We don't want to overstay our welcome. After all, I'm your boss," Kim said with a smile.

Tex looked at Tyler and asked, "What have we created?"

They moved to the next drilling site, which was fully operational. They uploaded their data and headed back to the hotel. It was getting late, and they had a flight to catch in the morning. Plus, they wanted to sync up with the team back home.

As they were leaving the field, they noticed a lot of military activity moving into the area. They waved to the soldiers, and the soldiers waved back. This needed to be reported. Why would they send the military to guard oil fields? It was bizarre.

HOTEL EVA - PERM, RUSSIA

Kim checked in with the Mission Operations Center when they arrived at the hotel and settled into their rooms. There was no update except that they had listened to the entire phone conversation today, received all the necessary updates, and were reviewing the intelligence. The plan remained unchanged.

Kim provided an update regarding the military presence in the oil fields, which they acknowledged, stating they would monitor the situation and pass the information on to Jenny's team. When Kim finished, she had fifteen minutes to prepare for dinner. She was starving, and a cold beer sounded appealing.

They met in the hotel lobby before heading to the Boston Café. The food was good, and they could sit outside and chat. They all ordered beers and discussed tomorrow's plan. The flight was set to depart at 10:35 a.m., so they aimed to be at the airport by 8:45 a.m. Since the drive to the airport took thirty minutes, they planned to meet at 7:00 a.m. for breakfast.

They talked about how fascinating the phone call had been earlier that day. Kim mentioned she had found a contact labeled Gazprom manager and had tapped the call button. On the other end of the line was a Russian-speaking agent. He seemed to know just the right things to say to ensure they weren't bothered and to end the conversation quickly.

"I need to find out how they knew what to say to that guy when we get back," Tyler said.

"Yeah, I'm sure they're going to tell you," Tex replied.

"They'd have to kill me if they told me, right? I'm being serious."

"So am I," Tex answered.

Everyone laughed.

The next day, they all met at 7:00 a.m. for a quick breakfast to discuss any last-minute updates on the day's activities. Before leaving her room, Kim logged in and saw that the only update was that they were trying to figure out where all the oil field equipment was being stored.

"How did everyone sleep?" Tex asked.

"Great," Kim replied.

"Me too, but the person in the next room was snoring again."

Kim hit him and said, "I wasn't snoring!"

Tyler quickly moved out of Kim's striking range. "How do you know? You were asleep!"

Everyone burst out laughing.

"Just kidding. Kim, you didn't snore." To his surprise, he hugged her, and she didn't push him away.

"Okay, you two. Let's eat and then head to the airport for our flight."

The drive was uneventful, and they arrived at Perm International Airport on time. They took only what they needed and left the rest in the SUV, which would be picked up later that day to avoid raising suspicion.

Tyler said, "I need to get myself one of these."

"Not on your salary!" Kim replied.

"Maybe I can find a sugar mama when I get back," he said with a smile. Kim clearly didn't appreciate that remark.

"Come on. I was joking," he added. Kim continued walking, not looking or speaking to him.

Tex glanced at Tyler, winked, and said, "Nice one!"

They arrived at the terminal, passed through security, and waited at the gate. The plane was already there, so they knew it would depart on time, which was good since they were on a tight schedule. The airline gate agent announced that the flight to Rostov-on-Don was ready for boarding. They found comfortable seats on the plane and waited for takeoff. Before they knew it, they were in the air, all trying to rest for another long day ahead.

MISSION OPERATIONS CENTER

"Looks like they made it to the airport on time and are heading to the terminal. We'll lose track of them once they enter. We might be able to catch them on the plane. We tested it here, and it worked," Andy said.

"Okay, thanks for the update," Marsha replied. "I'll be glad when they land and reach the next location."

22

PLATOV INTERNATIONAL AIRPORT – ROSTOV-ON-DON, RUSSIA

The short flight was a bit bumpy, but overall good. The plane taxied to its terminal, and the team soon disembarked, making their way to the parking lot to pick up their new ride. They didn't check in their baggage, so they left the airport within minutes.

As they walked to the parking area, Tex asked the team, "Did you guys get any sleep?"

Kim and Tyler replied, "A little." "What about you?"

"Nope. I was still wrapping my head around that well site yesterday."

"Yep, Tex, it was strange. It reminded me of a Hollywood western town. The facades were right, but there was nothing behind them," replied Kim.

They saw the sign for Parking Area 1 and looked for their white Mercedes with the license plate Y495YA 761. Fortunately, they had the license number. There were at least six white Mercedes with the Lukoil logo.

They used Alex's keys to unlock the Mercedes, and all the toolboxes, uniforms, and everything else were there. They were amazed at the level of detail Alex and Sonja could achieve in such a short amount of time. Typically, operations like theirs take weeks, if not months, to plan and execute effectively.

Tex drove with Kim in the passenger seat and Tyler in the back. They were headed to Ooo Planeta-Yug to meet their contact, Chief Engineer Antonov. Once they arrived at the refinery, Tex needed to give him the USB. The ride was only twenty-five minutes long.

"There's the main gate on your left," Tyler said. "I'm so glad we flew. That drive from Moscow to Perm was exhausting, even though I like driving."

"Me too," Tex and Kim agreed.

"Kim, what does that sign say over there?" Tyler asked.

"It says 'Company Vehicles Only,' so I guess that's where we park."

"Good catch, Tyler," Tex said.

OOO PLANETA-YUG OIL REFINERY (LUKOIL), RUSSIA

After the short drive to the refinery, they exited the SUV, grabbed their toolboxes, and headed to the main entrance. As at Perm, Kim did all the talking. Since she was the boss, Tyler and Tex put in their earbuds while walking to the gate in case they were asked questions. At the entrance stood two guards and a beautiful German shepherd Kim knew she wanted to pet.

She approached the guard, and they exchanged pleasantries. She complimented the beautiful dog, and the guard smiled as he petted it. "Do you want to pet her?"

"I would love to pet her if you don't mind. I love dogs," Kim replied. He responded, "No, please do. She loves it."

"What is her name?"

"Alexei."

"Defender of mankind! How fitting," Kim remarked. "Could you please let Chief Engineer Antonov know that Director Natalia Fedorov and her team are here to see him?"

"Yes, Director."

The guard promptly called and informed Kim that Antonov would arrive in five minutes. "Would you like something to drink? It's quite hot today."

She glanced at Tex and Tyler, who responded in Russian, "Yes, that would be great."

Kim leaned toward the guard and asked, "What's your name?"

The guard smiled and replied, "Sergey." He got up, went to the refrigerator, grabbed some cold water, and returned to his station, turning his head toward Kim and smiling again.

The chief engineer entered the office and said, "Thank you, Sergey."

He approached Kim, and before she knew it, he hugged her and said, "It's been too long! You should visit more often."

"I'd love to, but we are all busy these days. At least we have today, old friend."

"Sergey, I'll sign all of them into the refinery. They're with me."

Sergey smiled at Kim while opening the turnbuckle.

The chief engineer said as they walked, "Please call me Saul. Everyone does."

"Saul? That's not Russian," Kim replied.

"I know, but I love Breaking Bad," he said. "My first job out of university was as a chemist, and everyone here calls me Saul."

"Alright, Saul, it is then. Tyler and Tex meet Saul," Kim introduced.

"Saul?" they responded.

"I'll explain later," Kim assured them.

"First, let's head to my office. It's secure, and we can talk a bit before going out into the facility," Saul suggested. "Along the way, I'll give you a brief tour."

As they walked, Saul described the refinery's layout and production. "Did you know this refinery covers over ten square miles? It's massive. We have bikes and scooters to get around. You don't want to walk. It would take all day."

Once inside Saul's office, Tex handed him the USB and Alex's instructions. Saul quickly plugged the drive into his computer, copied the file, and took it to his sink. Before long, it was gone.

"We're here just to confirm some of our gathered intelligence. I wish I could be more forthcoming and provide you with additional information, but I can't," Tex said. "From your office, can you monitor the flow rate in and out of the refinery? What I mean is, if this much crude comes in, then this much final product gas, for example, must come out."

"That's a tricky question since we refine diesel, plastics, and other petroleum-based products," Saul replied. "Don't get me wrong—we produce a lot of gas. There has been a lot of unusual activity, and I mean visitors. Normally, we have visitors from Lukoil or one of our partners, but now it seems there are many military personnel, and I can tell, based on their logo, that they are from the logistics branch of the military. Even more atypical, I've also seen Chinese and Indian military personnel here in the last month or so."

"Interesting," Tyler chimed in. "That time frame aligns with some other strange things we've noticed. Sorry to interrupt."

"Typically, the three pipelines coming into the refinery provide us with the necessary amount of oil to process and maintain peak performance," Saul continued. "We now have four, but the overall amount of oil hasn't changed. Let me show you. You see these four gauges here? They display the amount of oil currently flowing through each pipeline. Let me show you the flow before the fourth one became operational."

He pulled a binder from his desk and opened it to show the previous month's production flow. Saul continued, "Here, take a look. Before the fourth pipeline, our flow was at this level. When they added it, there was no change. We didn't cut back the flow from the other pipelines or increase production at all."

"Are you suggesting, Saul, that the original pipelines weren't sending as much as your gauges show?" Tex asked.

"Yes. I didn't want to mention it because I knew you were coming here. This just started a couple of days ago."

"Do you know what source is feeding this pipeline?" Kim asked.

"Not exactly, but I think it's coming from Georgia."

"Is there any way we could access that pipeline?" Tex asked. "Let's say we have a tool to help and possibly answer the flow question definitively."

"If you don't mind getting dirty."

"Tyler doesn't mind at all, do you, Tyler?" Tex asked with a smile.

Tyler grinned. "No, I love it."

Saul said, "Let's go. I'll take you guys down to the pipelines. If you have any questions along the way, please ask."

They exited Saul's office and descended a flight of stairs to ground level. Once they arrived, he guided them to the pipeline, which was located between two others. From their position, they couldn't get close enough to scan it.

"Can we get a little closer?" Tyler asked.

"You can try to squeeze between the pipes if you want. Some workers do it, but it's a tight fit. Remember when I mentioned getting dirty?" Saul replied with a laugh.

"I'll give it a shot." Tyler placed his hand on the first pipeline. "You can feel the flow. It's moving fast. You know what, let me take a reading..."

He took the reading and transmitted the data to the satellite for Jenny's team to analyze. The ten-digit grid coordinates came along with the flow data, providing them with one-meter precision—sufficient for government work. He then began to navigate towards the second pipeline.

"It is tight," he remarked aloud.

They merely looked his way and smiled, pointing toward the second pipeline.

"If you get stuck, just pass the scanner!" Kim shouted.

"What about me?"

"Oh, yeah, I didn't think of that," Kim teased.

"Funny girl," Tyler said.

Tyler reached for the pipeline, placing his hand on it as he had with the first one, and noticed he couldn't feel the same vibrations as before. The flow was different.

"Saul, what does the gauge on your iPad read for this pipeline?" he asked.

"It's 9.8 kilometers per hour, which is correct."

"I don't think so. That's what we got at the first one, but this one is 3.3 kilometers per hour. Your app is wrong. Let me check the third one. Hell, I'm already stuck. This one reads 6.5 kilometers per hour. What does your gauge say?"

Saul shouted back, "9.8 kilometers per hour."

"Saul, something isn't right. There are huge discrepancies," Tex said.

"Can you close the app and relaunch it to see if something's going on with the app?" Kim asked Saul.

"Hold on," replied Saul. "Nope, same reading, Kim."

"Tyler, make sure you send the data!" Tex yelled.

"Already done!"

"Okay, now come out of there!" Tex waved his hand at him.

It took a few minutes of twisting and turning, but Tyler finally made it out. As they walked back to Saul's office, Kim said, "Tyler, you smell like oil."

"You mean I smell like money," he quipped, glancing at Tex.

Tex was laughing so hard that his eyes started to water.

"What's so funny?" Saul asked.

"Saul, my friend, it's a long story."

"Well, Saul, all we needed to do was confirm our initial observations. Let's head back to your office," Tex said.

In Saul's office, Tyler took photos of the gauges Saul had shown them earlier to help them understand the sensor readouts. The group returned to the main entrance, where the same guards were stationed.

Sergey poked his head out and said, "Have a nice day, Director Fedorov. I'll sign you out."

"Oh, thank you. Please call me Natalia," she replied.

Sergey's face brightened. The other guard punched him on the shoulder, said, "You dog," and laughed.

They thanked Saul and waved goodbye. Once they reached their SUV, Tyler drove to Krasnodar with Kim in the front passenger seat and Tex in the back. He intended to log in and send updates upon their arrival. They headed toward the M4 for the three—to four-hour drive, which would get them to Krasnodar before nightfall.

M4 TO KRASNODAR, RUSSIA

The traffic was light, and the weather was great, making driving excellent. Kim commented, "This place is so beautiful, green, and lush."

Tyler checked the gas gauge and decided they would stop for gas and a quick break halfway. He asked Tex if that was okay.

"Sure. Now put on some tunes," Tex said.

Tyler cranked up the radio. If they didn't know better, one might think they were all on a summer vacation. They felt great as they headed to their last stop before going home.

MOZART HOTEL – KRASNODAR, RUSSIA

As they walked up to the hotel, Kim remarked on the unusual main entrance located at the building's corner. "And look, they have an outdoor seating area right over there! I really like this place." Kim approached the receptionist, handed her their passports, and confirmed the room.

"Yes, Director Fedorov, your rooms are ready. You will be staying only one night, correct?" the receptionist inquired.

"Correct, but you have a lovely hotel here—very nice! I must come back," Kim replied.

"Well, you and your colleagues are more than welcome to return the next time you're in town. We have all three rooms on the second floor, near or across from one another."

"Thank you. Can you recommend places to eat within walking distance that have outdoor seating?"

"Of course! We are just a short walk to the banks of the Kuban River. There, you can find excellent dining options. What type of cuisine are you looking for?"

"Nothing special."

The receptionist continued, "Then I recommend Stephani Garden. It has a great river view, and you can even sit outside on a beautiful evening. It's less than a five-minute walk."

"Well, Stephani Garden it is," Kim decided.

She handed everyone their keys. They waved at the receptionist and went to their rooms.

"How about we meet downstairs in thirty minutes?" Tex suggested.

Kim and Tyler replied, "Sounds good."

"See you in thirty downstairs."

During their brief break, Tex logged in to check for updates or information. The only message read, "Reviewed pipeline flow—very interesting." As there were no updates from the team, he logged off and prepared for dinner and a cold beer or two.

Like clockwork, everyone gathered in the lobby right on time. The receptionist directed them toward Stephani Garden. Before Kim left the entrance, she asked, "This is a lovely sitting area. Is it open all the time?"

"Yes, you're more than welcome to sit out there," the receptionist replied.

She joined Tex and Tyler and said, "I think I'll sit outside when I get back, and you're welcome to join me."

They approached the hostess inside the restaurant. "If possible, I'd like to reserve a table for three outside," Kim said.

"Yes, but we have some open tables outside. Please follow me. Thank you for joining us tonight. Your waiter will be right with you," the hostess said. While they waited, they looked over the menu.

"Have you noticed all the cameras?" Tyler asked. "I mean, they're everywhere. I wanted to mention it yesterday but forgot. They were all over the drilling site, too."

"It's almost like a police state," Tex replied. "The president has been in power for nearly thirty years."

The waiter came and took their drink and dinner orders. As they waited for dinner, they spoke only in general terms. After their meal, they returned to the hotel, knowing that tomorrow would be another long day.

As they returned to the hotel after dinner, Tex said, "If we leave tomorrow at 7:00 a.m., we'll arrive between 9:30 and 10 a.m. I think we'll be on-site for an hour or two. I want to see some tankers leave the port and how high they ride. Once we're done there, we'll head to Sochi and be home in two days, sleeping in our own beds."

Tyler closed his eyes for a moment, thinking about his bed. Then he glanced at Kim and smiled.

"What the hell are you smiling at?" Kim winked and tossed her hair back.

"Mind if I sit out here with you?" Tyler asked.

"Sure, if you want to."

They sat outside for a few minutes and chatted about everything. After a pause, Tyler said, "I'd love to take you on an official first date when we get back home. What do you think?" Asked Tyler.

Smiling, Kim replied, "I was wondering what took you so long to ask me out. I was about to ask you out."

They both laughed and then got up. Tyler pecked her on the cheek. "That's it on the cheek," Kim said.

Tyler put his hands on her shoulders and turned her toward him. He looked into her eyes and kissed her on the lips. Kim put her arms around him without pulling away and pulled him closer to her. After a short time, they turned toward the hotel entrance. As they walked, Tyler put his arm around Kim, and she leaned her head on his shoulder.

Tyler and Kim were waiting for Tex in the lobby the following day.

"Good morning, you two. You both look well-rested. I slept like a log," he said. Tyler and Kim didn't respond. "Let's eat. We have a very long day ahead of us."

"I'm starving," Tyler replied.

After breakfast, Kim paid their bill, retrieved their passports, and hopped into the SUV for the relatively short drive to Novorossiysk. Tex drove with Kim in the front passenger seat and Tyler in the back. Before long, Tyler was fast asleep.

Tex said, "I wonder what's up with him? It's like he didn't even sleep last night."

Kim remained focused on the road, showing no emotion. Tex jumped on A146 to the shipping terminal.

MISSION OPERATIONS CENTER

"All right, team. They're heading to their final site today. Let's keep a close watch on them. I want them back in one piece," Marsha said.

23

SHIPPING TERMINAL - NOVOROSSIYSK, RUSSIA

It was 10:00 a.m. when they arrived at the shipping terminal. Tex parked their SUV in the lot next to the main building. Upon exiting the car, they were amazed at how large it was. The imagery alone had not conveyed the full scale of this place. They could see at least twenty storage tanks from their spot, but none of the berths for the ships to load oil. Their original plan was to walk to the shipping berths, but that was not feasible. It was far too distant and would take too long. They stood beside the SUV to devise a new plan. They all had badges, so gaining access was not an issue, but how to get transportation to the berths remained uncertain.

Tex outlined his new plan. "We walk in as a team, just as we have at every site. Kim, you inform them we are here for an unannounced inspection of fuel at any terminal they choose on this side of the bay. We need transport to that location. The inspection should only take about thirty minutes. We would prefer it if one of their drivers took us there and waited while we conducted our inspection. I believe asking for a driver shows we are not hiding anything, but I really don't want to get lost."

"Let's get to it," Kim said.

Inside the main office, they were greeted by the receptionist, a beautiful and charming young woman with blue eyes, long blonde hair, and a warm smile. Kim began, "Hi, I'm Director Fedorov from the Moscow headquarters. Where is your director or the manager of this location?"

The young woman replied, "Hello, Director. He isn't here and won't be for another couple of hours. He's flying in from Moscow."

"I see. So, who is in charge right now? We're here to inspect one of the oil terminals where an active oil transfer to a tanker is happening right now."

"Director, I'm the only one here right now. I can inform you that an active oil transfer is happening at the moment. It's at Pier Two. It started yesterday afternoon and should be completed within the next hour, if not sooner. Before I let you in, I need to call the assistant manager. He's on the other side of the bay. He can authorize me to grant you access to the facility if I can reach him. If I can't, you'll have to wait for him here, which may take a while."

"What is your name?" Asked Kim.

"My name, Director?"

"Yes, your name."

"It's Anastasia, Director."

"That's a beautiful name. I want to include you in my report," Kim said.

"Report, Director?" she asked, looking somewhat agitated.

Kim explained, "Yes, I would like to mention that your support allowed us to conduct our inspection within the specified time. That will enable us to move to our next location, where we have a meeting in ninety minutes. How long will it take to get to the terminal?"

"About ten minutes, Director," Anastasia replied nervously.

"A round trip would take twenty minutes. It takes thirty minutes for our inspection and another thirty minutes to drive to our meeting. That really cuts it close! I don't think the minister wants us to be late."

"Minister?"

"Yes, the minister of energy."

"Give me a minute, Director," Anastasia called out.

Within ten seconds, another woman entered the office and greeted them. "Hi, I'm Nadia, your driver. The truck is right outside. Anastasia said I should take you to Terminal Two. Is that correct?"

"Yes, it is, and please be at their disposal wherever else they need to go," Anastasia added.

"Anastasia, I foresee great things in your future," Kim remarked.

"Thank you, Director," she replied with a wide smile.

Kim spoke to Anastasia while Tyler and Tex looked dumbfounded the whole time.

With Kim in the lead. They all walked out of the main office and headed to the truck for the short ride to the terminal.

PIER 2 - NOVOROSSIYSK SHIPPING PORT

At Terminal Two, everyone got out except for the driver, who remained with the truck. She didn't care what they were up to. All she knew was that it kept her from doing paperwork. She turned down the truck radio and her walkie-talkie to avoid distractions before stretching out in the truck cab.

The team approached the tanker and exclaimed almost in unison, "This thing is enormous."

"I've been on a big cruise ship, but holy cow, this is so much bigger," Tyler said.

"How many barrels of oil do you think this can hold?" Kim asked.

"Tyler, where is this ship registered?"

"It looks like Panama. Her name is Dama Flotante," he replied.

Hmm, "floating lady," Tex thought.

"Tyler, be sure to include that information in our update. I want them to track this ship through the Bosporus Strait," Tex instructed.

"I've read that they can carry anywhere between 70,000 and 190,000 barrels. I'd estimate this one is close to 120,000 or so."

The driver yelled to Kim, "Director, the ship's first officer told me to inform you that this tanker is almost full and will be finished in the next twenty minutes, departing shortly after!"

"Thank you," she replied.

She said to Tyler and Tex, "That's great information. We can wait until it's full to see where she sits in the water. If she is really full?"

"Since this is a traditional load, all the activity is right in front of us," Tex said. "Over there is one of the pumps. Tyler, can you go to the hose and see if you can get a reading on the flow?"

"Give me a minute."

"Wait, I'll go with you," Kim said.

Kim and Tyler walked over to the fueling hose to take the measurement. Tyler looked at Kim and said, "You look very nice today."

"Shut up. It's time to get to work."

"It seems like the flow is about normal. Let me check the other one." They walked over to the other hose. "Hmm, not much flow in this one. It could be because they are almost finished. The holds its filling are nearly full, but I think you want to load them simultaneously to prevent the ship from becoming unbalanced or unstable."

Tyler uploaded the information to Mission Operations and received confirmation that it had been received. He thought this technology was impressive.

"Let's go see what Tex is up to. He's talking to one of the crew," Kim said.

As they approached him, they heard a strange language.

"Tex knows Spanish?" Tyler asked.

"I guess so."

Tex noticed them approaching, so he cut short his conversation with one of the ship's crew.

"We didn't know you spoke Spanish," Tyler said.

"Of course, who doesn't? I also speak Portuguese and French."

"What did he say?" Kim asked.

"They've been in port for a few days. He said a few holds in the middle of the ship store water, not oil."

"Why in the middle?" Tyler asked.

"Water is denser than oil. The molecules are packed closer together. Plus, the oxygen atoms in water are smaller and heavier than the carbon atoms in oil. So basically, it's for balance."

"Tex, that was a long explanation—you could've just said it's for balance," Tyler said.

"He said this procedure is new at this terminal, but at Primorsk and Ust-Luga, they've been doing it for years. He also mentioned they don't get liberty anymore while in port. Then he went on to say they are restricted to the ship. Very few crew members are allowed off the ship at the berths to monitor oil transfers. He was pretty pissed. Since they were allowed liberty in the past, something changed, and he had no idea why or what caused the change in protocol. He also mentioned it's not just this ship but all of them, regardless of what flag they fly, which has never happened before. He said, Hold on, I believe Russian, Chinese, and Indian vessel crews get liberty. The crew brought it up with the captain, who said he didn't know the reason and told them to drop it—he didn't want to discuss it. If they didn't like it, they could disembark when they got home, never to return to her or any other ship in the fleet."

"I need to send this with our report," Kim said. "I think our work is done here."

As Tex mentioned, the hoses were disconnected from the ship, and it was about to head out.

"Before we leave, snap a picture of where she's sitting in the water."

"Tex, did he say where they were going?" Tyler asked.

"Sorry, I forgot—India."

As they returned to the truck, they heard someone yelling, "Stay where you are! I'm the assistant manager and need to talk to you!"

Tex looked back and saw an overweight middle-aged man running toward them, slowing down significantly.

"Well, it's time to go. Come on, let's move. We have company, and he doesn't sound too happy," Tex said.

"Nadia, hurry back to the main office, please," Tex said as everyone climbed back into the truck. It only took a few minutes to reach the main office. As they drove, Kim glanced back and noticed another company truck about 100 yards behind them, which she assumed the assistant manager was driving.

At the main office, Tex said, "Thank you, Nadia," as they exited the truck. At the same time, Anastasia ran out of the office.

"Do you have a minute? Can you come into the office? The assistant manager is on his way," she yelled.

While the team was at the terminal, Anastasia called a friend at the Ministry of Energy in Moscow. They knew nothing about the minister being out of the office—he was in his office. She hung up the phone and sat still for a few minutes, contemplating what to do. Something felt wrong, so she decided to call the local FSB office. Anastasia gave them the details, descriptions, and names of all three inspectors, along with the backstory Director Fedorov had shared with her. Satisfied that they had enough information to begin an inquiry, they asked her to try to stall them until they could get a couple of agents on site.

The local FSB officers accessed the facility's cameras and ran them through their facial recognition software. Since using the standard search protocol would take a while, they narrowed the search to other Lukoil facilities. Since it would still take at least a couple of hours, they sent a unit to follow the visitors.

"Sorry, we need to rush to our meeting with the minister," Kim said.

"The minister is in Moscow, not here! It would be best if you came with me now," Anastasia insisted.

The team acted as if they hadn't heard and quickly climbed into their SUV. Tex took the driver's seat, Kim occupied the passenger seat, and Tyler settled in the back. She chased after them, noted their car's description and license plate number, and hurried back into the office just as the assistant manager parked his truck.

As he entered the office, Anastasia remarked, "Your face is beet red. Are you alright? You need to sit down."

He replied, huffing, puffing, and gasping for air, "I, I, I tried to stop them at the pier."

∽

"Kim, that was a fantastic performance back there. You deserve the Academy Award for playing an American agent posing as a Russian," Tyler remarked.

"Tex, why was she running after us? Do you think she called us in?" Tyler asked.

"You know what? I don't know, but let's get the hell out of here." They didn't notice the FSU agent's car drive right past them in the opposite direction. They were focused on getting to Sochi and heading home.

∽

The FSB agents arrived just as the team was leaving. As they drove up, Anastasia rushed out of the office. The assistant manager sat at his desk, struggling to catch his breath as a sharp pain radiated from his left jaw, through his shoulder, and down his arm.

She sprinted toward the FSB agents and shouted, "You just passed them! They're in that white Mercedes!"

By the time they stopped, she was standing next to their car. The lead agent got out and asked, "Are you Anastasia?"

"Yes, you fools! You drove right past them. Didn't you hear me? They were in that white Mercedes!"

"Hold on, lady, before I take you in. Now tell me everything, quickly. I want the short version."

They followed procedure, reported to their command center, and were assigned to track them down.

Anastasia walked back into the main office and then into the assistant manager's office. As she entered, she saw him leaning back in his chair, mumbling, "Call a doctor. I think I'm having a heart attack."

She took out her cell phone and called for an ambulance, thinking, "What a wonderful day. I should have stayed in bed."

MISSION OPERATIONS CENTER

Sean spoke up. "It seems they're heading down to Sochi, but now is not the time to let our guard down. Stay completely focused on the mission, everyone—we have about twenty-four hours left."

24

ON THE ROAD TO SOCHI

The team had just completed the reconnaissance of their final objective at Novorossiysk. They transmitted their intelligence to the satellite, which sent it back to mission operations for analysis. On their way to the safe house in Sochi for the night, they planned to head to the airport for their flight to Istanbul. From there, they would travel to Dulles in the morning before returning home the following day.

As they left the terminal, the same black sedan that arrived at the port was instructed to follow the suspects without engaging. At first, they didn't notice it because the heavy traffic—mostly trucks—made the sedan challenging to spot. Additionally, it seemed as though everyone in the area drove either a red or black car. As they merged onto the A4, the traffic thinned out. They were on the move and enjoying themselves. They estimated the drive would take about six hours, aiming to reach the safe house around 8:00 p.m. Tex decided to take the first driving shift. Kim sat beside him in the front seat while Tyler slept in the back.

Tex asked Kim, "How does he fall asleep so quickly? It's as if he doesn't have a care in the world."

"I don't think he does. He goes with the flow. Sorry for the pun."

After about two hours of driving, Tex stopped at a Gazprom station in Bzhid to get gas before continuing south on A-147 to Sochi, their last stop before reaching the safe house.

MISSION OPERATIONS CENTER

"Director Fields, it appears they've stopped in Bzhid. Everything looks normal and on track with the mission timeline."

"Thanks, Andy. Don't be so formal—it's Marsha. They should arrive in Sochi around 8:00 p.m. their time, which is about 1:00 p.m. our time. Please keep me updated. I'm heading to the office and will return here by noon. Do you want me to bring lunch?"

The others declined.

"See you all in a few hours." Before she left, she called Sean over. "Is everything prepared in case we need to extract them? The longer they're in-country, the more likely they'll be uncovered."

"Everything's set, and we're ready."

BZHID ON THE ROAD TO SOCHI

After Tex finished fueling at the Gazprom gas station in Bzhid, they were on their way in less than fifteen minutes, with Kim now driving. As they pulled out of the gas station, Tex sat beside her and noticed a black sedan with two occupants. It looked to him like they were watching them. Hell, he was tired, so he pushed it out of his mind and thought, *Damn, I'm getting paranoid.*

He told Kim, "As we pull out, check to see if that black sedan pulls out, too."

"Will do, Tex. Is everyone ready? Buckle up," Kim replied.

"I highly advise buckling," Tyler added. "I drove with her."

"A-hole." She stepped on the gas and got back on the road. The black sedan remained parked as they drove off.

As Kim drove along the Black Sea Coast north of Vokonda, she said, "Look at the view! It's beautiful."

The sun was hitting the water just right. Tex glanced in the side mirror and saw the same black sedan from the gas station, the sun reflecting off its windshield. It was no more than fifty yards behind them. Since he was so tired, he had to ensure his mind wasn't playing tricks on him.

"Kim, slow down a little."

"Why, what's going on?" Kim asked.

Tex replied, "I swear that black sedan behind us was at the gas station where we stopped."

"Are you sure, Tex? We're all tired," she said. "Tyler, can you turn around and check?"

He turned around. "I see it. It's not getting any closer. It's maintaining the same distance."

"Crap! Okay, Kim, speed up and let's keep an eye on it for a bit. We don't have to act like we suspect anything. It could just be a coincidence. Take the next exit and turn left at the first street to confirm."

Kim exited the highway, turned left onto the street, and continued increasing the distance between them and the sedan.

FSB BLACK SEDAN

"They just took a left," the passenger said. "Follow them. Slow down a little, but don't lose them."

The driver asked, "Do you think they suspect anything?"

"Why would they? We're keeping our distance, and everyone drives a black or red car. They've picked up their speed and haven't changed their plans. Just maintain your distance," the passenger replied.

INSIDE THE MERCEDES

Tex and Tyler continued to watch as Kim drove along.

"Hey, Tex, that sign said we're only fifty kilometers from Sochi. What do you want me to do?"

"Pull off at the next rest area if there is one. If not, we'll need more gas at the next station."

"We have plenty of gas to reach the safe house," Tyler chimed in.

"We've got half a tank," Kim replied. "We should be fine, but let's stop and see what they do."

"If my hunch is right, we're not getting to the safe house," Tex said.

They drove for another five minutes when Kim spotted a Gazprom station and pulled off.

Tyler noticed the black sedan continuing down the highway as they pulled off. "It looks like they kept going."

Tex sighed. "I still want to top this off. It's an old army habit—I can never run out or have less than half a fuel tank."

After they had filled up, Tex noticed the black sedan no more than three kilometers down the highway. They had pulled off at the next gas station, and it seemed they had just finished filling up before merging onto the highway.

It was getting dark, but it was still tailing them. Tex's keen sense of observation had been sharpened when he was a cav scout in the army.

"I think we've been made, so we're heading to the emergency pick-up location southeast of Khostinskiy, near Dubravnyi, a hilly wooded area. It's a perfect spot for extraction. Let's go through Sochi via A148 and get off at Pyatigorskaya Ulitsa. I'll tell you when."

"Where are we headed?" Tyler asked.

"A nice little guesthouse."

"Alright, Tex, have you been here before?"

"Sure have. Remember the Winter Olympics in 2014?"

"I remember. I love watching ski jumping and downhill skiing," Tyler said to Kim. "Did you watch them?"

"I sure did. I enjoy watching speed skating, but I'm not much of a skier. I've gone a couple of times, and I always seem to fall on my butt."

"I was on a special mission detail in Sochi and got to know my way around," Tex said. "That's why I picked this as our last stop. Okay, the exit will be coming up. Take it, head south, and stop in the parking lot of the guesthouse. Let's see what our friends are up to."

MISSION OPERATIONS CENTER

As Marsha returned, she heard Sean say, "Something's up. They went past the safe house."

"What? Are you sure?" Marsha asked.

"Look. They're at least five kilometers away from it and not moving now. Get me Blueberry Hill on the secure channel," Sean ordered.

25

AM BLUEBERRY HILL - BLACK SEA

Loitering thirty miles off the coast of Khostinskiy, a converted cargo ship registered under the Liberian flag, named AM Blueberry Hill, remained at slow speed in a figure-eight pattern. One might assume it had seen better days and that it was time for the scrap heap to claim it. However, the 550-foot vessel was state-of-the-art, equipped with the latest technology, and utilized by the CIA and Special Operations Command. They could accommodate mission packages there, ranging from fighting terrorism to deploying boots on the ground and getting those boots off the ground. This mission aimed at getting boots off the ground.

She had sailed through the Bosporus Strait from the Sea of Marmara into the Black Sea just ten days ago, with no one giving it a second glance. The manifest indicated it was headed to Sochi with a load of sugar and pepper to drop off, after which it would pick up tea and wheat. No one noticed she was two days late. She traveled at her slowest speed, unhurried. The captain wanted her off the coast of Khostinskiy, where the flight time for the MH-60L and AH-64E v6.5

Apache in her holds would still meet the mission's timeline. The birds had to reach the extraction site in fifty-five minutes or less.

The executive officer said, "Yes, we have priority traffic for you in the Combat Information Center."

"Tell them I'll be there in two minutes or less."

"Roger, Skipper."

Captain Richards made his way to the Combat Information Center (CIC).

"Sir, here you go. This is Blueberry Hill."

On the other end of the secure communication link came, "Please stand by."

"Blueberry Hill, this is the farmer. The berries are ready for pickup at position Charlie, I repeat, Charlie's. What is your ETA for starting the harvest?" Sean asked.

"We can start picking in forty to forty-five minutes. When will the berries be ripe?" the skipper replied.

"It looks like forty-five minutes," Sean said. "They have stopped growing for some reason. We are monitoring them. Stand by for the green light."

"Roger, that will do. Standing by," replied the skipper. "Get me, Chief Ryan. Have him and Captain Lynn Vogel come here ASAP and prep the birds for a possible lift-off in five to ten minutes."

"Will do, Skipper," he replied. Soon after, the chief and Captain Vogel entered the CIC. "Hey, Skipper."

"Hey, Chief Ryan,"

Lynn said. "We received your message, and the birds are getting ready. They will be prepared to launch in ten minutes. The crews are setting everything up and have already been pre-flighted."

"Let's quickly review the plan," the skipper said. "After that, we can launch if necessary—though I hope we aren't needed. This is going to be a tough one."

"Absolutely, Skipper," Chief Ryan replied.

Lynn laid out the plan. "We'll depart the ship and head east, flying fifty feet above the water at 110 knots. This should get us to the extraction site when they arrive, if not sooner, and set up security. Once we cross the coast, we'll proceed to the extraction location at nap-of-the-earth altitude. The chief will touch down and wait for five minutes while I hover in the northern tree line."

"Lynn and Chief, I want to inform you that we will launch an RQ-21 Blackjack drone from the ship's stern using the indoor catapult system," the skipper added. "We'll launch it in about five minutes to provide visuals and reconnaissance utilizing infrared and thermal imaging at the site before your arrival. The video stream will be displayed on your instrument panel."

"It will be dark tonight, and there's no moon," Lynn remarked.

The chief said, "Hell, yes. We love it dark—we are night fighters! It's our friend."

"The weather report indicates light winds from the east, unlimited visibility, and low humidity," the skipper said.

"So, what you're saying, Skipper, is that it's perfect flying weather," the chief replied.

The XO entered and informed the skipper, "We're launching the drone now." Everyone gathered by the monitor in the CIC to watch. The launch went off without a hitch, and the UAV was heading to the extraction point.

The drone pilot stated, "She is on the preplanned flight path, and the sensor specialist has reported that all sensors are online."

"Let's go below deck, get in the birds, and wait for our launch instructions," Lynn suggested.

FSB BLACK SEDAN

"They're pulling off the road. Should I follow?" the driver asked.

"Yes. Let me radio the local police to get a car here. They might be heading to their safe house. Speed up! Don't lose sight of them."

"They stopped at the guesthouse. Should we get out?"

The passenger replied, "Yes, I think it's time to introduce ourselves."

They exited the car, walked to the team, and said, "Hi, can we see your papers and passports?"

Tex responded, "Sure. Who the hell are you?"

"We're from the federal police." They opened their jackets to reveal their MP-443 Grach pistols.

"Well, since you put it that way . . ." Tex glanced at Kim and smiled.

He delivered a right hook, knocking the first agent out cold with an uppercut to his chin, while Kim executed a freaky-fast kick to the head of the other. He dropped immediately. They both went down like sacks of potatoes, unconscious. Tex leaned over and collected both their pistols. He handed one to Kim and kept the other.

"You guys just knocked those sons of bitches out cold! Kim, that was awesome! You kicked the crap out of him! I have never seen a kick that quick. You should be an MMA fighter," said Tyler.

"Thanks, Tyler. I have to say that it was gratifying. I needed that," Kim responded with a smile as she tucked the pistol into her waistband.

"Hey, where's my sidearm?" Tyler asked.

Tex replied, "Just focus on driving, my friend, just drive."

"We need to get out of here," Tex said. "I'm not sure if they informed anyone about us, but I wouldn't be surprised if they did."

"Do you hear that?" Tyler said.

"What?" Kim asked.

"Police cars!"

"Back in the Mercedes!" Tex barked. When Tyler slid into the driver's seat, he rummaged through his backpack, pulled out his favorite baseball cap, and wore it backward.

"What are you wearing?" Kim asked.

"This is my racing hat. I wear it when I play DiRT Rally."

She shook her head, her facial expression revealing she wanted to say something but held back.

Tyler gripped the steering wheel. "Hold on!" He shifted the car into gear, confirmed it was in four-wheel drive mode, and exited the parking lot in the opposite direction of the police sirens. The tires screeched as he took off.

The local police arrived at the parking lot, unaware of the white BMW's exit. Spotting the downed FSU agents, they exited their vehicle to assist. As they approached, they began to regain consciousness.

The lead agent asked one of the local police, "Did you see anyone leave when you pulled up?"

"No, there were some taillights in the distance. I don't know if it was who you were looking for. They went that way," he said, pointing to his right.

The two agents jumped back into their car and drove in the direction the policeman indicated without saying a word.

Puzzled, the policemen exchanged glances when, suddenly, the taller one asked, "Do you want to follow them?"

They replied, "No, it's almost quitting time, and there would be so much paperwork. Plus, they're a-holes, and I don't like those guys anyway. Want to grab a drink?"

"Sure, let's go."

MISSION OPERATIONS CENTER

"Marsha and Sean—they're on the move again," the duty agent reported.

"Which direction?" Marsha asked.

"Looks like they're headed toward the pickup location, 'Charlie.'"

"What's their ETA to the extraction point?" Sean inquired.

"Based on their current speed, about forty-five minutes."

As the team sat in the ops center, the feed from the UAV was on the large monitor. They could now see in real time what was happening on the ground in Russia.

AM BLUEBERRY HILL

"Skipper, we just got the go-ahead," the XO said.

"Roger, and thank you. Let's get the birds in the air. Open the portside launch pad."

Blueberry Hill had a unique method for launching helicopters. Instead of lifting off from the back deck, the ship's side lowered to create a balcony over the water. The ship could move sideways, enabling it to put the wind over the deck. Helicopters could take off and land without being above the ship's profile, thus avoiding detection and tracking their radar signature.

"Skipper, the birds are away."

"Great, we have communications with them. Where's the drone?"

"It's five kilometers from the target location," the XO replied. "Let me bring up the feed."

"That image is like watching a National Geographic documentary. It's so clear," the skipper said. "It looks like it's approaching the location. Do you see anything unusual?"

"No, sir. We'll go into orbit and focus on the road leading into the extraction location."

BLACK FSB SEDAN

The lead agent grabbed the radio microphone and said, "Attention all units. We are following a white BMW SUV. We are traveling toward Khostinskiy. Request a road block going east.

26

EN ROUTE TO THE EXTRACTION POINT KHOSTINSKIY, RUSSIA

As they got back on the highway, less than five hundred meters behind them was the black sedan racing straight toward them.

"Tex, it looks like we have company to our front," said Tyler.

In front of them, a black sedan was parked across the entire road. There was no way around it. It looked like the end of the road for them and their mission.

"Tyler, can you get around them? The road we need is a quarter mile behind them. It will be to your left," said Tex.

He replied, "Hold on, everyone." Tyler floored the excellerator, and the Mercedes lurched forward. As they got closer to the road block, the FSB agents started firing in front of them, hoping to slow them down. But the Mercedes sped right toward them, going faster as it got closer.

After scanning left and right, Tyler decided to go right at 100 feet from the roadblock. He pressed the brake and grabbed for the hand brake, but there was none. Turning the steering wheel hard to the left, the SUV fishtailed around the roadblock, missing the treeline by inches. Back on the road, they sped off, leaving a trail of dust.

With the bullets flying past them as they drove down the country road. Kim asked, "Tyler, where in the hell did you learn to drive like that?"

"The Internet, of course. YouTube is awesome," he replied, laughing.

She thought *he was not right, but I like him a lot.*

Smiling, Tex said, "I'm going to have to watch you at work and your Internet traffic."

Suddenly, the back window was blown out by bullets from the FSB agents. Shards of safety glass went through the passenger compartment.

"I'm alright. How are you guys?" Asked Kim.

"I'm good," replied Tyler

"Me, too," said Tex.

BLACK FSB SEDAN

Seeing what was occurring right before their eyes. The lead FSB agent got back on the radio and said, "You fools. Move your car and follow us."

EN ROUTE TO THE EXTRACTION POINT KHOSTINSKIY, RUSSIA

After "Tyler, turn left here," Tex ordered. "These backcountry roads might give us an edge."

Kim was peering out of the back window, providing updates.

"How much longer to the extraction point?" Tyler asked.

"Fifteen minutes at this speed."

"Will they catch up to us by then?" Kim inquired.

"They haven't closed the gap," Tyler replied. "This thing can really move on these roads. The four-wheel drive is a huge plus."

"Please send our last update, Kim, and then destroy the laptop," Tex said.

"Will do, Tex. I'm on it now," she replied.

Sitting in the back seat, Kim scrambled to ensure the last updates were sent and received. Once she verified this, she started the laptop's deconstruction sequence, destroying any potential evidence.

After only a minute, Kim said, "Done!"

"Here's the plan. When we arrive at the location, Tyler, you stop the car on the driver's side, facing the entrance. I want to try to block them from driving up on the choppers. There shouldn't be any way around us. They will need to stop and run toward us while we retreat, hopefully making us smaller targets. I recommend preparing to unbuckle your seatbelt. Leave everything in the car, don't take anything with you. Once we stop, we'll have no more than maybe fifty meters to our ride. When I say 'get out,' I mean haul ass. Tyler, you're getting out from the passenger side. You'll be the last one out. Don't look back. Just run like you've never run before," Tex said.

Tyler replied, laughing, "Like no one has ever shot at me."

MH-60 - LEAD HELICOPTER, OVER THE BLACK SEA

"Chief, we are five kilometers out," the co-pilot said.

"Roger. Signal Captain Vogel. She's choosing a spot in the tree line for overwatch to our left," Chief Warrant Officer James replied.

"Roger, I see it. I just sent the signal. She acknowledged."

As they reached the extraction point, Chief Ryan said, "Hang on, boys, this will be the ride of your life. Here we go."

Flaring the helicopter to slow from 110 knots to nearly a complete stop was a thing of beauty. Having flown MH-60s for almost twenty years, he could make them perform remarkable maneuvers. He positioned the helicopter in the field, hovering just above the grass.

Looking ahead with his night-vision goggles, he surveyed the area. The co-pilot scanned to the left, the crew chief monitored the right side, and the medic checked behind them on the left. They maintained a 360-degree field of observation.

"Do you see Captain Vogel?" Chief Warrant Officer Ryan asked.

The co-pilot replied, "Roger, Chief, she's below the tree line on our left. It's tough to spot her."

"One minute out from the extraction point," the co-pilot added.

In the Mercedes, the team prepared to exit the vehicle as soon as it came to a stop. They all unbuckled their seat belts, gearing up for a mad dash to the helicopter.

"Kim, give me an update," Tex instructed.

"They're two hundred meters behind us."

"When we stop, follow my lead. The birds will be at my one o'clock. Okay, everyone, stay close as we run directly to them."

As the Mercedes came to a halt, he yelled, "Ready!"

They burst from the vehicle and sprinted, not looking back.

"Skipper, we have visuals on them with the drone on our monitor," the co-pilot said.

"Are you sure?" the chief asked.

"Yes, three individuals: two males and one female."

"How can you determine males and females?" the medic inquired.

"Men and women emit different heat signatures."

"That's good to know," he replied.

"Is anyone following them?" the chief asked.

"One car about two hundred meters behind them and another further back."

"OK, let's keep an eye on them."

After a few minutes, the co-pilot said, "Chief, I have a visual of them at your one o'clock."

"Roger, I see them. I'm bringing her down." It was so gentle that no one even felt her touch the ground.

AH-64E - EXTRACTION POINT

Lynn radioed Chief Ryan. "I see them at my one o'clock. I'll take her up for a better view down the road."

She lifted her Apache just above the treetops, where she had a perfect view of the road leading to the extraction site. She asked her gunner, "Do you see that car?"

"Looks like two individuals getting out and moving toward the Chief's bird and behind our pickups," said the co-pilot.

"Get ready!"

"Roger. We are locked and loaded. There is another vehicle behind them and closing," he replied.

As Tex, Kim, and Tyler sprinted toward their ride home, there was suddenly a pop, pop, pop from the FSU agents' Glock 17s, which they pulled from the glove compartment. Rounds struck the ground beside them as they ran. Some whizzed by their heads, and one bullet found its mark.

Tyler collapsed to the ground. Kim and Tex looked back and shouted, "Tyler, let's go!"

"I can't walk... It's my leg. I got hit."

"You get up, you son of a bitch," Kim insisted. "We're all going home. You owe me dinner!"

"I can't. Go—go, please." Tyler looked down at his leg and passed out.

AH-64E - EXTRACTION POINT

The gunner reported to Lynn, "They're firing at them, and one is down."

"Gunner, Chain Gun," Lynn instructed. "Troops are in the open. Fire a short burst between them and those SOBs."

"Identified," the co-pilot confirmed.

"Fire."

"Roger."

All they could hear was Bang, bang, bang. It didn't take many rounds from their Chain Gun, which had a rate of fire of 625 rounds per minute, to neutralize the pursuers.

As soon as the second FSB team saw the tracer rounds impacting, they pulled off the side of the road.

Lynn commanded, "Cease fire."

"Roger."

"Great shooting!"

AM BLUEBERRY HILL

"Skipper, we just received word one is down," the XO said. "One of the assets is down."

"Are you certain?"

"Yes, sir. We saw the action on the monitor."

In the CIC, as the first rounds left the AH-64E, all they heard was, "Damn, that thing is wicked!" as the AH-64E unleashed a burst of 30 mm rounds.

As the bullets from the FSU agents impacted near Tyler, Tex ran back to where he lay bleeding from his wound. Suddenly, the FSU agents stopped shooting. Just then, bullets began flying, but they weren't coming from the direction of the FSU agents. When he reached Tyler, he lifted him over his shoulder in a fireman's carry and dashed toward the waiting helicopter—just a few more yards. Kim was running alongside them, trying to wake Tyler up. They were completely out of breath.

Tex laid Tyler on the floor when they reached the helicopter, and Kim jumped in, sitting beside him. Then, Tex climbed in.

"Chief, everyone is secure! Let's get out!" the medic said.

As soon as they lifted off, the Chief popped smoke to conceal their departure. As they ascended, they could still see the AH-64E holding its position. "What a beautiful sight," said the co-pilot.

The medic started to treat Tyler as Kim talked to him, saying, "Tyler, wake up, please wake up." Not one sound or movement from him, she thought. Could he have been hit somewhere else, and we didn't see it?

The medic started to check for other wounds for entry and exit points. He found nothing but the wound on the lower leg, and he was immediately put on a drip IV in his right arm. Knowing the blood types of everyone on the helicopter, he started to give Tyler some O positive in his left arm. At the same time, Kim was over him, shouting, "Wake up, Tyler!" She hit him on the shoulder. "Tyler, I was just starting to like you!"

"Ouch . . . that hurt. Why are you hitting me?" Tyler mumbled, smiling.

She hit him again.

"If this is how you show love, let me rethink this relationship."

Kim leaned over and gave him a big kiss.

The medic said, "Okay, guys, you can get a room later."

Gasping for air, "Is he going to be all right?" asked Kim.

"I think so. It looks like the bullet went in and out here, so we need to stitch him up. We can do that on the ship. I want to stop the bleeding. The entry point is near his femoral artery."

"Am I bleeding?" Tyler gasped as he looked at his leg again.

"Yes, Tyler, you got shot," the medic answered.

Looking at his leg, he replied, "It doesn't look too bad," as Tyler passed out.

"Do you want me to hit him again?"

The medic laughed. "No, I think he's had enough love for one day."

As Kim was about to hit Tyler again, "Hey, I was just faking. You're going to leave a bruise on me, Tyler said, laughing.

"Faking, right?" Kim replied as she touched his forehead.

The crew chief glanced at Tex and said, "Here, put these headphones on so you can talk to the pilot."

After Tex put them on, he said, "Thank you for saving us."

The Chief spoke up, "We are not out of the woods yet. We have about ten kilometers to the coast and a few miles after that to the ship. Hopefully, we'll be on board in thirty minutes or less. We have a nice tailwind."

AH-64 – EXTRACTION POINT

"We should destroy their car. Fire it up and make it glow!" Lynn said.

"I really hate to blow up a Mercedes," replied the gunner as he set his sights on the target and pulled the trigger. "But what the hell!" He pressed the trigger, letting a volley of 30mm rounds fly. As the rounds went down range, he continued, "Haven't blown anything up since Iraq."

What a sweet sound it was as the 30 mm rounds left the barrels of the Chain Gun.

The car burst into flames. Nothing would be left of it but a hulk of burning metal.

"Target destroyed."

"You think?" Lynn laughed. "Let's get out of here before the insurance company calls us."

FSB AGENTS - EXTRACTION POINT

As the agents kneeled behind their car, they saw the fire from the helicopter's nose. A second later, the car they had been chasing was destroyed, leaving no evidence. They moved away from their vehicle, hoping it would not be the helicopter's next target.

Once the helicopter departed, the agents got back in their car and called their commander.

"Sir, they got away," one agent said.

"What do you mean they got away?" the commander replied.

"Two helicopters were waiting for them."

"Two of our helicopters?"

"No, sir, not ours. Two American helicopters."

"How do you know they were American choppers? On Russian soil? Okay, how much have you had to drink today?"

The second FSB car arrived. The passenger got out and asked, "Did you see those helicopters?"

"I'm just assuming by the models: a Blackhawk and an Apache. Even though they look nothing like the photos I have seen, they were modified."

"Look at your phone. I just sent you a couple of pictures. Do they look like the ones in what I sent?"

The agent reviewed the pictures and replied, "Yes, sir, they look very much like the ones in the picture."

"Okay, they were Americans. Now, back to my other questions."

"None! We haven't been drinking all day. We've been following them all day since Novorossiysk."

"You're telling me that two helicopters picked them up and flew off?"

"Yes, Commander."

"Did you see which direction they are headed?"

"They headed towards the coast in a westerly direction. Also, we wounded one of them."

"What about their car? Did you get a chance to look through it?"

"No, sir. One of their helicopters blew it up. There's nothing left."

"I'm sending a team out to assist you," the commander said. "Stay where you are."

He hung up and called his superior, starting a chain reaction that reached the Ministry of Defense and, finally, General Popov.

His phone rang, and as he picked it up, he thought, "This had better be good. I have a lot to do today."

"General Popov, sir, I hate to bother you, but we have been informed of a situation near Sochi," his aide said.

"Go ahead, but what does it have to do with the Ministry of Defense?"

"The FSB started to track three individuals, two males and one female. They were identified at the oil shipping port of Novorossiysk, where they were seen in a couple of other restricted areas. Still, they had identification that allowed them to slip by security. Someone at the main entrance called the Ministry of Energy to verify some information. They told her it was false. With the information she discovered, she decided to call the local FSB unit. When the unit arrived, the individuals were seen leaving the parking area. That is when the FSB started to follow them."

"Why does this matter to the Ministry of Defense? Stop wasting my time!" The general shouted.

"Sir, they were... how can I say this? Well, they were extracted from Russia on American helicopters and flown out to sea in a westerly direction. The FSB ran their faces using the facial recognition software we acquired from China, including images taken at the port. The software identified their images at the airport in Moscow. They flew in a few days ago and have also been identified in the oil fields of Perm and the oil refinery at Rostov-on-Don. It seems they are very interested in our oil industry."

"You think so?" he considered. "Do we know where they are now?"

"No, sir. I reached out to the air defense forces in the region. They didn't pick up any unidentified aircraft entering or leaving Russian airspace. We also viewed images of up to fifty kilometers in the Black Sea, but no vessels could support helicopters. There were only transport vessels."

"We own the Black Sea. Find out where they landed. They couldn't have disappeared, now could they?" Not waiting for a reply, General Popov hung up the phone and yelled for his aide, "Take two messages and send them out when we are finished. Ready?"

"Yes, sir, I'm ready," replied his aide.

"Here's the first one to the commanding generals in Operation Moose. You have their names, I hope." He continued, "The timetable is moved up. Be ready to move in seventy-two hours. Report your status at once."

He went on, "Second message to Admiral Balakin. Commence Operation Moose. Report your status at once."

"Sir, I will send them out now."

"Thank you. Now get me a drink and one for you. In seventy-two hours, the world is about to change."

AM BLUEBERRY HILL

The XO informed Captain Richards, "Skipper, the assets are on board the bird and heading home."

"Radio, send a message to the gunship to destroy our assets' vehicle. We can't let the Russians get hold of the equipment in the Benz," the captain replied.

"They already took care of that, Skipper. The target is destroyed."

"Bring the drone back. There's no need to watch anything else. Great job, team."

"Skipper, the Mission Operations Center is on the line," the XO said.

The skipper said one sentence before he hung up: "The berries are perfect this time of year, but one is damaged."

MISSION OPERATIONS CENTER

Everyone in the operation center let out a loud yell and started to clap and shake hands.

Marsha said, "Now we are just waiting for them to be on board the Blueberry Hill. The message said one was hit. Did they say who or provide any other information?"

Sean replied, "We won't know until they get them back on board and check them out. It's a waiting game now."

Marsha acknowledged his response and sat down at her desk.

EN ROUTE TO BLUEBERRY HILL

Tex thought, "The pilot's voice seemed awfully familiar. Excuse me, Chief. What's your name? Your voice sounds so familiar."

"Are you getting old, Tex? You don't remember me?"

"Hey, hold on—Grumpy, is that you?"

"Sure is, Tex. Welcome aboard! How long has it been?"

"It must be over fifteen years."

"At least let me get you home, and we can catch up on the ship."

The co-pilot said, "Grumpy, I thought we were the only ones who called you that."

27

AM BLUEBERRY HILL

All the helicopters landed back on Blueberry Hill. The medics and hospital corpsman brought Tyler to sickbay, a state-of-the-art emergency room equipped with an operating room, while Kim followed closely behind. She glanced at Tex, who urged, "Go." Captain Richards greeted Tex and expressed gratitude to the chopper crew.

Tex then turned to Chief James, hugged him, thanked him, and said, "Let's catch up back in DC when you can." Next, he approached Captain Vogel to thank her and her gunner. After that, he returned to Captain Richards.

"Skipper, I really appreciate you getting my team out of there."

"No problem. We are happy to assist. By the way, we're headed to Istanbul and should arrive in a few days."

"Skipper, can you take me to your CIC?"

"Absolutely. Follow me."

"Please keep me updated on Tyler. I want to check on him, but I need to make a call first."

They made their way to the ship's CIC.

"Here you go, sir. This is a secure phone," the XO said.

"Is everyone on board? Is everyone alright?" Sean asked.

"Yes, everyone is aboard," Tex began, "but Tyler took a round to the lower left leg. The bullet went in and out. The medic on the helicopter did a great job. He stopped the bleeding and replaced the blood Tyler lost. He's in sickbay with Kim."

"Is Kim alright?" Sean asked.

"Yes, she's fine. She has a bit of a soft spot for the young man. Is Marsha there, Sean?"

"Do you want to speak with her?"

"Please," he said, then paused. "Marsha?"

"Yes, Tex."

"It's good to hear your voice."

"I agree—now get your butt home. You're taking me out, and we'll pick a date."

"A date." Tex smiled.

He said, "You choose one, and I'll be there."

"You got it. Tex, Sean wants to talk to you. Here you go."

There was a brief silence before Sean said, "We reviewed your intelligence, and wow, it got us thinking. We cross-referenced and examined it with the images and other intelligence we gathered from every source. What do you think is happening? We don't have a complete consensus yet."

He continued, "I believe Russia's reason for invading Ukraine in 2022 was a huge deception—they aimed to control the whole northern and eastern coast of the Black Sea and the Sea of Azov."

Tex said, "Hell, remember when they moved into Georgia? And what does Georgia have? Oil! Turkey is the only thing standing in the way of them controlling the entire region, and we know how friendly they've become. Basically, they want to control the movement of oil and everything in and out of the region into the Med."

Sean said, "I need to update you on what's happened since you left the country. We intentionally didn't tell you because we didn't want anything to taint your intelligence or analysis."

After a pause, Sean continued, "We've been monitoring some large Russian troop movements, and they're positioning supplies on the Jordan border with Syria—much more than what was reported in the news weeks ago. Additionally, the Chinese are moving along their border with Laos and relocating more troops into the region. The Indians had a large naval exercise in the Indian Ocean. While we already knew about this, it's strange timing, to say the least. It seems this activity has picked up in the last few hours. We're not sure what all this activity means, but we are monitoring."

"Is there any activity from Venezuela, Iran, or Iraq?"

"Nothing unusual. We're monitoring the Panama Canal."

"Why are we focused on the Panama Canal?"

"Over the past ten years, China has heavily invested in the infrastructure and ports on both sides of the canal: the Pacific and Atlantic. With China, Venezuela, and Russia closely aligned, we're worried they might attempt to blockade it. We've deployed additional naval assets to the region."

"So, what do you think all this signals?"

"Not sure, but do you want my take?"

"Absolutely," Sean replied.

"The troop movements are perplexing. None of the countries where the troops are stationed along the borders have grievances against Russia or China. I'm uncertain about India's role in this, aside from having a modern navy that can deploy significant assets to the region to support any naval or air operations. Their current naval exercises are the largest they've ever conducted. The exercises are taking place further south and east than originally planned."

"I'm confident all this connects with what you identified regarding Russia and oil. The question remains—why the troop movements? They can't just sit there forever. I believe we'll find out very soon what's happening. Our responsibility is to gather accurate intelligence and present it to the president. I'll say this: I think they want to control the global movement of oil."

"That makes sense, but why focus on oil right now?" Sean asked. "Everyone's shifting to green energy."

"Not really. Western Europe and the US are. Russia, China, India, and many others claim they are, but in reality, they aren't, and they will need oil for the foreseeable future."

"I need to head out and check on Tyler," Tex said.

"Get some rest, Tex, and we'll continue discussing the intelligence from your mission. If I have any questions, I'll reach out to the skipper. Just a heads-up. All the principals will be meeting the day after you return. We need to figure out what the hell is going on. We have to get something to the president soon."

"Sean, based on what you told me, we need to schedule a call with everyone tomorrow to discuss all the intelligence."

"You don't think we can wait until you're back? It's only about three days or so," asked Sean.

"I don't, so I can give it to you now if you'd like my initial assumption."

"I'd love to hear it, but I'll set up a conference call tomorrow at 3:00 p.m. your time. You do have a secure location on the ship, right?" Sean asked.

"Yes, I'm going to check on Tyler and Kim."

"Please let me know how they're doing. I'll talk to you tomorrow. Try to get some rest—the world is changing, my friend."

After hanging up, Tex headed to Sickbay to check on his team. He walked in and saw Tyler lying down, out cold. Next to him was Kim. She returned the corpsman's phone and asked him to send her the video she had taken.

"How's he doing?" Tex inquired.

Kim replied, "He's doing well. There are no major injuries from the wound, but they've got him on some strong meds. He should be up by the time we get to Istanbul."

"So he can fly back with us? I'll confirm with the doctor," Tex said. "Kim, how are you holding up?"

"I'm good—just worried about Tyler."

"I need to talk to the skipper, get cleaned up, grab something to eat, and rest. I want you to do the same. That's an order," he said with a smile.

"Yes, sir!" Kim responded.

"Oh, and before I forget, we have a conference call at 3:00 p.m. tomorrow. Let's meet at 9:00 a.m. in the SCIF for breakfast so I can bring you up to speed. A lot is going on."

"What about Tyler?"

"If he can be released and make it to the SCIF, that would be great. I want the entire team on the call. I need everyone's input."

"See you in the morning," Kim replied.

AM BLUEBERRY SCIF, BLACK SEA, EN ROUTE TO TURKEY

Tex entered the SCIF the following day, and lo and behold, there were Tyler and Kim.

"What the hell are you doing here?"

"I'm good—thanks for asking," he smiled. "I owe you for pulling me out of that field."

"That's what soldiers do—we don't leave anyone on the battlefield. How's the leg?"

"I'll be hopping around for a week or so. I just need to keep it elevated. I checked with the doctor. It looks like I can fly home with you guys, but I might need to be in first class—you know, to keep my leg elevated." He winked.

"You know what, Tyler? I think we all deserve to be pampered. I'll even pay for it!" replied Tex. "Good morning, Kim. You look like you're in a good mood."

"I'm doing great, Tex, and thanks for asking."

Tex smiled and said, "Tyler and Kim, the objective of the meeting is to reach a consensus on the current situation based on the intelligence we've gathered during our mission and the actions of other agencies. I haven't reviewed their intelligence, but I prepared a mission brief last night and made copies. Please read it over and share your thoughts. If necessary, we can adjust it before the meeting."

Tyler and Kim went over the mission brief.

"This looks great," Tyler remarked.

"Very concise and professional. Have you done this before?" Kim teased.

Tex chuckled. "Thanks, I have. Now, let's eat!"

28

BLUEBERRY HILL - SCIF

The secure communication link between Blueberry Hill and the Pentagon was established. The eighty-five-inch flat screen in the SCIF displayed both locations and the participants. In the Blueberry Hill SCIF were Tex, Tyler, and Kim. At the Pentagon, seated around a large oval wooden table, were Marsha, Jenny, Bob, Secretary of Defense Jesse Dorn, Joint Chiefs of Staff General Ralph Harris, Admiral Kevin Smith of Naval Operations, NIA Director Mark Chang, CIA Director Sean McGill, and NSA Director Peter Johnson. Alongside them were their deputies.

Tex opened the meeting by saying, "Good morning, everyone, from the incredible AM Blueberry Hill. We want to thank the skipper and crew for their professionalism, courtesy, and teamwork. Additionally, thank you to the folks at the Mission Operations Center. Great job."

"Can you provide us with a quick overview of how we got here?" Sean asked.

Tex summarized the events that had led them to their current position on the AM Blueberry Hill in the middle of the Black Sea.

He concluded, "And that's where we are today. Please feel free to ask if anyone wants a more detailed timeline of events. I believe everyone has reviewed the updates we sent while we were in country. I'd like to hear what everyone else has uncovered—the intelligence and your assumptions."

Sean said, "Once everyone here is finished, let's go around the table. I want Tex and his team to wrap up. After hearing everyone's insights, I would like them to give their best assessment of what's happening and then outline the next steps. Jesse, you're first."

"Jesse Dorn, the Secretary of Defense. We observe significant military movements along the border with China and Laos, with approximately one hundred fifty thousand troops being amassed." The SCIF displayed Jesse's images on the conference room monitor. "Here are images we received a couple of hours ago showing units composed of armor, infantry, considerable artillery, and support troops. We don't see any chemical or biological units, like decontamination squads."

"They've also flown in Mi-8 and Harbin Z-9 helicopters, along with Harbin Giant Eagle and Chengdu Cloud Shadow unmanned aircraft. They've moved at least five squadrons of J-20 fighters closer to the operational area. We haven't witnessed this movement level since the Sino-Soviet War of 1969, making this situation significant."

"In this next image, they have installed HQ-22 ground-to-air defense systems. We believe these systems could counter our aircraft if we engage in battle. Again, we suspect the HQ-22 will counter our aircraft in Laos or if they move into Thailand. We have not noted any additional movements of Chinese units, whether ground, air, or sea. The currently amassed troops seem to be the only ones in the fight."

"Do you have any idea what their objectives are if they decide to move into Laos?" Tex asked.

"We know they'll face no resistance in Laos since it is essentially a puppet state. It'll be a smooth ride. They built the road through their Belt and Road Initiative. They might be targeting Bangkok or heading down the Malay Peninsula. Once they pass through Laos, it's just 650 kilometers to Bangkok. Once they enter Thailand, the experience will differ from their passage through Laos."

"We currently have a carrier battle group and a contingent of marines in Singapore. We'll deploy them into the Gulf of Thailand if and when the Chinese advance. Additionally, we're relocating some B-21 Raiders from Barksdale to Andersen on Guam in the next few days. This is a long-duration training mission."

"What's in it for China?" Jenny inquired.

"It's not about oil—Thailand imports nearly all its oil. Besides, green energy is more valuable than oil at this point. Thailand is a major manufacturer of electrical components. Still, if the Chinese move down the Malay Peninsula to the Singapore Strait, they could control that critical choke point," he replied.

"Thank you, Jesse."

"Jesse, General or Admiral, has any significant movement of naval units?" Peter asked.

"They recently completed an exercise in the South China Sea near their Spratly Islands," Jesse replied. "As you know, they've militarized these islands. However, it appears that nearly all vessels except for four are returning to their home ports. Those four are headed to Da Nang, Vietnam, for a port call. We haven't observed any other activity, but we're monitoring with naval assets in the region."

"Well, there is one thing," General Harris remarked. "We've noticed increased activity around their strategic oil reserve locations —they're heavily guarding them. This is quite new. They have always had security but never a military presence. We're keeping an eye on this with Marsha and her team's assistance."

Marsha interjected, "Hold on for a second. I'll speak out of turn if you don't mind. I want to address what General Harris just mentioned. Earlier today, Jenny informed me that the oil fields Tex and his team recently visited have seen a buildup of Russian forces in the East Siberian oil region and the Timan-Pechora area."

She continued, "I've asked NRO to move an asset into position to monitor their strategic oil reserves in East Siberia. I should have an update within the next twelve hours. I will keep everyone informed. Wouldn't it be a coincidence if China and Russia did the same thing? Hell, we need to keep an eye on the Indians. I'll ask Sally at NRO about getting an asset to check them out. Sorry for barging in—please continue."

"No problem, Marsha," Sean said. "Let's talk about our friends, the Russians."

"There's been a large buildup of Russian troops along the border between Syria and Jordan," Jesse continued. "These troops are made up very much like the Chinese. However, we have seen some movement of their Spetsnaz reconnaissance units out of their garrisons near Moscow. Sean, can you provide any more insight into what's going on in Syria from the CIA perspective before I move into more of the military aspect?"

"Sure," Sean replied. "As you know, we have some intelligence assets in Syria and ground forces that the general can elaborate on if needed, but we've had them there since at least 2018. Our field operatives have reported that the Russian troops' morale is quite low, and some of their equipment isn't holding up well in the desert. Hell, we learned our lesson in Desert Storm. I remember putting pantyhose over our 120mm guns on our M1s, 25mm Bradleys, and M16A2s to keep the sand from getting into the barrels and clogging them up."

He continued, "They're also struggling to get water supplies. It's been a scorching year. Other than that, that's all I have. Oh, one more thing—we're seeing disinformation activity in Jordan aimed at escalating the anti-government protests. We believe Russian agents in Jordan are behind this activity. So far, the Jordanian government has managed to control it. If and when the Russians invade those areas, we're not entirely sure they can continue to contain them. We don't want another Arab Spring."

"What units can we position to counter any aggression if one of our regional allies asks us?" Tex inquired.

"Good question. I'll let Ralph take this one," Jesse responded.

"This couldn't come at a worse time," Ralph started. "We currently have the 2nd Armored Division and 4th Infantry Division transitioning to renewable energy. They are non-deployable and won't be available for deployment for another ninety to one hundred and twenty days. I'm working with the Army Chief of Staff and the Marine Corps Commandant to determine what units we can deploy."

"We have the 3rd Infantry Division, 1st Cavalry Division, and elements of the 1st Infantry Division, as well as the 1st and 4th Marine Divisions, that can deploy. I'm putting the 101st Airborne Division on alert. Most of the 82nd Airborne Division and the 2nd Armored Cavalry Regiment (ACR) are in Poland, and we have a solid assortment of Special Forces ready."

Ralph went on, "The Russian ground units are conducting a lot of live-fire exercises and vehicle maintenance. We believe this is in preparation for combat operations. Sean already pointed out their equipment issues. They've been flying reconnaissance missions very close to the border and have violated it at least three times in the last twenty-four to thirty-six hours, which coincided with getting Tex's team out of Russia."

"Regarding our troops in Jordan, we've put them on alert. I received an update from the commander: They haven't seen any unusual activity around their location. Guys, the Russians know where we're stationed. I doubt they want to engage with us. They will bypass us. If not, we have the Harry S. Truman Carrier Strike Group in the Mediterranean to deliver a level of pain the Russians haven't experienced since World War II," Ralph concluded.

"How can you say you think they'll bypass our troops?" Tex asked.

"We haven't seen any mention of U.S. forces or our locations in any of their communications. In fact, if we consider the most advantageous route to the Red Sea—assuming that is their objective—we are over 150 miles from that route. They could have chosen a quicker path, but it would have taken them close to our positions, and we are not moving!"

Tyler raised his hand.

"You're not in the fifth grade," Ralph said. "You don't have to raise your hand."

"Sir, what's your best guess on their direction once they reach Jordan? They could either head west into Israel or south into Saudi Arabia. Why would they choose one option based on what we've discovered? I mean, what do they hope to gain by turning right into Israel instead of going straight down into Saudi Arabia?"

"A great question, Tyler. Let's gather everyone's opinions, and I'll represent the Department of Defense. Israel and Russia maintain good relations, so I don't see them entering Israel. There's nothing to gain there except facing the fury of their army, and Russia knows we will ultimately support and defend Israel."

Ralph continued, "I'm still trying to figure out—or at least understand—where they currently are. It makes no sense. If they want to harm us, there are far easier methods. The Russians could move through Eastern Europe directly into Western Europe. Heck, the Chinese could come through Mexico or Central America! You don't believe for a second they couldn't bribe the cartels? Hell, I bet they could do it with fentanyl. This could turn into a proxy war if they desired. I'm not sure what the troop movements are meant for beyond controlling oil, but there must be something more. I can't pinpoint it." Ralph paused. "Peter, what do you think?"

"I agree. There's really nothing significant they would gain. Additionally, we haven't intercepted any chatter concerning Israel. I support the general's view. Marsha, you're up."

"I agree. Israel has significant natural gas reserves, but Russia has plenty as well. We haven't observed any unusual activity around those Russian reserves, such as in their oil fields." Mark said, "The DNI concurs that there's no substantial reason or justification for them to move into Israel. I'm glad you guys made it out of Russia. How's the leg, Tyler?"

"Sir, it's great! I'll be back to 100 percent before you know it. Kim's taking excellent care of me and the ship's medical staff."

"Good to hear, Tyler," Mark replied.

"What do you think, Sean?" Ralph asked.

Sean stood up. "I completely agree with these assessments. There's no evident reason, and we've been in touch with our regional partners. They don't see any reason, and Israel hasn't increased its posture along its eastern flank. Jenny, what's your take?" Sean sat down.

"I'm no military expert, but I don't see any reason for them to advance into Israel. I believe the Russians are after oil and the control or flow of oil from the region. Tex?"

"My gut says they're making a beeline to the Red Sea and down the Arabian Peninsula. There's no reason for them to move into Israel other than to get their butts kicked. But one thing's on my mind: Do you really think they've gathered enough force to carry out a full-scale invasion of that region along the Red Sea down to the Gulf of Aden? Unless the Saudis fold like a deck of cards, which I don't see happening. Hell, if I'm not mistaken, we have a defense pact with them. Are they in cahoots with each other? You know, the whole OEEC nonsense."

Ralph answered, "I don't think they have enough forces to hold the land they fought for. They don't want Jordan—it's just a quick way to reach their true destination. They're not looking to control any piece of land they just fought for, but we know the Jordanians will defend their territory. Why would you jeopardize your forces if you don't aim to control the land? It's crazy. It's almost as if they want us to focus on this while they're doing something else elsewhere. It's like driving down the highway, just passing cars without caring. You don't want to be overtaken by them. You keep going until you run out of gas or reach the next refueling station. You're not taking land—you're just trying to reach your final destination."

"General?"

"Yes, Jenny?

"How far can one of their main battle tanks go on a full tank of fuel?"

"We believe it's much like ours: about three hundred miles."

"They'll need to refuel before reaching Haql, Saudi Arabia, if not earlier?"

"Yes, they would take Highway 15 or 5. Maan is critical. Can we get some eyes on that area? They could establish a forward arming and refueling point (FARP). Refueling there would position them to launch a push deep into Saudi Arabia, and they could use their Mi-8s to transport the fuel."

"Well, once they enter Saudi Arabia, they'll control the Red Sea and might enable the Houthis and Iran to manage the checkpoints into the Gulf of Aden," Jenny noted.

"That was a sobering conversation," Sean observed. "Do we all agree that the final objective is to control the flow of oil in and out of the Red Sea?"

Everyone nodded.

"Admiral, can you deploy some assets to the region?" Tex asked.

"The USS Dwight D. Eisenhower Carrier Strike Group. Consisting of the USS Philippine Sea, a Ticonderoga-class guided-missile cruiser. USS Gravely and USS Mason Arleigh Burke-class guided-missile destroyers. Along with their air wings, Strike Fighter Squadrons (VFA) 32, 83, 105, and 131. All combined 65 - 70 aircraft. In addition, the USS Mason and USS Gravely are both guided missile destroyers. Plus, command and control elements along with subsurface assets. The entire CSG is currently in the region," Admiral Smith stated. "We'll extend their deployment for another ninety days. I'll accordingly position some additional support vessels in the region and elements of the 26th Marine Expeditionary Unit.

"Before we move on from discussing Russia, they currently have one of their two carriers, and its strike group has been in Hong Kong for thirty days, but we're starting to observe some activity around the berths. They recently recalled all their sailors and Marines to their ships. We believe they're going to get underway within seventy-two hours. We think they will head out to the Philippine Sea. We are relocating some of our assets to monitor them and have placed three P-8 Poseidons out of Pearl on alert."

"Thank you, Admiral," Sean replied. "Let's shift our focus to the Indian Ocean and India. General or Admiral, please continue."

"I'm going to let the admiral take this one," Ralph remarked.

"There's an increase in naval activity, even though it was planned in the Indian Ocean. We are beginning to pick up more communications within the units themselves—nothing unusual that we wouldn't notice on a normal cruise. The only out-of-the-ordinary aspect is the presence of the Marines. In the information they provided about the training exercise, there was no mention of any amphibious landings or anything the Marines would be involved in."

"They also completed significant renovations to the INS Vikramaditya to support unmanned drones that are the size of their carrier-based aircraft. It's the latest version of the Ghatak. It's a powerhouse and a force multiplier, without a doubt. We know they have ten on the carrier now and could land more on board if necessary. They have a solid stockpile."

"We're closely monitoring the Indian battle group and deploying several destroyers to track their movements. We've asked Marsha for a cell to oversee their activity," the admiral stated.

"That cell is up and running," Marsha replied. "They're tracking movements, and there haven't been any significant course changes."

"Admiral, do you mind if I step in?" Sean asked.

"Of course not. Go ahead."

"We've just received word that in the past twenty-four hours, China and India have reached an agreement concerning the Depsang region. They have committed to a complete cease-fire and have returned to their historical boundaries. They agreed to demilitarize the area, and both have pulled back. This is huge, folks!"

He continued, "They will become allies. We already know that India turns a blind eye to Russia and has purchased a lot of military equipment. Once this agreement is finalized, a military alliance involving Russia, China, and India will overshadow NATO, turning it into a mere neighborhood watch group. Hell, they all have nukes and depend on Russia for oil to run their countries, as well as China for green technology. I'm not diving into what's going on here. What do you think, Tex team?"

Tex responded, "I think we'd better figure this out. Beyond that, I'm curious about what's happening with China. Once I get that information, I can provide a better estimate. What do you think, Kim and Tyler?"

Both Kim and Tyler agreed, even though they were ninety percent certain about what was unfolding.

Sean asked, "What has changed? The only thing we can point to right now is when your team was pulled out of Russia."

"Are you suggesting that our presence in Russia relates to a potential attack from Russia, China, and India?" Tex asked.

"We can't say for sure, but your team and what you were investigating seem to have triggered a chain of events. Let's hear from the rest of the team, but I don't believe your actions are the reason for an attack. They've been building up to this for months. What I'm saying is that I think you forced them to accelerate their timelines. Peter, can you give us an update on signal intelligence?"

With a smile, Peter said, "Before I start, Tex, you look terrible—which, by the way, is the first time I've looked better than you. You guys did an excellent job."

"Hold on a moment," Jesse said. "The DOD has detected normal communications among their combat units so far, but the volume of communications is rising. Please continue, Peter."

"The NSA will confirm what Jesse just said—there are normal communications between units during any field training exercise, especially with this many troops involved. Something changed twenty-four hours ago. The level and frequency have increased by 25 percent. We are now intercepting more communications between countries—not just among units in theaters of operation and their command centers, but also messages from soldiers on the ground back to their families in Russia and China. This is both extraordinary and alarming. This trend has been steadily rising in the last few hours. Typically, this indicates a large-scale movement—we still don't know the direction yet."

"Hell," Sean said. "It looks like they're preparing for an all-out war, but all three fronts at once? We can't handle a three-front war. A two-front war would be extremely challenging, wouldn't you agree, General?"

"Yes, I agree," General Harris replied. "We'll have to pick our battles."

"Peter, anything else?" Sean asked.

"Not at the moment."

"Has there been any increase or unusual activity in the Russian naval forces?" Marsha inquired. "I'm particularly interested in their Northern Fleet. Are they moving anything to the Baltics?"

"Sean, I'll handle this one," the admiral said. "There's been no additional or unusual activity from their Northern Fleet out of Severomorsk, either on the surface or beneath it. All but two of their submarines are still in their pens: the Generalissimo Suvorov and the Perm. Other than that, it's very quiet up there."

"Do you find that odd?" Jenny asked.

"No, not really. All the activity seems to be concentrated in the Middle East, the Indian Ocean, and Southeast Asia. We are watching the Black Sea, the Baltic fleets, and anything coming out of Severomorsk. Again, we picked up one of their newest and largest subs a few days back, the Generalissimo Suvorov, along with an attack sub, Perm, who was leaving the port. Still, they are heading toward the Baltics, moving away from where the current activity is. It looks like a typical cruise."

"The only area where we're noticing increased activity is the Black Sea, which began about twenty-four hours ago. They're likely searching for a ship capable of launching and retrieving helicopters. We've informed the skipper of the Blueberry Hill to move closer to Turkish territorial waters. You should arrive in Istanbul by mid-morning tomorrow."

The admiral concluded, "That's all I have for now. We will notify the skipper if anything changes in the Black Sea."

"General, I have a question," Tyler said. "What about their airborne units?"

"We haven't noticed any significant movements of airborne troops at this time."

"General, is there anything you or the admiral want to add?" Sean asked. Both replied that they had nothing to contribute. "Okay, so why have Russia, China, and India moved their units into staging areas for a possible war?" Sean continued. "What's the root cause? Let's start ruling out the reasons. Peter, you're up."

"Based on all the metadata we've reviewed, we've seen no indication that any of the regions are in potential conflict," Peter stated. "Hell, just a few months ago, all regions were quiet. I reduced the teams supporting them. The only common factor is oil: transporting, producing, or processing."

"Thanks, Peter. General?" Sean prompted.

"I'll be blunt: We can't fight a three-front war. To me, this all relates to oil. I don't understand why they want to control every aspect of it. Russia has plenty, along with its allies, controlling over 90 percent. We could make up the other ten percent if we wanted to, but we don't even drill. We import oil. I'm done."

"Admiral?" Sean asked.

"I agree with the General. It doesn't make sense, but we are displaying a lot of power in the Mediterranean, Red Sea, and Indian Ocean. If that's where the fight will be, we're in trouble. We'll end up in the South China Sea by the end of the day. But is this all about controlling oil or its transportation?"

"Marsha, what's your take?" Sean asked.

"I would agree with everyone, but I believe it's 100 percent about oil. They don't want to occupy any land without oil or transport oil through it. The Russians and Chinese are protecting their drilling sites and strategic oil reserves. I bet the Indians are, too. We've never seen this before, and trust me, we've been observing them for years. Mark, you've been quiet. What are your thoughts?"

"You know I don't say much." Everyone laughed.

"Thanks for that—we needed a laugh," Sean said.

Tyler whispered to Tex, "Man, Kim, and Mark have some resemblances."

"What kind of drugs are they giving you?" Tex asked. "Some hallucinogens?"

"No, just painkillers and antibiotics."

Mark finally spoke up, "I agree there's something brewing. Based on their posturing, it looks like they want to attack. I've asked the president to hold a cabinet meeting within the next seventy-two hours to discuss these and other events. When I know, I will let everyone know the date and time."

"Tex, I think that leaves you and your team," Sean said.

"We know a few things. And please, Jenny, Kim, and Tyler chime in anytime. Don't worry about interrupting me.

He continued, "We knew a few things before our mission into Russia. First, a large number of the flare stacks at oil drilling sites were not ignited. Second, several hundred pumpjacks were not operational, and third, when the flare stacks ignited, the flame temperature was incorrect. It was too low to burn off any gas from the well."

Kim added, "There wasn't the usual activity around the drilling sites. There wasn't much maintenance happening."

Tex replied, "Kim, you're right. During our little Russian vacation, we discovered that those wells aren't just non-operational. The holding tanks are empty, too. The pumpjacks' sucker rods were only about twenty feet long—there's no way they could have been extracting any oil. Now, that's just what we identified in the fields. The refinery wasn't processing the amount of oil they claimed it was."

"Excuse me, Tex, but really, did they think anyone would actually raise an eyebrow at this?" Tyler asked. "Are they trying to pull off one of the biggest cover-ups in history? I have a theory about why."

"What a team! Thanks, Tyler," Tex said. "At the terminals in Novorossiysk, we noticed they were putting water in some holds while leaving others empty. They filled the holds to stabilize the ship in the water, but no oil was inside. Plus, the crews had no liberty while in port. We observed that one tanker, the Dama Flotante, was filled, yet it wasn't sitting where it should be in the water. Tyler took a picture, and I'm sure everyone has seen it."

"Tex, I have another update," the admiral interjected. "A couple of weeks ago, Bob asked us to monitor some oil tankers leaving Novorossiysk through the Bosporus Strait. Almost all of them were sitting higher in the water than they should have been based on the weight of the oil, considering how much fuel they would have consumed from Novorossiysk to Istanbul. I'm saying they didn't have as much oil as listed on their manifests."

Tyler stood up, cane in one hand and the other on the table for support. "Can I tell you what I think is going on? And remember, I just got shot and am on some strong meds."

"Go ahead, Tyler. What do you have for us?" Tex humored him.

"I think the Russians are running out of domestic oil reserves. Think about it—the flare stacks just stopped burning and started back up with an alternate fuel source. Those flames shooting out of the flare stacks are just a deception. The pump jacks don't work, and the ones that do aren't producing oil. Their entire process is bogus, and their transport ships don't carry the amount of oil listed on their manifests."

"Look where their troops are and pay attention to the positions of the Chinese and Indians. They're moving to control all the oil choke points at sea—dragging us into what could be World War III! We can't let this happen, or can we, since we're becoming a renewable energy nation? What about the other countries that can't make the shift to renewable energy? Are they just going to be controlled? How much will that cost us?"

"That still affects us—we still get oil from them and will continue to for the foreseeable future, especially since we've capped almost all of our wells," Tyler said.

Kim stood while Tyler sat down.

"When you think about oil—just gas and diesel to power our machinery—consider this: almost everything we use daily is made from petroleum. They could control manufacturing. If they wanted to stop the exporting or producing tires for our cars, they could do it. That's a scary thought. What if the Chinese stopped shipping solar panels to the U.S., Germany, England, and other countries they don't favor? Where will we be in just a few years?"

No one spoke.

"I'm done," Kim said. "Sorry for being so passionate."

"Mind if I share some new intelligence we just analyzed today?" Jenny asked.

"The more we have, the better advice we can give the president," Sean replied.

"We've been examining several oil storage tanks in the Baltic Sea," Jenny began. "We chose this location because it has two of the four primary oil storage sites in Russia, and since Tex and the team were in Western Siberia and the Black Sea, we opted for this one.

"What we discovered, using some new technology—I mean really new!—is that over 25 percent of the storage tanks are empty. Instead, they contain another substance that has the same consistency as oil but is neither oil nor a petroleum product. So, when they claim their storage tanks are full, they may be full, but not with oil. We're trying to understand the nature of that substance."

"That's very interesting," Tex said, "but I think we should take some time before we go back in."

"Anything else, Jenny?" Sean asked. "Great information."

"We're analyzing the other two sites in the Black Sea, and the Far East should be examined within the next few days."

"Great work, Jenny and the team," Tex said. "Does everyone agree that Russia has significantly reduced or overestimated its oil reserves?"

Everyone exchanged glances and nodded.

"Sean, what are the next steps?" Tex asked.

"We need to get this to the president today. I'll draft a secure message about what we discussed and agreed upon in this meeting. To clarify, we all agree that Russia is running out of oil and that everything we've seen has been a deception. We believe they, along with China and India, plan to control oil transportation along sea routes because they are the only three that understand the depth of the falsehood we are aware of."

"How much time do you think they have regarding their underground deposits and strategic oil reserves?" Jesse asked.

"There's no way to know for sure, but I would estimate one to three years," Tex replied.

Everyone agreed.

****Top Secret****

Message Begin
   From: CIA – Sean McGill – Director of the CIA
   To: POTUS (Command Structure)
   Title: Overestimation of Known In-Ground Russian Oil Reserves

Based on recent intelligence from imagery and human sources, the DNI, CIA, NGA, DOD, and NSA consensus is that Russia has been perpetuating a lie to the world: it has in-ground oil reserves that will last for many decades. However, we believe it only has one to three years of supply remaining.

This is the reason for the Russian troops amassing along the Syrian-Jordan border, the Chinese soldiers on the China-Laos border, and the naval movement of the Indian Navy.

We recommend a war cabinet meeting within the next forty-eight hours.

End of Message

****Top Secret****

Sean said, "Does everyone agree that this is the message we want to send the president?"

Everyone nodded.

Sean pointed at Tyler and said, "Hey, Tyler, great job! I think I'm going to hire you to work for me."

Tex stood up and declared, "Those are fighting words! He works for me, but you can borrow him sometimes." With a smile, he slapped Tyler on the back.

"Everyone, we'll see what this message to the president brings. I suggest you each get on a war footing and start working on new plans. If you have any old ones, dust them off and update them.

"Tex, I will send one of our Gulfstream G550s down from Germany to get you all and bring you to D.C. We can have a secure conversation on the plane if needed. I'll send all the logistics to the skipper within the hour. Safe travels," Sean said. "Thanks, everyone. If you need me, please reach out." The conference bridge was disconnected.

Tex, Tyler, and Kim sat in the SCIF, looking at each other.

Kim said, "I think that went well."

Everyone burst out laughing.

"That's exactly what I wanted. I needed a good laugh," Tex said.

"Hell, we've been here for three hours," Tyler replied.

"Your observation and analysis of what the Russians are doing is top-notch—you nailed it. I didn't connect all the puzzle pieces as quickly as you did," Tex remarked.

"Thanks. I'm not just a pretty face," Tyler responded. "See, Kim, I told you it was a puzzle!" He slapped his knee. "There's a saying in German that fits perfectly: Ich glaub' mein Schwein pfeift."

"When did you figure it all out?" Kim asked.

"About halfway through today's meeting, I suspected something like this a week ago. I just kept it to myself. I wanted more information, and each place we visited reinforced my hunch."

"Let's go, team," Tex said. "Time to eat! And I need to talk to the skipper first. I'll meet you in the galley in ten minutes."

They all got up and walked out of the SCIF. Kim put her arm around Tyler to ensure he didn't fall—or maybe she just wanted to be close to him. Tex headed to the bridge. The skipper was sitting in his chair when he noticed Tex approaching.

"How is everything?"

"Great. Sean is sending over some logistics for our travel arrangements. What's our ETA for Istanbul?"

"We should be in port by 0800—I mean 8:00 a.m. tomorrow. We're making good time."

"Perfect. I wanted to thank you for everything you guys have done. I've already mentioned it to Sean, Ralph, and Jesse."

"Thanks, Tex, but we're just doing our job. You're not the first," he said with a wink.

"I'm headed to the galley. Want to join me and the team?"

"I'd love to, but I need to prepare for docking tomorrow."

Tex went to the galley alone, where Kim and Tyler sat and ate tacos. "Damn, those look good. I'm starving."

"They're awesome. You can eat as much as you want! Hell, I've already had four," Tyler replied.

"What about you, Kim?"

"I haven't had as many as Tyler, but I can vouch for them and get you a couple, Tex."

They sat, talked, and ate for an hour. They needed to relieve some stress from the mission.

"We'll be docking at 8:00 a.m.," Tex said. "Shortly after we disembark, we'll head to the airport. Tyler, did you get cleared by the doctor?"

"I sure did. I spoke with him before meeting you at the SCIF, and he wants me to see a doctor when we get back home."

As expected, the AM Blueberry Hill docked in Istanbul at 8:00 a.m. Tex, Tyler, and Kim thanked the skipper and crew before walking down the gangplank to the waiting black Suburban. They climbed in and headed to the private section of the airport.

"I wish we had time to sightsee," Tyler sighed. "This city is so beautiful and historic. Fun fact: The Hagia Sophia was originally a church. Now it's a mosque."

"Very nice," Kim replied.

Reaching the G550 parked in a secluded airport area took just over an hour. Although this wasn't the standard terminal—it was the VIP terminal—they still needed to go through customs, which posed no issue. The paperwork had already been taken care of.

The crew welcomed them and mentioned they could sit anywhere they liked. Once in the air, they were treated to plenty of food and drinks. They buckled into their seats for the long flight home.

"This is better than first class! I can even stretch out my legs," Tyler exclaimed as the plane lifted off the ground.

ACT THREE

29

49,000 FEET ABOVE HALIFAX, NOVA SCOTIA

Once they lifted off, the pilot informed them that the flight would last approximately eleven hours nonstop. The G550 reached its cruising speed of 575 mph at an altitude of 49,000 feet and flew westward. For the water portion of the flight, the flight path took them over southern Europe, Germany, the UK, and the Northern Atlantic. Next, they passed over the southern tip of Greenland before heading down the eastern seaboard to Dulles. Flying at 49,000 feet ensured a smooth flight. After dinner, they reclined in their seats and dozed off. With only eight hours remaining, they were scheduled to land at Dulles at 2:30 p.m.

Tex, Kim, and Tyler woke up after a few hours of sleep.

"Man, I slept like a log. How about you guys?" he asked.

Kim replied as Tex nodded, "Same here, man. This is the way to travel."

"Captain, we just got this message from Langley."

The pilot stepped out of the cockpit. "Good morning, everyone. Sean wanted me to update you that there has been no increase in

Russian or Chinese military unit movements. However, India is deploying its naval forces into the Eastern Indian Ocean. He believes this could signal the initial phase of ground movement."

The captain handed Tex a piece of paper.

> Russian forces have not entered Jordan, and China has not entered Laos. Still, India is moving naval forces into the eastern Indian Ocean outside the training plan it filed. Everything is coming together. Please inform your passengers if they are awake. If not, don't wake them. They can't do anything at 49,000 feet anyway.
>
> Signed,
>   Director of the CIA
>   Sean McGill

"Thanks," Tex replied. "How far are we from Dulles?"

"We're two hours out and should land on time. The weather is beautiful. I'll update you when we start our descent."

"Thanks, Captain." Tex thought, *Should I call Sean? Hmmm, no, I'm hungry. I'll call after we eat. There's nothing I can do up here.*

DULLES INTERNATIONAL AIRPORT – DULLES, VIRGINIA

After the long flight, the G550 landed smoothly. The pilot, who had once been an Air Force pilot, utilized the entire runway. He finished taxiing, stopped in front of a nondescript hangar, and then parked inside. When they came to a stop, the crew opened the cabin door. Tex was the first to exit. As he looked up, Marsha stood there with open arms.

She walked up to him, hugged him, and said, "I'm really, really glad you're home. I missed you. I'm making you a home-cooked dinner tonight."

"Sounds great. I missed you."

Kim was next, followed by Tyler, who wasn't as quick as he used to be. Kim helped him down the stairs.

Marsha released Tex, hugged Tyler and Kim, and said, "Thanks for bringing him home in one piece. How are you, son?"

Tyler replied, "I'm good, thanks for asking!"

"I need to get him to his doctor's appointment at 4:00 p.m. today."

"What doctor's appointment?" Tyler asked.

"I made one for you before I went to sleep on the plane," Kim answered.

"There was a phone?"

Everyone laughed.

"I have an SUV ready to take you where you need to go. I don't want to see anyone in the office until tomorrow," Marsha instructed.

"So we're off for the rest of the day? With pay, right?" Tyler asked.

"Yes, with pay, Tyler."

Everyone got into the SUV, and after a short drive, Kim was the first one dropped off at home.

"Tyler, I'll pick you up at three-thirty."

"See you then," Tyler replied.

The driver then dropped off Tyler and asked, "Where should I drop you off, Tex?"

"Just take us to my car. I'll give him a ride home," Marsha replied.

"You got it."

"Marsha, is there a secure phone I can use?"

"Of course. Here you go."

Tex dialed quickly and held the phone to his ear. "Any updates, Sean?"

"Hello, stranger. Welcome home. Let me get Ralph on the call, too. Hold on a second. . . . Hey, Ralph, I have Tex on the line. Do you want to update him?"

Ralph spoke up, "There have been significant movements. The

Russian troops along the Syrian-Jordan border are positioning supplies, food, ammunition, and medical equipment along the line of departure. The Jordanians have reported increased air patrols of both manned and unmanned aircraft. They are also moving some of their armored vehicles and anti-aircraft units closer to the border and have recalled reservists. It's about to get ugly."

"Ralph, what units are we moving, if any?" Tex asked.

"The 173rd Airborne Brigade is relocating from Vicenza, Italy, to Sicily. This will position them closer should we need to deploy them to Jordan. Keep in mind that Jordan must request our presence before we can be on the ground. However, the brigade should arrive no later than tomorrow, just in case. We have informed our logistics contractor in Kuwait to prepare our vehicles that are in storage. I've notified the First Cav and Third ID for deployment to Kuwait. Both units are sending advanced parties as we speak. The situation with China is slightly different—they won't face any opposition when or if they move into Laos."

"Let me add something here," Sean said. "We've received some information that the government of Laos is requesting China's assistance in a border dispute with Thailand. This would effectively greenlight their ability to deploy troops into Laos. Their movement into Laos will coincide with Russia's deployment into Jordan. So, we're pretty much stuck for now."

Ralph jumped in, "The Thai government could request military assistance from us. We have a strong relationship with them and have held a joint military exercise called Cobra Gold since the 1950s. So far, they haven't made a request, but if they do, we're looking at the Marines stationed in Okinawa to deploy them to Thailand. We put them on alert."

He paused momentarily and then continued, "We are deploying a squadron of B-21s and B-52s from the 5th Bomb Wing out of Barksdale and from the 307th Bomb Wing out of Minot to Guam. One squadron of B-52s from the 2nd Bomb Wing out of Barksdale to Diego Garcia and two squadrons of F-22s from Hickam to South

Korea. Additionally, we are deploying a squadron of B-1-Bs from the 7th Bomb Wing out of Dyess to RAF Fairford, UK. We are holding our B-2s for now, but they can hit anywhere in the world out of their base in Missouri. We already have KC-135s Tankers deployed to support the flights to their locations and will be linking up in flight."

Jesse added, "Honestly, you can't trust North Korea, and if they get froggy, we could inflict some real damage on the North Koreans. The 2nd Infantry Division is staying put. We stationed four B-1Bs from the Seventh Bomb Wing out of Dyess Air Force Base last week for scheduled training. We've informed them we're extending it for another forty-five days. Ralph, do you have anything to add?"

"Nothing much except that we'll keep monitoring this region, but the Indian Carrier Battle Group is heading at full speed toward Singapore. We're just observing and alerting units for potential deployment, ensuring we don't overextend ourselves. Any questions, Tex?"

"No. Thanks, guys," Tex replied. "I'll be in the office tomorrow if things don't go sideways between now and then. Talk to you all tomorrow. Have a great day."

Just after Tex hung up, the phone rang.

Sean was on the other end. "Change of plans, Tex—meet me at the White House. How long until you can get there?"

"Alright, Sean, I can be there in thirty minutes."

"Sorry," Sean replied. "I'll see you there. They expect you, so getting through the gate won't be an issue."

"I assume this is about our last call and the memo to the president? Who will be attending?"

"Exactly. Ed Mullings, the Secretary of Energy, will also attend the meeting. Again, welcome back."

"What a political hack . . . see you in about thirty," Tex said before hanging up.

"Damn, let me know when you're done. I can pick you up," Marsha offered.

"That's alright. I'll take an Uber or a taxi."

30

WHITE HOUSE OVAL OFFICE

As Tex entered the White House, he was greeted by Mark, the Director of National Intelligence, Sean, and Ralph. "Hey, Tex, glad you could make it."

"Did I really have a choice?"

"You know you love us," Sean replied.

They were welcomed by the president's Chief of Staff, Jim Neal.

"This is Tex. He's leading this mission," Sean said. "He just flew in from Istanbul with his team."

"Great, nice to meet you. The president is busy, so we must keep this brief. We have a reelection fundraiser to get to by 3:30 p.m., so you have about fifteen minutes."

"It's Jim, right?" Tex asked. "You can call me when Jordan has more time. Sean, I'm leaving."

"Jordan?" Jim said. "That's Mr. President to you."

The president walked into the Oval Office, approached Tex, and hugged him. "Where are you headed, Tex?"

Tex leaned in and replied, "Jim said we only have fifteen minutes. He mentioned you were going to a reelection campaign event—we need more time than that. Can you spare us an hour?"

"Don't worry about Jim. He's a tool—I'm the mechanic. You have as much time as you need. I got Sean's message, and it's very concerning."

Still hugging Tex, the president glanced at Jim and said, "Sit over there and let them know I'll be late."

"Yes, sir," Jim replied. He had no idea that the president and Tex had known each other for over twenty years.

Just then, Ed Mullins, the Secretary of Energy, walked in. "Have we started yet?"

"Yes, and you're late, so please sit down and listen," the president responded. "Sean, you have the floor, but before you begin, let me share my initial thoughts and concerns. As you can see, I invited Ed since I might have questions regarding our energy posture. Ed, are you prepared to answer those questions? If not, get someone on the damn phone who can."

"Mr. President, I can answer your questions," Ed replied.

Tex glanced at Sean and Mark and whispered, "Hack." Sean and Mark burst out laughing.

Mark chimed in, "Hey, be nice."

The president turned his attention and said, "Ed, you're about to learn why you're here. This conversation doesn't leave this room. If I see or hear of a leak, someone is going to jail. Do you and everyone else understand me?" Everyone nodded.

He continued, "The gist is, if I interpreted your message correctly, Russia is running out of its in-ground oil reserves, and they've known this for years. We're not sure how much longer they can last, right?"

Ed stared in disbelief. "How can you possibly say that with a straight face, Mr. President? Are the Russians running out of oil? We monitor that, and there are global organizations that track the reserves! John McCain once said, "It's a gas station masquerading as a country." Of course, we sometimes revise those figures, but never to the extent of claiming a country has been lying about its reserves. I mean, that's the only thing keeping Russia afloat."

The president said, "Tex, please fill Ed in on the intelligence."

Tex replied, "Sure, let me review the intelligence. If you have any questions, my team or I will address them. Sound good?"

Without a response, the president said, "Yes, please continue."

Sean quickly interjected, "Mr. President, let me add something. Peter from the NSA has been examining metadata for the last twenty-five years to see if he can find anything that might help. Hell, it's worth a try."

"Good call," the president said. "I agree. Now, Tex, let's review the intelligence and some images."

Tex began the briefing by stating, "Sir, this image was taken a few weeks ago before one of our imagery analysts noticed the strange behavior. As you can see, the number of operational flare stacks and pump jacks remains well within historical norms. Now, look at this one, which was captured two days later. Over half are not burning, and the pump jacks are nonoperational."

Tex reviewed all the intelligence with the President, Ed, and Jim. When he finished, their expressions were priceless.

It took Ed a moment to ask, "Tex, do you or anyone else think the troops in Syria and Laos are related to this? What are your thoughts?"

"We believe this is closely related. We think their mission is to control the choke points for oil movement in strategic locations worldwide. If they control these areas, they can determine who gets oil, how often, and at what cost. We can't do much at the moment because these countries have not requested our intervention or assistance. We have prepositioned some units and relocated others to strategic positions that allow us to respond quickly. However, we cannot engage in a three-front war."

Ed responded, "That's a lot to absorb."

"How much is currently in the strategic petroleum reserves?" the president asked. "I know we've been using some to ease high gas prices, which hasn't been one of my best decisions."

"Mr. President, I just checked, and we're at sixty-three percent capacity right now," Ed said. "If you'd like, I can authorize the purchase to increase that to eighty to ninety percent. Of course, we'll be buying it from the Middle East."

"Go ahead and make those purchases, but route them through one of our purchasing companies. I don't want this getting out. What about opening some of our leases on federal land or asking domestic oil companies to ramp up production? What about pipelines? How much oil are we currently importing from Russia? I know we paused after the Ukraine invasion, but we ramped up again afterward since they returned within international boundaries," the president paused. "And how long would it take to cover that shortfall?"

"Sir, last year we imported around twelve to fifteen thousand barrels of oil a day from Russia," Ed replied. "It would take us at least a few months—I'd estimate six to twelve—to ramp up and notice any significant increase in domestic oil production. We need to finish a lot of the infrastructure we halted a few years ago. That will take time, but we can get there, perhaps with some initial hardship."

"Coordinate with the secretaries of transportation and the interior, and let's get those pipelines moving. Look into increasing domestic oil production," the president stated. "Inform them this directive comes from me, and I'll reach out. I want those reserves filled as soon as possible, and I expect the plan on my desk by 6:00 a.m. tomorrow."

Jim responded, "Mr. President, that might not be a good idea. You campaigned to transition to a green economy and reduce our dependence on petroleum products. This could impact your reelection. Your donors, not to mention the members of your party, might react negatively and withdraw their support from your campaign."

The president raised his voice, "Hell, Jim, in two years, it might not even matter! We might not even have a country by then. After just two months, it really might not matter. I'm not going to worry about politics right now. That's hard for me to say, but there's too much at stake."

"Sir, your base will turn against you unless they understand the exact reason for your actions, and I don't think we can disclose this information right now. I'm just sharing my opinion, Mr. President."

The president replied, "You know what, Jim? You can go. I'll call you when I need you."

"Damn, Lieutenant—I mean, Mr. President. You still have a pair." Tex whistled.

The President turned to Mark and asked, "What's your opinion? What do you think is the right course of action? Before you say anything, let me tell you that sanctions don't work. We tried that in 2022."

Mark responded, "I think we should consider oil production here. Mr. President, I'm not sure if you've noticed, but we've been experiencing frequent and intermittent short power outages over the past few weeks to a month. I believe this highlights the reliability concerns regarding our green initiatives in this country."

The President sighed. "We will keep this under wraps with a small group of individuals for now. We'll monitor those borders, and let's produce more oil. We also need to get to the bottom of these intermittent power shortages. Mark, can you look into this?"

A knock on the door abruptly interrupted the conversation. His Chief of Staff opened the door and said, "Sir, before I leave, you know the press will find out about troop movements. What will our response be?"

"Hell, Jim, that's what I pay you for. If asked, we acknowledge the troop movements, and we believe they are conducting training maneuvers with their allies like we have done in the past and will continue to do. If they ask about Russia, China, or India, say we are monitoring them, and our deployments and training have nothing to do with them," he paused.

He continued, "Now, if and when they move into sovereign countries, we will address that, but I recommend you start thinking about that response. Now, if you don't... mind."

Mark replied, "Yes, sir, getting back to your question now. I will investigate."

"Sean and Ralph, let's continue positioning our units. Let's act as if we're going to deploy somewhere, even though we're unsure where that is."

The President picked up his phone and made a quick call. "Jim, I need to know what's happening at the State Department concerning the embassies in Jordan, Thailand, and Saudi Arabia."

The President hung up and continued, "That's about it for now—I fully understand what's happening. Great intelligence briefing, Tex, Sean, and Mark. If there are no questions, let's stand by and see what unfolds in the next forty-eight hours. I think that's when they will decide whether to go. They are going. How could they not? They'll never admit they're running out of oil."

The President paused. "Our dilemma is... do we spill the beans? If we do, what does that gain us? They'll say we're lying and want to start a war, so we're repositioning units. It's the old Catch-22—damned if you do and damned if you don't. We'll let them make the first move. Agreed?"

Everyone nodded. The president leaned back in his chair. "I'll expect updates from every agency and department within the next twenty-four hours. Damn, it's still hard to wrap my head around this... oh well, it is what it is. Stay close to your phones. Tex, do you have a minute before you head out? Sean, I'll arrange for Tex to get a ride home." Everyone left the Oval Office except for Tex and the president.

"Tex, I just want to thank you. Tell your team I'd like to meet them next week if the world's still in one piece. So, where can we drop you off? Your place or Marsha's?" He smiled and patted Tex on the back. "I talked to her while you were in Russia. I'm happy for you two. Will I be invited, like last time?"

"At Marsha's," Tex replied, "and hell, yes."

Tex exited the Oval Office and the White House and hopped into the waiting car. He pulled out his phone and called Marsha. "I'm on my way home. I'll be there in thirty minutes."

31

MINISTRY OF DEFENSE – MOSCOW RUSSIAN

It was 11:30 p.m. in Moscow. General Popov sat at his desk while General Patel and General Chen were on the conference bridge.

"Hello, my friends. I apologize for the unexpected call. We are on the verge of a new world order and a great reset—one where we will control the flow of oil across the globe—not just oil, but energy as a whole. We can turn the spigot on and off and control the lights at will. Our allies will thrive while our enemies wither on the vine. I want an update on your units and their readiness to commence combat operations twenty-four hours from now, Moscow time. General Patel, let's start with you."

"We're ready for combat operations. Our carrier battle group is moving into position and will reach our staging point northwest of the Andaman and Nicobar Islands in twelve hours. We can support General Chen's forces with air assets when they begin their movement down the Malay Peninsula."

"And have you noticed any unusual activity from the Americans?" General Popov asked.

"No, not in our general area, but we have observed some positioning of their bombers and tankers at Diego Garcia, which could impact us if they chose to. However, they are older bombers, the B-52s. We can track and neutralize them if necessary."

"General, I wouldn't underestimate the B-52. The upgrades they have made are impressive."

"Point taken, General Popov."

"Great, thank you. General Chen, you're up."

"We are in position and can move at any time. We will not conduct any combat operations until we pass through Laos with the assistance of our allies. They have prepositioned fuel and supplies along our route, and we are prepared to occupy our battle positions along the Thai border. We will wait for the orders to move, but we are fully prepared."

"Any updates on American activity?" General Popov asked.

"No. Just like General Patel, we have observed no activity in the region. However, we have noticed increased naval operations in the South China Sea, and they are preparing their carriers in Japan for deployment. They have recalled all personnel from shore leave and alerted them. Additionally, they have moved more B-52s and B-21 bombers to Guam, where they can project power. I don't think they intend to."

"Excellent news, General. We have positioned our Spetsnaz and are ready to move. Once they receive the signal, they will advance into Jordan and be prepared for subversive activities," General Popov said.

He continued, "The Americans have relocated the carrier Harry S. Truman and its battle group to the eastern Mediterranean, north of El Arish. We've learned that the USS Eisenhower Carrier Battle Group will stay in the Red Sea region. I want to clarify that our goals do not include engaging the Americans. If we engage them, it will likely provoke both them and NATO to move into Eastern Europe. We can't fight a two-front war—we're still recovering from our invasion of Ukraine and the ongoing stalemate. Whether or not to engage U.S. forces is up to you. However, we will support you in any way we can. After all, we're allies. Please inform your nation's leaders that Operation Moose will begin in twenty-four hours. There is no turning back once we start."

The conference bridge went silent.

The general pressed the intercom button. "Get me Admiral Balakin on the line," he said, rising from his desk and walking toward the window.

In the time it took him to reach the window, his aide knocked on the door, peeked in, and said, "Sir, the Admiral."

"General, what can I do for you?"

"Operation Moose starts now," General Popov stated. "Please commence operations, and let me know when everything is in position."

"Yes, General. Are we still aiming for a twenty-four-hour timeline?" Admiral Balakin inquired.

"Yes. Once you're in position, we'll begin communication with the Americans. We plan to move ground units into position and reclaim what is rightfully ours. We believe the Americans have already taken the bait. They're deploying forces where we and our allies have positioned ours."

"General, has there been any activity from the 25th Infantry Division, the 2nd Infantry Brigade of the 11th Airborne Division in Alaska, or the air wings?"

"Interestingly, they've deployed a battalion to South Korea. I find it amusing how they always fret over them. They serve as a great distraction. One day, they'll realize the North Koreans are following our orders, or they'll face starvation. Maybe one day we will unleash them, but not yet today."

"Yes, sir," the Admiral replied. "Any other orders?"

General Popov responded, "No. You've done an outstanding job, and your sister says hi. We look forward to your visit next month. Stay safe, my friend."

Two days earlier, the mimics had left their pen, heading for the Norwegian Sea for a routine training mission. Two hours after their departure, when American satellite coverage was at its weakest, the Generalissimo Suvorov and Prem submarines left their pens, heading for the Beaufort Sea. After leaving their pens, they moved into the staging area and awaited their order. Once they get the order, it's only a matter of hours before they are on station. As they await orders to move into their attack positions, the Americans tracked the mimics as they made their way to the Baltic Sea. Everything was proceeding as planned.

"Get me, General Chen, on the phone. . . . General Chen, is Qi ready?"

"Yes, General. We will execute it in twenty-four hours." He hung up the phone.

General Popov leaned back in his chair, resting his hands behind his head as he took a long, deep breath. *It's so tranquil . . . but that is about to change in twenty-three hours and forty-five minutes.*

He reached for his humidor, opened it, and took out a hand-rolled Cuban cigar. Bringing it to his nose, he savored the rich aroma of the tobacco. He pulled his cutter from the humidor and clipped off the end of the cigar. After placing it between his lips, he lit it, and with a long drag, the cigar came to life, filling the room with fragrant smoke that transported him back to a simpler time in Cuba as a young captain. He closed his eyes, reminiscing about his young Cuban mistress. A few minutes later, he opened his eyes and glanced at the clock on the wall. In just a few hours, the world might be on the brink of war again. It would be up to the Americans.

OPERATION MOOSE – EAST SIBERIAN SEA

Generalissimo Suvorov and Perm's captains received orders to execute Operation Moose simultaneously. The crew aboard both submarines prepared to move from their initial staging areas to the combat locations in the Beaufort Sea off the coast of Alaska. The journey would take less than twenty-four hours. The crew on the Generalissimo Suvorov had been running battle drills and ensuring that all the equipment was ready. Only a select few among the crew knew of their new weapon, a laser cannon mounted on the submarine's bow. They were eager to get into position and try out their new asset.

Meanwhile, the crew on the Perm was busy conducting drills and searching for any American attack submarines that might be stalking them. It would be a game of cat and mouse, but they were there to protect the Generalissimo Suvorov. They led the way, positioned five hundred yards off the bow of the Generalissimo Suvorov.

THE COMMANDERS of Russian troops in Syria, Chinese forces on the border of Laos, and the naval commander for India all received their marching orders and the timeline for Operation Moose. They created operational orders and sent them to the unit and vessel commanders. They would begin combat operations in twenty-three hours.

32

SYRIAN BORDER WITH JORDAN

Twenty-three hours later, the deafening sounds of the Russian and Syrian artillery's 152mm cannons echoed, and the ground shook as flames from the muzzles painted the predawn sky a crimson hue over the countryside southeast of Nassib, Syria. This was merely the first of many volleys from the artillery battalions targeting Jordan—an unprovoked invasion of another country by Russia once again. This time, Syria, acting as its puppet state, was providing a safe haven, additional firepower, and supplies. The other artillery batteries were firing from their positions in Koayiah, Zaizoun, Tal Shihab, and east of Daraa along Highway 5, one of the main routes into Jordan.

Never again would Russia endure a prolonged war and defeat as it did in Ukraine after more than three years of fighting. Since they had not fulfilled their goals, they returned to their garrisons in Russia, Belarus, Crimea, and the Donbas region. This time, their supply lines and movements would not be hindered or slowed, and the plan would be executed precisely.

The light-blue MiG-35 fighter jets flew overhead on their way to designated targets. First introduced in 2019, the MiG-35 is equipped with precision-guided munitions and unguided bombs. It has been upgraded with enhanced targeting, advanced weapon systems, and the latest avionics, allowing for all-weather combat capabilities. With a speed of 1,305 mph and a service ceiling of 52,000 feet, it can provide close air support or achieve air superiority. In just minutes, the fighters can reach any location in Jordan and influence a battle in seconds.

Hours before the shelling began, Russian Spetsnaz reconnaissance units quietly positioned themselves to provide forward observation for the artillery and assess the effectiveness of the bombardment. They called in fire missions with lethal accuracy. Behind them, infantry in their BMP vehicles waited for the order to advance from their staging areas and cross the line of departure into their maneuver zones and battle positions, not anticipating significant engagements or counterattacks from the Jordanian military. They began moving from their positions toward their first objective: King Hussein Air Base. The quickest route was down the M5 through Jaber as-Sirhan, which faced heavy shelling, and then to Mugayir as-Sirhan toward the air base, which took direct hits from the 3M-54 Kalibr cruise missiles. The BMPs advanced along with the ZSU-23-4s armed with ground-to-air machine guns. Their mission was to eliminate any Jordanian helicopters, Bell AH-1E/F Cobra gunships, or low-flying, fast F-16 ground-attack aircraft.

The objectives were to capture the oil fields, control oil refining, manage oil movement out of Saudi Arabia, and restrict access to the Red Sea. They also aimed to avoid becoming bogged down in Jordan. The final objective was to take control of the substantial strategic oil reserves in the Kingdom. The assault and campaign would move the forces from Jordan to Tabuk and Medina, capturing Jeddah, Taif, and Jazen along the route. There, they would rendezvous with allied insurgents along the Saudi Arabia-Yemen border. The Houthis are in position and waiting. We have supplied them with enough supplies through Iran to keep the Saudi forces very busy.

The only way to achieve their goal is for the Americans to refrain from deploying their troops, even if the Jordanian government requests assistance. The Russians understood that the Americans had little desire for another war in the Middle East, and with military recruitment at an all-time low, they felt prepared to confront a seasoned army. Success would grant them full control over the entry to the Red Sea, cutting off oil shipments to the West and beyond, thereby managing a significant portion of the world's oil reserves. They would also control Bab-el-Mandeb, through which over 4.8 million gallons of oil transit daily, creating a choke point between the Arabian Gulf and the Gulf of Oman. With Iran controlling the Strait of Hormuz, over 16.8 million gallons of oil pass through that checkpoint daily.

CHINA'S BORDER WITH LAOS

All the brigade commanders convened to review the initial attack plan, and once the meeting wrapped up, the mechanized units of the People's Liberation Army swiftly moved into action. They quickly united and crossed the border without facing any resistance. The PLA's ground units and air assets were deployed, totaling over 160,000 active personnel, most of whom were conscripts. This force surpassed the initial plan of 150,000 participants in the operation, with an additional fifty thousand in reserve. The PLA Navy vessels entered the Gulf of Thailand on their way to the Java Sea to rendezvous with the Indian Navy. The day prior, they had quietly departed from Da Nang, Vietnam.

The local populations waved and smiled at the troops, a significantly different reaction from that experienced by the Russians in Jordan. The Chinese couldn't provide any troops or supplies to assist them. Each country operated independently and shared only one common goal: oil.

The PLA utilized the recently completed upgrades to 1A near Hepingzhai, China, toward Ban Souanteng, Laos. This upgrade, part of China's Belt and Road Initiative, enabled heavy tanks to move swiftly to Pak Nam Noy, one of their staging areas north of Tazoum, along 2E, then along 2W to the final staging area at Muang Ngeun before advancing into Thailand. The destination was the Gulf of Thailand.

Stiff resistance was not anticipated. The Thai government has forged strong economic and military ties with China in recent years, and the march to the Gulf of Thailand could occur in just a few days. However, U.S. Special Forces had trained the Royal Thai Army, and their loyalty to the government was uncertain. If they were to rise, they primarily consisted of infantry, artillery, combat engineers, and long-range reconnaissance units. They could pose a significant threat to the PLA.

The Gulf of Thailand would provide China with access to and control over the oil fields in the gulf, furnishing them with crucial oil reserves since the United States had long ceased exporting oil to safeguard the environment.

BAY OF BENGAL

India's population was nearly 1.5 billion, and maintaining its infrastructure and growth required energy. Coal and oil were essential fuels for powering factories and other infrastructure, and India imported approximately seventy percent of the oil necessary to operate the country. It needed oil—and a substantial amount—and the only way to secure this was by aligning with China and Russia.

The INS Vikramaditya had departed from its port in Chennai seven days earlier. She and her accompanying task force navigated through the Andaman Sea and into the Bay of Bengal. Their journey took them down the Malacca Strait, where over 15.7 million gallons of oil were transported daily. This location was where they intended to rendezvous with the Chinese Navy south of Singapore. Along with the regular task force, this one was bolstered by the INS Jalashwa, Magar, Gharial, Cheeta, and Kumbhir—all amphibious ships, landing vessels, and their full complement of marines.

Controlling the strait would enable India to manage and direct the transportation and movement of over sixteen million barrels of oil flowing through it daily, supplying them with the oil needed to power India and sell to other countries at their desired price. The ultimate goal was to control upwards of thirty-seven million gallons of oil daily, in addition to cargo, through these checkpoints.

33

PENTAGON – ARLINGTON, VIRGINIA

Army Major General Kurt Robinson walked into the Pentagon's Situation Room, looked at the monitors on the wall, and asked, "What on earth is happening?" The room featured streaming satellite imagery, live feeds, news channels, and video conferences on large wall-to-wall monitors. Robinson analyzed satellite imagery from all regions and areas affected by Russia, China, and India's militaries.

The movement and massing of troops had been ongoing for the past six months. However, since they were either stationed in their own countries or allied nations, the U.S. could only provide intelligence to its partners.

General Robinson began to receive signal (SIGINT) and human intelligence (HUMINT) from various regions and was updated on the current situation. "Get me NATO, Central Command, Far East Command, and others within the Combatant Commands that are affected or could be affected now! Have we seen any movement in Europe or along the DMZ in South Korea?"

"No, sir. Nothing seems out of the ordinary in those areas."

"At least that's some good news. I hope it stays that way," General Robinson replied.

"The Chinese are currently focused on Laos."

"Hell, that's going to be a cakewalk," General Robinson stated. "The real trouble will arise when they get to Thailand. Any signs of movement by China toward Taiwan?"

"Last week, the Chinese Navy completed a significant naval training exercise north of Taiwan. This was a planned exercise, and we were forewarned. After the exercise, they moved through the Taiwan Strait, with most vessels returning to their ports in China, but four ships continued toward the deep-water port of Da Nang, Vietnam. As of yesterday, they were still in port."

"Please provide me with an update on those ships in fifteen minutes. Also, which ships are they?"

"Absolutely, sir. I'll obtain their names, types, and classes."

"What about Cuba? We know that Venezuela has deployed at least three brigade-sized units and air assets."

"Sir, I'll update you in thirty minutes—actually, let's make it fifteen."

"I need that information. We're aware of the close relationship between Russia and Venezuela. I want surveillance on Cuba. Contact Director Fields at the NGA."

"Yes, sir. Director Fields is currently in a meeting but will call you in five minutes."

"Has the president been briefed on any of this?" General Robinson inquired.

"The briefing will commence in the Situation Room at the White House. We'll join remotely via a secure link."

"Give me a moment to organize my thoughts and notes."

A FEW MINUTES LATER, the briefing began.

"General Robinson," the president said. "Can you tell me what the hell is happening and why we didn't see this coming?"

"Sir, as far as we can determine, this is a highly coordinated movement of military units from Russia, China, and India. The reasons for this are yet to be established, as no discernible motivations exist for these activities. There haven't been any provocative actions or events to justify these movements. As far as we know, there have been no hostilities among them. They have not made any overtures toward our forces."

Throughout, the president understood why the attacks had started, but he couldn't disclose anything just yet. The timing needed to be perfect, and it had to precede any contact with China, Russia, or India.

The general continued, "The INS Vikramaditya and its task force set sail last week. We noticed that but were informed it was part of a planned military exercise with its regional partners. Mr. President, we will have more information within the next few hours. We are collecting intelligence from various agencies."

The president replied, "Okay, keep me updated and alert me if there are any significant developments."

General Robinson's aide said, "Sir, I have an update on the Chinese vessels."

He handed him a piece of paper that stated: They all slipped out of port late last night after our previous satellite passed. The ships include two destroyers, the Yan'an and Wuyi, one corvette, the Luan, and the amphibious ship, the Mount Lu.

The general stopped the aide and asked, "Does the Luan have its full complement of Marines onboard?"

The aide responded, "Sir, yes, we believe so."

"Believe?" shouted the general.

"Sir, let me get back to you on that." He continued, "They are going full steam ahead and are currently located between Da Nang and Na Trang, near Quy Nhon. They're heading to Singapore and should arrive in three to three and a half days. This will allow them to link up with the Indian naval task force in the Malacca Strait.

"That's just damn great," the general said. "Do we have any assets near Singapore? I sure hope so. Get the navy on the line."

"Sir, I'm working on that now."

The president replied, "General Robinson, give me your best guess based on what you know right now."

"Sir, it's hard to say, but it seems like they're all moving... well, at least the Indians and Chinese are heading south of Singapore where the Strait of Malacca and the South China Sea converge."

"And why do you think that area matters?"

"Mr. President, about sixteen million barrels a day pass through there. If they control that, they control roughly ninety percent of the oil flow to Asia."

"Okay, what about the Russians?"

"Sir, that's a bit more complicated. It depends on which route they take out of Jordan. They could either turn right into Israel or continue south into Saudi Arabia, which might suggest they aim to control the southern part of the Suez Canal and/or seize the oil fields and potentially the entry point into the Red Sea. They would require support from the Yemeni government, which we doubt they possess."

The president responded, "They don't, but Iran does."

"Yes, sir, that's accurate."

"General, what if they managed to control those two choke points?" asked the president.

"About 30 percent of the world's oil and gas supplies transit the Red Sea. Consider what the Iranians can achieve in the Strait of Hormuz, where twenty-one million gallons pass daily. The upside is we have ample resources in those two areas."

"Is there anything else, General?"

"No, sir. We'll keep your staff updated."

"We have a meeting in the Situation Room tomorrow at 8 a.m.

Please join via conference call, not in person. You have way too much on your plate, General."

The video and conference line went silent.

General Robinson ordered, "Get PACOM on the line now."

THE PRESIDENT LEANED BACK. *We were right. Let's see their next move. They don't know what we know.*

He yelled, "Get everyone here tomorrow at 8:00 a.m.! Heck, make it 7:00 a.m. and set up a call with Presidents Yang, Stovol, and Singh tomorrow at 8:30 a.m. I don't give a crap what time it is where they are—it's time to play poker."

34

WHITE HOUSE SITUATION ROOM

The president hurried into the room at 7:00 a.m. to meet with his security advisors. "Hey, everyone, we've got ninety minutes before our call with China, India, and Russia. Let's put a game plan together and execute it. Before we kick off, do we have everyone?" As he scanned the room, he noticed Mark was missing. "Does anyone know where he is?"

Mark walked in. "Sorry, I'm late, Mr. President. The traffic is terrible at this time of morning."

"Let's get down to business. Who's going to go first? All right, Defense, you're up. Ralph, please begin, and then Jesse. I'd like to hear both of your perspectives."

"Well, Mr. President, we need to determine or at least have some idea of their end goal. Maybe we should just come out and ask: Is it about oil? We think we know, but why not ask them? This is a blatant violation of territorial integrity by China and Russia. India has not encroached on anyone's territorial waters. They are now in international waters. There's nothing we can do about that. So, we need to focus on the goals of China and Russia in collaboration with India."

The president sat with a stony expression. Although he wanted to confront the three nations, a good leader always listens to his advisors.

"Okay. Jesse? What do you think?"

"I completely agree with Ralph. We need to confront them, ask about their goals, and find out if it's about oil. Honestly, we know it is. I'm sure they'll deny it. Wouldn't we do the same? So if we ask them if it's about oil, they may assess whether we're aware of the oil situation in Russia. This could make them reconsider their strategy or compel them to go all in."

"Let's hear from the CIA. Sean."

"We concur with the Pentagon. We aren't detecting any activity in Syria that suggests they're considering attacking anything near our forces. In fact, it's quite the opposite—they're actively avoiding us. This is also true in Iraq, where we have some Special Forces units. They are steering clear of us, which is odd because they could quickly eliminate and overtake them. We need to play our cards right and see if we can get them to acknowledge the Russian oil issue."

"We don't need to disclose all our intelligence. We can play dumb," Sean continued. "There's a way we can turn the tables to assist them until they can transition to a greener energy source. I don't believe the Russians, Chinese, and Indians want an all-out war. Do you think the soldiers, airmen, marines, and sailors understand why they're fighting? We should initiate disinformation campaigns in those countries and spark some protests. That could prevent them from moving more units to the fight, which they'll need to maintain internal control. Let me know, and we can get right on it."

"Go ahead, Sean, and thank you. What about you, Peter?"

"Thanks, Mr. President. We've been researching and analyzing metadata going back about twenty-five years for any phone conversations made within or coming out of the Ministry of Energy. It took a few days, but we uncovered something less than an hour or two ago. There are two conversations. Here's the recording of the first one."

""Petrov, this is Andreev. I just read your report. I won't go into any details about it. I'm just asking you a few questions. Just answer yes or no—no details or extended conversation is necessary. Do you understand?"

"Yes, sir."

"Are you one hundred percent sure that everything in the report is correct and accurate?"

"Yes."

"This is extremely important. Has anyone else seen it?"

"No."

"How many copies of this report did you produce? If more than one copy, who has one? Do you have any in your possession?"

"No copies. You are the only one. It's the original."

"Have you verified everything in the report? Did you explore and examine more than one location in the basin?"

"Yes, and yes."

"Thank you. Don't share or discuss this with anyone."

"Yes, sir."

"Hell, that's not even the best part," Peter said. "Right after that, the minister called his contacts in the FSB. I'm going to play that one now."

"Here is his address. Please pick him up. He is not needed anymore."

"There were no further calls after that. We believe they presented the information from the report in person," Peter said. Everyone in the situation room sat silently, unable to believe that what they had just heard was recorded in 2001.

The president stood up. "This is unbelievable! They've known they were running out of oil for over twenty years and kept it a secret. We can't keep anything secret here in Washington. I have to give them credit. Peter, do we know who he was talking to?"

"Petrov—the ministry's chief petroleum engineer. We will work with Sean to see if we can learn more about him and what happened to him. Based on some initial research, he hasn't been seen since mid-2001, shortly after the call with the minister of energy."

"Thanks, Peter. That was a great update. Have you noticed increased communication between Moscow, Beijing, and New Delhi?"

Sean took out his phone and sent a short text to his team at Langley.

> I need all the information on the last name Petrov, a high-ranking official at the Ministry of Energy in Russia circa the early 2000s.

"Nothing unusual, sir, but we are monitoring it very closely," Peter replied.

"Great. Marsha, what do you have?"

"The NGA continues to monitor the Western Siberian Basin and the other oil fields in Russia. We're also examining the strategic oil reserves of Russia, China, and India to detect any additional capacity or anything unusual in those areas. In the Western Siberian Basin, the flare stacks keep turning on and off, almost like a random timer—similar to what you would do at home. Regarding the strategic oil reserves, we've seen a lot of construction to increase capacity in China and India. In Russia, however, we haven't observed any new capacity being built. Unlike the other two, it's as if they are concerned about running out of oil. It's perplexing, to say the least."

"Thank you for the update, Marsha. Tex, can we hear from you now?"

"Before I begin, Mr. President, I'd like to introduce two team members, Tyler and Kim. Could you both stand?" Everyone in the Situation Room stood and applauded.

The president approached them and shook their hands. "Tyler, I heard you took a hit to the leg. How are you doing?"

"Mr. President, thank you. I'm doing well," Tyler replied.

The president said, "If not for both of you identifying early on what was happening in Russia, we would have been completely caught off guard. Your efforts in Russia with Tex's team have given us enough time to develop a plan and understand why these three countries are jeopardizing the world and potentially triggering World War III. So, I want to extend my gratitude. The nation appreciates your hard work. I also want your thoughts on this situation. Go ahead, Tex."

"I agree with everything so far. We should probably confront them early, as it might lead them to reveal their intentions sooner than they would like. This could also give us more time to position some units and resources in case our allies request assistance. I have one question: Where are they getting the fuel for this operation? Without our knowledge, this must be depleting a significant amount from their stockpiles, or they've been hoarding it for a very long time. Alternatively, they could get it from another participating country, but that remains in the shadows."

Sean stood. "Tex, that's it! We need to determine where they're getting their fuel supplies—Venezuela? Iran? Iraq?"

The president said, "Ralph, I need you to blockade Venezuela immediately. I don't want anything going in or out—only humanitarian aid and food. I mean by land, sea, and air. We need our friends, the Colombians, to help us with the Trans-Caribbean pipeline to ensure that no oil transported through it reaches those three countries, even through a middleman."

"Yes, Mr. President. I'll handle it," Ralph responded. "We currently have some vessels in the region. We're conducting drug interdiction, but we can relocate them and some additional units to start the naval blockade. I'll contact my Colombian counterpart and see what we can do. They've been accommodating since they're very concerned about Colombia becoming another Venezuela."

"Kim, Tyler—which of you wants to go first?"

"Mr. President, since we've identified their scheme," Kim said, "we should confront them and ask why they're increasing their oil reserves and the deception in the Western Siberia basin."

"I agree with Kim. We should lay out what we know," Tyler said. "So far, there's been some unusual activity regarding production in the West Siberian oil basin. We know they aren't moving as much oil through the pipeline or refining as much as they claim. We know their oil transport ships aren't fully loaded with fuel. We know there's increased construction activity at their strategic oil reserves. And finally, we know they also tested pulling oil from storage tanks in Germany, which no one even noticed."

"I believe this provides them with enough information. Let's take the initiative. It could be just the icing on the cake if we inform them about the intercepted message from 2001 between the Minister of Energy and the chief petroleum engineer, which didn't seem significant at the time. However, considering what we know, it's the corner piece of the puzzle we've been trying to solve. And perhaps, just perhaps, Russia hasn't been entirely truthful with its partners. Maybe we can sow some discord and create cracks in the glue that holds them together."

The president leaned over to Tex and said, "I like these two."

"So do I. And please keep your hands off them." He smiled.

The president replied, "Tyler, I must say I like your plan. We have ten minutes before we call them. Does everyone agree with this approach? Mark, do you have anything before we proceed?"

"No, Mr. President, I agree with Tyler. I think we can create a little division among the three of them. That might help prevent them from continuing or, worse, expanding."

"All right, everyone, it's game day."

Sean felt his phone vibrate in his pocket, so he pulled it out and read the message. He put it back in his pocket and said, "Sir, about our friend Petrov. He was discovered floating in the Volga River a week after his conversation with the minister. It was ruled an apparent suicide," Sean stated.

"Well, the plot thickens," the President replied.

BEIJING

Halfway around the world, Commander Ai Yin sat beside the lead developer and instructed him to execute the code. The cyber warrior entered a few commands on his keyboard to unleash Qi on the Americans again in thirty minutes on a preselected power grid. He set the duration for sixty minutes and pressed Enter.

It was initiated at 8:30 a.m. in Washington, D.C., thirty minutes after the conference call began. After giving the instructions to the developer, she waited. The results should be instantaneous once the command is executed on the endpoints.

35

WHITE HOUSE SITUATION ROOM – 8:00 A.M.

The atmosphere in the room was tense. No one knew the true intentions of the Russians, Chinese, or Indians. However, one thing everyone agreed on was that an all-out shooting war was imminent.

"Sir, we are starting the feed from President Yang of China, President Stovol of the Russian Federation, and President Kumar of India." Each of them said in turn, "Hello, Mr. President."

"Hello, Presidents Yang, Stovol, and Kumar. It seems you've all been busy today. Let's get straight to the point. What are your intentions regarding the military movements and invasions you initiated today? If you could please provide some details, that would be appreciated. If not, I will clarify why we believe you invaded."

President Yang replied, "Well, Mr. President, we were invited by the Laotian government. We have done nothing wrong. We haven't invaded anyone. We haven't crossed into any other territorial boundaries. We aren't obligated to give you any reason for our actions. In fact, we basically control you, and soon you'll see just how much we do."

"Now, now, President Yang," warned Russian President Stovol, "there's no need to get angry or hostile. After all, we are rational men."

"President Stovol, I'm going to be perfectly blunt with you. We know why Russia, China, and India have begun these military confrontations: you're running out of oil."

Silence enveloped the conference feed. The expression on the Indian president's face spoke volumes—there was no mistaking his thoughts.

President Kumar looked into the conference video camera and said, "I would like to learn more about this. We were completely unaware of it. When these plans were drawn up, and we were asked to take part in the military actions, I was informed that it would ensure safe oil transport along the route south of Singapore. Considering the rising pirate activity in the region, this would allow secure passage for everyone. Others in my government, specifically the military, conveyed that to me. Evidently, they were lies, and I'm certain you both had nothing to do with this—did you?"

He continued, "I want to assure you, Mr. President, we didn't know Russia was running out of oil. One would think they would have informed us since we get 80 percent of our oil from them, so please continue, Mr. President."

The president thought, "This is the start of the crack in the glue that binds them." "President Kumar, you know both of these individuals have lied before, so this is par for the course."

"President Kumar, you were not given the real reason for your troop movements. I would find out why you were misled and by whom," the president said.

He nodded and muted his microphone. Everyone could see he was yelling at the top of his lungs.

Mark's pocket began to vibrate. "Mr. President, I need to take this call. It shouldn't take more than a moment."

"Go ahead, Mark. You know what we're going to discuss anyway. Come back as soon as you can."

Mark left the conference room and read the text.

> 8:30 EST, 60 minutes, and the same area to be affected.

As before, he removed the SIM card and destroyed the burner phone. Then, he took out his work phone and called the DHS director to inform him about an impending attack on the Northern Virginia and DC power grids.

"It's happening in thirty minutes and will last for sixty minutes. Please ensure that contingency plans are in place. This is a test of our response, nothing more."

Mark walked back into the Situation Room and sat down. As he entered, the president explained why he believed Russia was running out of oil.

"Feel free to interrupt me if you'd like to jump in. There's a lot of unusual activity in the West Siberian oil basin concerning flare stacks that are either malfunctioning or not producing the proper heat signature for the type of gas that should be burned off. Some oil sites have pump jacks that aren't even drilling into the ground! Secondly, the amount of oil flowing through your many pipelines is less than you claim to the world. It's only half. Third, the oil tankers at your terminals aren't filled according to what the manifests indicate. They are thousands of gallons short. However, this only applies to ships flagged by friendly nations to Russia, like China, for example. These nations have been covering for you, either willingly or unwillingly."

"Fourth, we have noticed increased activity regarding your strategic oil reserves, but only in Russia and China, not India. Lastly, we reviewed some conversations we recorded about twenty years ago. We discovered one conversation between the Minister of Energy and the Chief Petroleum Engineer concerning a survey and study he conducted in the West Siberian oil basin. It was very cryptic at the time, but now, putting all this other intelligence together, the pieces fall into place. For some reason, since then, the Chief Petroleum Engineer, Mr. Petrov, has not been heard from until we discovered he committed suicide shortly after providing the report to the minister. Yes, Mr. President Stovol. We know about the report the minister received that fateful day, and you know because he delivered it to you in person, Mr. President.

President Kumar rose from his desk, approached the camera, and declared, "We are halting military operations immediately. We have been foolish! I will deal with General Patel and anyone involved in the cover-up."

The president continued, "President Kumar, there are no consequences for your forces. You have done nothing against us or any of our allies. As long as your ships return to port, we can restore our amicable relationship."

President Stovol spat, "We don't need you anyway. Get out of here before we sink your pathetic navy."

Ralph stood up from the conference table and left the Situation Room. He pulled out his cell phone and called General Robinson, "I need you to confirm whether the Indian naval forces have started turning back and are returning to their home ports."

After confirming, he walked back into the Situation Room.

"Mr. President, it appears they have turned their naval armada around and are heading back to India."

"Can you verify this? What about their air assets?"

"Let me check quickly. Sir, their aviation assets are returning to the carrier, and some ships have already begun returning to their home ports. We will continue monitoring this movement and update you on their arrival. They will take a few days to reach their home ports but aren't moving further toward Singapore."

The president merely nodded.

"We'll get right to it," President Yang declared. "As you know, we're securing all major shipping routes and choke points to control the oil flow to much of the world. This will be accomplished within days, and you cannot stop us."

"Very nice, Mr. President, you've figured out some of our plans," replied Stovol.

President Stovol added, "Our oil reserves are diminishing, but there are others from which we can source oil. We will reclaim what is ours, starting in about five minutes. You'll soon understand why buying all your green technology—solar panels, wind turbines, charging stations, and the software to run them—probably wasn't a good idea from China. You went from energy independence to depending on other nations for your oil needs, and now you rely on China for your green energy requirements! You can't make this stuff up. We'll be in touch in twenty-four hours."

The line went dead.

"What on earth was he talking about?" the president said.

"Mr. President, you know we get over 85 percent of our renewable energy components and technology from China, right?" Tex replied.

"I know we do, but they go through strict security checks to ensure no malicious software on any components. Are you suggesting they could control our power grid? Turn it on and off whenever they want—one day in Arkansas, the next in Kentucky?"

The silence in the room was deafening. Everyone glanced at each other.

36

BEIJING, CHINA

Commander Ai Yin pulls up the electrical grid map of the United States and says, "Let's concentrate on Washington, DC, and Northern Virginia. Let's see Qi in real time," Commander Ai Yin stated."

All solar farms, wind farms, and charging stations were currently active, bright green, and operational. A cascading series of events would begin when these power generators went offline. Lucy couldn't believe they had this much power at their fingertips. Within five minutes, all the lights turned red. It was like tossing a stone into a pond. It started rippling, and then, just as planned, everything turned red. The program functioned flawlessly.

WHITE HOUSE SITUATION ROOM

"What the hell was that?" the president asked.

"The lights just flickered. I'm not sure, but the generators just turned on," Jim replied.

"Do you think this is what they were talking about? We need to find out what's happening. Is there any information about the surrounding areas? Have there been any power outages reported in DC and Northern Virginia?"

Suddenly, the lights went out across the greater Washington, DC, and Northern Virginia areas. It was the early morning rush hour when all the stoplights began to fail. Chaos ensued on the streets of Northern Virginia and the D.C. area. Every light was out in nearly every building. Only hospitals, select businesses, and government buildings had any power, running off generators for a limited time. The alert issued by the DHS came just in time. Critical infrastructure had managed to withstand the power outage, and all precautions had succeeded. The blackout was, at most, a minor inconvenience.

"Sir, we have reports of a complete power outage in Northern Virginia and D.C.," Jim said. "It's affecting millions of people. It appears that the government's critical infrastructure—federal and local—and hospitals and a local municipality were forewarned of a potential power outage. So, they took the necessary precautions when the outage began. The DHS issued an alert."

The president responded, "You're telling me they were warned about this potential power outage? Were they notified of a possible cyberattack, or was it just that a power outage was likely to occur? Let's get to the bottom of this. But right now, does anyone know how long these generators will last? What about the generators at the hospital or other critical infrastructure?"

"Sir, the White House can sustain power for twenty-four hours, but we can switch to propane if necessary," Jim said. "I believe the generators at other critical infrastructure locations—federal, state, and local—are rated for twelve hours."

"Well, let's hope this doesn't last twelve hours. Let's focus on a contingency plan." Plan."

Mark glanced at his watch and smiled.

"Mark, what are you smiling about?" asked the president.

"Nothing, sir, nothing. However, I need to step out for a moment."

He took out his phone and typed a short text. This time to someone else individual.

> Is everything in place for extraction?

He received his reply in under a minute.

> We are fueled and ready. Waiting on the package.

He placed his phone back into his pocket and re-entered the Situation Room.

~

The power outage lasted only sixty minutes, and then, just like clockwork, the lights came back on.

Ed said, "Sir, Potomac Electric Power released a public statement about the outage. They explained it was caused by a construction company cutting underground cables, that it was repaired, and that there wouldn't be any further disruptions."

However, the internal discussion was quite different. This was a cyberattack, and the experts in the Security Operations Center sprang into action to determine what had just occurred and whether it could happen again.

"General, we need to alert the National Guard for possible mobilization within the next twelve hours," the president said. "If they turn the lights out like a rolling blackout in other regions of the country, we all know what happens—the freaks come out. Hell, these riots will make the demonstrations of the summer of 2020 look like a frat party."

BEIJING, CHINA

After sixty minutes, all the lights turned green. Everything was back online. Qi operated according to specifications. Commander Ai Yin thought *Those North Koreans are damn good!* Just as she sat in her office and began to pull out one of her burner phones, there was a knock on her door. Without waiting for a reply, a figure entered. It was her commanding general. She immediately stood and assumed the position of attention, her heart racing.

"Good morning, General Yen. To what do I owe this visit?"

"Good morning, Commander. You look startled. Is everything okay?"

"No, no, sir, not startled—just surprised. I didn't expect you. In fact, I didn't know you knew where my office was!"

"I thought I'd take the short trip here to see my number one commander."

"Sir, I don't know what to say, but that is an honor," she replied. "Sir, please sit down."

"Thank you, Commander. Ai Yin—may I call you by your first name?"

"Please do, sir."

"May I ask what gives the program—I hear you call it Qi—the ability to remain undetected? We've conducted numerous cyberattacks worldwide, and the security teams or the governments detected nearly all of them. However, we conducted a few tests with Qi, and there were no detections. Why is that? I'm very interested and curious at the same time. I have questions about its future use. However, first, I want to understand why it is undetectable. Before you begin, I know about indirect and direct malware, phishing, man-in-the-middle attacks, and DoS attacks. What are we using?"

"We are utilizing the Internet of Things Attack," she said. "The difference is that we are the ones inputting the code. We are the manufacturers, so we're not trying to exploit a vulnerability from the outside. Our code has many jobs and processes that run randomly, providing information, statistics, and other details to the users and the power companies."

She continued, "We added another process that allows us to determine when, how long, and what location to cause an outage. The new process operates like the others but doesn't do anything until we give the command. It's not that the security team sees and flags a new process. It has always been part of the application. There's nothing new. We updated it as we have before and will continue to do so. In fact, we want to make it easier. Generally, if we wanted to, we could fully automate it and allow it to run randomly from one power company to another. That would only require a few lines of code."

"Exciting, Ai Yin," he said. "Let me ask you a question."

"Yes, General, anything."

"Since we provide almost all the technology for electric cars, could we do the same for them? For example, we could limit the times someone drives in a region. In Los Angeles, we might program a certain number of cars to be on the road simultaneously, regardless of whether they are fully charged, or restrict how far they can travel from home."

"Yes, General, we can do that. In fact, we could program those smart refrigerators to show a temperature of 5ºC, although it might be much hotter overnight, causing the food to spoil. Sir, we could exert that much control over everything if we desired."

"Ai Yin, since we own most of the meat-packing companies and other agricultural firms and farms, we could control the prices of nearly anything. America will be ours—the future is bright for China. Anyway, Ai Yin, I need to run. You've given me a lot to think about. By the way, I've put you in for a promotion, which shouldn't be an issue for approval."

He stood up and walked out the door. Looking back at her, he said, "Keep up the great work! I expect a proposal on my desk next week regarding electric vehicles."

She stood at attention, waiting for him to leave so she could catch her breath. Afterward, she went back to her desk and sat down. Wow, that was close. She paused for a few minutes to regain her composure, then pulled out one of her burner phones, opened Telegraph, and typed her latest message:

> Code to be changed.

She clicked Send, removed the SIM card, and destroyed the phone as usual. Leaning back in her chair, she placed her hands behind her head and took a long, deep breath. There was so much to do. She needed to start now. She had forgotten to inform the general about the successful last test. I need to call him, but I'll wait a moment.

∽

THE MESSAGE WAS READ, and the phone was destroyed. Everything was going according to plan—there was one more message before notifying the president.

BEIJING, CHINA

She thought just one more fix to the program would be better than a hundred percent. Her heart raced and pounded in her chest. She logged into her computer, opened the code editing software, and accessed Qi. After making a small change, she saved it. She then copied it to two USB drives, one of which she placed in her purse. The other she intended to take to her lead developer. Before logging out, she created a new user and password to access the network, a back door into China's classified system. Once that was completed, she initiated a command to schedule a program to wipe her hard drive clean. She logged out of her computer and picked up her phone.

"Get General Yen on the secure phone, please."

"Commander, he's on the line."

"Sir, I forgot to tell you that we achieved one hundred percent success."

"Ai Yin, thank you. We're experiencing the same. I will pass on the information. Stand by for phase two—it starts in twenty-four hours. Please don't forget my proposal for next week."

"Yes, sir, we'll be ready, and the proposal will be on your desk next week."

The line went dead.

She stood up from her desk. She walked down the hallway, paused at a portrait again, and said, "I just want to make you proud, Uncle."

She handed her lead developer the latest software version and instructed him to distribute it to all the manufacturers so they could send it to every endpoint. "Commander, why are we changing the code?" the lead developer asked. "The last version worked flawlessly."

"Do I now have to justify my actions to you? Just do your job, soldier. I'm your commander, and you need to follow my orders. We want one hundred percent, not ninety-nine."

"Yes, Commander, I didn't mean any disrespect."

"We are doing this for the Chinese people," she replied.

"Yes, Commander." He felt proud, thinking he might get promoted. The update would be deployed to all the endpoints within four hours.

"Excellent. Now that we have completed our mission, everyone can take the rest of the day and tomorrow off. General Yen's cyber warriors are now in charge of Qi," she told her lead developer.

"Yes, Commander, I will let the team know. It's a great day for China!"

She returned to her office, took out her new burner phone, and typed a new text:

> It's a dry time of year in 4 hours.

This indicates that updating all the endpoints properly would take four hours. She tapped the Send button, and the message was directed to a different number than the last one. Like before, she removed the SIM, destroyed it, smashed the phone, and tossed it in the recycling bin. She knew it wasn't recyclable, but what could they do to her? Put her in jail? She laughed. She left her office, hopped in a cab, and instructed the driver.

THE CAB CARRYING Ai Yin pulled up to a secure area at Beijing Capital International Airport (PEK), an area dedicated to private, designated areas and services for business aviation, including VIP lounges and dedicated handling for private jets. Waiting there at the terminal was an unassuming G700. She paid the driver his fee, gave him a very nice tip, exited the cab, and walked over to the jet. As she walked to the plane, the door opened. The stairs extended, and she walked into the jet. Before she entered the cabin, she turned around and smiled. Not knowing if she would ever return to China.

As she entered the cabin, the co-pilot said, "Hello, Fugu."

She replied, "Hello, I'm ready."

The pilot taxied out to the runway, got his clearance, and added power to the twin Rolls-Royce Pearl 700 engines. He then rolled down the runway, pulled the nose up at 165 knots, and headed northeast. The co-pilot pulled out his cell phone and sent a short text.

37

NORTHERN COAST OF ALASKA - ARCTIC CIRCLE

One hundred miles off the northern coast of Alaska in the Beaufort Sea, approximately three hundred miles from Anwar, Alaska, the Akula-class nuclear-powered ballistic submarine Generalissimo Suvorov and the fast attack submarine Perm of the Northern Fleet were both at a depth of four hundred feet, just deep enough to avoid detection by satellites. The Generalissimo Suvorov, armed with sixteen ballistic nuclear missiles that have a range of thousands of miles, stood by, awaiting orders. Additionally, she carried conventional and nuclear cruise missiles.

The Perm was positioned to provide overwatch and remain submerged throughout this mission. She was fast and sleek, equipped with a full complement of Type 53 torpedoes.

Fifty miles northwest cruised the Ural, a nuclear-powered icebreaker converted into a troop transport for amphibious landings in the Arctic Ocean. On this voyage, 350 highly trained Arctic marines from the Northern Fleet were onboard. The aft deck had been transformed into a helipad, where an Arctic Mi-8AMTSh-VA was stationed to transport troops and supplies and provide close air support.

Below the deck, the Marines reviewed their objectives while checking their weapons and supplies.

Generalissimo Suvorov's captain sent a message to fleet headquarters stating they were in position and awaiting final orders.

Once Admiral Balakin received confirmation that the subs were in place and the icebreaker was moving into its battle position, he knew it was time to alert and position his airborne units. He sent out the message to begin loading the aircraft.

WHITE HOUSE SITUATION ROOM

When Mark's phone began to vibrate, he exited the Situation Room. He retrieved the burner phone, powered it on, and read the message. He thought to himself, I guess it's time. He returned to the Situation Room door just as power was restored. Before Mark Chang became the Director of National Intelligence, he served as the station chief of the CIA's China office for covert and field operations. He was fluent in Mandarin, Cantonese, Russian, and German.

The president looked at his cabinet. "What the hell! Get me, General Andrews. Isn't he the commander of your cyber command?"

"Yes, sir, I'll get him on the line," Ralph replied.

The president asked, "General, have you identified the cause of the outage? Is it a computer virus?"

"No, Mr. President, we haven't detected any network activity or cyber attack vectors from China, North Korea, Iran, Russia, or other malicious actors who might have been responsible," General Andrews responded. "We reached out to one of the regional power companies affected by the outage, and they informed us yesterday that the firmware on their devices had been updated as part of a new release and bug fix."

"Anything else?"

"The manufacturer just issued another update in the past hour or so. The affected power companies reported that they couldn't prevent the updates. There's a flaw in the updating process that typically follows a change control procedure."

"Where did the update originate?" the president inquired.

"Their headquarters is in China. It was a routine firmware update, business as usual, and nothing was flagged by their or our antivirus, malware, or threat detection systems."

"Did they install it? Or how was it installed?"

"The power companies aren't responsible for the updates according to their manufacturer contracts. All updates are done by the manufacturers in China." General Andrews paused. "Sir, we do have an idea."

"Yes, let's hear it."

"We're considering moving the infected devices back to a known good state. However, they don't know when that was, so they're researching when the short-duration power outages started. Hopefully, they have a backup, but they're not certain if they can back up so many devices. They've never attempted it before."

"Never tried it?" the president asked.

"No, sir,"

"Okay, everyone, I want all critical infrastructure to test their disaster recovery plans within the next ninety days, and I mean every one of them. General, is disconnecting the communication link between the devices and the manufacturers possible?"

"A connection is necessary for failover monitoring of the devices on the power grid, allowing the manufacturer to reboot or update them if the power company loses connection. If we take them offline, we're uncertain about returning them online."

"Wow, they thought of everything," the president remarked.

"We can attempt to restore them to the last known good state. Let me get back to you in an hour."

"Okay, General, you got it. What sort of contingency plans do we have? How much backup power can we draw from generators?"

"We don't have any contingency plans for this type of scenario," Ed replied. "We never considered a complete power outage, just one on a regional scale that impacted the Northeast in August 2003."

"And what was the plan that came from that power outage?"

"Make sure critical infrastructure has backup generators that can function for twelve hours without refueling."

The president stood up from the conference table, approached Ed, and regarded him closely. "That's all? No alternative power sources from other regions, like a failover?"

Ed looked up. "No, sir, nothing was mandated."

The president paced around the conference table, stopped, turned, and stared at the monitor. He turned back and took a deep breath.

"You're kidding me. We haven't mandated any backup plans. Well, that's ridiculous. You'd think we would've learned something from the major outages in Texas in 2021 when they faced that severe freeze. Hell, even the windmills and wind farms were impacted—they froze!" he scoffed. "This is just great. What are you guys doing all day? I can tell you what you're doing today—get me a damn plan! Now, get the hell out of here and get to work. Is that understood?"

The president paused. "Where's Mark?"

"Sir, I'm right here."

"Sorry, I didn't see you sitting next to Kim."

"Sir, I had to step out for a minute."

Kim leaned over and said, "Hi, Daddy."

Tex and Tyler looked over and mouthed, "Hi, Daddy?"

Tyler leaned over to Kim and asked, "Daddy? Your last name isn't Chang."

"Long story, Tyler. I was married before—it didn't last long. We can talk about it later if you'd like."

"No need to, I understand. All I care about is we are together now," he replied, smiling.

She smiled warmly.

"Mark, I think we have a plan to reduce the number of power outages next time. I'm not sure what it is, but we will, if possible, restore a backup of the affected devices. We are testing it now."

"Mr. President, please hold those plans."

The president stood up straight and slammed his fist on the table.

"Hold them? Do you have another plan, or should we just let them execute the software again? Please answer me. Damn, Mark, are you messing with me? It's been a long day."

Mark was known for showing little to no emotion—his nickname was Mr. Spock.

"No, sir, I'm not messing with you. I'm about to tell you the most guarded secret in U.S. history. More people knew about the atomic bomb than what I'm about to discuss. It's only known to three people: me, Sean, and Fugu."

"Who the hell is Fugu? Why wasn't I informed of this?"

"Plausible deniability, sir, so that you can deny any knowledge of it."

The president said, "Okay, I understand."

Director Chang opened his briefcase, pulled out a large file, placed it on the table, and began briefing the president.

"As you know, Mr. President, I was stationed in China for a considerable time during the latter part of my last assignment. I met someone through her parents. At that time, she was young and still in school," Mark said.

He continued, "I assisted her with her homework and shared stories about America's greatness. She expressed her hope that one day she could visit, and I gave her my phone number, which remains the same today. One day, I went to her house, but she was gone. Her parents informed me that officials from the Ministry of State had come for her. I wasn't aware she had excelled in her classes and was being prepared for military service with a focus on cyber warfare. Let me fast-forward."

"Yes, please, you have three minutes," the president replied

"Out of the blue, I received a phone call about a year ago. Fugu mentioned she only had a minute but needed to speak with me in person the following week when she was home for a holiday. I asked her how in the world she remembered my number, and she replied, 'I have a photographic memory. I'm good at remembering numbers, dates, and so on.'

"I cleared the travel with Director McGill, and she and I met up once I was in China. She told me she was working on a project related to renewable energy on the software side, focusing on controlling all the components necessary to manage the solar panels, wind turbines, charging stations, and everything else. She believed it could control the entire unit—not just the input or output, but also determine how long to generate power and where to send it."

"She assisted with the specifications for all the various parts of the program. Once the specifications were finished, they would be sent to North Korea to finalize the code. We didn't have much time, so I showed her a list of numbers from burner phones at the CIA. There were about twenty that I controlled. I asked her if she could memorize them, and she said she could."

"I told her to text me when she had important information and advised her to get some burner phones. However, I also told her she didn't have to do it because it was dangerous and could lead to jail—or worse. She replied, 'They've taken everything from me—everything.' She started crying. I didn't know what to say. I just hugged her. "You're all I've got in this world," she said as she walked away. Five weeks ago, the first burner phone on the list started to buzz. There was a message on Telegram."

The president turned toward Mark. "Wait, she remembered the number after all these years? That's unbelievable. She should work for us. Please, go on."

No one in the Situation Room made a sound.

Mark continued, "The message stated she had just received all the bits and pieces of the code from the developers in North Korea.

Her team would assemble it into one application for distribution and testing."

"North Korea had a hand in this?" the president asked. "General, you know what to do. Please continue, Mark."

"She mentioned that her team had less than thirty days to finish, after which it would be tested. Exactly twenty-one days later, she sent another text saying that the test would occur the next day and that they would turn the power off for less than a minute. I timed it. It was precisely fifty seconds. Sir, everything she has told me has been 100% accurate."

The president placed his hands behind his head. "So, the code is being used to disable all these wind turbines, solar panels, generators, and charging stations? Essentially, it stops all renewable technology from functioning, and the Chinese can dictate where and for how long. I wish we'd thought of that."

"A week or so later, I received another text indicating that the next test would be longer and where it would take effect—five minutes in Northern Virginia."

"She sends you the time, duration, and location?" the president inquired.

"Yes."

Tex stood. "Damn, I remember that! Marsha and I were at the Yard House."

"The other day, she texted to say the next one would be for sixty minutes, and they would notify the president before proceeding and outline their demands. This is the one that happened today."

The president stood. "Sean, do you know all of this and the demands?"

Sean replied, "Yes, I knew. I don't know the demands. But I have a hunch, and we will find out very shortly."

"Why didn't you let me know about the one today?"

"I was just about to, but things started happening quickly," Sean said. "Sir, let Mark finish, please."

"I'm a bit stressed today." The president sat back down. "Go ahead."

"I had already worked it out with Fugu. She developed a code to prevent the application from functioning after the sixty-minute test. I just received confirmation that the new code is finished, and the firmware was updated just a few hours ago."

"Well, hell. It seems like it hasn't," the president replied.

"Sir, we wanted the Chinese to think they had us over a barrel—forgive the pun. That's why the power outage worked. It's part of our plan. After the last test today, she had her lead developer send the update with her code to the manufacturers."

"Mark, is that the firmware update from a couple of hours ago?"

"Yes, sir."

"You understand what happens if she fails? When the lights go out, the worst among us come out to play, and they have their own rules."

"Yes, Mr. President, I do." Mark glanced down at his phone, looked up, and smiled.

"Okay, how in the world can you trust her to ensure that the United States has power tomorrow? Can you please explain that to me? Because I feel like taking drastic action against those bastards."

"Sir, Fugu is my niece, my sister's daughter. I'm all she has left—me and her cousin Kim."

Kim looked over at her dad, hugged him, and said, "I have a cousin in China!"

"Yes, but not anymore. She's on her way now and should arrive tomorrow."

"We got her out?" the president asked.

"We did—I just received confirmation."

The president says, "Get me General Andrews on the line."

"General Andrews, please stop what you're doing. We have a new plan."

"Yes, sir. We couldn't get into the firmware anyway. It's locked."

The president smiled and winked at Mark. "That was a fascinating story, but what do we do next, guys? We have eighteen hours and need to figure out our next move and theirs."

"They mentioned something about taking back what is theirs," Tex said. "What the heck does that mean?"

"What do we have that belongs to them?" Marsha asked. "We haven't taken anything from them."

"We didn't take it, but we bought it from them in October 1887 for 7.2 million dollars—that's 125 million today. But its true worth can't be measured in dollars. Commonly called Seward's Folly," Tyler said.

Everyone turned to Tyler.

Kim asked, "How do you know that?"

"I watch a lot of TV."

Everyone burst out laughing. They couldn't believe he just said that.

"I think you're right," the president said. "They want Alaska back. There's a lot of oil in Northern Alaska, that's for sure. Marsha, do we have any eyes on that region? If not, can you relocate those assets? Just contact NRO and, with my approval, have them move anything they can to that area. I want the most advanced and newest satellite, if possible. We need some excellent imagery and real-time footage. General Harris, what division do we have in Alaska?"

"Sir, we have a brigade from the 25th Infantry Division participating in a joint exercise with elements of the 1st Marine Division. We also have some F-35s stationed at Eielson, just outside Fairbanks. The 11th Airborne is in Alaska but is not yet combat-ready."

"Great, place the 25th on alert along with the Marines and gather intel on Anwar. Don't advance any further than the northern coast. I don't want anyone getting hurt right now. How long will it take to deploy them?"

"Twelve to sixteen hours, sir," General Harris replied. "We can have the F-35s up there in thirty minutes or less and start some recon missions."

"That's cutting it close. What other units are available?"

"We're somewhat limited since we've deployed many of our armored and infantry divisions to Eastern Europe to bolster our troops in Western Europe. Additionally, some non-deployable units are transitioning to renewable energy."

"Hold on," said the president. "Where do all the components we install in our vehicles come from? If you say China, halt the transition immediately—not one more component—and start retrofitting them back to being petroleum-driven. Sorry, General, please continue."

"We have deployed Marines to South Korea," the general said. "In response to the movements of China and Russia, we have deployed or are deploying naval assets to the Mediterranean, Red Sea, Arabian Sea, and the South China Sea. There are no additional units available for deployment right now. We need to activate the National Guard, which would take a few days to mobilize. However, we may need them to manage looting in the event of widespread power outages.

"Sir, with your permission," the President said. "You have it without hesitation. I approve."

The General continued, "Roger. I want to deploy the Second Battalion of the 75th Ranger Regiment from JBLM to Fairbanks, Alaska. They can be in the air in six hours, with a flight time of a little over three hours, meaning they can be on the ground in nine hours. We can deploy from there if needed."

"So, they could be on the ground in time?" the President asked. "Do it. General, I want the Third Battalion on alert for deployment to Colombia if we need to take action regarding Venezuela."

"Yes, sir, I will implement it now."

While General Harris spoke, the Chief of Naval Operations stood behind him, leaned over, and whispered in his ear.

General Harris turned to face him and asked if he was 100% sure. He nodded. "Mr. President."

"Yes, General. Do you have anything else to say?"

"Sir, we have been monitoring two Russian subs off the northern coast of Alaska. We are prepared to strike if necessary. Do we have your authority to proceed?"

Once again, without hesitation, he replied, "Yes."

He stood up, surveyed the room, and said, "Move to Defcon 2 - We are now in 'Fast Pace.' Alert all units, and be prepared 'Cocked Pistol, Defcon 1. I want an update in 30 minutes."

38

WHITE HOUSE SITUATION ROOM

With everyone in the Situation Room, the President entered, sat down, and said, "Update, folks. I want your updates. Is everyone at 'Fast Pace'?"

Everyone gave a thumbs-up, one by one. The United States was on the brink of World War III.

"All right, everyone, we have two hours until our next meeting. Does anyone have a plan?" the President asked.

"Jordan—I mean, Mr. President, I have an idea," Tex said.

"Let's hear it, Tex. And Jordan is fine," he replied with a smile. "I'm all ears."

"We know where their strategic petroleum reserves are located. Most of them are above ground, unlike ours. We store our underground salt caverns along the Gulf Coast in Texas and Louisiana. We could take out a couple of storage tanks in Russia and China to show them we understand the stakes."

"Can you bring up a map showing eastern Russia and northern China? Thank you. In Eastern Siberia, the Russians' SPR is located here and here. In Northern China, theirs points to a location west of Datong. These sparsely populated areas will help us minimize collateral damage to the population and infrastructure. We can even warn them if you'd like. We're not taking all their reserves—just enough to inflict damage. It will take them years to replace those at a significantly higher cost."

"Okay, hold on for a moment," the president said. "Let's get the Department of Defense's input."

Jesse replied, "This looks promising. It hurts them but doesn't annihilate them. I need to involve the Air Force and provide them with some options. Can you give us four hours?"

"We don't have four hours. Get them on the line now and bridge them in."

The Air Force Chief of Staff was on the phone bridge. Tex instructed him not to visit the White House but to have the U.S. Strategic Command (STARTCO) representative attend the Pentagon meeting.

"S<small>IR</small>, we have three B-21s from the 96th Bomb Squadron at Barksdale Air Force Base, LA, conducting a long-duration flight to test our new hypersonic air-to-ground missile. They are currently en route to Anderson AFB in Guam. Please bring up a map of the Northern Pacific. They will need to complete a midair refueling to cover the extra distance, but we have a KC-135 tanker moving into position to rendezvous with the bombers. I understand what everyone is thinking, and yes, it's a long flight. With the missiles' range, we can shift them slightly closer to the targets, incorporate a refueling here, and be in position in just over two hours. We need your approval to move them to launch, Mr. President."

"Go ahead and get them refueled. I want them in position just in case. We'll need the exact coordinates for the targets," the president replied

"Hell, General, we are the NGA. We have every coordinate known to man!" Marsha yelled. Everyone laughed.

"I'll have them for you in ten minutes," Marsha added.

"Okay, here's the plan," the president said. "We'll move our bombers into position after refueling and deploy the Rangers from JBLM to Fairbanks. A battalion from the 25th Infantry and a Marine battalion will be moving very shortly. General, I want a brigade from the 82nd on the ground as soon as possible. Listen up, everyone: Any soldier, Marine, or airman will have the right cold-weather gear. We're just lucky it's not the dead of winter."

He breathed and continued, "We have a couple of F-35s ready to launch to give us some eyes on the ground. I have also asked the NRO to reposition an asset, which should be ready in about thirty minutes. We're lean right now and don't have many more options. I believe their military movements are nothing more than a ruse to draw us away from their real objective."

"What do you think their real objective is?" Tyler asked.

Everyone turned their attention to the president. "Alaska. Our oil there would compensate for their shortfall and provide them with a land bridge into Canada and then down to the tip of South America. It's one of the hardest places in the world to defend, and we don't have a strong presence there. We rely on early warning, naval assets, and air superiority. I'm shocked that we haven't detected anything up there, have we, General?"

"Sir, we only have the two submarines we've tracked and are monitoring. There's also a nuclear-powered icebreaker on its maiden voyage that we've been aware of for some time. But there are no surface ships along the coast," the general replied.

"Marsha, I need eyes on the icebreaker. I want to know how many people are on board. I'm curious if there might be an attack force there."

"Got it. I'll handle it," Marsha replied.

"However, I just learned that we picked up a flight of thirty IL-76 Candid aircraft from five different Russian airbases, moving over the Chaun Bay at four hundred knots so that they could land in three hours or less. NORAD will soon detect them on our radar and surveillance systems, allowing us to track them more effectively," said General Harris.

"Great, now we know about their submarines. Have we detected anything besides subs near Alaska or off our east or west coast? Other than the icebreaker?" the president asked.

"No, sir, not a single one. However, we have positioned another fast-attack sub at their battle stations off the northern coast of Alaska," General Harris replied.

"Thanks, General. I want to know if any of their transport planes have fighter escorts." He continued, "I want our jets to get up close and personal with them, enough that they can read the jump master's name tag. If they enter our airspace, that's a whole different ball game. Get the Prime Minister of Canada on the line—I need to update him. We might need them to move some units toward Alaska."

"Additionally, contact the NATO secretary-general. Once we can determine with absolute certainty what is happening, Russia will need to strengthen its Western Front. I will invoke Article Five of the NATO Charter, alert our European forces, and prepare for initial battle positions. I'm not joking around."

"Sir, I'm going to activate the Alaskan National Guard to secure our pipelines in Alaska," the general stated

"Do it, General. All right, we all know what needs to be done. Now, execute the plan and keep everyone updated. We'll start the call in ten minutes."

"Sir, when Tex and the team were in Russia, my field agents gave them a USB stick to pass on to our contacts at the facility in Rostov-on-Don," Sean said. "I want to inform Tex, Tyler, and Kim that we got Saul out—he's in a safe location. The USB stick contained a computer program we could execute remotely to shut down the entire site. From there, it will spread to other refineries. We'll take them out one by one. I need the order to execute."

The president replied, "You have my permission—execute now. How long until they or we see the results?"

"Two to four hours. They'll soon notice their refineries going down, Mr. President. The execution will happen while we are on the call. We can observe their reactions in real-time."

"Great—it's time to go on the offensive."

39

AIR-TO-AIR REFUELING OVER THE NORTH PACIFIC

The lead B-21 had just received orders to move to the refueling location "Charlie" and relayed the information to her flight.

"Skipper, we should be good on fuel. Why are we getting topped off?" the copilot asked.

"If I were a betting girl, I'd say our mission has changed. This is going to be interesting."

The three B-21s, known as the Gremlins, descended to 28,000 feet to link up with a KC-135 Stratotanker from the 92d Air Refueling Wing out of Fairchild AFB on its way to Kadena Air Force Base, Okinawa. When they received flash traffic, they positioned themselves at the refueling point Charlie.

As the flight of B-21s descended, they reduced their speed. They needed to be at 350 knots to connect with the tanker. The tanker's copilot began communicating with the receiver aircraft using secure channels.

"Gremlin Five-Six, this is Panther Two-Two. Please continue your descent to twenty-eight thousand. You are five miles out. Keep reducing speed to three hundred fifty knots. It's a little bumpy, but clear skies, over."

Panther Two-Two's co-pilot muttered, "I'm not too fond of clear air turbulence."

"Roger, Panther Two-Two."

"Gremlin Five-Six, Panther Two-Two, let's review emergency breakaway procedures. During a breakaway, we will ascend and turn left by twenty degrees. The receiver will descend and turn right by twenty degrees. The other two, left and right, will move away from the tanker and position themselves two miles out."

"Panther, roger. Over."

"Just what we need. It was so smooth up there at forty-nine thousand," the co-pilot remarked. Air-to-air refueling is already tricky, but light turbulence at night makes it even more challenging in the pitch-black sky.

Master Sergeant Green, the boom operator, had amassed over nine thousand hours of flight time during his eighteen years in the role. There was nothing he preferred more. Tonight's mission felt different. While en route to Japan, he was instructed to relocate to a refueling point, Charlie. Refueling a flight of B-21s was not part of their original mission or flight plan from Fairchild. He slipped on his new flight gloves, having cut off the fingertips weeks ago, as he did with every pair of flight gloves issued to him. He needed to feel the controls. He extended his fingers and twice clenched his fists, gripping the joysticks to maneuver the boom into position with the receiving aircraft. He remained calm while guiding the receivers into place. Three miles from the tanker, the boom operator in the airplane's tail had the best view of everyone on the tanker, looking back and down. He took over communications with the receiver aircraft and contacted Gremlin Five-Six.

"Gremlin Five-Six, this is Panther Two-Two. You are three miles out and closing. Maintain three hundred fifty knots, over."

"Roger, Panther Two-Two. There are three of us. I will be first, with Gremlin Five-Nine on your left and Gremlin Five-Four on your right."

"Roger, Gremlin Five-Six. Do you have visuals?"

The pilot and copilot strain their eyes to spot the tanker. Their eyes are weary, as they have been in the air for over twelve hours.

"Skipper, there she is at our eleven o'clock, five hundred feet above us."

"Panther Two-Two, roger. We have visuals. Moving into position."

"Gremlin Five-Six. I also have visuals. Please move into position."

"Roger, Panther Two-Two. Sergeant Green, is that you?"

"Gremlin Five-Six, roger. Good evening, Major."

"Panther Two-Two, I feel much better now. Let's do this."

As Gremlin Five-Six moved into position with the precision of a Swiss watchmaker, Sergeant Green controlled the stabilizer wings on the boom, guiding it into the fuel receptacle behind the cockpit. Once positioned, Gremlin Five-Six relied on the boom operator's expertise.

"Gremlin Five-Six, steady. Forward. Up five. Steady—damn, it's bumpy. Steady."

In Gremlin Five-Six, the pilot and copilot remained silent, focused on aligning the tanker and getting fuel.

"Gremlin Five-Six, steady. I have a green light and am starting the fuel transfer," said the boom operator.

"Break, break, break!"

When the refueling boom connected and was securely seated in the refueling port on Gremlin Five-Six, it encountered a pocket of turbulence. The KC-135 suddenly lurched violently up and down. Gremlin Five-Six came within feet of the tanker. When she heard, "Break, break, break!" she veered to the right and down, moving away to a safe distance from the tanker. Inside the tanker, Sergeant Green pulled the boom receptacle back toward the aircraft, and once they were level again, he wiped the sweat from his brow, took a deep breath, and exhaled. He clenched his fist and grasped the joysticks for attempt number two.

"Gremlin Five-Six, please line up two hundred and maintain three hundred fifty knots."

Inside the Gremlin, the copilot thought, this guy is as cool as a cucumber. We almost had a midair collision, and he acted like it was nothing. I want to buy him a beer or two. They both snugged their safety harnesses a little tighter.

"Panther Two-Two, roger."

Gremlin Five-Six maneuvered into position behind the tanker. After the last attempt, everyone felt a bit on edge. The boom made contact with the receiver and began taking on fuel.

"Gremlin Five-Six, green light. We are giving you nine thousand pounds. Credit card, please, over."

"Panther Two-Two, send the bill to Uncle Sam. You make it look easy, over."

"Gremlin Five-Six, all green here, and fuel is flowing. It looks like around twenty minutes. You should be topped off after that, and then we can refuel the rest of your flight. Who's next, over?"

"Panther Two-Two, Gremlin Five-Nine off to your left will be next, over."

Gremlin Five-Six completed the fuel transfer, broke away from the tanker, and took up a position next to Gremlin Five-Four. They could relax for now.

"Panther Two-Two, thank you. Sergeant Green, you are a master, my friend. Have a great night, over."

"Roger, Gremlin Five-Six. By the way, I was told never to feed Gremlins after dark, out."

The other Gremlins refueled without any issues and received their new orders. Their training mission has just become operational.

"Gremlins ascend to forty-nine thousand. Once there, reach 575 knots at 260 degrees out."

Panther Two-Two radioed back to command, "Topped off and on our way."

The KC-135 crew resumed their cruising altitude and waited for any further instructions as they flew toward Okinawa.

40

WHITE HOUSE SITUATION ROOM

General Harris leaned over to the president and said, "They're on their way."

The conference call included the Chinese and Russian presidents, the president's National Security Council, and the CIA, NSA, DOD, NGA, and DNI.

President Stovol said, "Good morning, Mr. President. I hope you're well."

"Cut the crap, Stovol." He replied,

"As you Americans put it, I'll 'cut the crap' and get straight to the point. We've made significant advances in our military campaigns over the last twenty-four hours, but you already know that. We will have total control of the shipping lanes within forty-eight hours. As you can see, we're going to great lengths to ensure no U.S. or NATO countries are involved. We want no contact."

The president responded, "What about the cyberattack here? Are you really going to claim it wasn't you, President Yang?"

"No, it was us, and we'll do it again and again if you don't provide us with the oil in northern Alaska," President Yang replied.

"We don't want everything, just our fair share, which Russia has guaranteed," he smirked.

Everyone in the Situation Room thought *it was about Alaska and our oil.*

"President Yang, you know you're screwed," the president warned. "You can't trust them. In 2020, we couldn't understand why you became powerful allies, considering your history of conflicts over your borders in 1969 and the Sino-Soviet border war. I guess we know now."

"Like you've never befriended our enemies. Cut the small talk. Here's our proposal. We want to offer you a solution to our current issue. We believe Alaska is ours, and we want it back. We only seek everything north of the Arctic Circle. We are generous and only desire peace. That's it. In fact, as a sign of goodwill, we will return the $7.4 million you paid for it."

General Harris stood up, leaned over the president, tapped the mute button, and whispered, "The two identified subsurface vessels have moved within a hundred miles of Prudhoe Bay, Alaska. We suspect they are Russian subs. We can't guarantee they are Russian, but we cannot identify the type of new signatures that haven't been detected before. Additionally, that nuclear icebreaker is speeding toward the coast of Alaska. Their helicopters will be within range of the norther coast of Alaska in thirty to forty-five minutes."

"You don't know what kind they are?" the president whispered. "Is there any activity on the West Coast?"

"Sir, we've never encountered them before. Right now, there's no activity off our western coast. I've notified the Coast Guard to initiate their coastal watch protocol. Sir, we are starting to receive the feed from our NRO asset. We'll need dual screens for the conference and the satellite feed. It's in real time."

ARCTIC OCEAN – PRUDHOE BAY

Inside the Generalissimo Suvorov, the captain sounded battle stations. He aimed to make a grand entrance and ordered an emergency surfacing. The crew braced themselves. Those crew members who had experienced this kind of surfacing before knew what to expect, but those who hadn't were in for the ride of their lives. The sub's bow broke through the surface at almost seventy-five degrees vertical, rising above the waves before crashing back into the water. The sub settled on the surface. Below deck, the crew busied themselves, completing all the checks on the ballistic missile launch tubes, which remained closed.

The Perm was still waiting and watching beneath the water at a depth of two hundred feet, listening for any sound from the American fast attack subs, with its crew manning battle stations.

WHITE HOUSE SITUATION ROOM

The team was watching the feed from the satellite.

"What the hell," Tex exclaimed as Generalissimo Suvorov lurched out of the water.

"What's that thing on its bow? There have been numerous modifications to her. She doesn't even resemble a sub in the traditional sense," Jesse remarked.

The call was still muted when the president stated, "Damn, that's a clear picture."

Peter unmuted the call.

"We assume you can see our sub. Isn't she beautiful?" President Stovol continued. "As you can see, we made a few minor modifications to her. Do you see that bubble on her bow? Watch this."

At that moment, the bubble emitted a pulse of bright light, and the satellite feed disappeared. The U.S. was now blind.

After releasing the light pulse, Generalissimo Suvorov dove to a missile-firing depth of 160 feet in the icy Beaufort Sea.

"What the hell did you do to our satellite?" the president asked.

"We don't like being spied on, Mr. President."

The line was muted just then, and the Russian president's facial expression was priceless. He was waving his fist and pounding it on the table, and it looked like whoever he was yelling at was in some serious trouble.

Muting the line, Tex leaned toward the president and said, "I guess they just had a refinery—one of many—go offline." He chuckled, and then everyone joined in the laughter. It was America's turn.

The lines were unmuted again. "President Stovol, is there anything we can assist you with? By the way, we are tracking your airborne units en route to Alaska. I will tell you this once: Not a single airborne troop will land in the United States alive. Is that clear?"

"You will not make me look like a fool, Mr. President. We know you don't possess military units to repel our forces. We don't mind sending them to their demise. We will land, and we will take what is rightfully ours. "

Throughout this entire conversation between the Russian and U.S. presidents, the Chinese president sat there, appearing as if he were watching a ping-pong match. He didn't need to say a word. It was about time to go all the way with Qi. He was waiting for them to stop talking.

President Yang said, "Gentlemen, this fighting will get us nowhere. Why do you think we have signed every carbon and green treaty and agreement anyone could ever dream up? We know the U.S. will abide by all requirements and stipulations. We know you will go far beyond, and at the same time, you know we won't. It's almost comical."

"Hell, we built several artificial islands in the South China Sea. They are only two feet above sea level. We don't think the ocean will rise to overtake the islands, and if it does, that's fine with us. All we wanted you to do was buy all your green technology from us, and you have, so thank you. You are now as dependent on us as you were in the mid-seventies with the Middle Eastern oil-producing countries. You never learn from past mistakes. Right now, I'll show you just how dependent you are on us."

He looked to his left and signaled his cyber warriors to activate Qi. At the same time, he monitored a screen displaying power grids in the U.S. and waited for them to turn from green to red. Nothing happened. He began to look very agitated, and it was clear his blood was about to boil.

"Get General Yen and tell him to find Commander Yin and the lead developer now!"

President Stovol was not even fazed. He didn't care whether it worked or not. He didn't care about "going green." All he wanted was oil and, more than that, Alaska. He was ready to do what he had to—nothing was off the table.

BEIJING

"President Yang, she isn't here and can't be found. She left this morning," said his aide.

"What do you mean?" President Yang replied.

"Sir, she is gone, along with her team. She gave them all permission to leave the barracks."

"Who the hell authorized those passes? I sure as hell didn't approve any passes! Find her now! I want her arrested and brought to me."

Earlier that day, Commander Ai Yin Chang had slipped from Beijing to a secure section at Beijing Capital International Airport thirty-five miles outside the city. Waiting at that airport was a G700, painted in the colors of the People's Republic of China, with a range of 7,500 nautical miles and a speed of 600 miles per hour. She made her way out of China in less than an hour and a half. Her destination was Joint Base Andrews, with a stop at Elmendorf AFB to switch planes before the final leg of her journey.

President Yang understood that they could do nothing against the United States. Without their cyber capabilities, they were a paper tiger. He had to eat crow.

"Get me President Jones on his cell."

WHITE HOUSE SITUATION ROOM

"Gentlemen—I mean, President Stovol. I don't see President Yang in the conference right now. I have authorized a strike on your strategic oil reserves. I suggest you get as many people out as you can. You have one hour," the president stated. Sean muted the conference and leaned over to him. "The feed from China is down."

41

45,000 FEET OVER THE NORTH PACIFIC

The general gave the bomber crews the go-ahead before the meeting. Three B-21s flew over the Northern Pacific Ocean at fifty thousand feet, near the Bering Sea. The air defenses in Russia and China detected nothing. The B-21's stealth technology made them the size of small birds, avoiding detection by Russian or Chinese air defense forces. If, by chance, they were spotted, the flight would resemble every other training mission from Barksdale AFB in Bossier City, LA, to Andersen Air Force Base in Guam, appearing as just a typical extended training operation.

The B-21s were equipped with three stealth hypersonic air-to-ground missiles. With enhanced fuel storage and a speed exceeding 3,800 miles per hour, the missiles could cover 6,000 miles and hit their target in under an hour.

The bomber crews finished their launch checklist, confirmed the target coordinates, and armed the missiles. "Skipper, we are ready for launch."

The trailing B-21 opened its ordinance bay doors and released a payload of three stealth hypersonic missiles en route to Russia's strategic oil reserves in Eastern Siberia.

The copilot announced, "Missiles away."

They fell from the bomber to a predetermined altitude before the motors ignited. All the crew saw was a white smoke trail, and then they were gone, traveling at twice the speed of a bullet fired from an M4 rifle. They were headed for Russia's strategic oil reserves.

At the same time, the lead B-21s in the formation executed the same procedure, launching missiles at China's strategic oil reserves in northern China.

"Sir, the crews report no aborts and all missiles are en route to their predefined targets. They didn't need to fire the additional missiles, which saved us some money. Mr. President, sir, they are on their way. Now we wait."

The conference bridge went silent. There was no turning back now—the president just hoped it wouldn't escalate.

Suddenly, his chief of staff leaned over to him. "Sir, President Yang is on the phone."

"What phone?"

"Your cell."

"How in the hell did he get my cell phone number? Never mind." He went off-camera. "Please hand me the phone. President Yang, how may I assist you?"

"We are withdrawing from the agreement with Russia. We never intended to inflict any physical harm on the United States. We hope to collaborate with you in the future. We will help remove the code from your devices and all other components."

"Thank you, President Yang. I could have our missiles detonated and self-destruct to spare you the damage to your strategic oil reserves, but I won't. You can cover the shortfall in your reserves by purchasing from us. Naturally, at our prices. Have a great day."

"We have started evacuating the civilians. We will contact you soon." The line went dead.

The president turned to Tex and said, "Don't mess with Texas."

"Jordan, I'm not from Texas."

"I know, Tex, it's a joke. I'm from Texas. We have eyes on both locations, right?"

Ralph replied, "Yes, sir. We're receiving some early bomb damage assessments from both sites."

"Did we hit all targets with maximum effectiveness?"

"Yes, sir. From initial observation, a successful surgical strike was carried out with the expected results. However, we'll have more details and information once they stop burning in the coming days or weeks."

42

STRATEGIC PETROLEUM RESERVES – EASTERN RUSSIA AND CHINA

Russia's strategic petroleum reserves exploded in Eastern Siberia, sending a fireball over ten thousand feet into the air. The subsequent explosions were even louder, causing the ground to shake for hundreds of miles from the blasts. Everything within a five-mile radius was obliterated in this very remote location, explicitly chosen to minimize civilian casualties.

Since China's oil reserves were situated in a valley, the fireball engulfed the entire twenty-square-mile area. It shot straight up and could be seen as far away as Datong. Given the proximity of the oil storage tanks, it appeared as one massive explosion. The blast rattled dishes off shelves in Hohhot, one hundred miles from the epicenter. The Russians made the critical decision following the last explosions in the Russian strategic oil reserves. President Stovol ordered all strategic missile forces, both land and sea, to full alert and commanded the launch of their missiles toward intended targets in the United States.

OFF THE NORTHERN COAST OF ALASKA

The captain of Generalissimo Suvorov received the orders and began executing them. He confirmed they were at firing depth. Once reached, they opened the launch tube doors and prepared to unleash her sixteen ballistic nuclear missiles. The captain and the missile officer moved to the launch controls. Both inserted their keys and awaited the launch orders.

WHITE HOUSE SITUATION ROOM

"Sir, the Russian submarine has opened its launch doors," General Harris reported.

"General, is our submarine in a position to fire?" the president asked.

"Yes, sir. It is in position and waiting for orders."

"Take them both out."

The general passed the firing orders to Naval Operations.

Aboard the Generalissimo Suvorov, the crew was tossed from side to side without warning. All the lights went out, and the damage control light illuminated the sub's interior.

The commander yelled, "What the hell was that?"

Those were the last words spoken by any crewmember on the Generalissimo Suvorov. The sub's hull began to buckle. She started taking on water and was heading to the bottom fast. There was nothing the crew could do. Everything went dark as the Generalissimo Suvorov imploded.

Two hundred feet below her, the Perm met the same fate. Her crew never picked up SSN-770, the USS Dallas, a fast-attack submarine. With her new stealth technology, she had moved in behind the

Perm, waiting for orders to attack. Her highly trained crew eagerly awaited their battle stations.

MOSCOW RUSSIA

"The subs have stopped communicating."

"What? Give the order to fire the missiles again," yelled the Russian president.

"Sir, they received the order but never executed it."

OFF THE NORTHERN COAST OF ALASKA

The USS Dallas departed the area, and no one ever picked her up. She glided silently toward the icebreaker to intercept and, if needed, sink her.

Inside the submarine, the XO remarked to the captain, "Damn, that focused sound wave cannon was incredible."

The sound wave from the cannon traveled at 1,480 meters per second, faster than any conventional torpedo. It could fire at multiple targets simultaneously, and the subs never knew what hit them. There were no residual aftereffects. The subs appeared as if they had just imploded, ensuring the nuclear core remained intact with no nuclear radiation or material leakage. They were clean kills.

WHITE HOUSE SITUATION ROOM

The feed from the Kremlin went dark.

Jesse Dorn, the Secretary of Defense, stated, "Sir, NORAD has just indicated a potential missile launch from Russia. What do you want us to do?"

"Have they launched yet?" the president asked.

"They haven't. We're on alert because their silo doors are open."

"How long until they strike if they launch?"

"About thirty minutes. Sir, we need to get you out of here now!"

"No, we aren't going anywhere. Move to 'cocked pistol.'"

OFFICE OF THE PRESIDENT IN THE KREMLIN – MOSCOW, RUSSIA

Igor Volkov, the energy minister, burst into the president's office. "Sir, wait! Please, don't do this. I have some excellent news."

"What is it? This had better be good, or I will shoot you myself," as he pulled out a pistol from his desk.

"Sir, a couple of months ago, I authorized exploring some sites east of Chayanda in Eastern Siberia based on outdated data. I had a hunch. Sir, we discovered what we believe to be Russia's most significant oil discovery! We are not running out of oil. We have more than ever beneath our soil. We don't need anyone else's."

President Stovol gazed at the energy minister. "It's too late. We're going out with a bang. I have nothing to lose. I can't afford another defeat. I'll be dead in a matter of weeks anyway. I'm dying from cancer."

Just as he was about to turn the key that would initiate the launch of their nuclear missiles, Igor sprinted forward and shouted, "Stop, stop, we have the oil!" He lunged at the president, hitting him with full force. The blow knocked the president off his feet, and as he fell, he struck his head on the edge of the desk. He landed on the floor with a loud thud. His lifeless body lay on the floor as the blood flowed from his head. The president's guards heard the commotion, rushed into the office, and stared at Igor.

They drew their pistols.

"Stay where you are! Don't move."

"Is he dead?" Igor inquired.

One of the guards bent down and checked for a pulse. There was none.

"Yes, Minister, he is dead!"

"I didn't mean to kill him! I didn't!" he shouted. "What have I done?"

As the guards took Igor into custody, the vice president entered the president's office and commanded, "Let him go. He is a hero."

"Sir, President Stovol is dead, and he killed him," the guard responded.

"That pig on the floor was about to kill us all. Let him go."

They released Igor.

"Minister, I heard and saw everything you said. Russia owes you. Please take a seat. I need to call the President of the United States, but first, we need to stand down and halt all military movements."

He called his military command and ordered them to cease combat actions and movements, returning to security level 1. He also ordered the arrest of every general or admiral involved in this operation. Finally, he picked up the red phone on the desk, the same phone that was installed after the Cuban Missile Crisis.

THE PRESIDENT REACHED for the ringing red phone and muttered, "This thing actually works?"

"Mr. President, the Russian people owe you and the United States an apology. We acted without regard for our people. Our actions do not reflect those of a civilized country. We will pay reparations for any damage we cause. I have ordered our military worldwide to stand down and return to their bases. I'm sure you can confirm that now. Additionally, we have had a change in leadership—President Stovol is no longer with us. Again, please accept my apologies. I believe it's in our best interest to meet in person to discuss our future, which I believe is bright."

"Mr. President, I presume?" the president queried. "The extent of destruction and suffering you and China have inflicted is astounding. The anxiety you generated worldwide hasn't been seen since you invaded Ukraine. In fact, think of the Cuban Missile Crisis. You need to rebuild trust with us and the world. Your actions will speak louder than words. We await your next move."

Turning his gaze, he inquired, "General, can you confirm they have begun withdrawing to their garrisons? Once you do, lower our Defcon to Level 4 'double take.' Notify Dallas to monitor the icebreaker, but don't engage at this time."

"Yes, sir, I will get right on it."

"If you can verify, General, stand down our units and keep them in place. Also, the secretary general of NATO should be contacted and informed that the Russians and Chinese are de-escalating. There's no need for Article Five. I will reach out to the prime minister of Canada to express my gratitude for his assistance."

Everyone in the Situation Room was stunned. Tex was the first to speak.

"Anyone up for a beer? I'm having a bachelor party."

Everyone exclaimed, "What?"

The president chuckled. "Who would marry you, Tex?"

Marsha stood up. "Me! I love that damn fool."

"So, where's the party?" Tyler asked.

"Right here," the president called out. "Jim, set it up now! How does next Tuesday at 6:00 p.m. sound?"

"Before we plan Tex's party—and by the way, everyone is invited—I think we've reached a critical moment for the future of the United States. Please believe me, I want to transition to renewable energy, but we must be smart about it—we can't just flip a switch. In the last twenty-four hours, we were almost ready to act. Well, frankly, it seems like someone doesn't want us to succeed. I can't let that happen, so I've decided to address the nation tonight and present a new plan to become energy-independent, utilizing both fossil fuels and renewable energy. Additionally, we will develop the technology ourselves, from the components to the software and everything in between. I must say, we haven't seen any coverage of what has transpired on cable news or the major networks. Maybe this was one secret we managed to keep."

Everyone laughed.

"So, good idea or bad?"

Tex spoke. "Jordan, I think that's a great idea. Americans love a transparent president. I'm behind you on this address to the nation."

In unison, everyone said, "Do it!"

"Jim, reach out to the networks. The address will be at 8:00 p.m. EST. I need to write this address myself. Jim, no speechwriters—this one is coming from the heart."

Mark's phone vibrated in his pocket. He took it out, read the message, and smiled. He exclaimed, "Fugu's plane is scheduled to land in forty-five minutes! Who wants to come with me to pick her up?"

"Mark, I'm sorry but I can't keep calling her Fugu. What's her name?"

"Ai Yin Chang, but I call her Lucy."

"Ai Yin Chang," replied the president.

Mark leaned over to the president and said, "Commander Ai Yin Chang."

"Lucy is good," replied the president.

"Excuse me," said the president, "How will you get to Andrews in forty-five minutes? Is it lunchtime? Before you say anything, Jim, get The Beast. They need a ride."

"Who's going with me?"

Tex, Marsha, Tyler, and Kim replied, "We are!"

"Tex, do you have a minute before you take off?" the president asked.

"Of course."

"I have been thinking about this for the last couple of days. Everyone recognized the value you and your team brought to the fight. The intelligence was remarkable, the imagery was cutting-edge, and the intelligence from Russia was exceptional. You all accomplished something I wouldn't have authorized. What "Fugu" did for this country was a once-in-a-generation event and attested to her love for freedom. I want you to consider something: I'd like to assemble a team of you, Tyler, Kim, and Lucy, and you would work for the DNI on emerging threats from unusual requests made by other agencies."

"Jordan, thank you so much, but I need to run this by the others, including Marsha. I require her approval. By the way, I think that would be an amazing team."

"Did you think I would bring this up without consulting Marsha? She's completely on board."

"I'm in then! I'll talk to Kim, Tyler, and Lucy and get back to you as soon as I can."

"Great, just let me know, but take as much time as you need."

43

JOINT BASE ANDREWS – MARYLAND

The C-17 landed at 1:30 p.m. at Joint Base Andrews, and Lucy stepped out. The flight from China took just sixteen hours, with a layover in Alaska. After disembarking from the aircraft, she gazed at the C-17 and said, "This is the most beautiful 'Moose' I have ever seen."

Director Mark Chang and three others welcomed her. She ran to Mark and exclaimed, "Uncle! I hope I made you proud."

He embraced Lucy. "You made the whole world proud! Well, not everyone, but most," he replied with a smile. "I want to introduce you to your cousin, Kim."

She gave Kim a big hug.

"Thank you, Lucy."

Lucy leaned in and said, "My English isn't the best, but who are those two handsome men?"

"That's Tyler on the right and Tex, our boss. Let me introduce you. Lucy, this is Tyler, my boyfriend."

Tyler put out his and said, "Lucy, it's a pleasure meeting you. I can't wait to pick your brain."

Lucy took his hand and replied, "Pick your brain?"

Sorry, Lucy, it's a figure of speech, replied Kim.

Kim continued, "This is Tex. He's our boss."

"Hi, Tyler and Tex. It's a pleasure to meet you both."

As they walked to the waiting cars. Kim whispered something in Lucy's ear.

As they got to the cars, Lucy said, "Thank you, everyone, for getting me out of China."

Tex replied, "Lucy, the risk you took to help the United States. Getting out you was nothing."

"Tex, can I ask you something?" Lucy asked.

He replied, "Of course, ask away?" As they got into their car.

"Tex, why do they call you 'Tex'?" she asked innocently as they got into the car.

Looking at Kim, Tex replied, "Funny, did Kim put you up to this?"

"It's a long story. We'll have plenty of time to discuss it as we prepare for our next mission."

"Next mission? Where's our next mission?" Lucy asked.

"Our next mission? Are we a team?" Kim replied.

"Yes, if you're on board. That includes you, Lucy."

Everyone, in unison, exclaimed, "YES!"

"Well, if we're a team, every team needs a name, and I have the perfect one," Kim added.

"What would that be?" Tex inquired.

"Texarkana! Here's my reasoning: You're named Tex—Tyler's from Texas. I'm marrying someone from Texas, and Jenny likes the Dallas Cowboys. And let's not forget, Tex, you hail from Bald Knob, Arkansas. It's that simple!

"Texarkana, it is." Kim asked, "So, where's our next mission?" Tex replied, "China." "China? Oh crap!" "Just kidding, Lucy. Hey, your English is really good." Everyone burst out laughing. Lucy asked Kim, "When and where is the wedding, by the way?" "Not sure. Maybe the next place our mission takes us! Tex will let us know." "I know of some great spots," Lucy whispered to Kim

"Let me call the president," Tex said to the group. "Sir, you have your team. We call ourselves Texarkana."

"You guys start next week. Take the rest of the week off. I'll see you soon, and thank you."

44

WHITE HOUSE

The President entered the Oval Office. Waiting for him was his wife of thirty-seven years.

Martina said, "Hi, Schatz," as she walked toward him and embraced him. "Is everything okay? It's been a busy couple of days. I haven't seen much of you."

"Yes, Schatz, everything is good, and you're right. It's been a long couple of days. I'm going to address the nation tonight."

"What are you planning to say? Who is helping you write it?"

"Schatz, no one it's all me. We as a nation must rethink what 'energy' means to us. We were on the brink of World War III over energy in the last few days, and almost no one knew. The American people need to understand what our strategy is going to be. Some won't like it—hell, some will hate it—but it's something we must do, and it's my job to make sure our country has the energy it needs today, tomorrow, and in the future."

"I support you, and so will the American people because you have their best interests at heart. What time are you presenting it?"

"At 8:00 p.m. I haven't even written it yet," he admitted with a smile.

She could sense the last few days had worn him down. She was so glad they only had two years left in the White House before returning to Texas.

"If you need me, just give me a call. I love you."

"I love you, too, and thank you for everything."

"Don't forget, the grandkids are coming this weekend."

"Damn, I forgot. I can't wait."

His wife left the Oval Office while he sat behind the Resolute Desk. This would be the first speech he had written since his initial campaign for Congress. He glanced at his watch—only three hours until the address.

He took a pen from its holder on the desk and put his thoughts on paper. His heart was pounding, but it had nothing to do with the speech he was about to deliver to the American public. It finally struck him just how close they had cut it. He thought, *What happened in Russia for them to back down so quickly?* He resolved to uncover what it was another time. He leaned back, took a deep breath, placed his hands behind his head, and closed his eyes.

A loud knock on the Oval Office door startled him awake. He looked at his watch. 7:30 p.m. Damn.

"Mr. President, it's 7:30 p.m. We need to prepare you for your address and set up the office. Can we come in?"

"Yes, give me a minute." He had to wipe the sleep from his eyes. He looked down at the blank piece of paper. He hadn't written a single word. "Come in!"

"Sir, can I have your speech?" Jim asked. "I need to load it into the teleprompter."

"I don't have a written speech. This one comes from the heart."

"Do you want me to cancel?"

"Hell, no! Let's get ready. We have twenty-five minutes."

"My fellow Americans, there has been deep division in this great country over the past several years. That is about to change. We are a united country not just because of the magnificent land God has given us but because we share common goals of peace, prosperity, kindness, and love for one another, regardless of our background, race, religion, or where we live or come from in this great nation.

"I was elected to help propel us towards a greener world with less pollution and cleaner air and water for us and future generations. I am responsible for ensuring peace and prosperity for everyone from sea to shining sea. I'm committed to this but will also dedicate myself to making the United States one hundred percent energy-independent. We will no longer depend on foreign oil from people who don't like us and whose governments are unstable or poor stewards of the environment. Bad geopolitical decisions, war-torn areas, and corrupt governments will not influence prices at the pump and home heating bills. This results in uncertainty and higher costs, creating anxiety for everyone, especially the poor and middle class."

"Being energy independent in a safe and environmentally friendly manner is the right course of action. We will open up ANWR and other areas in Alaska, build more pipelines to safely transport oil products, increase offshore drilling, open up federal lands, and unleash our God-given resources. At the same time, we will advance nuclear energy, solar, and wind, though these alone cannot power this great nation or many of our allies. However, I'm confident it will be effective in the future—but we're here now!"

"No country on earth can produce cleaner energy than the United States. We have signed every climate agreement known to humanity. We meet every obligation and, in many cases, go far above and beyond, while other countries that signed the same agreements do not and have no intention of fulfilling their requirements. Meanwhile, they sell us nearly every component of the green technology needed to power our nation. Thus, we become dependent on them."

"My question is: If they produce it and can send it to us for use, why can't they install it in their own countries? Don't they believe in it? Why are they constructing islands two feet above sea level in the South China Sea? Aren't they worried about rising oceans? I can tell you firsthand that they aren't concerned about the rising ocean levels. These are multi-million-dollar projects that we have helped fund."

"My fellow citizens, we need to shift our perspective. There is a term used in supply chain logistics: the last mile. We have become 'last mile' thinkers. We only notice the delivery trucks at our favorite stores, plug in our appliances at home, and fill up our cars at the gas station. Yet, there is so much more involved in stocking those stores, delivering electricity to your homes, and providing gas at the pump to fill your car. We don't consider where the items in those trucks originated or how the electricity you use daily is generated. It's time to change our mindset from the 'last mile' to 'the first and the next mile.'"

"The jobs created will lift many of our friends, family, and neighbors out of poverty and into the middle class, generate tax revenue to support those less fortunate and improve schools so that the next generation can foster greater technological innovations. Consequently, their children and grandchildren will inhabit a cleaner world. As Ronald Reagan often said, we strive to find that 'shining city on a hill.' We will become that shining city on the hill known as the United States."

"Thank you, and God bless the United States. Please keep our men and women in the military and our first responders in your prayers."

THE END

EPILOGUE

ONE YEAR LATER – EAVESDROP BREWERY, MANASSAS, VIRGINIA

The American public still had no idea how close they and the rest of the world were to World War III. Nevertheless, tensions remained high between Russia and China. The U.S. president still didn't fully trust them and likely never would. He kept his promise to the American people by opening up ANWR for drilling under the strictest environmental standards. Following the completion and opening of the Keystone pipeline, more and more green energy was produced in the U.S. New small modular reactors were safely brought online, leading the U.S. to become energy-independent and export energy to its allies.

The world appeared safer, or so it seemed.

∼

Tex, Kim, Tyler, Lucy, Jenny, Mark, and Marsha gathered in the beer garden at Eavesdrop Brewery on Centerville Road in Yorkshire,

Virginia, to celebrate Lucy's becoming a US citizen. The weather was beautiful: the sun was shining, and the temperature was 80 degrees, making it a perfect day for celebration.

Everyone stood up and raised their glasses. Tex said, "To the newest US citizen! You were a patriot long before becoming a citizen. Thank you, Lucy."

"That's not the only good news," Marsha added. "We're adopting a puppy!"

Everyone raised their glasses again.

"Here's to your puppy! May it bring you happiness and joy, along with weekly outings to pick up brown rocks," Tyler toasted. They all burst into laughter.

The news continued with Kim. "Tyler and I are getting married in August, and everyone is invited!"

"It's about time," Jenny said.

Everyone raised their glasses again. "To Kim and Tyler."

Over the past year, Tex, Lucy, Kim, and Tyler had sharpened their skills and become an even better team. By leveraging their individual skills and shared knowledge, they were prepared for any mission.

Tex felt his cell phone vibrate in his pocket, took it out, and read the message. "Be in my office tomorrow at 8:00 a.m."

Tex looked up from his phone and said, "Drink up, my friends. We have more work."

Welcome to Team Texarkana

GLOSSARY

ANWR is a national wildlife refuge on Gwich'in land in northeastern Alaska, United States. It consists of 19,286,722 acres in the Alaska North Slope region.

Boeing 777 (Triple Seven)—Commonly referred to as the Triple Seven, the Boeing 777 is an American long-range wide-body airliner developed and manufactured by Boeing Commercial Airplanes. It is the world's largest twinjet.

CIA—The CIA is the world's premier foreign intelligence agency. Our work is vital to U.S. national security. The CIA collects and analyzes foreign intelligence and conducts covert operations. U.S. policymakers, including the President, make policy decisions based on the information we provide.

CIC – Combat Information Center on a ship.

Delta Force - Officially known as 1st Special Forces Operational Detachment-Delta (1st SFOD-D), is one of the U.S. special missions' units primarily focused on the counterterrorism mission.

DHS – Department of Homeland Security.

DMZ - a strip of land running across the Korean Peninsula near the 38th parallel north.

GLOSSARY

DNI - is a senior-level agency that oversees the intelligence community.

DOD – Department of Defense.

ETA – Estimated Time of Arrival.

EU—The European Union (EU) is an international organization comprising 27 European countries that governs common economic, social, and security policies.

FMV - Full-motion video. FMV can be collected from a myriad of sensors packaged on aerial or ground assets. It refers to live video that can be analyzed in near real-time to provide decision-makers with up-to-the-second intelligence.

GEOINT—Geospatial intelligence is information derived from analyzing images and data associated with a particular location. It uses imagery to survey and assess human activity and physical geography anywhere on Earth.

Green Berets - Special Forces are guerrilla warfare experts who use unconventional techniques to fight terrorists abroad.

HUMINT—Human intelligence is derived from human sources. To the public, HUMINT remains synonymous with espionage and clandestine activities; however, most HUMINT collection is performed by overt collectors, such as strategic debriefers and military attaches.

IOCs - Indicators of compromise (IOCs) are forensic evidence of potential intrusions on a host system or network. These artifacts enable information security (InfoSec) professionals and system administrators to detect intrusion attempts or other malicious activities.

IP Address – A unique address that identifies a device on the internet or a local network. IP stands for "Internet Protocol," which is the set of rules governing the data format sent via the Internet or local network.

JBLM – Joint Base Lewis McCord, located south of Seattle, WA.

Log4j - Used by developers to track what happens in their software applications or online services. It's basically a massive journal

GLOSSARY

of the activity of a system or application. This activity is called 'logging'; developers use it to monitor user problems.

Metadata - data that provides information about other data but not the content of the data, such as the text of a message or the image itself.

NATO—North Atlantic Treaty Organization—was the first peacetime military alliance the United States entered outside the Western Hemisphere. After the destruction of the Second World War, European nations struggled to rebuild their economies and ensure their security.

NATO Article Five - Article 5 provides that if a NATO Ally is the victim of an armed attack, each and every other member of the Alliance will consider this act of violence as an armed attack against all members and will take the actions it deems necessary to assist the Ally attacked.

NGA - The National Geospatial-Intelligence Agency (NGA) delivers world-class geospatial intelligence (GEOINT) that gives policymakers, warfighters, intelligence professionals, and first responders a decisive advantage.

NORAD - North American Aerospace Defense Command is a combined organization of the United States and Canada that provides aerospace warning, air sovereignty, and protection for Canada and the continental United States.

NORD Stream 2 - a 1,200km pipeline under the Baltic Sea, which will take gas from the Russian coast near St Petersburg to Lubmin in Germany.

NRO - U.S. Government agency in charge of designing, building, launching, and maintaining America's intelligence satellites.

NSA - The National Security Agency provides guidance, products, and services to protect classified and unclassified national security systems against exploitation through interception, unauthorized access, or related technical intelligence threats.

PACOM - United States Indo-Pacific Command is a unified

GLOSSARY

combatant command of the United States Armed Forces responsible for the Indo-Pacific region.

Portside – Left side of a vessel.

POTUS – President of the United States.

Qi - Translated as "vital energy" or "life force.

SCIF—A Sensitive Compartmented Information Facility (SCIF) is a secure place where sensitive information can be viewed and discussed to prevent outside surveillance or spying.

SIGINT - the collection and analysis of electronic signals and systems to gather intelligence

SIM – An integrated circuit (IC) intended to securely store the international mobile subscriber identity (IMSI) number and its related key.

Sojwa – Officer Rank in the North Korean Army equates to a major in the US Army.

SPR – Strategic Petroleum Reserves.

STRATECO – Strategic Command is one of the eleven unified combat commands in the Department of Defense.

TDY – Temporary Duty Travel is a designation reflecting a United States Armed Forces Service member's travel or other assignment at a location other than the traveler's permanent duty station as authorized by the Joint Travel Regulations.

XO – Short for Executive Officer or the second in command of a military unit.

3M-54 Kaliber – a family of Russian cruise missiles.

AH-1E/F - an American single-engine attack helicopter commonly called 'Cobra.'

AH-64—The Boeing AH-64 Apache is an American twin-turboshaft attack helicopter with a tailwheel-type landing gear arrangement, a tandem cockpit, and a nose-mounted sensor suite for target acquisition and night vision systems. It can carry a crew of two.

B-1-B - a supersonic variable-sweep wing, heavy bomber by the United States Air Force. It is commonly called the "Bone". It is one of

GLOSSARY

three strategic bombers serving in the U.S. Air Force fleet, along with the B-2 Spirit and the B-52 Stratofortress.

B-21 – the Raider is the newest stealth heavy bomber for the United States Air Force.

B-52 - an American long-range, subsonic, jet-powered strategic bomber for the United States Air Force.

BMP – a tracked Russian Infantry Fighting Vehicle.

C-17 - a heavy lift four-engine transport for the United States Air Force.

Chengdu Cloud Shadow - also known as Wing Loong-10, is a series of unmanned aerial vehicles of the High-Altitude Long Endurance type featuring a stealthy airframe.

F-16 – 4th generation multi-role fighter for the United States Air Force.

F-22 - 5th generation American single-seat, twin-engine, all-weather stealth tactical fighter aircraft developed for the United States Air Force.

F-35 - 5th generation American family of single-seat, single-engine, all-weather stealth multirole combat aircraft intended to perform air superiority and strike missions.

Harbin Z-9 - a Chinese military (NATO Name – Haitun) utility helicopter with civilian variants. It is a licensed variant of the French Eurocopter AS365 Dauphin and is manufactured by Harbin Aircraft Manufacturing Corporation.

Harbin Gian Eagle - high-altitude, long-range UAV is a reconnaissance aircraft designed by Beijing University of Aeronautics & Astronautics and Harbin Aircraft Industry Co., Ltd. The PLA Navy and PLA Air Force use it.

HQ-22 Ground Air Defense - China's air defense missile system.

IL-76 Candid – a Russian multipurpose, fixed-wing transport aircraft.

J-20 – a twin jet all-weather stealth air superiority fighter with precision strike capability.

KC-135 Stratotanker - provides the United States Air Force with

GLOSSARY

its core aerial refueling capability and has excelled in this role for over 60 years.

M1 - the Abrams is a third-generation American main battle tank designed by Chrysler Defense and is the main battle tank of the US Army.

M230 Chain Gun - is a 30 mm, single-barrel chain-driven autocannon that uses external electrical power to cycle the weapon between shots.

MH-60 - Sikorsky SH-60/MH-60 Seahawk is a twin turboshaft engine, multi-mission United States Navy helicopter based on the United States Army UH-60 Black Hawk and a member of the Sikorsky S-70 family. The most significant modifications are the folding main rotor and a hinged tail to reduce its footprint aboard ships.

Mi-8 - is a medium twin-turbine helicopter, originally designed by the Soviet Union and now produced by Russia. In addition to its most common role as a transport helicopter, the Mi-8 is also used as an airborne command post, armed gunship, and reconnaissance platform.

Mi8AMTSh-VA – a variation of the Mi-8 for extreme cold climates.

MiG-35 – a Russian multirole supersonic fighter.

MP-443 Grach - a semi-automatic short recoil locked breech pistol used by the Russian internal intelligence agencies.

P-8 Poseidon – Anti-submarine warfare aircraft, an American maritime patrol aircraft developed and produced by Boeing Defense, Space & Security, modified from the 737-800ERX.

RP-21 Blackjack - The RQ-21A Blackjack provides the warfighter with dedicated day and night Intelligence, Surveillance, and Reconnaissance (ISR) coverage, target acquisition, and communication relay via a dedicated and cost-effective airborne sensor system capable of delivering actionable intelligence to the tactical commander in real-time.

ZSU 23-4 – a Russian radar-guided anti-aircraft lightly skinned tracked vehicle.

ABOUT THE AUTHOR

Travis Davis is an award-winning author for his World War One Historical Fiction Novel, One of Four: World War One Through the Eyes of an Unknown Soldier. He is also an Air Force brat who grew up in Arkansas, Spain, New York, and California. He joined the U.S. Army at 17 years old as an Armored Reconnaissance Specialist and was stationed at various forts in the United States and Germany, where he met his beautiful wife. During his three tours in Germany, he conducted hundreds of border patrols along the East-West German border and the Czechoslovakia-West German border. He saw firsthand communism and its oppression of its citizens. He retired from the U.S. Army, where his last duty assignment was as Assistant Operations Sergeant of the 2nd Armored Cavalry Regiment at Fort Polk, Louisiana. He is a lifetime member of the Sergeant Morales Club. Travis has received multiple awards, including the Meritorious Service Medal and five Army Commendation Medals.

When he is not writing or working, Travis enjoys exercising, traveling (he loves a good road trip), baking different loaves of bread, making ice cream, and relaxing in his backyard with friends and family while having a cold beer. He currently lives in Allen, Texas, with his wife of over 37 years. He has three adult children: two daughters living in Arkansas, one son living in Northern Virginia, and many wonderful grandchildren.

"Travis never met a stranger," his wife always says.

ALSO BY TRAVIS DAVIS

One of Four: World War One Through the Eyes of an Unknown Soldier

From New York Harbor to the battlefields of France, relive World War One through the eyes of an unknown soldier, as told through his diary. See how the 100-year-old diary brings a father and his estranged son back together by tracing his experiences fighting on the battlefields of France in 1917 - 1918 to his final resting place, the Tomb of the Unknown Soldier at Arlington National Cemetery.

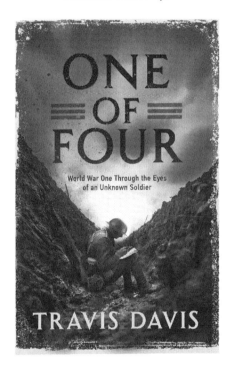